Auggie drew in a big breath that expanded his (awesome) chest. Then he said, "Pepper, the last thing I wanna do is freak you. I just managed to nail down my first date with you. And that task took me three years."

Three years.

I couldn't stop the smirk I gave him.

He definitely noted my smirk, if his nostrils flaring in a sexy way had anything to say about it, but he kept talking.

"But like I told you, I'm taking this serious." He flicked a hand in the spare space between him and me. "That means, in my mind, I'm making you mine. Juno mine. You're both gonna be in my life. And I look after the people in my life that I care about. You're out of this mess, whatever is going on there, so it can't touch you in one way. If it's what we think it is, though, it can touch you in another. It can upset you. Upset Juno. And I gotta do what I can to make that not happen. And if I can't do that, make it so the blow is as soft as I can possibly manage."

Ummmmmmmmm...

"Did you just say that?" I asked, my chest warming, and other places warming too.

"I just said that," he affirmed...*firmly*.

So of course, I pulled his mouth down to mine and I kissed him.

PRAISE FOR KRISTEN ASHLEY

Praise for *Dream Chaser*

"Series fans will be pleased to return to this high-octane world and check in with familiar faces."

—*Publishers Weekly*

"Stream-of-consciousness prose and propulsive, action-packed plotting will please old fans and draw in new readers."

—*Kirkus*

Praise for *Dream Maker*

"The excellent first romance in Ashley's Dream Team series… Those who like a dash of sweetness in their suspense will be delighted."

—*Publishers Weekly*

Dream
Keeper

Dream
Keeper

KRISTEN ASHLEY

A Dream Team Novel

FOREVER
New York Boston

Copyright © 2021 by Kristen Ashley
Cover design by Daniela Medina. Cover photographs © Shutterstock. Cover copyright © 2021 by Hachette Book Group, Inc.

Forever
Hachette Book Group
1290 Avenue of the Americas, New York, NY 10104
read-forever.com
twitter.com/readforeverpub

First Edition: November 2021

Forever is an imprint of Grand Central Publishing. The Forever name and logo are trademarks of Hachette Book Group, Inc.

The publisher is not responsible for websites (or their content) that are not owned by the publisher.

ISBNs: 978-1-5387-3395-0 (mass market), 978-1-5387-3396-7 (ebook)

Printed in the United States of America

CW

10 9 8 7 6 5 4 3 2 1

*To all those who helped guide
my journey back to me.*

Dream
Keeper

PROLOGUE
Parent Trap

AUGGIE

Auggie stood at the front of the church and watched her walk down the aisle.

The bridesmaids' dresses Lottie chose were very Lottie. Sleek. Sexy.

Baring.

All the women looked great in them, but none of them looked better than Pepper.

And he thought that even before Pepper, as she strutted down the aisle, caught sight of her daughter, Juno, and shot her girl a huge smile.

Pepper Hannigan was gorgeous.

Anytime she was with her daughter?

Knockout.

They were the next in the line of Lottie's matches.

Auggie and Pepper.

Mo and Lottie were the obvious firsts (Mo was one of Aug's four best buds), and Lottie earning the love of Mo had been all Lottie's idea.

Mo never thought he'd find anyone as fantastic as Lots, would never go for it, until Lottie talked him around.

Now Mo was standing at the front of their line, waiting to make her his wife.

Once Lottie got her happy ending, she set about giving the same thing to Mo's friends...fixing them up with her own crew.

And so far, she'd done a bang-up job.

Mag and Evie, the second couple, were living together and getting married.

Boone and Ryn, the third, were tight, and further, they were in business together.

Axl and Hattie, the fourth, were as good as living together, and practically inseparable.

It was him and Pepper who were the holdouts.

This was not for lack of trying on Auggie's part.

Once he'd met her, Auggie saw no reason not to go for it.

She was gorgeous. She was funny. She spoke her mind. She was laidback. Together. She didn't seem to have any hang-ups.

But Pepper saw reason not to give it a shot because she had a kid.

He got it. She was being careful. Whatever had torn her and Juno's dad apart had made her skittish.

So yeah.

He got it.

That didn't mean it wasn't torture.

Like right now, when her eyes caught his, the smile that she gave her kid still in them, and Auggie felt that.

He *felt* it.

Damn.

It wasn't even aimed at him in any real way, and that residual love she'd targeted at her daughter was so big, it took forever to fade away.

He'd never felt that kind of love.

Not once in his life.

And he wanted it so bad, the backs of his teeth hurt with the need to taste it.

He lost her attention when she shifted to take her place at the front of the church and Auggie tore his gaze away from her to watch the next woman, Hattie, march down the aisle.

On its way, his gaze snagged on Juno.

Dark hair to her mom's blonde, she was all dressed up, her hair curled—her mom was a bridesmaid in a big wedding with all the prep that entailed, but it was clear Juno had not been forgotten.

She was staring at her mother, beaming with pride.

Seeing that beam made Auggie want even more of what he'd never had.

From the both of them.

*   *   *

"No one should enjoy this song that much," Axl noted.

Auggie and his bud were sprawled in chairs next to a table that had a scattering of smeared cake plates, abandoned drinks, and a sprinkling of the personalized M&M's that had been Lots and Mo's wedding favors.

Lottie and Mo had taken off a couple of hours ago, but the party was not winding down in the slightest, which wasn't a surprise, considering the guest list was made up of Rock Chicks and their posse, and Dream Team and their crew.

Lottie and Mo might be long gone, taking off to go all night somewhere else.

But their wedding reception was going to kiss the dawn.

At least.

Case in point, it was after midnight, "Celebration" by Kool and the Gang was playing, and the dance floor was packed.

Callum Nightingale was the center of attention. To his mother and her friends egging him on (and his father and *his* friends standing on the sidelines shaking their heads, but grinning), Callum was actually breakdancing, and the kid rocked that shit.

But Auggie wasn't watching Callum.

He was watching Juno and Pepper goofing off.

No woman in a dress cut that low with a slit that high should be able to pull off acting that big of a dork.

But Juno had selected the air trumpet, and Pepper had decided on the air saxophone, and they were jamming *out*.

No stale air guitar or lead singer nonsense for those two adorable goofballs.

They were about the horns.

And they were having the time of their lives.

They were in the midst of a huge celebration, and still, they were a party of two.

Fuck, why did his gut ache?

"Aug?"

Auggie stopped watching Pepper and Juno singing "Yahoo!" into fake microphones while still holding on to their fake instruments and looked to his friend.

The minute he did, Axl's head ticked, and he murmured, "Buddy."

There you go.

He didn't hide the ache.

Aug swallowed, turned his attention back to the dance floor, and focused on Luke Stark breaking up some situation happening with his daughter, Maisie, and Tack Allen's son, Cutter.

"She's still stonewalling you," Axl guessed.

"Said it before, Axe. She's got a kid. I get it. If you're a mom," *like Pepper was a mom*, he didn't add, *not like my mom was a mom*, "you protect your kid."

"She'll get there," Axl declared.

Auggie was beginning to doubt it.

"Seriously, man, she'll get there," Axl pressed.

Aug rolled his head on his shoulders and looked back to the dance floor, but not to Pepper and Juno, just the general wave and hum of happy people expressing that happiness physically.

Then he said, "If she doesn't, she doesn't."

"She looks at you when you're not looking at her, Aug, and when she does, she has the same expression on her face you just did."

That got Axl Auggie's full attention.

"No shit?" he asked.

Axl shook his head. "Would I shit you about that?"

No, he would not.

"You haven't noticed it?" Axl asked.

He hadn't.

Aug couldn't stop it. His eyes shot right to Pepper.

And damn.

When they did, he caught her quickly looking away.

His gaze dropped to Juno.

She didn't look away.

She was staring right at him, big grin, and when she got his attention, she waved.

He returned her smile and waved back.

The song changed to "Can't Stop the Feeling!" and suddenly Hattie was in her man's space.

"Babe, not gonna—" Axl started, right before she yanked him out of his chair.

"You too!" She pointed at Auggie as she dragged Axl to the dance floor.

She kept her eyes on him while waving at him to hurry it up even as she shoved her man where she wanted him to be.

That being among the dancers forming a big circle, and when Auggie noticed Pepper bending forward and pressing her hands between her knees, her mouth wide open with laughter, he got off his ass and joined the party.

When he did, he saw, in the middle of the circle, Smithie was cutting loose. And probably unsurprisingly, considering the man ran a club, he could bust a move.

Dorian joined his uncle in the circle, snapping his fingers and moving practically nothing but those and his shoulders. Even so, Ian ratcheted up the cool factor of this mess immeasurably. He was just that guy.

They faded out when Jagger and his woman, Archie, took Jag's little brother, Wilder, in, and Wilder did what the kid often did. He went wild.

But Archie's moves took cool to a place where it was hot.

Jagger's brother, Dutch, was dragged in by Dutch's girl, Georgie, and they crashed that particular party.

Bikers and their babes cutting a rug.

Only at a Dream Team wedding.

As the song carried on, it went like that with Lots's brother-in-law, Eddie Chavez, standing on a chair at the edge of the circle filming it on his phone, which was good.

Mo and Lottie were undoubtedly down with whatever they were doing right then.

But they wouldn't want to miss this.

It ended as it should.

Hattie heading out for a solo.

She'd lost the four-inch heels, and partly because she was classically trained, partly because she was Hattie, she pulled off something that was hip-hop, disco and classical ballet that had everyone hooting, shouting, catcalling and clapping, it was just that damned *awesome*.

But Aug stopped watching Hattie in order to watch Axl doing it.

And...

Auggie also wanted *that*.

Pride.

And lots of love.

Aug felt something which made him swing his head the other way to see Pepper glancing away again.

When he caught that, it wasn't the first time he did it that day.

It wasn't the first time he did it genuinely that day.

But it was the best one he'd felt that day.

He smiled.

* * *

PEPPER

"She's got a talent with it," Auggie teased, his black eyes lit with a playful light as he gave guff to Ryn.

"I gotta admit, she does," Boone agreed on a mutter.

"Uh, becoming a gazillionaire flipper doesn't work if you buy a fabulous house that you maybe change a chandelier in," Ryn remarked. "The house needs to be a mess. A disaster. It wouldn't be fun if it wasn't a challenge. So yeah, I have a talent with finding a challenge or why would I do it at all?"

"We could have called Guinness with the amount of rat droppings at this current flip," Auggie put in. "And that was before Hound nearly fell through the floor in the bathroom after they pulled up the linoleum."

"Yeah, that sitch with Hound wasn't awesome," Ryn mumbled.

I stifled a giggle.

"Is that your goal, to become a gazillionaire flipper?" Now it was Boone who was teasing.

"No, love of my life," Ryn retorted, and at hearing those words uttered by his woman, Boone didn't look as roguish anymore. He looked something else and that something else was dreamy. "My goal is not only to become a gazillionaire flipper, but also to have my own show on some DIY network."

With that last bit, Boone was no longer giving his woman loved-up eyes.

He was giving her WTF eyes.

"You want a home improvement show?" he asked.

"Uh." Ryn flipped a hand at Boone. "Look at you. You're camera-ready *all the time*. We'd have fan clubs in, like, *a day* and a line of my personally designed décor at Kohl's in a month."

"I gotta admit, you're totally camera-ready all the time," I entered the conversation. "Both of you."

Boone shot me a *you're not helping* look.

Aug audibly bit back laughter.

I turned to him.

He winked at me.

I felt that wink explode in my sternum.

I want you so bad, I wake up thinking that, and go to sleep grieving that I don't have it, my mind practically whimpered after catching that wink.

I shot him a lame smile and looked away.

Looking away was hard.

He was insanely beautiful. Like, Michelangelo-would-stop-in-his-tracks-and-get-on-his-knees-and-beg-him-to-be-a-model beautiful.

But it was more.

Augustus Hero was easy to be with.

He was just…

A nice guy.

A good guy.

Good sense of humor. Good with people. Good at making conversation. Good with kids. A good friend.

A *good guy*.

And he liked me.

He didn't hide it, and not only the times he'd asked me out.

He was open. Ready for me to go there.

To take us there.

I want to go there, my mind whispered.

No, I need *to go there,* it shouted.

I could not go there.

Not now.

Not with my ex, who was also my baby daddy, being a huge jerk.

Not with my beloved daughter caught up in his shenanigans.

Corbin had a revolving door of ladies.

That wasn't going to happen at Mom's house.

Stability.

Safety.

That was what Juno was going to get from her mom.

"I'm not going to be on a house-flipping show," Boone declared, and I could have kissed him for breaking into my thoughts.

"We'll see," Ryn murmured.

"We won't," Boone replied.

"Okay, honey," Ryn said and then gave me big eyes.

I smiled at her, and even though they were being cute, my mind was at a place where I hoped that smile didn't look fake.

Because I was sitting by Auggie, and he was a good guy, he was my friend.

But my gut ached.

"What about you?" Auggie asked, his voice lowered in a way that I knew that question was just for me.

I turned to him, thinking about how much I liked his voice, and finding he'd leaned a little into me, so I also caught his smell.

I liked his smell too.

He smelled like...

"Well?" he prompted.

"What about me, what?"

"Any plans for a reality show?"

Not unless people suddenly found it fascinating to watch someone meditate.

I shook my head.

"No plans to take your rad air horns section on the road?"

I blinked, confused. "Sorry?"

"You and Juno. At the wedding. I'm pretty sure Kool and the Gang would hire you and your girl just to add some pizzazz to their act."

A surprised giggle erupted from me. "Did you just use the word 'pizzazz'?"

He shrugged. "I call 'em as I see 'em."

"I must say, we're full of pizzazz," I admitted.

"The synchronized kicks were my favorites," he noted, making that ache achier, at the same time adding a warmth I decided to ignore at how open he was in communicating he was paying attention. Open but without pressure. Auggie had a knack with that. "And you were always on beat with your 'Yahoos.'"

"You can't mess up the 'Yahoos,'" I stated with mock gravity.

He chuckled and the sound, the sight of his humor was so beautiful, I died a little.

To hide it and move beyond it, I shook my head again, this time (fake) smiling, and asked, "Do you have any plans for a show?"

He shook his head too.

"You'd kill on a reality show," I noted.

His brows went up as his gorgeous lips quirked. "Yeah? Why?"

"Uh, have you looked in the mirror?" I teased. "You wouldn't have to do anything, except maybe flex a biceps every once in a while, and *bam!* Instant droves of fans."

I was so busy trying to be funny, I hadn't noticed how his eyes shut down as I was talking.

Um.

What was that?

"Did I—?" I began.

"What are you two whispering about?" Boone asked.

I tore my attention from Auggie and caught Ryn giving him a look that stated plain she was just stopping herself from giving him a *don't interrupt them!* shove.

But no, none of this matchmaking.

From anyone.

Auggie was my friend. He was cool with Juno. He was a great guy to know. He knew we were the last match, destined for each other, and I couldn't go there, and he understood why I couldn't go there, and he was cool about that too.

And as much as I wanted more, that was all I could have.

I figured he'd eventually find someone else, but I didn't think about that (at all, *ever*).

As I'd learned in my life, I had what I had, and I had to find a way to be good with it.

And I had to have the patience to wait until that time (should it ever come) where I'd get what I wanted.

Just a little bit of it and I'd be happy.

Nothing as big as all that was Auggie.

That...

Well, that would only happen in a perfect world.

Not in my world.

Auggie was the impossible dream.

* * *

"You've gotta go."

His breaths were still labored.

So were mine.

But his face was in my neck so I could feel his.

They felt beautiful.

He was also still inside me, mostly because he just came.

And so had I.

That felt even more beautiful.

"Sweetheart," he whispered.

This shouldn't have happened.

This never should have happened.

What had I done?

Why had I been so *weak*?

I pushed against his chest.

"Auggie, you have to go."

He lifted his head and looked down at me through the dark.

"Pepper, that was good."

No.

It was *so* good.

Frantic, I-can't-wait-to-be-inside-you, I-can't-wait-to-get-you-inside-me wall sex right inside my front door?

That was not about ending a dry spell.

That wasn't even about a weak moment.

That was about Auggie.

Auggie and me.

Auggie and me and how *unbelievably fucking good* we were together.

I'd denied it. I'd denied him. I'd denied me. When I looked at him. When he looked at me. When I was with him.

But it couldn't be denied.

We'd just proved it.

We were *unbelievably fucking good together*.

On this thought, with a fair sight more desperation, I pushed again at his chest, trying to squirm away from him.

He kept hold.

And put his mouth to my ear.

"Baby, that was hot, but it was fast, and it was done before things were said. Now we gotta talk."

"No." I shook my head. "No talking. No nothing. That was a mistake."

"It wasn't a mistake."

With desperation mounting, I declared, "It was totally a mistake. *You* are a mistake. *This* is a mistake. It's all a huge *mistake*."

He lifted his head. "I'm a mistake?"

I hated the tone of his voice.

Disbelieving.

Kinda pissed.

A thread of hurt.

God.

But I couldn't go back on it.

I couldn't.

This shit was not going to happen to me again.

And I wasn't going to put Juno through it.

Why had I given in?

I knew why. A night with Boone and Ryn being cute and so very together, sitting with Auggie, denying myself.

Then, he was so sweet to me, as he always was, eventually letting myself pretend we weren't there as friends, but we were there . . . *together*.

Eventually, I'd had just that little too much to drink to make it safe to drive home. Before my right mind, my good-mom mind, my take-care-of-priorities mind could tell my stupid, selfish mind to stop it, I turned my head and asked him to drive me home.

Now we were here.

In my foyer.

Just having had sex.

And it was *me* who'd jumped *him* on my front stoop after he'd done the gentlemanly thing (see! he was perfect!) and walked me to my door.

Then I'd dragged him inside.

"Yes, Auggie." I squirmed again and this time I got away.

My panties were somewhere on the floor. Fortunately, the skirt of my tank t-shirt dress was easy to shimmy back down.

I went to my front door that Aug had slammed after he'd stalked me into my house and before he'd pinned me to the wall.

And the reminder of all of that sent quivers down my inner thighs.

I opened the door and stood abreast of it, eyes to my feet.

"Pepper, sweetheart, you don't want me walking out that door," Auggie warned.

No, I don't, I thought. *I really, really don't.*

But I couldn't have what I wanted.

I never could.

I'd learned that repeatedly.

Why had I forgotten?

Don't reach, you might get it and find out (A) you didn't want it in the first place, or (B) it didn't want you.

So I said nothing.

He stopped in front of me. I could see the toes of his boots close to mine that were exposed by my flat sandals.

There was something very . . . *wonderful* about that.

His boots.

My sandals.

His masculine.

My toenails painted pale pink.

Him right there.

With me.

"Pepper, look at me."

"You've gotta go," I repeated.

"Juno's with him."

That made the back of my neck itch.

Then again, whenever my girl was gone, doing her time with her dad, I had that feeling.

"Yes, she is."

"So we can talk."

"We're not talking."

"Pepper—"

My head shot up and I snapped, "God! I shouldn't have to say it again! Get out, Auggie! That was stupid and it was weak and it's not happening again. I'm already mortified enough I let you fuck me. You're just making it worse."

For a second, he seemed shocked.

Shocked and hurt.

My heart squeezed.

That wore off fast, he got in my face and growled, "I'm not gonna play this game."

"I'm not playing a game."

"I know women like you. And yes, you are."

He knew women like me?

I didn't ask, mostly because he didn't give me the opportunity.

"Thanks for the hot fuck, babe," he said. "At least that made it worth putting up with this bullshit play."

And then he was gone.

I closed the door behind him.

Put my forehead to it.

"Huge mistake," I whispered.

But I knew.

I could tell myself that again and again and again.

But I'd seen the girls with their guys.

So I could repeat it for eternity, and I'd never believe.

No, Augustus Hero was not a mistake.

The mistake would be if he took a chance on me.

Now *that* would be a mistake.

Huge.

Because I was a mess.

My family was a mess.

My ex was a mess.

There was only one thing that wasn't a mess.

The home I gave my daughter.

And that was also the one thing I was determined never to make a mess.

Therefore, I had to do everything in my power to keep things good and safe and right for my girl.

Including denying myself a great guy named Auggie.

* * *

JUNO

She'd messed up.

She'd sat at the big, round table in the corner of the coffee area of Fortnum's Used Books.

This meant it was like she had a big light shining on her.

Or signs pointing at her.

Or whatever.

That was bad.

She wasn't supposed to be noticed.

She should have hidden in the bookshelves. Or got close to someone else so the people that worked there would think she was with her mom or dad.

Making things worse, the ladies that worked there, she could tell, were moms.

Toe-tah-*lee*.

And that was also bad because you couldn't pull things on moms. Moms figured stuff out.

And then there was the big, crazy-looking bearded guy behind the coffee counter.

Oh man.

Juno had a feeling that guy didn't miss *anything*.

Including the fact she'd walked into the store by herself and sat by herself and she'd been there awhile.

Truth: she was tall for her age.

She was still only eight years old.

They all kept looking over at her.

They were going to ask her where her mom or dad were, she knew it.

Man...

Oh man.

He needed to get there.

Right away!

She couldn't know he'd come.

Her mom and her mom's friends talked (and they'd talked about him). Juno listened. It wasn't like they acted like Juno was a baby and she couldn't understand what they were saying, or they didn't think she was important, so they forgot she was there. They were cool around her. Natural. Just them. And they thought Juno was cool too.

Unlike her dad (sometimes), her mom knew Juno was with it. She had a brain. She wasn't a little kid anymore.

And she and her mom were a team.

They'd always been a team, but now that she was growing up, they were *more* of a team.

Like, Juno helped with the dishes, and sometimes even helped her mom cook.

And she kept her room tidy so her mom didn't have to tell her to (anymore).

And when Juno asked, Mom began to teach her how to do the laundry. So Juno told her that when she did her own, she could also do her mom's. After she said that, Mom gave her one of her big, tight hugs, so Juno knew that'd help out *a lot*.

Juno had gotten really good at dusting and she never (well, not *never*, but not as much as she used to) forgot to spray the shower with that after-shower spray her mom said helped keep the shower clean so she didn't have to do it all the time and the glass would look all clear and pretty.

So Juno's mom knew Juno could handle stuff.

It was just that Juno knew, in their team, her mom handled most of the big stuff.

Okay, that was because she was the adult. She was the *mom*.

The big stuff in life, Juno had learned, was not about forgetting the shower spray.

The thing was, there was a lot of stuff her mom had to handle.

Like, way *more* than other moms had to handle.

Which was why Juno was there, right then, at Fortnum's.

It was why, a couple of days ago, she'd grabbed Auntie Ryn's phone real fast when she'd put it down. Nabbed it before it shut off, doing this so Auntie Ryn wouldn't see.

Doing this so she could run to the bathroom with it, find his phone number and write it down.

Why she'd sent the text she'd sent to that number half an hour ago.

A text to the guy she thought could help.

Because Juno knew her mom needed a break.

Juno's mom, Pepper, needed a lot of stuff.

And Juno knew *exactly* what she needed.

Mom just wouldn't go for it.

So Juno had decided *she*, *Juno*, was going to *make* her go for it.

Not in a mean way.

Hopefully, Mom wouldn't even know it was happening.

But she couldn't do it without a little help.

She couldn't do it without him.

And she had this one chance to talk to him without her mom knowing...

If he came.

He had to come.

Uh-oh.

Oh no!

One of the moms that worked there was approaching. The blonde one. The one the crazy-looking guy kept calling "Loopy Loo," which couldn't be her name (but could be proof the crazy-looking guy was just plain crazy).

Juno was either going to have to get out of there, or she was going to have to lie to the blonde lady.

Juno hated lying.

She had to do it with her dad (sometimes) because he was just so...so...*gah!*

But she didn't like it.

And she didn't want to do it to the blonde lady. She was real pretty and dressed cute and looked like she was nice.

Man!

Why couldn't he have just come when Juno—?

Before "Loopy Loo," with that worried expression on her face (which said totally that she was nice), made it to Juno, the bell over the door chimed.

Juno looked right there.

And even though she'd never met him, only ever heard her mom and her mom's crew talking about him, she knew it was him.

It was the suit.

No one else in that place was wearing a suit.

She jumped up from her chair and ran right to him.

So all the people who'd been watching her since she got there would know she was okay, Juno threw her arms around his hips, pressed her cheek to his stomach, hugged him tight and cried, "Finally!"

She felt a hand wrap around the back of her neck (it was a big hand, and it was warm, so it felt nice) and the deep voice of the man she was holding asked, "Juno, is everything okay?"

She tipped her head back and looked into his eyes.

He was worried too.

And she could tell, not even knowing him, he was worried about 5,287 times more than Loopy Loo was.

And Loopy Loo was a mother!

There it was.

Proof.

Juno had done right.

This was the guy to ask.

Of course, in her text, she'd told him he'd had to meet her there *right away*, and the way she did that made it sound like there was something to worry about.

This didn't feel very good because it wasn't a nice thing to do, scaring someone like that.

But sometimes you had to do what you had to do.

Right?

"You know me," she stated, something else that proved she was right.

It was him. He knew her. Even if they'd never met, like she knew him, he knew her.

He *so totally* was the person to ask.

"I do, honey, now answer me, are you okay?"

Juno nodded, fast and happily.

He watched her do that, but he didn't seem to get any less worried.

"Is your mom all right?"

That time, she didn't nod fast and happy.

She shook her head, slow and not happy at all.

Because her mom was not all right.

She tried to hide it, but she was never all right.

If it could be just them, Pepper and Juno, the dream team, they'd be okay. *When* it was just them and her dad didn't mess things up, or her grandfather, or all that other stupid stuff, it was *awesome*.

But it wasn't just them.

Juno's mom had to put up with so much more and it was a serious *pain*.

And she thought Juno couldn't help her, and the sad truth was, for some of it, Juno couldn't.

But her mom couldn't do it alone.

Not anymore.

It wasn't fair.

It wasn't fair all the stuff Juno's dad pulled, and it wasn't fair all the crap her mom's family did.

None of it was fair.

It was too much.

And Juno's mom was strong. The strongest mom *in the whole world*.

But she needed a break.

His body seemed to get tight at her answer before he asked, "Why are you here alone? Is she—?"

Juno let him go and stepped away. "She's fine. She's home. I'm supposed to be at a friend's house. My friend is covering for me. She lives close to here, so she's there...covering. And I walked here to meet you. But I need to get back before her parents figure out what we're doing."

"You're here alone?"

Juno nodded.

Unluckily, but not surprisingly considering the look on his face and the fact he was a grown-up, he kept talking about that.

"You walked here from a friend's house...alone?"

Oh man.

"Uh..."

"Can you explain why you did that?" he asked.

"You're Mr. Cisco, right?"

He nodded but said, "You can call me Brett."

Um.

She didn't know about that.

Mom didn't like her to call people by their first names unless they were super close friends or family.

When they talked about him, Juno could tell Auntie Ryn and Auntie Hattie and Auntie Evie liked Mr. Cisco a lot.

But Juno never called a grown-up by their first name, unless her mom said it was all right.

(Though she did call Auntie Ryn, Auntie Hattie and Auntie Evie, Rinz, Hatz and Ehvz, but only because her mom said she could.)

"Okay then, uh…" she started. "I did that because I need you to help me."

"Help you with what?"

"Help me make Mom fall in love with Auggie."

Mr. Cisco's head ticked as his brows shot *way* up.

And it was then, in a big-guy, too-old way, she thought he was kinda okay-looking (and on top of that, she liked the suit he wore that had a vest—she'd seen Chris Evans in a suit like that, and Chris Evans was *the world*).

She thought Mr. Cisco was more okay-looking when his expression suddenly changed, and she liked the way his eyes got. They made her *feel* like one of her mom's brownies warm out of the oven *tasted*.

And he replied, "I'm all in."

Juno felt something inside her get all loose when she didn't know it had been tight and hurting.

But it had been.

And she sent a silent message to Heaven, something that she would never in a million, billion, *trillion* years admit to her stupid grandfather she did (though, she did it a lot, it felt nice sending messages to Heaven).

Thank you, God.

But in real life, she smiled so big at Mr. Cisco, her face hurt.

And he smiled back at her.

CHAPTER ONE
A Perfect World

PEPPER

My phone chimed with the eleventh text I'd gotten in an hour and I *just* managed not to pull it out of my purse and throw it in the nearest garbage can.

Okay.

All right.

Deep breath and...

Center.

Bottom line: I needed to get over it because I didn't want to be a hater. Hating was such an ugly thing. I didn't like how it made me feel and I didn't want it around my daughter. And when the world at large was so full of negativity and hate that it was pushing in sometimes on an hourly basis, the best way to keep that kind of thing from burying my little girl was, when I had her, do my all not to be a hater.

So I had to guard against the hate.

Even if the holidays were coming up and it always got bad during the holidays.

Bad in the sense of these texts I was currently getting from my sister, because she (and Mom and Dad) always thought holidays were the perfect time to win me around to their way of thinking.

Or, to be blunt (and honest), indoctrinate me and Juno into their way of life.

A way of life I'd turned my back on years ago.

You had to hand it to them, they never gave up.

But that was a stretch for a silver lining because it was also a not-great thing that *they never gave up.*

And it couldn't be denied, I hated it (rephrase: disliked it intensely) when they put my sister forward to appeal to me in a sisterly/generation-sharing way.

Making this worse, I had to divide my time with my daughter, giving some of it up to her father, which was never fun, but especially unfun during the holidays.

In a perfect world, my baby would be with me all the time.

In a *perfectly* perfect world, my baby's daddy would not be a liar and a cheater, and we'd all be together all the time.

It was not a perfect world.

This year, I sensed holidays were going to be even worse because her dad had a(nother) new woman in his life, and from what I was getting, she was all in to win Corbin by showing she could be the best stepmom in Denver.

That happened a lot (the new woman and her wanting to win Corbin by using Juno) and it always involved messing with Juno's heart. And then, when Corbin dumped her (and he would eventually dump her), part of Juno's heart would go with her.

It hurt my baby girl.

It hurt to watch.

It also hurt because I was powerless to do anything about it.

In the beginning, I'd tried to talk to Corbin and warn him about introducing his girlfriends to our daughter too soon.

He didn't want to hear my advice on how to father.

Though, even if he didn't want to hear my thoughts on parental issues, he spent a lot of time making sure I heard from him on a variety of subjects that had to do with co-parenting (and other topics).

This regardless that Juno was eight, and for the most part, we had it down.

I didn't need any of this right now.

It was career day for Juno's class and Juno loved me. She thought I could do anything. As such, she did not get that her mom—who had been a stripper, but was now a featured dancer at a former strip club (even so, you could absolutely still describe what we did as exotic dancing, we just no longer bared all)—was not the person teachers wanted talking to their kids about their future career prospects.

But Juno thought I was cool.

Juno thought I hung the moon and that my besties, Lottie, Ryn, Hattie and Evie, were the stars (all of them also dancers, except Evie, who used to be one, but now she was a student).

So Juno didn't hesitate to ask me to come and chat with her class.

I had a little presentation to give. It was a lot about the chore-ography, costumes, lighting, music choices and working with the stage technicians, and less about how I found new and interesting ways to take off most of my clothes (obviously).

But I was nervous.

I could dance while disrobing with a crowd watching, but standing in front of them and talking?

Nope.

Making matters worse, they were having career days all semester, one each Tuesday. The kids invited parents or other folks in their lives to come in and chat with the class. Thus, I knew Juno had asked her dad to come that day too, and as referenced earlier, he and I did not get along.

Juno was probably trying to see to my feelings and instead of telling me her father was going to be there, she'd warned me "someone else is coming."

It was a little weird she didn't just say, "Dad's coming to bore everyone with anecdotes about being a baller real estate agent."

But sometimes she got a little weird when her dad had a new woman in his life.

Therefore, during these times, I had to let her be how she needed to be, even if that was weird, and be prepared to pick up the pieces after.

This was what was on my mind after I got past checking in at the front office and was walking down the hall toward Juno's classroom.

But even if my headspace was taken up with all of that, when I turned the corner to the hallway where Juno's classroom was, nothing would have made me miss the astonishing and totally unforeseen fact that Augustus "Auggie" Hero—hot guy, ex-military, current-commando, man I was supposed to be dating since Lottie tried to fix us up ages ago, man I'd broken down and had wall sex with not long ago and then ended that episode *very badly—that* Auggie Hero was holding up the wall beside the door to Juno's classroom with his broad shoulders.

But his head was turned, and his black eyes were on me.

Oh God.

Now there…

Embodied in that man…

Was a true perfect world.

But I felt my heart start racing and that had nothing to do with the fact he was gorgeous.

What was he doing here?

It was important to repeat that he was a current commando.

A commando who, for unknown reasons, was loitering in the hallway of an elementary school.

Was...?

God!

Was there some threat to Juno?

Completely forgetting how disastrous our last encounter had been (which was now a couple of months ago—we'd both independently instigated Operation Avoidance since then), I rushed to him, my high heels echoing against the tile in the quiet hall.

And I didn't hesitate to grab on to his forearm that was crossed on his chest and lean in close so I could say low, "Is everything okay?"

He stared down at me.

Then he tipped his chin and looked at my fingers curled around his forearm.

He looked back at me when I squeezed his sinewy flesh and snapped, "Auggie! Is something wrong? Is Juno unsafe?"

At my question, his face changed.

In my panic, I hadn't really registered his expression before, but now it couldn't be missed that it was hyper alert.

I was already hyper alert, but I did not take it as a good sign he'd gone hyper alert even if it wasn't a surprise, considering all that had been swirling around the Dream Team for nearly a year.

That Dream Team being Evie, Ryn, Hattie, Lottie...and me.

And it was important at that juncture to mention that all the drama that had been swirling around the Dream Team included death and dirty cops and kidnappings and stalking and shoot-outs, and it bore repeating...*death*.

As in *murders*.

So...yeah, Auggie Hero, Badass Extraordinaire, standing outside my daughter's classroom freaked me.

Big time.

His voice—something I particularly liked about him, it was deep but smooth (not silky and elegant, instead soft and calming)—came at me.

"Is there a reason Juno wouldn't be safe?"

My voice was rising. "I don't know! You tell me."

"Pepper, I didn't come up to me and ask if Juno was safe."

Okay...

Wait.

What?

"Then why are you standing outside Juno's classroom?"

His strong, heavily stubbled chin jutted slightly to the side.

"I'm here for career day," he declared. "Juno called. She wants me to talk to her class about going into the military."

I blinked up at him.

"You didn't know?" he asked.

No.

I.

Did.

Not.

Know.

That.

My.

Daughter.

Asked.

Augustus Hero.

To talk to her class on the same day I was going to talk to her class!

How did Juno...?

Why did Juno...?

What the hell?

"Her father isn't coming?" I asked Auggie.

He shook his head once. "No clue. I just know I'm here and now you're here. That's all I know."

I stood there, staring at him, at a loss for words because my daughter had somehow found a way to call Auggie and ask him to come and talk to her class during career day.

She did not have a cell phone.

As far as I knew, she didn't use my mobile.

Though, we were one of the last of a dying breed that had a landline, also as far as I knew, Auggie's phone number was not a part of the collective conscious.

How did she call him?

Further, I didn't know if she had a quota on how many people she could ask to come speak to the class, but if she did, and considering the fact that her father was not there, that meant possibly she'd picked Auggie over Corbin.

Even if Corbin was a cheat and an asshole and I had many (what I thought were) serious questions about his concept of parenting, Corbin was good-looking. He was confident. He dressed well. He had encyclopedic knowledge of Bruce Willis films, *Seinfeld* and *The Office*. And he was indeed baller at real estate. So he was interesting, could hold a conversation and probably had motivating tidbits to share with a third-grade class.

Auggie, on the other hand, was the most beautiful man I'd ever laid eyes on and every time I saw him I was reminded of this fact.

That thick black-black hair that curled at the ends. His hooded brow, deep-set onyx eyes and dense eyebrows that had a wicked-gorgeous arch. The slight flare to the nostrils of his strong, attractive nose. His excruciatingly perfect lips. His tall, lean, muscled body that was not too tall or too lean or too muscled, it was all *just right*.

Not to mention, Auggie was funny.

Auggie was playful.

Auggie liked to tease.

There was some boy to this man that would never go away.

And there was something so insanely compelling about a man who was downright beautiful in a classical sense (he looked like a Greek god, for goodness sakes) being the kind of guy you knew would make you laugh in bed. Who would get into the spirit of

Halloween and Christmas in a way the joy would never go out of it. Who wouldn't sweat the small stuff and would guide you to that same.

I dealt with a lot of small stuff in my life every single day.

It'd be good not to sweat it.

And he wasn't only a veteran, he was currently a commando.

He'd been on the team that had rescued Evie from a kidnapping, and that effort had reportedly included smoke bombs and confusion tactics, so I had secondhand knowledge that he was the real deal.

He was probably the single coolest person you could ask to speak at a third-grade career day.

The only cooler person I could think of would be Hawk Delgado, Auggie's boss, because I had suspicions that the cover story was false to protect his identity and Hawk had single-handedly found and eliminated Osama bin Laden.

But as such, and for other reasons, he probably couldn't talk to eight-year-olds about that.

"Pepper, you're touching me," Auggie stated unhappily.

At these words, I shot back a step, letting him go, but I did this still staring at him.

Now in horror.

Oh God, how had I forgotten?

The last time I'd spent any real time with him was when we'd had sex in my foyer.

And then I'd kicked him out and he did not want to be kicked out.

I'd made a pact with myself.

No men in Juno's life until she was mature enough to sort through that emotionally.

I had decided this would be when she was around fourteen or fifteen, though I'd consider it at thirteen, but also possibly push it back to sixteen if she was having a difficult adolescence.

I knew this was going to be a *very long* row to hoe for me (case in point, standing right there with all the perfection that was Auggie Hero and not being able to make him mine).

But there were sacrifices you made as a mother that were necessary.

This was one of them.

I had told not one single soul about this pact I'd made with myself.

None of my friends were moms, they wouldn't get it.

Added to that, none of my friends had started a family with the love of their lives, or even had just settled in with the love of their life, sleeping beside him for years, only to learn he'd been cheating on them *the whole time they were together*.

Yep.

The *whole* time.

They didn't get what it felt like to have your heart broken, your trust decimated, all your dreams for your future shattered *and* have to watch your daughter experience the same thing.

They didn't get that.

I went through that.

But more importantly, Juno went through it.

Top all of it with the shit my dad, mom and sister pulled on a regular basis and okay, sure. Maybe I was overprotective. Maybe this pact was over the top.

Maybe.

But as a single mother, I didn't have the luxury of dealing in maybes.

"I'm taking it Juno didn't tell you she asked me to be here," he remarked, breaking into my explanatory (justifying?) thoughts.

"No," I mumbled.

"You got a problem with me being here?" he asked.

I absolutely did.

I had not gotten into how hard I'd climaxed when he'd done me against the wall of my foyer.

Or how fantastic of a kisser he was (the promise of those perfect lips delivered, believe you me).

Or how good he smelled when you got up close to him. The only way I could describe it was he smelled *warm*. Like he was the human embodiment of a sunny day.

And I'd gone into detail on how good he looked.

But I also did not have a problem with him being there.

Because he was single-handedly going to make my daughter the coolest kid in school, possibly until she graduated from high school.

Therefore, I answered, "No."

"Good," he grunted.

"Uh, how did Juno call you?" I asked. "Was it on my phone?"

He shook his head. "Nope. A number I'd never seen."

"Can I have that number?"

As he pushed away from the wall to fish his phone out of his back pocket, he shot me a glance that no mother wanted to get. It said, *How do you not know how your eight-year-old kid is making phone calls?*

He wasn't able to get his phone out and I wasn't able to broach any further subject, like continuing our discussion on Juno asking him there without me knowing it. Or how it'd be nice for us to go back to what we were before we'd let the dam break on our physical attraction that stupid night in my stupid entryway.

And this couldn't happen because the classroom door opened, and Juno was coming through it.

"Mom!" she cried, darting to me and giving me a hug around the middle.

I loved, adored and cherished my daughter's hugs, even when she'd done something I wasn't so sure about. And I never missed a chance to glory in one.

However, I wasn't able to return the hug before she'd popped back, whirled and threw herself at Auggie, giving him a hug too.

"Auggie!"

Shit, shit, shit.

At this juncture, it had to be noted that Auggie was always great with Juno.

He kidded around with her in cute ways and always had time for her. Even if she interrupted him talking to someone else (something she wasn't allowed to do, but I'd noted, and lamented, she got very animated when she was around Auggie), she immediately became the center of his attention in a way that never failed to make my stomach feel gooey. Last, he was casually affectionate with her in a manner that didn't make my stomach feel gooey.

It made my heart feel light.

He might be unhappy with me, but the expression on his face as he bent his neck to look down at my daughter...

Nope.

No.

I was not going to process that.

"Ms. Hannigan, Mr. Hero, uh, well..." Juno's teacher, Ms. Linn, cleared her throat and I took her in, the way she was pinching the fabric of her skirt, fidgeting and looking in Auggie's vicinity without actually looking at Auggie.

Not to mention, being unable to speak.

I felt her pain.

Seriously.

Auggie had that effect on people.

Juno forged into the breach, beaming up at Auggie and crying, "Come talk to my class!"

With that, she took Auggie's hand, reached out and grabbed mine, and pulled us both in, tethered to her, a long string of connected human beings, man, child, woman.

My walking dream.

My current nightmare because it wasn't meant to be.

God, please, strike me with lightning, just don't hit my baby (or Auggie).

"All right, everybody," Ms. Linn said crisply as she followed behind us, obviously having gotten it together. "Our career day series continues with Juno's mom and stepdad, Ms. Hannigan and Mr. Hero."

On the word "stepdad" I stopped dead.

Auggie did too.

He also whipped his head around, his eyes coming right to me.

I knew this because my gaze was glued to him.

Okay.

All right.

What was happening?

"Ms. Hannigan is a professional dancer and she's going to be speaking on that and we will all be thanking Mr. Hero for his service, as he's a veteran of the United States Marines, and he'll be sharing about that."

I was staring in Auggie's eyes as he stared in mine and we were both so caught in this, neither of us moved or said a thing.

I suspected this lasted awhile. However, I was still so flipped out about Juno telling her teacher that Auggie was her stepdad that I couldn't stop it.

Auggie was evidently experiencing the same thing.

"Who's going to go first?" Ms. Linn prompted.

"Mom," Juno said, tugging at my hand, which finally made me look down at my daughter. "You go first and Auggie can go last."

"Okay, honey," I murmured.

It was then, she let my hand go but didn't let Auggie go. She walked him to the side of the room where Ms. Linn was standing and only then did she let him go. But she did it in order to stand next to him and *lean into him*.

Auggie planted his feet, stood strong and crossed his arms on his chest, but somehow made that seem not like it was a dis of her physical affection but simply that he was the man she could (and did) lean on.

And they looked cute together.

My stomach started feeling funny.

Not the gooey funny (exactly).

Another, better, kind.

"Mom, you can go now," Juno encouraged.

Okay...

Shit.

I turned to the class, pinned a smile on my face, and thanked God that I'd written out bullet points and practiced speaking about them in my bedroom last night, then in the bathroom mirror this morning, not to mention in the car on the way there.

The words came forth and I hoped they made sense.

We'd been told to keep our presentations to about ten to fifteen minutes in order to have time to take some questions and not exceed the kids' ability to pay attention.

I probably talked for ten. There were only a couple of questions.

And then I was ridiculously thankful when Ms. Linn said, "Thank you so much, Ms. Hannigan."

"Now, Auggie, your turn!" Juno cried excitedly.

I wandered toward my daughter.

"Yes, now class, welcome Mr. Hero, who is going to talk to you about being a marine," Ms. Linn reminded them.

Auggie strode to stand in front of the room as the class singsonged, "Welcome, Mr. Hero."

It was then I realized, when I'd been talking, I'd had some of the girls' attention but none of the boys', because right then I could see Auggie had *all* their attention.

In fact, the vast majority of the class was leaning forward on their desks like he was a magnet luring them to him.

I looked at him.

I'd gone into detail about how gorgeous he was.

I did not share that he was wearing black cargo pants. Light-weight black utility boots were on his feet. A black quarter-zip wicking pullover with a gray stripe that ran over the shoulder and down the arm covered him up top.

And a serious expression was on his face.

In other words, I did not share that he looked like he'd strolled into that classroom direct from some maneuvers, like, say, rappelling down the side of a high-rise building.

He launched in.

"I appreciate your teacher saying you'll be thanking me for my service, but you don't need to do that. Because we all should serve our country in some capacity. I chose to do it enlisting, doing drills, learning how to shoot a rifle, going to class and listening to lectures about strategy and tactics, and being deployed and put in situations where I would eventually have to put everything I'd learned into action. I also do it by voting. When you turn eighteen, one way you can, and should do it, is by voting. You can also do it by keeping informed about what's happening and staying on top of your representatives by sharing with them what's important to you. You can do it by knowing the laws and obeying them. You can do it by becoming involved in some sort of civil service or with an organization that does good work to keep the will of the people, not the will of special interests, foremost in our representatives' minds."

Some boy in the third row interrupted him by calling out, "But you know how to shoot a gun, right?"

Auggie nodded shortly. "I know how to shoot many different kinds of guns. I've shot all those guns. And I've shot people."

I sucked in a breath, so did Ms. Linn and pretty much every kid in that room.

"And it was not fun," Auggie went on. "What it was, was nec-essary in the worst form that can take. But what's more important for you to know about that is not me lifting a rifle and pulling the trigger. It's the foreign policy that put me in the position to do something so terrible. It's the decision-making path that planted me in that desert. And each and every one of you, when you can vote, will bear responsibility for where any soldiers' boots hit ground. Now, you can handle that responsibility responsibly. Or you can choose not to give a crap. But you'll still be responsible for where he or she goes, who they shoot, and who shoots at them. My advice, having had my boots hit ground in a lot of places that weren't a barrel of laughs: Give a crap."

"Um . . ." I started nervously, then called, "Auggie, honey."

He looked to me.

Yes, his expression was very serious.

However.

"Maybe dial it back a bit?" I suggested.

"No way!" a kid cried. "Like, *we* send soldiers to deserts and jungles and stuff?"

Auggie turned back to the class. "Not now, but you will. But now, your parents do. And you will when you're no longer a minor and you can assume your responsibilities as a citizen."

"That's crazy!" another kid said. "The president sends soldiers places."

"And who votes for the president?" Auggie asked.

There was a powerful, collective sense of *Hmm* throughout the classroom.

"My uncle was like, you know . . . he was in the army and he went somewhere," another kid said. "He came back, and Mom was mad because he did it without a hand. And it messed up his head. And she and Grandma and Granddad said he shouldn't have been there in the first place."

"Maybe he shouldn't, but maybe he should," Auggie said. "Sometimes, it's ugly work, but it's gotta get done. Do you wanna know what cost your uncle his hand? What was so important he was somewhere that could happen? Why someone who will never pick up a rifle decided to send him somewhere where he'd not come back all in one piece?"

"Yes," the kid said quietly.

"Yes," Auggie agreed. His voice gentled when he asked, "Where did he go?"

"A place called Sylia."

"Syria," Auggie corrected kindly. "And maybe one day you can have a conversation with your mom and grandparents about it and they can explain why they feel the way they do. But there are very bad people in Syria doing very bad things. And I'm sorry your uncle lost his hand. That's terrible for him and everyone who loves him. But from what I know about what's happening there, there's a good chance he was fighting the good fight."

The kid bit his lip.

Auggie gave him a second for any follow-up if he needed it, but when the kid stayed quiet, Auggie continued.

"Enlisting in the marines was the best decision I've made in my life so far. Before that, I could mess around and when you do that, you mess up. I had no direction and had no idea what I wanted from my life. In the marines, I learned discipline. And I'm not gonna lie. Shooting a gun is fun. Shooting a rifle is more fun. But you shouldn't ever do either unless you know what you're doing and you're in a safe space to do it. The marines taught me that too. Basic training isn't easy, but it's good for the body. It's good for the mind. It also teaches you not only how to rely on yourself, but how to be on a team. *Really* be on a team. There are good things to learn when you play a sport, and your teammates depend on you to shoot a basket or make a touchdown. There are better things to learn when the team you're on depends on you to stay alive."

Now, for better or worse (and with one glance at Ms. Linn, it was clear, albeit surprising, she thought it was for the better, alternately, she could be mesmerized by Auggie's lips moving, which happened), having their rapt attention, Auggie kept talking, and when he was done, he took questions for a lot longer than I did.

When it was time for us to go, Ms. Linn broke in and ended it. She thanked us. She told the class to thank us. And she allowed Juno to walk us out the door.

Whereupon Auggie got another hug and a "You're the best, Auggie! That was great!" from my daughter.

Auggie gave her a one-armed, but still warm, hug then let her go.

She popped back, gaze aimed up at him, and announced, "And I signed you up to help build the sets for the Thanksgiving show."

I felt my insides seize.

One of Auggie's wickedly awesome eyebrows went up.

"They said they needed people who could build things and you helped Auntie Ryn with her house, so I figured you'd be great!" she finished.

"Uh…" I didn't quite begin.

Because she turned to me, I got a hug and a "See you tonight, Mom!"

And then my daughter—who had pulled two big, whopping fast ones—shot me a dazzling smile like nothing was amiss, and bopped back into the classroom, her long dark hair swinging down her back.

I watched her go and then took another step into the hall as, with a thankful good-bye smile (that lingered on Auggie, unsurprisingly), Ms. Linn closed the door on Auggie and me.

Stiffly, still reeling about all that had gone down over the last hour, including my girl's final bombshell, I turned to Auggie only to see him striding resolutely down the hall.

Okay.

Hang on a second.

A lot just happened.

But not lost in that was the fact that my daughter had been around this man over the last year at parties and get-togethers, celebrations and just hanging out. She did not hide she liked him, he in turn was great with her.

I didn't allow myself to process this in any proper way considering the fact, to me, they were just my kid and an adult that was a part of my posse. The end.

He didn't come over to my house for wine nights or to watch TV or in some capacity where he'd eventually be tucking her into bed. He was just around. He wasn't (I told myself) important, to me or Juno.

But I was wrong about that.

For me.

And, it would seem, Juno.

I had fucked him, then kicked him out.

And somewhere along the line that I'd missed, Juno had claimed him.

Shit.

This needed to be discussed.

A lot needed to be discussed, including how Auggie and I could move on from what we'd done in my entryway.

We shared friends. We shared time. We shared space.

We'd *been* friends.

And my kid obviously liked him a lot.

We had to sort our shit.

Now.

I hurried after him in my heels, calling, not loudly (seeing as I was in the hall of an elementary school), "Auggie."

He didn't break stride.

Now, he wasn't *too* tall, like Mag and Mo tall (Mag was six four, Mo seemed even taller, but it could just be that Mo seemed bigger all around because Mo was a pretty intense-looking guy).

But Auggie was tall. Taller than me and I wasn't short by a long shot, being five eight.

So he had long legs.

Long legs that took him away from me quickly.

I hastened my step.

"Auggie!"

Nope.

He was out the front door.

Dammit.

I dashed after him, giving a quick wave to the ladies at the front desk who did not see me wave since their eyes were glued to the door Auggie just walked through.

Understandable.

"Auggie!" I called again, sharper and a bit louder this time.

I also cursed that I'd worn the pumps I was wearing.

They were sleek, stylish and high-heeled. I thought they said Professional Mom, even if for the most part I wore them with jeans because they made me feel like Cool Mom.

The pencil skirt I was wearing that I didn't think was too tight until I had to semi-run in it didn't help.

"Auggie!" I snapped as he opened the door to his silver Kia Telluride.

Finally, he turned to me.

I stopped a couple of feet away, huffing and puffing, such was the effort of running in heels and a pencil skirt, and this said something, considering I danced in the former nearly every night.

"I'm thinking there are things we need to discuss," I announced, I thought, unnecessarily.

I was going to suggest we go have a cup of coffee or ask him if he'd had lunch (I had not) and maybe offer to buy him a late lunch.

I did not get that chance.

Auggie spoke.

And tore me apart.

"I fucked you and you were a sweet fuck. But you were clear after it was over, and having had time to consider it, I'm glad you were. I also agree with what you said. So I'll be clear now and stick to your theme."

That was the definition of not a good start.

Alas, he continued.

"Your daughter's got some ideas and it's on you to sort her out. I'd appreciate if you did that. But you and me, however you've decided to work that, is not gonna happen. I've got no time for game playing and no patience for people who play. And I fucking hate cockteases. Even though you finally let me get in there, you're not gonna lead me around by my dick for the shot at another go. Your kid is cute. I like her. They need help with their Thanksgiving thing, I'm in. As long as I don't have to spend time with you. If you're around, you gotta find a way to tell her I'm out. Are we clear?"

I stood solid, marveling that I managed to do that because every word he spoke felt like he was pummeling me with stones.

Hefty, jagged ones.

"Pepper?" he clipped.

Oh no.

Nonono.

My sinuses were stinging, my eyes felt funny.

Shit.

I was going to cry.

"Crystal," I whispered, whirled on my thin heel and started booking across the parking lot toward my Hyundai.

I managed to get my keys out of my purse and bleep the locks of the Tucson, all without falling flat on my face, which was a downright miracle. I also managed to get the door open.

But the tears were streaming.

Shit.

I was about to adjust to get around the door and hike my ass into the seat when the door was slammed shut in front of me.

I whirled again, only to find Auggie *way* in my space.

"These are the games I'm not playing," Auggie warned low.

"I told you I understand," I replied, my voice husky.

"Do not forget, you were the one who kicked my ass out. Before that, you were the one who shot me down, repeatedly. And that night, you were the one who came on to me."

I did do that.

And I didn't have some lame excuse (but at least it would be something to blame it on), like I was drunk.

I was lucid and with it and all there.

I was just tired of denying myself.

I just wanted to feel attractive.

Desirable.

Womanly.

And not in a stripper way.

In the opposite of a stripper way.

In a let-a-man-like-Auggie-touch-kiss-and-have-sex-with-me way.

No, no, no.

Honesty.

In a let *Auggie* touch, kiss and have sex with me way.

I closed my eyes tight, but when I did, more wet leaked from them, so I opened them again.

Why hadn't I put on my sunglasses?

Auggie was staring at my cheeks.

"I hear you, Augustus. I'm processing what you say," I promised. "You can move away now. We can be done."

"Why are you crying?" he asked.

Was he insane?

Considering the answer was obvious, I didn't respond to his question.

"Just let's be done, all right?" I requested.

"Why are you crying, Pepper?"

I shook my head.

He took half a step back, saying, "Yeah, this is a game I'm not playing."

Can you love me?

Can you do it in a way that I'll be able to trust you?

Trust that you won't step out on me?

Trust that you won't break my heart?

Trust that you can love my daughter like she's your own?

Trust that you won't break her heart either?

Do you have it in you to build a home and a life with me where I can look after you, you can look after me, we can raise my baby and maybe make more, and all of us will be safe and happy and together forever?

Can you take me to that perfect world?

In other words, this is far from a game.

You don't gamble everything on everything.

Which is why I can't gamble anything on you.

"It would figure, when she's been batting a thousand, I would be the one Lots tried to hook up with a woman who just wants to yank my chain."

And again...

Ouch.

"Nothing to say?" he taunted.

I stood there and did nothing, but swallow.

"Yeah," he said softly, looked me up and down...

And then he turned and walked away.

CHAPTER TWO

Gonzo for God

PEPPER

O h my God, I'm gonna kill her," I muttered to myself, eyeing my sister standing on my front porch as I drove up to my townhome in my boring townhome community where every structure looked like the next.

Except for how everyone was trying to outdo everyone else in outdoor home ornamentation.

Including me.

Halloween had just gone, but Thanksgiving was around the corner.

Therefore, I had my eye-catching wreath made of nothing but a dense circle of profuse orange berries on my door.

I also had a swirl of a fake, thin branch that had an attractive straggle of fall leaves artfully swagging over the beam at the front of my porch.

I further had the charmingly painted board leaning beside the front door that had the word GRATEFUL running down it and big pots filled with crowded sprays of button mums in the colors of burnt-orange and cream. These were interspersed with orange and white pumpkins on either side of the door.

And the brick steps leading to the porch had more of these pots and pumpkins carefully strewn along the sides. Interweaved with them were fairy lights timed to go on when the sun went down.

Steps that right now led up to my sister standing on my porch among my autumnal efforts to keep up with the Joneses at the same time give a homey home to my daughter so one day she'd be able to say, "My mom was so awesome. She *loved* the holidays. She went all out every season, decorating the house like you wouldn't believe! She's the greatest mom *in the world*!"

Yep.

That was my goal.

At least the last part was.

In other words, my décor was not the best in the complex, but it far from sucked.

I was not glorying in my holiday décor as I hit my garage door opener, and this was not only because my sister was there.

We could just say on the drive home I had not been able to find my center.

I had also not breathed and mentally retreated to my heart where I should always be safe.

Nope.

I had cried until I wondered why on earth I was crying and then I started to get mad.

Because seriously...

What in *the* hell?

I did not deserve that from Auggie.

No freaking way.

So his bestest buds were Mo, Mag, Boone and Axl.

And Lottie had fixed them up with fantastic women, and they were all living various versions of happy.

And some version of that didn't happen for Auggie and me.

But not because I was playing games.

Not because I was *yanking his chain*.

It was because it wasn't just me in this scenario.

And I had *explained that to him*.

I did this during those times I sadly, but yes, repeatedly shot him down.

Now, one could say I was glad that happened with Auggie in the parking lot of Juno's school because I realized while driving home that it was good we never gave it a go.

Because he was *a dick*.

And at that present moment, for obvious reasons, I really didn't need this, whatever it was, with my sister.

I needed to go up to my room, light some candles, get cross-legged, close my eyes, shut it all out and *breathe*.

I didn't even have the car turned off before I touched the remote to lower the garage door just in case I needed to cut her off at the pass.

But by the time I hit my kitchen, the doorbell was ringing.

Part two of my bid to be all I could be for my kid in order to give her all I could give: although our townhome complex didn't structurally have all the originality in the universe (however, the Battle of the Seasonal Outdoor Décor had grown to epic proportions, so it didn't lack personality), the inside of our townhome was, if I did say so myself, *everything*.

From the garage you walked into a sea of clean white cabinets in a substantially sized kitchen. There was a shiny taupe tile backsplash set in a herringbone pattern. The island in the middle had some fun shelves on one side where I put plants, picture frames and cookbooks. The appliances were gorgeous brushed stainless steel. And the light fixture above the island, with its five bright bulbs encased in an open metal frame, was a showstopper.

The family room fed right off the kitchen.

It featured a shag rug in mushroom that was *divine*. Juno and I had picked a pink couch (it was more of a blush, so it was semi-neutral, not outright gaudy) with a fluffy pillow back. A circular coffee table sat in the middle of the rug and was decked with a matte blush vase filled with faux-but-didn't-look-it milky dahlias and spikes of eucalyptus leaves. A white built-in with our books and TV and knickknacks was against the wall opposite the kitchen. And on the floors, there were some pink poofs and huge woolly-crochet-covered pillows for lounging. Peanut-colored comfy armchairs sporting big square pillows of snowy fake fur rounded that area out.

It was clean and tidy and serene and feminine, but it still had character, was warm and welcoming.

I loved coming home.

I loved cleaning our home.

I loved cooking in our kitchen or lazing on that pink couch and bingeing TV.

I did not love my doorbell ringing incessantly.

Dammit.

She'd seen me arrive, she was my sister, and it was uncool to avoid her.

Considering why she was probably there (to ask me to church, demand I go to church, or a prayer meeting, or a sit-down with their creepy-ass pastor, or some combo or variation of the above, all of which I had, for an entire decade now, in a variety of ways from kind and gentle to impatient and curt, refused to do), it was uncool of her not to avoid me, that was true.

But I tried in any situation to be the least uncool one.

On a deep exhalation of breath, I walked to the hall that was flanked on the right side with a set of stairs and fed into the aforementioned entryway, which was actually quite large and grand, considering the entirety of the townhouse was less than two thousand square feet.

Off one side was a hall closet, a powder room, and to the other side, a small office that I had set up as a dual zone. One supremely girlie desk where Juno could do classwork or crafts or play on her purple laptop or whatever floated her boat. One slightly less girlie desk where I could pay bills and write letters and online shop.

Tech wasn't allowed anywhere else in the house.

Outside the office, we spent time together or with books, magazines, television, crafts or our own thoughts.

That was the only way I was a hard-ass mom.

But no way in hell was my kid going to get beaten down by social media or lose half her time to YouTube when there was so much more life had to offer.

Like living it.

Fortunately, she was still a little too young to care about this.

But I had to get that seed planted now and gird my loins because it was coming, I knew it.

I pulled open the door, and unfortunately for my sister, Saffron, when I did, I was raring to go.

It didn't help that she was wearing a crewneck sweater, a corduroy blazer over that, a scarf not wrapped jauntily around her neck, but instead wrapped to hide the skin there and a wool A-line skirt that fell precisely two inches below her knee. However, no skin showed there either because she had on low-heeled boots. She also wore no makeup and her hair was pulled back in a knot at the base of her skull.

If I didn't know her, I would expect her to try to hand me a pamphlet and ask me about my relationship with God.

Even though I knew her, it would not surprise me if she handed me a pamphlet and requested we talk about my relationship with God.

In fact, my guess was, she was there, without the pamphlet, but in her church-girl getup, ready to talk to me about my relationship with God.

"Saffron, I cannot do this now," I snapped.

"Mom has cancer."

And yet another time that day I was stunned immobile. But this time, it felt like my insides were shrinking.

"What?" I whispered.

"She has cancer and it's not good. The family needs you, Pepper."

I shook my head slowly.

She misunderstood my headshake, which was all about the fact that I could not process that my mother had cancer and it was "not good."

"No, really," she went on. "*We need you.*"

"I...I...what kind of cancer?" I asked.

"Breast, but it's moved to the lymph nodes."

Oh God.

Lymph nodes were bad. Everyone knew that.

I stepped out of the way, arcing an arm down low in front of me to invite her in.

She came in but didn't move any farther than the entryway, her usual MO, for, my guess, she feared beyond that she felt she would be tainted by my den of iniquity.

I closed the door and turned to her. "I can't believe this."

"I couldn't either. But it's true."

"I...my God." I pulled myself together. "Okay. What do you need? More, what does *Mom* need? Do you want to come and sit down? I can make us some coffee."

"Pepper, you shouldn't use the Lord's name like that. And the Lord frowns on drugs and you know caffeine is a drug."

I closed my mouth.

"And really," she carried on, "you need to be careful about that. All of that. We need you pure for the prayer circles."

Uh-oh.

"The prayer circles?"

She nodded. "We also need to find Birch. *Immediately*. Have you heard from him?" she continued.

Birch was our older brother and I had not heard from him in years.

Neither had anyone else.

"No, I haven't, Saffron. Listen—"

"We have to find him. As soon as possible. The full family has to be there to complete the circle."

Yep.

Uh-oh.

"Saffron, *listen*," I hissed. "I need to know what's going on. When was Mom diagnosed? Where? Have her treatment options been explained to her? Have you all—?"

"She was diagnosed last year."

I gasped because...

Well...

Last year?

And I was only hearing about this now?

What the hell?

"*Last year?*"

"Yes," she said briskly. "And back then, she wanted to try the treatment the doctor suggested, so Dad allowed it."

"He *allowed* it?" I echoed.

She nodded, also briskly. "Yes. And things looked good, then they didn't. So it's obvious to everyone this is not in the doctor's hands, it's in God's. Which is why we need a *full* circle."

Okay.

My dad and sister thought my mother's cancer was in God's hands.

And they were right.

It was.

The thing about that was, He'd given that disease to my mother. He'd given it to our family. It was on Mom to take care of the precious life He'd also given her. And it was on us to take care of the precious life *that was my mother*.

And although I expected God would be hip to a prayer circle, He was probably expecting a whole lot more from all of us.

Right.

Time to center myself and breathe.

Saffron didn't breathe.

She kept talking.

"Therefore, we need you. We also need Birch. We must start right away."

What *I* needed was to focus on the important things, so I did that. "How is she?"

"She's losing weight and her energy levels aren't great."

Saffron had always been very close to Dad. As had Mom, so naturally, to be with Dad, and to make Dad happy, Saffron and Mom spent a lot of time together.

Honestly?

I had no idea if my sister was close to my mother. My family was not showy with affection (well, those three weren't, Birch and I had been to each other).

God (or their God) frowned on that kind of thing.

But a mom was a mom.

I wasn't close to Mom and this news had me reeling.

I took a step toward my sister, lifting my hand to touch her, starting, "Saffron—"

She leaned toward me and bit out, "I don't wanna hear it."

I stilled, my hand raised, and looked in her eyes.

Her crazy Gonzo for God eyes that would not let anything else in.

Because that was what made Dad happy.

So that was what Saffron, and Mom, gave to him.

"Are you going to help Mom, or not?" she demanded.

I dropped my hand and said quietly, "Of course I want to

help. I'll be there for her. I need to think about how I want Juno involved, because she's growing up, but this is a lot for a little kid to understand. But I don't think that a prayer—"

Saffron cut me off.

"You have those friends, those . . . *men*. They can do things. Can they find Birch for us?"

Birch had vanished over a decade ago with not a single word or sighting.

Auggie and the commandos could probably find him in an hour.

Suddenly, a phone scenario, unbidden, crowded my head.

Me calling Auggie.

Ring, ring, ring.

"Hello, cocktease."

"Hello to you too. Listen, my mom's got cancer, and apparently, it's bad. We need a full, pure prayer circle but no one knows where my brother is. Can you do me a favor and find him?"

"Your mom has cancer?"

"Yes."

"That's convenient."

"Not really."

"I mean convenient for you to have an excuse to connect with me so you can keep yanking my chain."

"I got what you meant."

"A prayer circle?"

"We never got around to me explaining my family are Gonzo for God. It might seem crazy to you, but they believe praying for her will get God to step up and cure her cancer. I usually don't get involved with this kind of thing, but this time, I might have to allow myself to be roped in. If only to have some time with Mom. Because she's Gonzo too, but she's still my mom. And so I also need to find some way to locate my brother who escaped all this crazy years ago and rope him in too. Can you assist with that?"

Long pause.

"*Nice try, player.*"
Hang up.
"Pepper!" Saffron snapped.
My body started and I refocused on her.
"Can you ask them to help?" she pushed.
I could totally ask Mo. He looked like the evil henchman to a Bond villain, but he was a sweetie. And if I went to him through Lottie, he might even keep it from the other guys.

Mag, Boone and Axl, I likely could not ask because they'd be all in to help, but they'd share it with Auggie.

As for Auggie...well, that was obviously a big, fat *no.*

"Let me think about it," I said to my sister.

"We don't have time for you to think on it."

My insides started shriveling again and my voice had dipped low when I asked, "What do you mean, we don't have time for me to think on it?"

"I told you, Mom has cancer."

"I heard you, but—"

"You don't kick back with cancer."

Like tackling it with a prayer circle?

"So, will you ask them to help find Birch, or what?" she pressed.

Okay, I made really good money as a stripper.

Bought myself a nice townhome in a nice complex with great landscaping and the War of the Seasonal Décor happening, awesomely furnish that townhome, keep my kid (and myself, I had to admit) in trendy/stylish/good quality clothes type of good money.

I even made a monthly deposit into the savings account Corbin and I started when Juno was born that I wrested from him when she was five and I found out he was still fucking his high school sweetheart. And when I used the word "still" I used it in the sense that he hadn't quit *since high school.* And at that time, I was twenty-five and he was twenty-eight.

If I could keep those deposits up and play with that money, shifting it around in high-interest CDs and the like, it would take the pressure off financially should Juno go to college or a trade school. And if she didn't, then it'd be a nice nest egg for her to set up for life, saving her from credit card debt she might accrue because she needed pots and pans and a couch.

What was left over from my earnings was little and it was firmly set aside for a rainy day. And because it was sparse (though growing) and anything could happen, I never touched it.

But I supposed when your mother had cancer—and Saffron was not hiding that things were bad—you considered it a rainy day.

Birch no way, no how would come home to join hands and kumbaya God.

That said, my brother was a good guy. Funny and smart, and until he took off, he and I as the outcasts of that crew were thick as thieves.

I got it. I didn't hold a grudge. I totally understood why he vanished.

But if I knew my brother, he'd want to know this was going down with Mom.

So rainy day time, maybe I should use that extra to hire a private investigator.

If Auggie and the guys, trained in all sorts of things, could find Birch in an hour, so could another PI.

I mean, how much would an hour and a few computer searches cost?

"I'll figure something out," I told Saffron.

She stared at me.

"Promise," I went on.

Saffron sighed.

"I'll give Mom a call," I said.

"Fine. But I'm your point person about Birch. Dad and I don't want you upsetting her."

It never felt good, being that daughter who "upset" her mother.

I did it a lot by just being me.

"I'll try not to upset her," I replied.

She sighed again, this one about five notches above the last one in the level of beleaguered she was, before she walked to the door.

When she had it open, I put my hand on the edge, and shared, "I can help with other things too, you know."

Having moved over the threshold, Saffron turned to me.

"We need your and Birch's spirit and guiding light. That's what we need."

"Okay, I'll consider that. So now let's talk about what *Mom* needs."

That got me Saffron's fuck-you face (though she'd never used the F-word in her life, still, that face totally told me to ef off).

Then she turned and strode on her sensible heels to her minivan that she selected herself, even if she had no husband, no children, but did on occasion need to cart a number of carcasses to revivals.

I watched her get in.

I watched her drive away.

Then I closed my door, rested my head against it, and gave myself a second to gather some strength in the midst of my seriously shitty day.

After that, I went to the phone and called my mother.

I did not mention Birch.

I did offer to make casseroles to help feed her and Dad, as well as come over to clean if she thought that might help.

She declined and asked me to Sunday's service.

I declined and asked if I could come and visit sometime outside of church time.

Considering I'd just failed in my goal of not upsetting her, she shared I upset her by not saying, "Of course, darling! Come over straight away. I'm scared and anxious and the best thing for me would be time spent with my girl."

She told me she'd think about it.

She then said she had some corn bread to make, and she had to go.

Wanting to do what I could for my mother in this time, I did what she asked.

I let her go.

CHAPTER THREE

"Stepdad"

PEPPER

It was not even a half an hour after my sister left, I was sitting at my desk in the office zone when I saw the car pull into my drive.

My desk faced the window so Juno's desk could face a carefully, and prettily, constructed gallery wall of corkboards, chalkboards, whiteboards and cute shelves, all hers to use to be creative and express herself.

And I was at my desk so I could be at my laptop and do a deep dive into Facebook.

I'd unearthed my high school yearbooks from my freshman and sophomore years (the years I shared the same school with Birch), so I could remind myself of the names of his friends.

From there, I tried to find them on Facebook and see if Birch followed them.

In the past, I had (more than once) tried to find him on every social media platform there was.

No go.

So I was perusing profiles and pictures of people who weren't super big on privacy settings in hopes my brother was keeping in touch (maybe under a different name) with old friends.

Okay, so it was a figurative rainy day, but I didn't have to pay a PI to do a Facebook search I could do myself. And if I could find him myself, when I got a flat tire or the hot water heater went out, I didn't have to sweat it.

This was what I was in the throes of when the car pulled into my drive.

Shiny.

Black.

Expensive.

BMW.

Corbin.

For the first time ever, I wondered if my love of the Lord as practiced through meditation and prayer and taking my daughter to our nondenominational Christian church was not enough and maybe I *should* be Gonzo for God.

Because I'd somehow karmically earned a really freaking bad day.

I was standing in my opened front door before Corbin made it from his car to the porch.

This meant I was in position to watch Corbin walk up my steps.

I'd always known I was pretty. No conceit, just fact. I was tall and slim, but I had good tits, round hips, a nice booty and long legs. Added to that, I had long, thick honey-blonde hair that was almost, but not quite, strawberry and I had features that put me firm between a California Surfer Girl and a symmetrically gifted, local-gigs-only (thus not super) model.

All great attributes for a stripper.

All *fantastic* attributes for attracting assholes.

Corbin having been one of those assholes.

My ex was a wolf in sheep's clothes.

A sheep's *expensive* clothes.

He, too, was tall. Dark. Good-looking and built in a rough-hewn way, like he was a lumberjack in a suit.

And he was affable.

Very affable.

He could talk to anybody.

Get on an elevator with him and he'd know how many kids you had, their names and your favorite restaurant before you got off.

In this time, if you were a woman, you'd feel listened to and your confidence would have received a healthy boost that this handsome man was talking to you in a way that was just that tad bit flirtatious. If you were a man, you'd feel listened to and wonder if he golfed because you needed another guy to complete your foursome.

You'd also be in possession of his business card.

Yes.

That was Corbin.

When it came out that he'd betrayed me, my heart had been so shattered, I'd lost my mind and I hadn't gained it back until I met Auggie.

Because Corbin had made me feel beautiful and listened to, he was great in bed, he was driven, an excellent provider, and he changed lightbulbs, never missed the yearly rotation of switching out batteries in smoke alarms and took out the trash without being asked.

Thus, he was a good lover, a good partner, and he made me feel like we were a great couple who could tackle the world and face our future strong and together... always.

As such, I'd been a mess when I found out that was so far from true, it wasn't funny *and* I'd lost what I thought was (but was not in truth) a really great guy who took care of me, Juno, gave me orgasms (most of the time) and was not hard on the eyes.

Then I'd met Auggie and all pining for Corbin and the life we'd had was gone.

Now, all I saw was a grifter.

And for reasons unknown, he was on my porch.

"Hey, honey," he said.

Okay, so I was over Corbin, and as such, he shouldn't have any power over me.

But it pissed me off no end that on occasion he still called me "honey."

He had at times, since we broke up, tried to pretend all was hunky-dory, we still had love and affection, we just lived in separate houses now.

All was not hunky-dory and not because we were broken up or *how* we had broken up.

Because our parenting styles differed vastly.

One could just say tech was not limited for Juno at Corbin's house, mostly so he could use it as a sitter.

And I'd already gotten into the women.

"Corbin," I returned, not leaving the doorway. "What's up?"

Suffice it to say, I did not want to know what was up.

In the time I had between now and Juno coming home, I had Facebook searching to do, not to mention I had to research private investigators, also figure out how I was going to talk to my daughter about the stuff she'd pulled that day at school with Auggie. Primarily, *why* she did all that, but also *how*.

I didn't have time for whatever was up with Corbin.

He looked beyond me with his attractive mostly-green-but-still-hazel eyes, then down went his gaze to the mums and gourds on either side of the door, and finally up again to me.

"Cute pumpkins," he said on what was once (to me) a panty-melting grin.

Someone was in a mood.

And it was a mood I was suspicious of because, after I'd

preliminarily lost my mind at our breakup, I'd gone cold, he'd gone alternately cheerful (to get his way) and remote mingling with asshole-y (when he wasn't), and we'd sometimes gotten along and other times (that being most times) not.

"Thanks," I replied shortly. "Now, what's up?"

"Can I come inside?" he requested.

"Corbin, I haven't had the greatest of days. Just tell me what's up that you couldn't text or phone about, but instead, you're a surprise guest at my house."

"Yeah, Pepper, I get bad days considering today some other guy showed at my daughter's career day, that guy not her dad, that dad being me."

Well...hell.

I stepped aside.

Corbin came in and did not have issue with the abode of sin my sister thought my house was, therefore she didn't let full immersion blemish her pure soul.

He walked right to the great room in the back.

I had failed to share that our backyard was practically nonexistent. It was just a patch of grass and a small, covered porch surrounded by a high dark-gray fence with interesting horizontal slats.

The view over the fence was to the units on the next block.

But since the entire back wall of my lower floor was windows, and my daughter needed cool outdoor space for her and her buds, my backyard was also dotted with big pots filled now with autumnal mums. Farther, on the patio, we had a corner sectional sofa with plenty of seating and lounging space with some poofs for feet or asses and neutral-colored stools to put down drinks or books. Rounding this out was a calming blush-and-powder-blue rug. And for evening times, there were not only more fairy lights (these with pretty shades), but also ground lighting against the fence.

And it sucked in a huge way that Corbin, standing in his nice suit in my kickass kitchen with the backdrop of my small but totally awesome yard, looked like he belonged right there.

Auggie might look like he belonged there too. Woefully, I'd never know. But odds were high he would, considering he'd looked like he belonged in front of a third-grade classroom and I wouldn't have called that either.

Corbin started it.

"So, apparently, our daughter has a stepdad."

Dammit.

"Corbin—"

"Baby, did you think I wouldn't find out?"

At that, my shoulders jerked back, and my head bounced on them because of it.

He had never stopped calling me "honey."

But he'd stopped calling me "baby."

That was the first "baby" I'd gotten since I kicked his ass out three years ago.

"Juno plays her cards close to her chest with us," Corbin continued, then he raised a hand, palm out to me. "And I'll own it, that's on me. I'd been stupid. I'd fucked up. And after I fucked up and lost you, I realized how badly I *really* fucked up. I then slid into denial. But I can no longer deny the parade of women since we ended was to try to hurt you like I thought you'd hurt me after you refused to try to work things out between us, when I'm understanding now that I hurt myself. And you. And Juno."

I wasn't proud of it, but my mouth had dropped open.

And I was so stunned with the stuff coming out of *his* mouth, I couldn't close my own.

He took a step closer to me, which didn't bring him close-close, but the gesture was not lost.

"But I know my girl," he said, his voice quieting. "If you had a man that was going to assume that role in Juno's life, you'd tell me. Face-to-face."

"I would," I forced out, still stuck on being called *his* girl.

Something shifted in his face that I was not sure about.

"Right," he said. "So who is this guy?"

"He's...in my crew. A friend of Lottie's husband, Mo. And he's a veteran. A former marine."

Corbin's lips tipped up as he said, "Ah. The cool guy. Dads are rarely the cool guys."

"Corbin—"

"So the teacher got it wrong," he stated. "Just a friend. But Juno didn't tell me because she didn't want to hurt my feelings."

Once he'd worked that out on his own, something he could have done through getting the necessary info he needed by texting me, he took another step toward me and this one made me brace because he had long legs and it brought him close-close.

I didn't know if I should retreat because of what that might say about how I felt regarding his proximity, or if I should stand my ground and declare that his being close didn't affect me at all.

I chose the latter, because it didn't, outside making me feel weird.

And his voice was still quiet, but now it was low in a way I was very familiar with in our past life.

It was his persuading voice.

Like, say, he wanted to persuade me that he needed to have that long weekend in Vegas with his buds (which was probably a long weekend with his other woman).

And like, say, when he wanted to persuade me to have sex.

I'd been a pushover for both. The first, because I'd trusted him and loved him and wanted him to have a good time with his buds. The second, because I liked having sex with him.

But it had to be said, it was also because I'd always liked the way his voice sounded when he spoke like that.

"Okay, now, if you've got time, I wanna talk about something else."

I shook my head. "I don't have time. Juno will be home soon."

"The bus doesn't drop her off until three thirty and it isn't even three."

I hadn't checked a clock, but this was probably true.

Still.

"Corbin, if you have something to discuss, text me, we'll set up a time to discuss it. But before Juno gets home, I have some things to do."

"Are they more important than talking to your daughter's father?"

"Actually, yes."

That surprised him.

Okay, I'd neglected to mention that Corbin was also far from dim. As such, it didn't take him long to put things together.

"You'd mentioned a bad day, is everything okay?"

No, it wasn't.

My daughter played me.

She'd played Auggie.

Auggie thought I was playing him.

He'd called me a cocktease and generally been a massive dick.

My mother had cancer that had spread to the lymph nodes.

And I had to find my long-lost brother and convince him to join a prayer circle.

To share all of that without sharing any of it, I said, "It's just that today has been a lot."

He reached out and cupped my upper arm in order to rub it up and down in a soothing manner as he urged, "Talk to me."

Right.

Now was the time to retreat.

I carefully removed my arm from his touch and stepped away.

"Pepper—"

"What's going on, Corbin?" I asked.

"This is what I want to know from you," he replied.

"Just pointing out, I didn't show up at your house unannounced."

He bobbed his head. "All right. I heard word Juno's stepdad visited her class today, and since I didn't know she had a stepdad, I came here to understand how that happened."

We'd gone over that but . . .

Hang on a second.

"School isn't over," I pointed out. "And Juno doesn't have a cell phone. Regardless, she obviously isn't sharing with you about this. So how did you hear the teacher called Auggie her stepdad?"

He erased the minimal distance I'd put between us.

I took another step back and nearly tripped on our fabulous shag rug.

He erased that step too.

"Corbin!" I snapped. "What's going on?"

"Paula called and told me. Her daughter has a cell phone."

I was confused.

"Who's Paula and what does her daughter have to do with it?"

Corbin hesitated. I saw his eyes working, the gray matter behind those eyes came up with a solution and that was what came out of his mouth.

"Right, what I'm going to say is going to seem like it will fuck us up even more, but I swear to God I'm going to unfuck us."

Uh . . .

Us?

He kept going.

"Paula is the mother of one of the girls in Juno's class. I met her after the parent/teacher conference. When we were done with Ms. Linn, you went to your car, I had to use the restroom, and when I came out, we ran into each other. We've been seeing each other ever since."

Okay.

All right.

Um...

"You're dating a parent of another kid in Juno's class," I stated, just to be sure I'd heard him correctly and it wasn't some *other* mother of some *other* kid who hopefully was *not* in Juno's class, or better yet, not in Juno's entire *grade* or even in Juno's *entire school*.

"It wasn't smart, Pepper, but I'd just spent a whole half an hour sitting next to you and you barely looked at me so—"

I stepped wide and to the side and shouted, "*Are you stupid?*"

He turned to me and tried a conciliatory, "Pepper—"

"Does Juno know this?" I demanded.

"Paula has met Juno. I have not met Paula's girl. But Juno doesn't know Paula's girl is in her class."

"Well, Paula's girl knows about you, or she wouldn't be calling her mother about Auggie talking to the class," I pointed out.

Corbin had no response to that.

Translation: Paula was probably a good mother who was being careful with her daughter and Corbin was lying to his daughter because, if things progressed, Juno would eventually find out her dad was dating the mom of a kid in her class. However, Paula's kid knew, so this was a time bomb waiting to explode.

"So, when you scrape this woman off," I began, "and she's pissed or heartbroken or whatever she's going to be, and her girl knows her business, which is *your* business and then she'll be negatively affected by that business, Juno is no doubt going to be wrapped up in all that mess, what then?"

"I'm scraping her off, as you so enchantingly put it, tonight. Since the girls aren't really involved, there won't be any issue. But it doesn't matter. We're done because you and me are going to try again."

Okay.

All right.

"*What?*" I shrieked.

He took another step to me, but I pivoted and took three steps from him, lifted my arm his way in a *back off* gesture and shook my head for good measure.

"Stay where you are," I demanded.

"Listen to me," he demanded in return, but at least he stopped moving.

I dropped my arm but only to put both hands on my hips.

"No, Corbin. It's over between us."

"We were good together."

"We were never good together."

He looked hurt. "How can you say that?"

"Oh, I don't know, because you were fucking another woman the whole time we were together?"

"Baby—"

"*Stop it*," I hissed, taking my hands from my hips and crossing my arms on my chest.

In other words, *closed for goddamn business, buddy. You're never getting back in.*

I'd forgotten that not only was Corbin astute, he was also confident, stubborn, and if there was something he wanted, he pulled out all the stops to get it.

"It's been a long time coming," he said. "I'll admit it. Realizing I'd made a massive fuckup. I'll admit that too. But when I heard 'stepdad,' it all clicked into place. My part in this, my responsibility for it, but most importantly, my responsibility for putting it right."

Now we were getting somewhere.

"When you heard 'stepdad' you had this epiphany?"

"Yes."

"So you're jealous."

To my shock, he copped to that immediately, just not in a way I'd expect.

"Of course I'm jealous. You're the mother of my child and the love of my life."

My eyelids closed even as my eyebrows went up.

The love of his life?

"Pepper, honey—"

I opened my eyes quickly because his voice was closer.

"Not another step," I warned.

He stopped again.

"The love of your life?" I asked.

"I know I didn't act like it, but we were young. I wasn't ready for that commitment. Settling down. Being a father."

I opened my mouth, but he got there before me.

"I'm not blaming you for getting pregnant. It takes two. I'm just saying, shit happened, and I wasn't ready to deal. And instead of getting it together, I tore things apart." The persuasive voice came back. "I mean, Pepper, honey, I was only twenty-three when we got pregnant with Juno. And you were nineteen. Thinking on it now, that's young. No one has it together that young."

"It's good for you in your future growth and for your future relationships that you understand your part in that, but that does not negate the fact that what we had is done," I informed him.

"It's not done," he informed me.

"It is, Corbin. It's done. It's over. It's dead. It cannot be resurrected."

"You can't say that unless you try."

"I so totally can."

"Really? Then tell me why, since we ended, you haven't had another man."

That wasn't true.

I had.

Auggie.

But I didn't think throwing Auggie in his face would be a sterling move at this juncture.

"That's none of your business."

Another expression change, this one not hopeful, but borderline triumphant, and he took one step toward me then stopped.

"You lost your shit when we ended," he said softly.

"Yes, because the man I loved, the man I lived with, the man I committed to, the man I gave a beautiful daughter was fucking another woman and had been since I met him."

He winced at that.

But his recovery was quick.

So I had to be quicker. "Now I've found my shit, and I'm happy." Not entirely. "Juno's happy." Though, that was in question after what happened at her school that day. "And I'm not going back, not because I don't want to rock the boat. I'm not going back because I no longer wanna be *in* that boat."

"You know what we had was good," he remarked... *firmly.*

There it was.

The explanation for the triumphant look.

He thought he'd ruined me for other men.

"What we had is over."

"So why haven't you moved on?" he asked, a smile playing at his mouth.

"Because my daughter has to put up with the women who drift in and out of your life. She's social. She's got a big heart. She likes people first and asks questions later. So the four, five, six, how many has it been, Corbin?" I didn't let him answer, I kept talking. "Women who've drifted in and out of your life did the same in hers and I'm not going to make her deal with that when she's with me."

His smile was now gone. "I was trying to replace you."

"An endeavor doomed to fail. There's only one me and you've lost me irrevocably."

He stared at me.

I stared at him.

This lasted way too damned long.

I uncrossed my arms to throw my hands out to my sides and started impatiently, "Corbin—"

"We'll see."

Oh hell.

"I'll talk to you soon, honey," he said as he walked toward me.

I turned with him as he walked by me and I followed him as he kept walking.

Time for the big guns.

"Mom has cancer," I announced.

He stopped abruptly and pivoted to face me.

"I think it's bad," I shared. "I just found out today. I'm not sure they're handling it right."

"Not a surprise," he murmured.

"But whatever," I kept going like he didn't speak. "I need to focus on that. Focus on how to share that with Juno. Focus on what that means for us and for them and how we'll fit into how they plan to tackle that. I don't need you messing with my head."

"In dealing with them especially, you used to lean on me."

I did.

I *so* did.

That was the part where he made me feel listened to.

He thought they were as crackers as I did and it felt good having someone validate my decision to put a firm boundary between them and the part of them that might harm me, and, when she came, my child.

Back in the day, Corbin was that boundary. He was stalwart in that.

In that, he'd never let me down.

Now...

"I'm sorry about your mom, honey," he said. "And I hope it goes without saying that if you need me in any capacity, I'm there."

"After you scrape off Paula, of course," I noted.

He didn't even flinch.

He just concurred, "Yes, after I end things with Paula."

We went into another staring match that lasted until I sighed.

Corbin smiled.

I had learned that in men, there was good cocky—the confident kind that was so confident, the little swagger that went along with it was attractive.

There was also bad cocky—the overly confident kind that was just annoying.

Guess which one Corbin was.

(Hint: not the first.)

"We'll talk," he said.

"We won't," I replied.

"We will," he refuted. Another smile and, "Hang in there, honey. You need me, you know how to get to me."

And with that, he turned again and walked out of my house.

I stared at the door he closed and belatedly realized that Juno would be going to him on Monday, which was four days away, and I probably should have told him he could not talk to our daughter about the possibility of reconciliation.

Any decent father would know to be extra cautious about broaching such a subject with their child, doing so only upon mutual agreement and doing it in a way that was also mutually agreed.

I couldn't depend on that with Corbin.

This sent me to my phone on my desk whereupon I typed in a text that shared he was not to bring this up with Juno under any circumstances.

Probably texting while driving, he sent back, *Of course not. Later, baby.*

And yet again I had the urge to take my phone to the garbage bin and drop it in.

I couldn't do that.

Instead, I sat back down at my desk, woke my laptop and did some Facebook sleuthing at the same time keeping my eye out for my daughter's bus because I had hopefully one last unfun thing to do that day and it was going to happen around the time my daughter was expelled from a Twinkie on wheels.

CHAPTER FOUR
Desperate Times

JUNO

Juno thought it was really, super nice that, whenever she called him, he answered by the second ring.

"Hey, Juno."

"Hey, Mr. Cisco," she whispered.

Her door was closed. Her mom was downstairs. Juno was sitting on the floor on the opposite side of the bed from the door and hopefully beds absorbed noise.

But it was late. Nearly time to go to sleep, also almost time for her mom to go to work.

This meant soon Mom would come up and check on things, like Juno brushing her teeth and hair and having her book bag ready.

She didn't have a lot of time.

"How did things go today?" Mr. Cisco asked.

"I don't think good," she told him.

"Why don't you think that?"

"Okay, well, um...first, I watched out the windows after they left school and they talked by Auggie's car then Mom took off to her car real quick and Auggie followed and they talked there and, um...well, he was in my way and I couldn't see her. But when he took off, she was crying."

"Damn." Mr. Cisco was now whispering.

"Yeah, but, um, okay, see, things are even more bad."

She swallowed and her mouth tasted funny when she did.

She knew that taste.

It tasted like tears.

"Can you tell me?" Mr. Cisco asked.

Juno took a breath and then another one because the first one was all hitchy, but the second one was better and that meant she could talk.

So she did.

"Well, I got home, and Mom wanted to know how I called Auggie and why I did and why the teacher called him my stepdad."

There was a pause before, "Why *did* your teacher do that?"

Yeah.

She'd taken that too far.

"Well, uh...I kinda told her he was. You know. Like, if it's said out loud, maybe he'd get some ideas."

Mr. Cisco sounded proud when he stated, "Brilliant tactic, Juno."

"It didn't work."

"That's all right, sweetheart. This kind of thing takes commitment and time."

"Okay, but Mom was crying."

"I'll look into that."

He didn't sound proud when he said that. He sounded kinda mad.

Juno forged ahead.

"So, I got home, and when she asked, I told her my teacher got it wrong and I used a friend's phone to call Auggie and got his number from Auntie Ryn's phone, which was mostly all a lie."

In the sense it *was* all a lie, except for the part she *could* have gotten his number from Auntie Ryn's phone, she just didn't. She got it from Mr. Cisco.

"Again, as we discussed, in your life, I hope there are very few times where lying is the way forward," Mr. Cisco said. "But now is one of those times when it is. Have you heard the saying 'Desperate times call for desperate measures'?"

"I don't think so."

"Well, they do. Do you understand that?"

"Kinda."

"Okay," he muttered.

She had to keep going or they'd run out of time. "So there's the lying but also I . . . well, Mom doesn't usually keep things from me. She talks straight. She doesn't have anything to hide. So I hear things. But I don't go trying *to listen*."

Another pause and then, "What did you hear?"

"Mr. Cisco, it's not right to listen when someone doesn't know you're listening."

"You're right. It absolutely is not. However, we're in the middle of an operation here, Juno. And in every important operation, information is key. Are you with me?"

He was right.

This *was totally* an important operation.

"I'm with you."

"So what did you hear?"

She swallowed again.

Then she said, real low, "My grandma has cancer."

She actually heard him suck in breath.

Whoosh.

"Mom was talking to Auntie Lottie on the phone and she . . . she . . ."

Juno tasted tears again.

"It's okay, Juno. I can guess how she was."

"And then she got on the phone with Auntie Ryn, and she told her Auggie was super mean to her."

"How mean?"

"She called him a..." Juno pushed up, looked over her shoulder and the bed to her door, saw it still closed, the light coming from under it uninterrupted by something like feet, then she sat back down and breathed out a word she wasn't allowed to say, "*dick*."

"Hmm..."

"And he called her a corktease."

"What?"

His question was swift and very sharp.

So she was kinda scared when she said, "He called her a—"

"No, Juno. You don't have to repeat it. I heard you."

At his tone, Juno got quiet, though she didn't get it, like she didn't get why her mom was so upset Auggie called her a corktease.

And she didn't get why he'd call her that.

Her mom liked wine but that just seemed weird.

But she couldn't stay quiet, because, outside Grandma being sick, and her mom crying, there was *another* worst part she had to tell Mr. Cisco before she had to get off the phone.

"And Dad came over before I got home from school and he wants to get back together."

Now Mr. Cisco was quiet.

That lasted so long, and it was teeth-brushing time, so she had to call, "Mr. Cisco? Are you still there?"

"I'm here, Juno."

"Dad has a girlfriend."

"I know, you told me."

"He needs to stay with her."

"Yes, you told me that too. She's the mom of a child in your class, and if they broke up, that might make things unpleasant at school."

Juno was feeling funny.

And not because her dad thought she didn't know he was seeing Emma's mom, and that didn't feel good. It felt like he thought she was stupid or something. It also made her realize how her mom would feel if she knew Juno was lying, because her dad wasn't *lying* lying by not telling her Paula was Emma's mom. It was still *kinda* lying.

But now there were bigger things to worry about.

"No, I don't care about that. He needs to stay with her so he's not in the way so Auggie can be with Mom."

"Okay, sweetheart. You're right. That's a curveball. I need to think on that one."

She got on her knees, turned and faced the door, just in case she couldn't hear Mom coming, and that funny feeling got funnier.

And she knew what it was.

It was what Mr. Cisco said it was.

Desperation.

"What are we gonna do?" she asked. "Grandma's sick and Mom's family is weird, but Grandma can be sweet, and Mom loves her. And Mom and Auggie didn't talk for very long and Mom was crying. Did Auggie make her cry? Why was he mean to her? And why is Dad saying he wants her back when he has a girlfriend?"

"Juno, honey, listen to me, okay?"

"Okay."

"You did what you could do. Now, I need to do a few things. Keep checking your phone. I'll text you if we need to talk. But leave this to me for now. All right?"

"You're going to do a few things?"

"Yes."

"What things?"

"Just leave those to me. Okay?"

She thought about it.

He'd said he was all in and he'd gotten her a phone and everything, which totally proved he was.

And she liked him a whole lot.

When they were at Fortnum's, he'd looked into her eyes when she talked, and he nodded a lot to make sure she knew he heard her, and he had a really nice smile.

So she said, "Okay."

"Okay."

She didn't want to ask.

But now she was getting that desperate times thing.

So she had to ask.

"Should I, um...listen to Mom more and then tell you what I hear?"

"No, sweetheart," he said real fast. "You just be normal with your mom. I'll take it from here."

When he said that, that thing inside that had gotten tight again after she saw her mom crying in the parking lot and Auggie walking away looking all mad, then got tighter when she got home and had to lie, and then even tighter when she heard her grandma was sick and her dad was going to *ruin everything*, got loose again.

"Thanks, Mr. Cisco."

"You don't have to thank me, Juno. Good people deserve to be happy. And anyway, I owe your mom one."

"What?"

"Never mind. Now, sleep good, all right?"

"You too, Mr. Cisco. And I promise, I'll check my phone as often as I can. Goodnight."

"Goodnight, Juno."

She hung up and then shoved the phone under her nightstand.

Then she jumped up and left the room to go to the hall bathroom, which was hers and she never had to share it even though they had a guest room. It was just that no one ever stayed over anymore, mostly because Aunt Saffron was no fun (so it was mean, but Juno was glad she didn't come and stay like Auntie Ryn used to do on girls' nights). And now Auntie Ryn had Boone so she never stayed over either.

Juno was done with her teeth and hair and in her pajamas and lying on her stomach on the bed with her big box of Prismacolors and the coloring book (that was not a kids' coloring book, it had a lot of tricky flower pictures in it and Mom colored in it too) when Mom came in.

"Right, kiddo. You good to go?" she asked.

It was nearly time for her mom to leave for work, which meant Flossy, Juno's sitter, would be there soon.

Juno liked Flossy, even though she didn't get to see her much because she was asleep most of the time Flossy was there. And Juno probably wouldn't be able to talk to her much even if she wasn't asleep because Flossy was in college and she hung out at their house to be there for Juno, but most of the time, she was studying because she was going to be a doctor.

Her real name was Florence, and Juno liked Flossy, but everyone knew Florence was better because of Florence + The Machine.

But it wasn't her name so she didn't get a say.

"I'm good to go," Juno replied. But she put her pencil down and sat up on a hip and asked, "You okay, Momma?"

Her mom sat on the bed with her, answering, "Sure, Dollface. Why do you ask?"

Juno looked away.

"I don't know," she mumbled.

Liar, liar, liar! her mind yelled.

Mom shoved some hair off Juno's shoulder and Juno looked back at her.

She was the prettiest mom of any of the kids in her class. By far.

And Juno had the best house of all her friends, even Megan, whose parents were *loaded*.

And Juno's room was *awesome*.

Her favorite bits were the big pillow that said FOLLOW YOUR HEART and the stenciling on the wall just to the side of her bed that said SLEEP TIGHT KNOWING I LOVE YOU.

Her mom was the best decorator *in the world*. Their whole house and the whole outside of it proved it.

But Juno's room was best of all.

"Are *you* okay?" Mom asked, looking at Juno too closely.

"I'm good. I just think maybe I did wrong asking Auggie to talk to the class. The thing is, I love Dad, but he doesn't have that interesting of a job. You know?"

Mom smiled. "I know, baby. And you didn't do wrong, even if you didn't go about it completely right. It seemed like the kids got a lot out of what Auggie had to say. Though, tomorrow, you should call your dad and explain things to him. He needs to hear from you why Auggie was there."

That wasn't something she wanted to do.

But her mom told her life was full of somethings you don't want to do.

The key is, get them done, so you can get to the things you do *want to do,* she'd say.

"Okay," Juno agreed.

The doorbell rang.

"That's Flossy," Mom said, bent in, kissed Juno's forehead, and sat back. "I'll go let her in and come up and kiss you goodnight."

"I'll come down with you."

"You keep coloring until you need to shut those eyes. Flossy'll get set up downstairs and come up and say hi."

"All right, Momma."

She smiled at Juno and Juno smiled back.

Then her mom hustled out of the room.

Juno looked down at the coloring book she was trying to color in like Mom colored, with shading of different hues in the petals and on the leaves.

It didn't look near as good as her mom's did.

Things come with time, practice and patience, kiddo, Mom had said. *If you don't think something is right, just work at it until you get it right. Maybe you'll find along the way that it isn't about it being right, it's about how good you feel that you worked at something. I promise you, something you worked for feels way better than having something that didn't take any work at all.*

Yeah.

Her mom had said that.

And sitting there in her bed in her awesome room, Juno thought about the way she saw Auggie look at her mom sometimes, and how she saw her mom look at Auggie sometimes, and how they never looked at each other that way when they were both actually looking at each other.

And she really, really, *really* hoped her mom was right.

CHAPTER FIVE

The Dark

AUGGIE

When his phone rang, Auggie was in his SUV taking a short ride to attend to some business at a high-rise downtown, and he was trying to keep his shit while he was doing it.

Looking at his dash, he saw who was calling.

Considering his mood, and his current mission, he would not normally answer it.

That day had not been good, him acting like an enormous asshole to Pepper being top of that heap, dealing with what he was on his way to deal with now and the possible reasons for that a close second, he didn't need more bad news.

But it didn't help to delay it. That just spread bad shit out longer.

And considering the long lingering case they were working on, not only his team but also others, including the caller, this couldn't be anything but bad news.

He took it anyway.

"Yo, Lee," he greeted Lee Nightingale, the man behind Nightin-gale Investigations, the premier private investigation agency in Denver.

"Hey, Aug," Lee replied. "Do you have a sec?"

"Sure."

Lee didn't bother with pleasantries, and Auggie wasn't sur-prised he didn't.

It wasn't that the man was rude. It was that it was late evening, and if Lee wasn't home with his wife and two kids, he'd want to get done what had to be done to get home. If he was home, he'd want to be with his wife and kids, not talking work on the phone.

A handful of years ago, the idea of Lee Nightingale, Family Man, would have had most of the men of Denver chuckling.

But there it was.

"Right," Lee began. "Shirleen just spoke with me. She told me your woman called."

This wasn't what he was expecting, and hearing what it was, Auggie nearly tried to find a place to pull over so he could fully concentrate on the call.

Because he didn't have a woman.

But he knew who Lee was talking about.

Shirleen was Lee's office manager.

And that meant Pepper was calling Lee Nightingale.

No one ever called Lee for good reasons.

Why was Pepper calling Lee?

"Not my business," Lee went on. "Not my place to ask, figure things have hit a rough patch with you two."

Not so much a rough patch as they hadn't ever been on a smooth one.

Except that night they'd been out for drinks with Boone and Ryn. Just friends together, one couple, one should-be-a-couple, but weren't.

At the bar, Pepper had not taken things out of where she firmly kept them, the Friend Zone.

Or as Auggie knew it, the Torture Zone.

She hadn't had too much to drink.

She still asked him to drive her home.

He'd agreed, not doing it thinking he was going to get himself some. Instead, thinking she was a mom and overly careful about drinking and driving, considering she had someone who counted on her getting home safe.

And he'd walked her up to her door because he was his father's son.

What happened after that was all on her.

Lee broke into his trip down memory lane.

"But I figure you'd wanna know she's looking for an investigation service to find her brother," Lee finished. "Shirleen said she balked at our rates and told her she'd have to call some other firms. So, to save her the time and money, you might wanna get on that for her, or if you two are going through some shit, punt it to one of your brothers."

The right thing to do in this scenario was explain to Lee that he'd gotten it wrong. That although Lottie had tried to hook them up, unlike all the others, it didn't take. Pepper and he were not an item, and with the way things were going, especially how he'd blown it today, they never would be.

He didn't do that.

He asked, "Did she tell Shirleen why she was looking for her brother?"

"Shirleen didn't share that, and she's taken off for the night. You got her number?"

Auggie was maneuvering into the front drive of the high-rise, his gaze on the valet, as he answered, "I have her number. I'm on something right now. Will she mind if I call her later?"

"Considering she's a woman who likes to be smack in the

middle of everyone's business, you could call her at midnight, and she wouldn't mind."

Shirleen was good people. She was also good at her job. She'd been such a good foster parent, she'd adopted both of her boys and they'd been nearly of age when she did it, so they picked her as plain as she'd picked them.

She was also good at being in people's business.

Even if he wasn't hip on people being in his, he'd learned a while ago that with his crew, it was impossible to keep folks out of it.

You picked your battles.

But Shirleen was already in and she might have something he needed.

So he wasn't going to dick around getting it.

"Thanks for the call, Lee," he said as he stopped at his destination.

"Hope you two work shit out and the reason she needs to find her brother isn't a bad one."

He hoped that too, on both sides.

But now he had to do this.

"Later, brother," he bid.

"Later, Aug."

They hung up and Auggie, having parked by the valet stand, shut her down and angled out of his vehicle.

"Here to see Mr. Rappaport," he told the valet, handing over his key.

"Gotcha," the valet replied.

Aug went into the grand foyer and saw straight through to the back, which was a wall of windows with a view to a manicured garden that had a lighting design second to none.

And in the foyer, there was a massive lime green rug on the shiny floor that had a subtle geometric design in cream. Dead center on it was a huge round black table with a gigantic flower arrangement sitting in the middle of it.

The elevator bays, one on each side, were discreetly tucked in the back. A seating area was between them. There was a member of staff that was probably another valet plus security hanging unobtrusively in a not-so-well-lit corner. And the concierge was sitting at a desk with two chairs angled in front of it so tenants and guests didn't have to do anything taxing, like stand, when they asked for their packages or dry cleaning.

He walked there, but before he opened his mouth, the concierge said, "Mr. Hero for Mr. Rappaport?"

Well…

Fuck.

Cisco knew he was coming.

But thinking on it, that wasn't a surprise.

Because Brett "Cisco" Rappaport didn't hide what Auggie had found. And if Cisco didn't want something known, it wasn't known. But Auggie had found it in no time.

So after what happened that day, he knew Aug would run it down.

And therefore, Auggie would be right where he was right then.

"Yeah," he confirmed.

The concierge looked beyond him, dipped his chin, and Aug looked over his shoulder to see the other guy moving toward the elevators.

"Mr. Rappaport is expecting you," the concierge declared. "Brandon will show you up," he finished.

"Thanks," Auggie muttered, moving to the elevators.

He got there, Brandon fobbed him up, and Auggie wasn't surprised "Mr. Rappaport," better known by his street name, Cisco, had a unit on the top floor.

Cisco also had a five-thousand-square-foot house in the mountains.

Because crime paid.

Auggie couldn't think about that. Thinking about that put him in a place where he had to consider what he'd learned about an hour ago. And he was there to deal with that, not lose his shit about it.

He'd lost his shit already today, and he regretted it. He'd rather have lost it with Cisco, and not Pepper, but he couldn't turn back the clock.

That said, maybe it was good he'd put a line under them.

He'd have preferred to do it another way.

But he was a Hero. Hero men weren't averse to fucking shit up royally.

You could ask his father.

And his mother.

Though, she'd gotten hers back.

A thousand-fold.

The elevator doors opened, he got out, saw another table, also round, much smaller, as was the flower arrangement on it (but it was fresh). He looked left and turned right.

There were only two units on that floor.

And he needed unit 2002.

He walked that way and hit the button by the grand double doors.

He waited around five seconds before one side of the doors opened and Cisco's driver, bodyguard and right-hand man, Joe, opened it.

"Hey, Aug," Joe said.

How Auggie had gotten to a point in his life a man like Joe greeted him like they were buds, he had no clue.

Wait.

He did.

Cisco, who was an equal opportunity felon (this meant he dabbled in anything illegal that might make him money) had kidnapped the women—those women being Evie, Ryn, Hattie and Pepper—because he'd been framed for a murder he didn't commit. And Evie had been pulled into that situation by members of her family.

After Cisco did that, Auggie's entire crew had been dragged into the search for a ring of dirty cops.

"Joe," Auggie replied.

"Come on in," Joe invited, stepping aside.

Auggie entered.

Short hall that widened exponentially to a big room with an insanely good view of the lights of Denver beyond which, during the day, would be an even more insanely good view of the Front Range.

Yup.

Crime totally paid.

Auggie walked to the landing above a sunken living room, the edges of which were all one continuous couch or bench, including right up to the window. You could lie there and be nose to view, feeling like you were floating over Denver.

The place was stylish, neat and minimal to the point it didn't look welcoming, comfortable or even lived in.

Aug knew Cisco didn't spend a lot of time in Denver. He preferred the mountains.

But he needed a place in town, primarily to conduct business.

And this place gave nothing away about the man, which was a strong tactical move in his kind of business.

"Joe, we're good."

He heard this from off to his left, and he looked that way to see Cisco walking down a long hall wearing suit pants and shirtsleeves.

The minute they locked eyes, Cisco greeted, "Hello, Auggie. Can I get you a drink?" like Aug was there to catch a game.

"You can tell me why a number that Juno used to phone me traces directly back to you. And then you can promise me you won't have anything to do with Juno at all, unless Pepper invites that, from now until the day you die," he replied.

Aug felt Joe hesitate, but Cisco glanced at him and shook his head.

Joe took off.

Cisco kept moving until he got to a side cabinet that butted a pristine kitchen that was entirely white. Gleaming white cabinets with no handles. Sleek white countertops. Glossy white backsplash. Three white light fixtures hanging over the island.

Cisco touched a panel, it sprang open, he pulled open its mate and revealed a wet bar.

He turned to Auggie.

"I'll repeat, can I get you a drink?"

"No," Auggie answered.

Cisco went about making himself a vodka rocks.

Auggie practiced patience while he did that.

He then lost his patience.

"Cisco," he warned.

The man turned with glass in hand.

"Juno came to me. I gave her the phone because I didn't want her conniving again with one of her friends to cover for her while she walked alone to someplace she could meet me, which was what she did the first and only time we met," Cisco shared.

Auggie stood unmoving and tried not to think of Juno alone on the streets of Denver, making her way to some meeting place that clearly not her mother, nor any other adult, knew about.

Aug was a kid guy. He loved kids.

It did not take deep reflection to understand he liked being around kids for two reasons.

One, because kids were awesome.

Two, because his childhood was so fucked up, he was all for being that guy you could have fun with, that guy who was never too serious, that guy who understood viscerally that you were only a kid once, and you should make the most of it, because it didn't last.

But Juno was more.

Juno was cute, sweet, open, funny, smiled quick, and her eyes were always bright and happy.

And she was Pepper's.

"We met at Fortnum's and Tex MacMillan would tear off his own arm if it meant keeping her from harm, even if he doesn't know who she is," Cisco continued. "And Tex was there. So she picked well. But mostly, she picked lucky. Since she was desperate enough to do that, I felt establishing a safe line of communication was in order."

"Why was she meeting you at all?"

"Because she very much wants her mother to fall in love with you and she was enlisting support in her efforts to make that happen."

Auggie felt his chin list back into his neck and his eyebrows go up. "Say again?"

"I think you heard me."

Cisco took a sip of his vodka then wandered to the island where he leaned a hip against it.

And then he kept talking.

"Now is the part where I would have told you, if Juno was keeping you from taking things forward with Pepper, or if she was what was keeping Pepper from taking things forward with you, neither of you have to worry about that. It's safe to say Juno is very much at one with the idea of you two being a couple, and I sense this has to do with the fact she very much wants her mom to be happy and thinks you can make her that way. However, I won't say that. Instead, I'll ask why in the fuck you called her mother a cocktease."

Goddamn shit.

"How did you know that?"

"Juno has ears and Pepper has girlfriends."

Goddamn *shit*.

He was going to catch it at work from the man of whoever Pepper called.

In fact, he was surprised his phone wasn't already blowing up.

Especially if it was Lottie who Pepper talked to (and Lottie would be the one doing the calling).

But also, if it was Ryn.

"Are you going to explain that?" Cisco pushed.

"I don't think I have to tell you that's none of your business."

"Sorry, but Juno has made it my business."

"Juno isn't your business either," Auggie returned.

"Pepper has a daughter," Cisco shot back. "You cannot be so connected to your dick you don't get she's cautious about relationships because, if they work, she won't be the only one in them."

"Again, Pepper and me are none of your business."

"As far as I can tell, there is no Pepper and you."

Shit.

That stung.

Auggie shook it off.

"That's none of your business either."

Cisco kept going like Auggie didn't speak.

"And there won't be if you continue to act like a motherfucker."

Auggie took in a deep breath, giving himself a second to process the fact he was having this conversation.

Then he made moves to extricate himself from it.

"You get that phone back from Juno," he ordered. "And you do what you gotta do to shut Juno down. I'm putting this on you for Juno's sake. If Pepper knew this shit was happening, she'd lose her goddamn mind and Juno is just a kid who wants good things for her mom. She didn't do wrong, as such. She just went about it wrong, and she shouldn't take too much heat for that. So sort it out, Cisco."

He'd said what he'd come to say, so he made a move to get out of there.

"Pepper's mother is dying of cancer."

He stopped moving and again focused on Cisco.

"I don't know how much Pepper knows," Cisco carried on. "Juno only told me she'd heard her mom talking about her grandmother being ill. But I made a few calls to a few sources who could look into a few files. Her prognosis is dire. There are treatment options, some of them experimental, but they're there and could prolong life, though likely not lead to her being cancer free. The family has opted to put her mother's health in God's hands."

"Shit, fuck," Auggie bit out.

He'd heard Pepper's family was religious.

But damn.

"She found this out today. Also, today, she found out her ex wants her back."

Auggie's entire body grew solid.

"I've no idea where Pepper is with that," Cisco continued. "But Juno does not want it. At all. She wants you for her mom. This desire of Juno's, and the lengths she'll go to achieve it, obviously needs to be explored. But with that, I'll say myself, it's none of my business. It's Pepper's. And if you'd get your head out of your goddamn ass, it's yours."

"I fucked shit up today."

Now, why did he say that?

"I figured that out," Cisco replied. "Considering Juno saw that you made her mother cry and heard that you'd called her a cocktease."

Oh hell.

Auggie looked away, put a hand to the back of his neck and rubbed, saying, "Jesus."

"She heard it as 'corktease,' and sounded confused, but I wasn't confused," Cisco explained.

Aug wanted to find "corktease" funny.

He just didn't.

Because where that came from flat-out wasn't.

He dropped his hand and looked back at the guy.

"She's impenetrable," he stated.

"No woman is impenetrable."

Literally, this was true, since Auggie had penetrated her.

Figuratively, not so much.

"What happened today?" Cisco inquired.

Was he going to talk to this guy?

"Juno asked me to speak to her class for career day."

He guessed he was going to talk to this guy.

And he kept doing it.

"Pepper showed looking gorgeous. First thing she did was touch me. A while ago, we'd had...a thing. It started fantastic. It got even better. But it didn't end well. I wasn't ready for her to touch me and act like we hadn't had that thing. Then, when I was doing my presentation, she called me 'honey.' She's never called me honey. It was sweet. I liked it. But it wasn't mine. So it got under my skin that I was not that to her, she wouldn't let me be that to her, but still, she thought it was okay to call me that, like I was that to her. And when all that played out and it was over, I was pissed and I tried to take off, but she followed me, pushed a conversation, and I lost it with her."

Cisco was watching him closely. "Do you lose it often?"

"If you mean, do I have a temper? Yes. If you mean, do I normally treat women like shit? No."

"This 'thing' you had, did you fuck her?"

Auggie didn't answer that but he gave the guy a look.

Cisco nodded.

Yeah.

He read the look.

Auggie spoke.

"I want her, and I'm frustrated. Which is not an excuse. She let me in and then kicked me out, which made me more frustrated. That's also not an excuse. Now, today, it's her getting in my space, touching me and calling me 'honey,' when the last time I saw her, she was closing the door on me, and my dick was still wet with her."

"This picture is coming clearer," Cisco muttered.

"Yeah," Auggie said shortly. "And, man, I have intimate knowledge of more than one woman who fucks with men's heads for whatever reason they do it. They don't know what they want. Or they get off on it. Or they're stringing him along because they want company and orgasms, but they think they eventually might find someone better. Whatever. And I do not need that shit. She knows I'm into her. She knows I want to give us a shot. She's cold. Then she's nice. She turns reserved. She switches to funny. She's friendly. Then she avoids me. Then she lets me fuck her against the wall in her foyer, not even allowing me all the way into her house, and *she* instigated that, before she kicks me out. And the next time she sees me, she's acting like that didn't happen. What the fuck?"

"You do know you can ask me this, but I can't answer primarily because," Cisco leaned toward him, "*I'm not her*."

"Pepper does not get into anything deep."

"She let you get deep, Auggie, and you're the only man since her breakup with Juno's father she let do that, so I have to say, I disagree."

Auggie did a slow blink before he asked, "How do you know that?"

Cisco shrugged, took another sip of his vodka and said low, "Axl was working late, Hattie asked me if I wanted to go to dinner, I said yes. Joe drove, she drank, and she gets talkative when she drinks."

Mag, Mo and Hawk did not understand why the women, all of them, dug Cisco as much as they did. As mentioned, the man was a felon, a very successful one, and you didn't get to his level in that world being a good guy.

But the women liked him so much, they hung out with the guy on the regular.

Though, Boone had a clue.

Axl flat-out liked him.

Auggie had been with Mag, Mo and Hawk in not wanting anything to do with the guy.

But now Auggie was getting it.

Cisco's voice was back to normal when he said, "So, you can take that as you have a lot of people in your corner on this because Hattie was sharing because she too is frustrated that Pepper isn't letting you in. And she didn't hesitate to add that she isn't the only one in your crew having these feelings."

"I can want it, they can want it, Juno can want it, but it's Pepper who has to want it."

"Her family is in a cult, did you know that?"

Shit.

He knew they were religious, but...

"A cult?"

Cisco nodded, drank more vodka, and then said, "It's not big. The head pastor, who's also the leader, is a nutjob. Not the kind of personality that attracts a lot of followers, say like a Koresh. But there are followers and Pepper's family has been a part of the group for a long time. Her father especially believes, to the point he's a deacon. Hattie told me that before they found this guy's god, her mom and dad were hippies, that's probably why Pepper is named Pepper. But something shifted and free love and eating special brownies and going to Dead concerts became an infatuation with something that was the exact opposite. Since Juno contacted me, I've been trying to find out about them, but the lid on that is closed tight. And I think we both get that is not good."

No, it was not.

Cisco kept going.

"Pepper felt stifled by that. She hated it. She was already her own woman when she was a girl and she escaped as soon as she could. Left that life. Got her license to do hair. Met her ex. Fell in love. Made a baby. And he's a man on the move. He was selling cars when they met. Started selling real estate. Opened his own brokerage when he was only twenty-seven. Now, he has eight agents working for him, does retail, commercial and residential, rentals and sales. And he's someone to watch."

Auggie was not feeling this, mostly because, if some miracle occurred and he could sort things out with Pepper, she should be telling him this.

He was also not feeling it because the guy sounded like a catch and he wanted her back.

"Cisco—"

"He also never quit fucking his high school sweetheart."

That hit him like a gut punch.

"You're joking," Auggie growled.

Cisco shook his head. "Not when he and Pepper were dating. Not when they moved in together when she was nineteen. Not when he got Pepper pregnant when she was still nineteen, but nearing twenty. And not when she had the baby, they nested, she stopped working, and only went part-time when Juno hit kinder-garten. Now she's in a nineteen-hundred-square-foot townhome in a decent mid-income development. And he has a thirty-two-hundred-square-foot modern build four blocks from Cherry Cricket in north Cherry Creek."

A trendy 'hood.

A tony 'hood.

This guy's pad probably cost millions.

Her pad, nothing close.

Cisco kept at it.

"She managed to get out of some significant mindfuck and dysfunction with her family and in with a man who could offer her a very stable life, at least financially. And she was all in, making babies and working for play money."

"So Hattie talks a lot when she's got a few in her," Aug muttered.

"She does," Cisco agreed. "But are you hearing me?"

Aug looked him right in the eye.

"She had a dad who put her in a shit situation while she was growing up that might have been and still might be dangerous, and she had to escape it. And she went right from him to a man who broke her trust in a way no man should and it's hard as hell to bounce back from. Yeah, I'm hearing you. But now put yourself in my shoes, where does that leave me?"

"Nowhere good, if you're calling her a cocktease."

Auggie opened his mouth but Cisco lifted his hand.

"I get it. Mixed signals suck. But, brother, what were you thinking?"

I was thinking I didn't want to be judged by her ex's deeds, and I didn't even know what they were then, I just didn't want his dark pushed on me.

I was thinking I'm not her ex, I didn't dick her over, and I shouldn't be treated like that.

I was thinking I'm not my dad, and I shouldn't be treated like him either.

And I was thinking that she's acting like my mom.

"Auggie?" Cisco prompted.

"She's not the only one with a complicated past, man."

Cisco studied him.

Auggie allowed himself to be studied.

Cisco ended it with, "I'll ask again, do you want a drink?"

Aug drew in a breath.

Then he inquired, "You got any beer?"

Cisco didn't smile. He didn't gloat. He didn't act like a dick at all. He queried, "Do you like Fat Tire?"

* * *

Auggie waited until he was home from Cisco's before he made the call.

Boone answered.

"Brother, what in *the* fuck?"

There it was.

Pepper had called Ryn.

"We can talk later, but for now, I need you to find time tomorrow to tell Pepper that Lee contacted us to take care of finding her brother, and we're on it. And by that I mean *I'll* be on it, but you don't have to tell her that."

"What?" Boone asked.

"She's looking for her brother and I fucked things up seriously today so she's not coming to me, and because of that, us. She's trying to hire an outside PI. I can dig around on him tomorrow, give you what I got, you can give it to her, and she doesn't have to lay out that cash."

"So you know, I heard you. And I'll connect with Pepper. But gotta share, the shit you pulled today, man, has made the rounds. Everyone is pissed as fuck," Boone told him. "Gotta admit, including me."

"I'll get on that too," Auggie promised.

"How did it get that dark?"

"If it was just me and some woman that is not a part of our crowd, I'd tell you. But for Pepper, I'm gonna keep the road to what happened to myself."

"What's that mean?"

"That means I fucked up, but there was reason. No excuse. But reason."

Boone didn't say anything.

Auggie did and it was to give him a reminder so Aug didn't get pissed at one of his boys.

"You know me better than that, brother. I'm not going to claim what I did was right. I'm just going to say it didn't happen out of the blue."

There was a pause before Boone replied, "Yeah, I said something like that to Ryn, that there's two sides to a story. I'll be keeping that thought to myself in the future."

Ryn was a strong woman.

Ryn was also a loyal friend.

"I'm gonna get on it and I'm not gonna waste time and let her sit on what I did today for too long," Auggie told him. "Considering how things have gone, I wouldn't expect miracles. But give me time. I'll sort it, one way or the other."

"All right, Aug. And I'll get the message to her that we're taking care of the brother thing. Does it have to do with her mom being sick?"

Yeah, word had gotten around.

"My guess, yes. But I don't know yet."

"If you need help with that, let me know."

"Will do. Thanks, bud."

"Anytime, Aug. Hang in there."

"Right. Later."

They disconnected and Aug went right into his contacts to find the number.

It rang twice before Shirleen answered with, "Shit, boy, I thought you'd never call."

That almost made him smile.

"I need to know everything Pepper said to you, Shirleen."

"Well, normally, I would not do this because it's clear you are not her favorite person. However, I got curious and started looking into things myself, and I gotta tell you, Augustus, I didn't find much, but I didn't like anything I found."

"If I bring the late-night snacks, you up for a visitor?"

"Moses and me are snuggled in for the night. But I can always use one of Tex's coffees to start the day."

"I'll meet you at Fortnum's. What time?"

"Nine."

"See you there."

"You got it, Auggie."

They hung up.

Aug put his phone on the charger.

Then he looked out the big window in his kitchen that had the view to his neighbor's garden. A vacant lot in a popular neighborhood they'd bought decades ago and transformed so it was part flowers, part vegetable patch. It included an arch covered in vines that bloomed all summer and a tiny koi pond with a fountain.

Probably one of the most expensive serene spaces in Denver, because that lot should have a house on it, and it was likely taxed like it did.

But it was good for Auggie because it was a great view.

And he needed a little serenity because the dark was surfacing in his brain.

A dark he never let rise.

Or it would consume him.

Possibly annihilate him.

And like always, he had to fight like hell not to let that happen.

CHAPTER SIX

Yet

PEPPER

It was five days Post Auggie Being A Dick.

Sunday.

The first of my two days off in any given week.

Juno and I had been to church that morning (*our* church). Now, she was down the street at my neighbor Jenn's house making cupcakes with Jenn and her two girls.

But Jenn had called a bit ago, they were almost done, and my daughter was going to be home soon.

So I was in my bedroom on my cushion at my meditation station.

This was not me-time.

This was my daily non-negotiable purposeful time.

It wasn't about de-stressing and confidence boosting (okay, it was, but it wasn't *just* about that).

It was a part of my existence.

If things were different...

Like Corbin hadn't cheated on me and I hadn't been solely financially responsible for myself and my daughter (right, not solely—Corbin paid child support for Juno, and I used all of that for Juno, but we could just say I thought I'd be in a life-partnership situation with man and family . . . and I was not).

At the same time providing her with an overall life where she didn't have to worry about Mom making ends meet. A life where she had good not only because her dad helped with that, but because her mom took care of business (all of this being what led me to stripping).

If I did not have to see to all of that, I would open a meditation studio.

And there, I would offer to others what I received from the practice. I would create and provide a place people could go in their day where they felt better for having been there.

Of course (as dreams had a tendency to do), I had it all thought out in great detail in my head.

What the entryway would look like, the music playing, the neutral colors, the plant wall.

The roomy, airy single meditation studios you could rent where you could select the music, the scents, the lighting, even tapes of guided meditations if that was your gig.

The group meditations being offered that would focus on different things: anxiety, sense of self, intention, creating a personal mantra.

And the yoga that did good things, as yoga always does, but more, it built your spirit, your awareness of your body and bringing balance to it to assist in bringing balance in your life.

I would sell teas that did not make any claims, they were just good teas.

And I'd offer cute clothing in all sizes that you felt good in and could be comfortable in.

And awesome bolsters, cushions and mats, candles and mindfulness gifts.

And I'd be one of the teachers giving classes.

Some versions of my dream had an additional sunshiny room filled with healthy plants, comfortable chairs and some tables. A place where folks could meet. There'd be a bar where I'd serve awesome smoothies and delicious teas and interesting coffee drinks, and folks could commune in a tranquil place. You could bring a journal, a book or a magazine, but no laptops or phones allowed.

My best, biggest, brightest dream versions had a garden where I'd also offer classes.

Maybe a Japanese garden (with a definite Zen element).

This was my dream.

This was also my spirituality.

This time belonged to me and it belonged to God in the personal way I thought He deserved.

I was not unaware this was a leftover of my upbringing.

But when I'd left that life, I did not turn my back on spirituality. I'd always felt very centered in that, even when I was younger.

It was just that I did not understand why anyone would follow a god that held some down (the women) while he lifted others up (the men). A god who turned his back on some of his children (gays, non-believers, those of other faiths) while promising to shower abundance and eternal life on others who toed his supposed line. A god whose fire and brimstone, judgment and hate outweighed his delight in his creations and his forgiveness, acceptance and love. A god who people could use to act on the former without giving thought to the latter.

Nope.

I didn't understand this at all.

So I found my God and my practice and my faith in my home and life and church and world.

And I didn't have a problem with dreaming about sharing that goodness with people.

Not pushing my God how I saw Him, but giving folks a place where they could find that peace in themselves, whatever form that would take, whatever higher spirit they turned to (if they had one).

Serenity.

Balance.

Safety.

That was what I'd do, giving that to others every day for a living.

But now, I was ending my meditation, coming back to awareness, moving fingers and toes, opening my eyes, and seeing someone standing in my bedroom door.

"*Gah!*" I screamed, pushing up on the sides of my feet in order to stand.

"Sorry, shit, you were so quiet, I didn't want to disturb you," Auggie said.

He'd been leaning on my doorjamb (like he'd been there for a while, watching me!) but when I jumped up, he shoved away from the jamb.

"What are you—?"

I stopped myself mid-question because the look on his face was...

Well...

It was downright hypnotizing.

I mean, the guy was gorgeous, but how he was looking at me now?

I stared at him.

He stared at me.

I stared at him more.

He stared at me more.

Neither of us moved or spoke.

"Mom!" Juno shouted from somewhere not close. "Auggie's here! I told him to go up and say hi!"

That yanked me out of my Auggie-Was-Looking-at-Me-Like-I-Dotted-the-Sky-with-Stars-and-I-Absolutely-Adored-That-Look Trance.

And my first thought was, *Why on earth would my daughter send a man up to our very personal space to say hi instead of calling me down to say hi to that man?*

"In case you haven't figured this out, she's trying to fix us up," Auggie stated like he heard my unspoken question.

He did this walking into my room.

Yes, Augustus Hero was *walking into my bedroom.*

"Fix us up?" I parroted, not sure what to be more shocked about. Him thinking Juno was trying to fix us up or him being in my room.

"Were you meditating?" he asked.

"Yes," I answered.

"Does that work?"

"Yes."

"I've never tried," he told me.

"You should," I told him.

"I've also never seen anything like that. You're even beautiful when you're completely still. Maybe more beautiful."

Um…

First, he'd *totally been watching me.*

And second, *wow.*

I mean, I knew he was attracted to me (obviously).

But…

Wow.

"I've never seen a room like this," he went on, glancing around. "It's fantastic. Seriously. It's the single most awesome room I've ever been in."

My legs were feeling weird. Like they would soon be unable to support me.

All right.

That was it.

I needed to get a handle on things.

"Auggie—"

He'd stopped a couple of feet away.

And he didn't get any closer when he said, "I have no excuse for the shit I said to you at Juno's school. I'd like to talk it through with you. I'd like you to understand where I was coming from, as an explanation, not a defense. And I hope you give me the shot to do that. But we have more important shit to talk about and I didn't know you were meditating when I came up here, but I still would have come up here. Because when we talk about it, I don't think Juno should hear."

Okay, I wasn't sure what was happening. I hadn't really recovered from the way he was looking at me earlier, definitely not him saying I was beautiful, he dug my room, the fact he was in said room and absolutely not him asserting that Juno wanted to fix us up (though, giving this cursory contemplation, considering her recent behavior, I had to admit it made sense).

But I did not forget what a jerk he'd been to me, the ugly things he'd said. And bearing in mind our shared friends, I knew we'd have to find our way beyond that to being able to be in each other's company without making everyone uncomfortable. But that was as far as I was willing to take it.

Or at least that was as far as I was telling myself I was willing to take it.

He cut me off before I could explain any of that to him.

And he did this by saying, "I found your brother."

At this news, it felt like the sun shone on me, warm and bright in my bedroom.

I was so happy to hear it, I bopped forward the distance separating us and grabbed his biceps with both hands, smiling up at him, saying, "Oh my God, really?"

"Baby..." he said softly, the word trailing from his lips, trailing in the room.

And trailing a finger of icy cold up my back with the tone of it and the new look on his face.

He moved his arms and I lost purchase, but he gained it, taking both my hands in his.

Uh-oh.

"Would you be comfortable with me closing the door?" he asked.

"Why?" I asked back.

"I think I should close the door." His voice was still super soft. "Are you okay with that?"

I stared into his eyes and my head moved in a distracted nod even if I didn't want him to close the door.

Not because I didn't want to be alone with him in my bedroom behind a closed door (though, there was that).

But because, intuitively, I knew I didn't want to hear what he had to say.

I feared it, so much that finger of cold had spread across my skin.

And so, when he gave my hands a squeeze and let go, I shivered.

He walked to the door, closed it, and came right back to me, taking up my hands again and holding them, warm and firm in both of his.

"Auggie, this is scaring me," I warned.

"I'm sorry. I've been trying to figure out how to share this with you since I started learning things about Birch and none of them were good."

My fingers tightened around his and I leaned slightly toward him, not losing contact with his gaze.

"Your brother didn't break from your family and keep his shit together to build a good life, like you did," he began.

"Wh-what's he been doing?" I stammered.

He gave my hands a squeeze and said, "Well, starting with the least bad stuff . . ."

Oh no!

"He's been married three times, and divorced three times, and he has five kids by four different women."

I felt my mouth drop open.

That was the *least* bad stuff?

I mean, Birch had been girl crazy, but I didn't think a lot about it, because at the time, I was boy crazy. Thus, I thought, what was good for the goose...

"And, well...*fuck*," Auggie bit off.

"What?" I asked.

He moved his head to the left like he was stretching out some tension before he straightened it and stated, "He's done some time."

Oh my *God*.

"Like...*jail* time?" I asked.

Auggie nodded.

My hold on him tightened. "For what?"

He hesitated and then shared, "Depends on which stint."

Which...*stint*?

Auggie continued, "But it started with a class four grand larceny charge, which, probably because it was his first offense, only bought him a year."

Only bought him *a year*?

A year *in prison*?

He hesitated (again).

I braced (more).

"And his last stint was for domestic violence assault."

I tore my hands from his as I took a step away, lifting one up to cover my mouth.

I did this so I wouldn't shout.

Or scream.

"How much do you wanna know?" Auggie queried, his words now quick and no-nonsense.

I pried my hand from my mouth, hugged my body with both arms, and croaked, "All."

Still quick and no-nonsense, he counted it down.

"The larceny charge was because he stole from an employer. Printers. Computers. Toner. Things of value, and lots of them, that he could sell that were easy to clear out in a hit he did at night when the office was closed."

Why on earth would Birch do that?

"Is he on drugs?" I asked.

"No," Auggie answered.

"*Was* he on drugs?"

"There was no mention of dope and no sign he has or had a problem with it in my searches."

"So he just stole to...*steal*?"

"I don't know why he did it, sweetheart."

Oh God.

"He later took an automobile," Auggie went on.

Oh God!

"I say 'took' because he returned it," Auggie said. "It was his girl-friend's. Or his ex-girlfriend's. Actually, one of his baby momma's."

"Oh God," I whispered, moving slowly until I knew my bed was there, and then I sat and the absurdly large weave of my chunky-knit throw that was folded over at the end of my bed poofed up all around my hips.

"Maybe I should stop," Auggie offered.

"No." I shook my head, not wanting it, but knowing I had to have it and wanting it to be over. "Keep going."

"Pepper—"

"Please, keep going, Auggie."

He studied me a beat.

And then he said, "The theft of the car he contends was a mis-understanding. But since his relationship with her went downhill after she found out she was the other woman...the pregnant other woman...and he was married at the time, it's unlikely that was the case. That said, they eventually got back together and made another baby."

"So he's Corbin," I said dully.

"Say again?"

I gave him the negative headshake, lifted a hand and rolled it at him to request he continue.

Regrettably, he did that.

"The domestic violence charge was levied on him by his last wife."

I dropped my head.

My big brother was a wife beater.

My God.

My awesome older brother *beat his wife.*

"Pepper." His usually smooth voice scratched over my name and that made me shiver too.

And then I felt him.

I lifted my head and saw he'd squatted in front of me, thighs splayed.

"Should we stop?" he asked.

"Is there more?"

"Yes." I must have made a face because he continued, "Not big shit. Bar fights. He went into business with someone and it went sour. He had some landlords that weren't his biggest fans, primarily because he didn't like to pay rent, and could be destructive. And that's it."

That wasn't *it.*

That was *a lot.*

"So he left and went completely off the rails," I remarked.

Auggie said nothing.

"That's kinda the definition of going off the rails," I asserted. "Twelve years, three marriages, five kids, jail time, bar fights and business disputes. That's a lot of not good to pack in that kind of time. To wit, totally and completely off the rails."

Auggie stayed silent.

I closed my eyes tight and tipped my head back.

Then I plopped back on the bed.

I took a second.

I took two.

Then I opened my eyes and the first thing I saw was the huge light installation over my bed.

When I first clapped eyes on it, I went on a mission, which included performing a bevy of lap dances in order to afford it because I *had* to have it.

It looked like a delicate tumbleweed, bleached natural in shade, spiky in texture, but in a soft way. This surrounded a low-watt bulb so in the daytime, you saw nothing but that bit of nature suspended almost like an earthen cloud over the room. But at night when you turned the light on, the slender twigs cast shadows over the room where it made you feel like you were in a forest. And the light was never bright, never invasive, it was soft and welcoming.

I loved that installation.

It gave me some peace just then.

Just not enough.

My brother was an ex-con.

He beat women.

He fathered copious children willy-nilly.

"Pepper, you okay?" Auggie called.

I got up on my elbows and looked at him.

He looked watchful and concerned.

He also looked out of place.

It was Sunday.

He wasn't wearing his usual commando attire of cargoes, utility boots and tight tee.

He was wearing jeans, a heathered-rust, long-sleeved Henley that was roomy at the mid-section, fitted at shoulders and biceps (in other words, the perfect fit), and on his feet were a pair of Nike leather Killshots with a navy swoop.

My room was a dream, and he was a dream and there was

something spectacular about him being all...*Auggie* in freaking Nike Killshots and a Henley, seemingly all action man even in casual clothes, standing in my place of serenity.

The dichotomy was perfection.

It was balance.

He was thunder energy. Fire.

(Mountain?)

I was water energy. Lake. Earth.

Another finger glided up my spine, but this one was not icy in the slightest.

"Pepper," he repeated. "Are you okay?"

"I thought Boone was looking into this," I said.

"I asked Boone to tell you he was looking into it in the sense that *we* were looking into it in the sense that actually *I* was looking into it. I did this because I started trying to find your brother the day after I acted like an ass to you and I didn't think you'd be down with me taking care of it for you."

This reminded me that I shouldn't be down with that because he did way more than act like an ass to me.

He'd been a total dick.

I pushed off the bed, probably highly ungracefully, considering he was standing close to it and I had to avoid him.

But avoid him I did.

I also put space between us.

He looked at my feet in my new position distant from him, then to my face.

And I prepared to thank him for his assistance and ask him how much I owed him for his time.

However, he spoke before I could get there.

"And now we need to talk..."

Oh no we didn't.

We weren't going to talk about what he said outside Juno's school and why he said it.

We weren't going to talk about an us.

Because there was no us and there never would be.

And he needed to finally get that.

"...about the situation with your sister," he finished.

I closed my mouth and blinked.

At my count, I currently had three situations: one old (Auggie and me not being a thing when both of us wanted to be a thing), one recent (Mom having cancer), one new (my brother being the definition of an asshole).

My sister, as far as I knew, was not a situation.

I opened my mouth again to ask, "What situation with my sister?"

"The fact she's marrying the pastor of that church they belong to," Auggie said.

I stood immobile, staring at him, I knew, in horror.

I knew this because I felt that horror.

In fact, I felt it so strongly, I thought I might throw up.

"What?" I whispered.

"You didn't know," he whispered back.

"*What?*" I shrieked.

He shot my way, took hold of my neck under my ear, fingers wrapped around and back, up in my hair, other hand on my waist, face in my face, and said urgently, "Quiet down, babe. Juno's downstairs."

My voice was no less horrified, even if it was a lot less loud, when I asked, "My sister is marrying Reverend Clyde?"

"Legally, no. Unofficially so he won't be prosecuted for bigamy, yes. He's adding her to his family, which already has five other wives."

My stomach dropped. "Holy hell."

"Yeah."

"He's, like, a hundred years old."

"Not quite. But he's way older than her. He's seventy-five."

"Holy hell."

"Yeah."

"When did they start doing that? The multiple-wives thing?"

His head ticked. "They didn't do it when you were younger?"

I shook my head.

Oh man.

His expression had changed again.

"What?" I asked.

He bit his lower lip. I could see the edges of his white teeth. They were spectacular.

I didn't have time for Auggie's spectacular teeth *or* how fabulous they looked pressing into his perfect lower lip *or* how much more fabulous they'd look pressed into *me*.

I had to know why he was biting that lip.

I curled my fingers in his Henley, used them to pull back and push forward at his pecs to get him to spit it out, and in case that wasn't enough, I added on a snap, "Augustus! What?"

"Your father has four wives."

"Oh my fucking *God!*" I screeched the final blaspheme.

"Babe, *quiet*," he ordered low, giving me a squeeze with both hands.

"Four wives *more* than my mom or four wives in total?" I asked in order to understand the full crazy of what I was learning.

"Total."

"When did this happen?" I continued.

"I don't know," he answered.

"This is *insane*," I declared.

"Yeah," he agreed.

"So, my brother is a felon and a wife beater. My sister is marrying the creepiest creepmeister in history, which, by the way, Reverend Clyde was that *way* before I knew he had multiple wives. A man who happens to be forty-nine years older than her and has known her since she was a little girl, which, I think we can both agree, ratchets up his creep factor by *a lot*. And my father has three wives I didn't know about, which is good for him, seeing as he has backups for when his first one dies of cancer."

"Baby," he said gently.

"It's official. My very recent meditation has worn off now."

And with that announcement, I fell forward and planted my face in his chest.

Immediately, Auggie wrapped his arms around me, one at my shoulders, one lower on my back.

He was warm and he smelled like the sun with hints of some fabric softener (or something), his chest was broad, his muscles solid and strong, his arms tight.

And instantly, I had a visualization of myself steady and sure-footed on an island standing under a sturdy structure that provided shelter as the winds blew, the rains came down and the seas churned around me.

Shit, shit, shit.

I tried to pull away but Auggie's hold tightened.

"Don't," he said, and it was a borderline groan, like my pulling away was physically hurting him.

I did not want to hurt him.

And I realized in that second, I never wanted to do that *ever*.

But my mind wanted to protect me. It wanted me to move away.

My heart had its own mind, and I stopped moving.

My head, though, fortunately, still had control of my mouth.

"You didn't act like an ass, Auggie, you shredded me. Corbin and I can get into it, and he can go low, but I've never been decimated by something he said like I was when you said those things to me. It isn't okay. There's no excuse for it. And there is no way I'm ever going to get into a relationship with a man who would speak to me that way."

"I take it Corbin is your ex?" he asked.

"Yes," I confirmed.

"You had his child, shit went bad, you two went your separate ways undoubtedly with broken promises and drama, and he's never hurt you the way I did?"

I clamped my mouth shut because I'd just started, and still, it was high time to quit talking.

"I've spent my whole life," Auggie began, "my whole life, Pepper, as far back as I can remember, watching my dad fuck shit up with my mom and then watching my mom make him pay for it. He'd cheat or he'd lose a job or he'd forget her birthday. They'd shout at each other. And eventually she'd leave him. He'd crawl to her, begging her to come back, promising he'd never do any of that again. She'd make him squirm. Hot. Cold. There, then a ghost. For him *and* for me."

Well, hell.

That sounded familiar.

He kept going.

"She'd get boyfriends who she'd rub in his face. Dump them and take Dad back. Move in and we'd be a family again. She'd snap her fingers and he'd dance, completely at her whim, until he was done with it. Then he'd do something stupid, and it'd start all over again."

Man, just when you thought your life threw you some curveballs, that your situation was really rotten, you hear someone else's, and you realize you had blessings to count.

And obviously I'd had my issues with things the way they were at home before I left, but hearing how he'd grown up, I was realizing I had blessings to count.

"Auggie," I said softly.

"And I need to make certain you understand that when I said 'my whole life,' I mean, in the time since I met you, she's left him twice and taken him back twice. It's still going on."

We'd known each other awhile.

But we hadn't known each other *that* long.

"Oh my God, that's the worst," I whispered.

"It is. And I gotta tell you, I know your ex cheated on you and the way he did was extreme."

The consequences of sharing a lot of friends, I should have known.

But still.

Damn.

"And now you know this about me," he continued.

I could tell he was gearing up for something.

I also could tell I wasn't going to like that something because I might absolutely love that something.

Therefore, I opened my mouth to stop him before he could start.

But he was on a roll and I couldn't get in there.

"Having a slew of Aunt Thises and Uncle Thats in my life because my dad would step out to get away from her games, or my mom would step out to strike back at him for hurting her, I would never do what your ex did to you. Not to you. Not to any woman."

Oh boy.

Mm-hmm.

I loved that.

"And," he kept going, "having those aunts and uncles fade in and out of my life, I know how important it is not to force a kid to live through a parent's relationships. It's disorienting. Temporary is not a concept in a kid's emotional range. Constantly having to learn new personalities, some good, some bad, and how to live with them is no fun. Not only dealing with the bad, which just sucks. But worse is the good. People in your life that mean something to you that eventually will be gone. So I get on a level even you don't how you're trying to protect Juno."

Yeah.

I loved that too.

"And I will always, Pepper, *always* handle your girl with care," he continued.

Shit, shit, shit.

I knew this to be true.

Because he was mad when he was at the school.

Mad at me.

But he'd hugged Juno and let her lean on him, and he not once gave her any indication that he was not at one with being there for her and being there with me.

He kept speaking.

"But, baby, you need to get, I am not your ex. And I need to get, you're not my mom or the other women who jacked me around."

The other women who jacked him around?

Oh boy!

He kept speaking.

"And you've been giving me vibes of my mom, sweetheart. I get why. But I let that get under my skin. I know you aren't her and I know the ups and downs you're experiencing are about your situation and Juno. I'm not your ex, you're not my mom. And I'm sorry. I really am. If I could rewind that time when we were by my car and replay it, I'd ask you to back off and we'd talk when I wasn't pissed and trying to cool down. But I can't rewind. Nothing erases me lashing out like that. And my goal is to help you learn that it's messing with my head this much that I did it, because I've never in my life done something like that to someone who didn't deserve it. So that means it is not a normal thing with me."

Messing with my head this much...

So much, to atone, he'd spent days finding out a lot of stuff about my brother.

So much, he'd also spent days learning dire news about the rest of my family, but even dire, it was important I knew it. Especially now, with Mom sick like she was.

And then there was...

It is not a normal thing with me.

Oh man.

Oh crap.

Oh boy.

Yes, I was loving all of this.

"Last, I need you not to mistake me," he continued. "I like everything I know about you. I want to know more. I really dig your kid. She's awesome. So you need to know I'm not in this for a quick fuck or a short-term situation where I have someone to pass the time with. I'm serious about you. About seeing if there could be an us. And I understand you'd come to me already as an us with Juno. And I'm standing right here with you in my arms promising you that if it doesn't work, I will not lay you out and I will not just be Uncle That to Juno. I told you I would handle her with care. What I'm telling you now is that you'll get that from me too."

Suddenly, I was finding it wasn't easy to breathe.

"And that's all I got," he finished.

I was relieved, because all he had was all good and I wasn't sure I could hold up.

I already knew a bunch of other stuff about Auggie that was all good.

It was piling up.

And I wasn't certain I could keep fighting it.

But it wasn't all he had because he kept going.

"Juno was walking home when I pulled up and she ran to me. She asked about it and I promised I'd help with the Thanksgiving show. Whether you're helping or not, I'm in. But for you for right now, I just gave you a lot that's gonna fuck with your head about your family and more to think on about us. And even if I don't want to, I have a feeling it's best for you if I leave you with it."

But he didn't leave.

He gave me just that perfect touch more goodness.

"But I'm not your touchstone for when times get tough... yet...and now I gotta let you be so you can get to that person or..." he glanced around the room again before he concluded, "...find where you need to be."

He finally shut up.

I did not start speaking.

Yet.

"Are you good for me to leave?" he asked.

I didn't move a muscle.

I just kept hearing him say, *Yet*, in my head.

He gave me a squeeze. "About your folks, your brother. That upset you, sweetheart. I sense you need space, but I can't go unless I know you're good for me to leave."

I started to shake my head (because I was *not* good for him to leave for more than one reason).

But I forced myself to nod.

He bent and pressed his lips to my forehead.

Oh *God*.

He then let me go, murmuring, "First meeting at the school about the Thanksgiving gig is Wednesday night. If you go, maybe we can catch a bite after."

I didn't say a word.

Yet.

He stopped at the door and turned back to me.

And he delivered his final silken blow.

"She's ready for you to find some happy for yourself, Pepper. Even if it isn't me, you're not doing her any favors by showing her that you don't think you're important enough to have that for yourself."

And with that, he opened the door, and he was almost through it before I called, "Auggie!"

He again turned back.

"Thank you."

Lame.

But in that moment, it was all I had.

And of course his reply was a smooth, tender, "Anytime, baby."

With that and a lift of his chin, he disappeared down the hall.

I stared after him.

I'm not your touchstone for when times get tough...

Yet.

So...

My mom was super sick.

Since I'd learned that, I had not been invited to spend any time with her and now I was wondering if that was because I had three stepmoms I didn't know about.

My sister was getting married to a man who was older than our father, and she was sixth in that line.

My brother had spent his years of liberation from all that crazy messing up his life as well as what sounded like a bunch of other people's lives.

And it did indeed seem like my daughter was trying to pull another fast one, throwing me in the way of Auggie at every opportunity, including inventing some. That not only bore more discussion with her, but contemplation about why she'd do it.

All this was going on and all I could think of was *Yet*.

I had never...in my life...had a touchstone.

I had never...in my life...had someone shelter me from any storm (at least not someone who was unbeknownst to me off creating his own storm I had to endure).

Now, I had to think about this.

I had to stop jacking Auggie around (even though I didn't mean to jack him around) and really think about it.

For me.

For Juno.

And definitely...

For Auggie.

CHAPTER SEVEN

A Mountain

PEPPER

Obviously, when shit got uber real in pretty much every aspect of your life, you had only one choice with how to deal with it.

You called in your girls.

Since part of what I needed to talk about was my daughter. And my daughter loved my girls, and vice versa, thus keeping them apart when there was a possibility to be together was impossible, the frantic group text message I sent after Auggie left included me begging them to show at my house for coffee and my famous cinnamon rolls the next morning after Juno went to school.

It would be nice to be able to be that TV mom who was best friends and shared everything with her kids without said kids having any emotional trauma from the fact their mom treated them like a bud instead of doing their best to give them direction as a parent.

But a friend was a friend.

And a mom was a mom.

So I had to find a time to work it all out with my posse when Juno wasn't around.

This I did.

Since Lottie, Ryn and Hattie also had the day off (or I should say, the night), they were in.

But even Evie said she'd sort it with her boss to show up.

Which told me how much they already knew. Because let us remember, Aug worked with all their men. He didn't strike me as a chatterbox, but if you worked closely with people who were also your friends, you talked.

Like I was about to do.

(That said, it might be about the cinnamon rolls, because they were only famous in my crew, but they were *seriously* famous in my crew.)

Promptly at 9:30, they began arriving. Evie first. Then Lottie and Hattie on each other's heels. And finally, Ryn.

After allowing time for hugs, hellos and coffee mug filling, I hustled their asses to my family room and shut them up by serving the cinnamon rolls still warm from the oven with the cream cheese frosting melting on top.

Obviously, they grabbed their plates and forks at once and nearly bumped heads going for the pan I placed on a hot pad on the coffee table.

So, when they sat back and were stuffing their faces, I launched in.

And I was so wired, I didn't even take a seat before doing it.

"I'm assuming you know some stuff, don't know other stuff, so I'm gonna run it all down."

I got four nods from four heads with mouths chewing.

Well…

Hell.

"Right, I don't know where to begin," I admitted.

"Start at Auggie," Lottie said.

"How's your mom?" Hattie asked at the same time.

Evie and Ryn were still chewing.

Auggie probably should be saved for last because, odds were, that discussion would take the longest.

So I started where all of this started.

Or at least the recent part of "this."

Hearing about my mom.

"I don't know how Mom is," I told them. "I haven't seen her. I've called every day since I heard the news. I've asked to see her. She evades. And then Auggie told me that not only was my sister set to marry Reverend Clyde, who's seventy-five years old—"

Gasps all around.

"—and she will be wife number six—"

More gasps, but with hers, Ryn sucked in so much breath, she started choking.

"—also, my dad apparently has three other wives as well as my mom. Something I did not know."

"Holy shit," Lottie said.

"Yeah," I agreed. "So I'm kinda at that place where I'm thinking I'll never be invited to go and spend time with my mom. And if Mom's as sick as Saffron says she is, she isn't feeling up to meeting me somewhere. Even here. And onward from that contemplation, I've realized I haven't been to their place for a long time. So long, it's been years. They come here. We meet at restaurants or parks. They show up at Juno's events. They try to get us to go to church. And now I'm thinking that's probably because my dad doesn't want me to run into his other three wives."

"This is..." Evie started but didn't finish.

"Insane?" I filled in.

"Yeah. That was the word I was looking for," she muttered.

"Unh-hunh," I agreed again.

"You know, the fundamental Mormons do that and it's part of what they believe," Hattie pointed out carefully.

"No shade," I said to her. "But if this was that, first, my father, mother and sister would not hide it from me. They never cared what I thought about how they practiced their faith. As you know, they've been trying to drag me into it, or *back* into it, since I left. If that was a healthy part of it, they wouldn't hide it. And second, my sister isn't choosing a man to be with who she loves who will also offer her sister wives. She's being married off to a guy old enough to be her *grandfather*."

"Have you talked to her since Aug told you this?" Ryn asked.

"No."

"So how do you know she doesn't want it? I mean, it's un-usual, with that wide of an age gap. But there are May-December romances that are real," she went on.

"Well, mostly I know because we're sisters. Growing up, we shared a room. And she might be religious, but she's still a woman who used to be a girl. And when she was a girl, she told me not only about the boys she had crushes on, she told me her hopes and dreams about her future husband. And some old dude was not any part of that."

"Mm-hmm," Lottie hummed then said, "I hear you."

"Whoa, Pez, this is *a lot*," Hattie noted.

It totally was.

"I haven't even scratched the surface," I shared.

I got a lot of big eyes at that and then they all settled in.

"Auggie found my long-lost brother," I declared.

Even if they'd just kicked back from the last bit o' news, when I made that declaration, I actually physically felt them brace.

Then again, they were my girls. They knew I not only loved my brother, I missed him.

I didn't hold back when I gave it to them.

"He's an ex-con, a serial husband, though not in the way his father is, in the way he divorced the *three* women he married since he took off."

"Oh shit," Ryn murmured.

"He's also a wife beater in the sense he did time for it," I finished.

"Oh Pepper," Hattie whispered, aghast.

"Yup," I said, popping the "p" in order to be perfectly clear how much I felt her aghast-ness.

Ryn reached long for a positive spin. "Okay, silver lining: I suppose it's safe to say your brother isn't invited to the prayer circle now, so you no longer have to worry about that."

Evie elbowed her and shot her an eye roll.

"I know, lame, but I got nothing else," Ryn muttered under her breath.

"Right, and now...do I tell my family my brother is that big of a mess?" I inquired. "Not only did he have three wives, he has five children. He's apparently a shitty business partner. And in his spare time, he jacks around landlords and gets in bar fights."

Hattie winced.

Evie (who, incidentally, also had a crappy brother) hung her head.

Lottie and Ryn looked like they were getting mad.

Evie lifted her head. "I'm understanding the cinnamon rolls now."

"If any situation screams *cinnamon rolls*, this is it," Hattie concurred.

"I'm not done," I told them.

Ryn's voice was getting higher. "Are you serious?"

"Oh shit," Lottie said around another bite of cinnamon roll (an aside: this was testimony to how good my cinnamon rolls were, because Lottie was eating them, and she and Mo treated their bodies like temples, except when it came to my cinnamon rolls).

"Yes, I'm serious. And yes, oh shit," I confirmed.

For fortification, they all dug into their rolls.

I waited until they had mouths full of ooey, gooey, cinnamony, doughy, frosting goodness before I carried on.

"So, I shared with you all what went down with Auggie and Juno asking him to career day and all of that," I began.

I got four head nods.

"And I just told you Auggie told me about my sister and my brother."

Four more head nods.

"I also told you Auggie came over yesterday, and this is one of the reasons why I asked you here today."

The head nods came again.

"What I didn't tell you was that Juno saw him pulling up. She let him in. Then she told him to come up to my bedroom to say hi. She did not shout up and say, 'Hey, Mom! Auggie's here!' She probably knew exactly what I was doing and sent Auggie right up to my room."

They stopped nodding and stared.

"I was meditating," I carried on. "He watched me."

"Oh man." Ryn.

"Cool." Evie.

"Hot." Lottie.

"Yikes." Hattie.

"When I finished, he told me I was even more beautiful when I meditated."

"Oh *man*." Ryn.

"Cool!" Evie.

"*Hot*." Lottie.

"Yippee!" Hattie.

I ignored them.

"He further told me that he loved my bedroom. And, after giving me the intel about my brother and sister, and doing it in a *really* nice way, even if what he had to say was *really upsetting*, he told me about his parents' crazy relationship that is hella dysfunctional. How they've dragged him along in that mess and were still doing it. Made some mention about how women jacked him around that did not sound good. Apologized for what he said to me at Juno's school. And when he did that, he did it in a way that I knew he really meant it and it wasn't just words. And finally, he made some promises I, for the life of me, and I gotta say between yesterday and now I've tried, cannot imagine he wouldn't keep."

"Yeah, Mo's told me all of this about Aug. His parents are serious assholes," Lottie corroborated.

"Mo told you? Mag didn't tell me," Evie said. "Does Mag know?"

"Probably," Lottie answered.

"Boone hasn't told me either," Ryn put in.

Hattie was semi-squirming.

Axl had shared with her.

"It's okay," I said to her. "Honestly."

"I felt bad not telling you. I really did," she replied. "But Axl told me and then he said it was Auggie's to give to you, and I agreed."

"That's why I didn't say anything too," Lottie added.

"Totally, it's okay," I assured them.

Because it was.

This was because Axl was right. It was Auggie's to give me.

Though...

"Someone told him about Corbin," I shared.

"It didn't come from Axl," Hattie piped up. "He knows it goes both ways."

"It might have come from Mo," Lottie admitted.

"Or Mag," Evie said.

"Or Boone," Ryn said.

"I don't mind," I promised. "It's not like I don't know we all talk about all sorts of stuff."

"But you mentioned it," Lottie pointed out.

"I didn't say it to make you all feel weird," I replied. "I said it because he knows, and he was very clear that he wasn't going to do what Corbin did to me."

"I don't think he'd ever do that," Evie said.

"Not ever," Hattie punctuated.

"If he did, he knows Mo would fuck his shit up," Lottie announced.

"Boone would too," Ryn said.

"Okay," I cut in, because I was right. The Auggie part was going to take the longest. "So..." I squeezed my eyes shut tight, then with a groan, plopped down on a crochet-covered pillow that was behind me before I put my elbows to my knees and buried my face in my hands.

"Pez," Lottie called me.

I took a deep breath and gave her my gaze.

At one look at her pretty face, I knew she understood precisely what weighed me down so much it physically took me down.

"Auggie's gorgeous. Have you ever considered that?" she asked.

"Of course. Like, every time I look at him. And, just to say, a lot of the times I'm not looking at him and just thinking about him."

"I don't mean that kind of consideration," she said.

I let my expression, which I knew was now confused, do the talking.

She heard me and began to tell a story.

"Before they met us, the guys used to hang at a bar. It was a local but also kind of a pickup joint. They had good TVs and the men were tight with the bartenders so they could tell the person behind the bar what they wanted to watch, and they'd change the channel. They could catch their games there and never run out of beer. And hot babes hung there. So, for obvious reasons, it was their regular place."

She took a breath.

No one said anything.

She kept going.

"There was a couple that hung there too. One of the times they were there, Aug told Mo that the chick was his thing. But she was taken, because she was always with this guy. Both Aug and Mo thought that was that. Except one day she came to the bar without her dude, and she sat beside Auggie. They struck up a conversation. They got on. She was his kind of people. She was meeting some friends that night, so she said good-bye and took off. But this connection meant enough, Auggie told Mo it happened."

I wasn't feeling super happy about this story, even though I had no idea where it was heading. I just knew the way she was telling it, wherever that was, wasn't good.

But I kept my mouth shut.

Lottie continued her storytelling.

"But she came back, again without the guy she was always with, and she sat with Auggie. She wasn't meeting friends that time, and made it clear she came back to hang with Aug. Like the first time they hung out, they clicked...big time."

She hesitated.

I got what she meant by "big time," so I nodded.

She carried on.

"And after he did her, he told her he wanted to see her again, and she admitted he was her freebie."

Uh-oh.

My back straightened because I had a feeling I knew what that meant.

I asked anyway.

"Freebie?"

Lottie nodded. "Freebie. Auggie's hot. She saw him. She wanted him. She had her guy. They weren't open, but they made a deal. Kind of a modified celebrity deal you joke about with your partner, but you do that because you'll never go there. For them, it was for real, and her seeing Auggie at that bar was what prompted it. Her dude got to pick a girl he could fuck no problems, no questions, no go-back-for-mores. She got to pick a guy. Auggie was that guy. She fucked him because he's gorgeous and she wanted that notch. That experience. That was all he was to her. A hot guy she fucked."

I felt chilly on the inside.

Lottie wasn't finished.

"Needless to say, none of the guys went back to that bar, and shortly after that, Mo met me. And that's the worst it's happened, but similar things have happened to Auggie and they happened a lot. We think guys like him who have the bod and the face and the hair and the clothes and they make good bank have it made. But women can be bitches. It's happened to all of them, even Mo. It's just that Auggie is movie-star gorgeous, so he got it more. He's a conquest. He's spoils. In other words, from that chick to some friend posse making him the prize in some game, the opposite of a dogfight, but the end result is the same, he's been seriously dicked around by women like you would not believe."

The opposite of a dogfight, but the end result is the same.

"Boone didn't tell me this either," Ryn whispered.

"Mag mentioned something," Evie murmured.

Hattie didn't say anything.

So I knew she knew.

As for me, I was utterly unable to move for fear of what I'd do if I did.

"And that's just *that* shit," Lottie went on. "There are others who wanted a guy who looks like him that they can parade around. They didn't want to get to know him. He didn't have a brain or thoughts or feelings or opinions. He was just their trophy."

Okay.

I'd had enough.

To express this, I didn't take my eyes from Lottie even as I lifted both hands and pressed my fingers to my lips.

I drew in a long breath through my nose, held it, and exhaled.

I dropped my hands in my lap.

Then I leaned toward her and screamed, *"Those fucking bitches!"*

Lottie's blonde hair swayed with her head jerk.

Ryn and Evie grinned at each other.

Hattie grinned at me.

See?

I knew I shouldn't have moved.

Too late now.

"Are you fucking serious with that shit?" I demanded of Lottie.

"I wish I wasn't, but I am," Lottie replied.

I shot to standing.

And then I started pacing.

And muttering.

"Oh my God, this is fucked *up*. I mean, I can't even believe this shit. Who would do that to somebody?"

"Maybe you should sit down and have a cinnamon roll," Hattie suggested.

I stopped pacing, whirled on her and snapped, "I don't want a cinnamon roll!"

"Okay, I'm feeling better about her and Aug now," Ryn stage-whispered to Evie. "Serious, if she's so upset on his behalf she turns down a cinnamon roll, she's in deep for him."

"Totes," Evie agreed.

"Oh my God, this isn't funny," I declared with extreme exasperation.

"It isn't," Ryn said. "But you are."

I turned on Lottie and asked (somewhat irately), "Why didn't you tell me this before?"

"Before, it was none of your business. Now, I sense you're finally wavering about him, in terms that you're finally going to let him in, so it is."

"He's fire and thunder and maybe mountain," I blurted. "And I'm water. Lake. Earth. We balance."

Evie, Ryn and Hattie stared at me (Hattie was even blinking in a bemused way I would have noted was kind of cute, if I wasn't freaking out).

Lottie spoke.

"I really wish I knew what you were talking about, because the way you're saying it, you sound like you mean it and it's important," she said. "But I have no clue what you're saying."

"The Tao," I told her. "The trigrams. The different energies. We all have the capacity to have each one flowing through us any given day, any given time in our life. The goal is achieving Tai Chi, having all of them flowing, having that balance. But we tend to gravitate to the energies that most define us. Fire energy is charisma. Confidence. Courage. Just the smallest light of fire can banish dark, and if you think about it, that's extraordinary. Thunder energy is power. Inspiration. Thunder makes things happen."

They were all staring up at me with rapt attention.

So I kept at it.

"Water is flow. Reflection. Healthy relationships. Boundaries."

"You've sure got that last," Lottie mumbled.

I shot her a look that might work on Juno but probably wouldn't on Lots, but even so, I kept on.

"Lake is positivity. Optimism. Joy. Balance. And earth is nourishment. Taking care of yourself and others."

"What's mountain?" Evie asked.

"Wisdom," I answered, then I held quiet, something nudging around the place of my heart. And that something took so much of my attention, when I kept on, it was like I was whispering to myself. "Constancy. Faith. Trust. A mountain has always been there, and always will be."

I fell silent and I had no idea how long everyone in the room was silent with me, but it felt like it took a long time before I finally stopped centering on my heart and came back into the room.

When I did, Lottie declared, "I'm a flipping Taoist."

"You totally freaking *are*!" Ryn agreed.

"Holy crap, like, maybe you balanced us *all* out," Evie said.

"I knew your fixups weren't random!" Hattie cried.

"Of course they weren't random," Lottie said, sounding miffed.

"I knew Boone and I weren't random, for sure," Ryn decreed.

"I totes thought you wanted to mess with Mag's head with me, but now I see it," Evie put in.

"Once I stopped being an idiot and got to know him, I also knew Axl was the balance of me," Hattie said.

"Uh...*hello*," I called.

Everyone looked at me.

"All that thunder and fire is awesome, definitely," I stated. "But it's the mountain energy I need."

"Auggie is *sooooooooooooo* a mountain," Hattie assured.

"*Soooooooooooooooooo*," Ryn asserted.

I wanted to believe that.

I *did* believe that.

But...

"I have to *know* that," I returned. "For Juno *and* for me."

"You can't *know* shit," Lottie retorted. "Though I will say that I agree that Auggie's a mountain. But what's really going on here, Pepper?" she asked.

"What do you mean?" I asked back.

"I mean, we got it." She flipped a hand. "Things have not been easy for you. Far from it. You have Juno to consider, and she's important. But he's been open with where he's at with you. He fucks up, and then he breaks his back finding your brother for you, and it's a dark bonus, but it's a bonus nonetheless, him discovering that shit about your family. And you lose your mind when you hear women have been bitches to him."

She shook her head in disgust.

And kept at me.

"And he's not dumb by any stretch. He might not know about

those energies, but with parents like he had, women fucking with his head, do you think he doesn't get that he needs nourishment, balance, someone looking out for him? Finally? Never having had that in his life? I mean, you're not only beautiful. You're not only awesome. You're a great mom. Auggie can put one and one and one together and want the three."

"I think I need a cinnamon roll now," I announced.

Hattie moved forward to pry one from the pan for me.

I went back to the cushions on the floor and dropped down on one.

Hattie handed me the gooey roll on a plate with a fork. I took up said fork and dug right in.

Lottie let me chew.

She let me swallow.

And then she didn't let me get away with avoiding what she said.

"What's really holding you back, Pez?"

I looked at her.

And I gave it all to them.

"I made a pact with myself. No men until Juno can emotionally understand what that means to me, and by extension, her."

"In other words, no men, so when you try again, and he dicks you over like Corbin did, she wouldn't be decimated, like she was when Corbin dicked you over," Lottie deduced.

I stopped looking at Lottie and turned my attention back to my roll.

"Pez," Lottie called.

I lifted my eyes to her.

"She didn't get where Daddy had gone," I said softly.

Lottie drew an audible breath into her nose and sat back.

I pointed to myself with my cinnamon-and-cream-cheese-frosting-smeared fork. "It hurt me, what he did. I loved him. Even if he'd just cheated on me once, it would have destroyed me. But he didn't cheat on me once. He cheated in a way he cheated on us both. He carried on a whole other life that didn't have us in it. And he had to go. But by getting rid of him, I kicked out my daughter's father. I took him away from her—"

"You did not, he did that," Ryn said firmly.

I turned to her.

"You get, though, that I had to live with her confusion, and she was only five. She didn't understand at all what was going down. But I know she hurt. And a mother cannot handle her child's hurt. It doesn't just get swept away by rational thoughts and understanding you're doing the right thing. When your baby hurts, *you hurt*."

No one said anything for long beats before Evie spoke.

"We haven't touched on that. The fact Corbin wants you back."

I shook my head and dug into my roll again, saying, "He hasn't followed up on it. Nothing. Juno goes back to him after school today. He and I are finally getting into a rhythm. We don't really speak anymore unless something comes up we have to speak about. The thing is, he's very competitive. I think he was just triggered by the idea of someone invading his turf."

"Do you mean his turf, as in you? Or his turf, as in, there might be a man in Juno's life?" Ryn asked.

"Me," I said. "And maybe both of us. It's not based in any reality, but Corbin is that type of guy. I've had the chance to think about it since he said he was going to fix us, and I should have known, in that particular sense, if I moved on from him, he would never take it lying down. He'd act up. It'd be a thing. Then we'd get over that thing."

"Do you think somewhere in the back of your mind you were considering this possibility, that Corbin would insert himself in the situation, and that was another reason why you didn't try things with Auggie?" Evie queried.

I thought about that.

Then I said, "Yes."

Everyone grew silent.

I ate my roll.

Hattie broke the silence.

"What now?"

Of all of this, that question was easy.

"What now is that I have to doubly consider where I'm at because I don't want to be one of those bitches who jacks Auggie around," I stated.

"Oh my God," Ryn groaned as she fell back to the couch.

Evie rolled her eyes at Hattie.

Lottie glared at me. "Are you serious right now?"

"Yes!" I cried. "I mean those women—"

She clapped. "Babe." She clapped twice more. "Stop it."

"You did not just clap at me," I said low.

"You're making excuses," Ryn decreed. "Before, like Lottie said, we got it. Now . . . it's bullshit."

"Totes," Evie agreed.

"I'm not a mom," Hattie started, "but I get that hesitation. And when Axl told me about what women did to Auggie, I hurt for him. But I have to say, it sounds like you're fishing for ways to protect your heart."

"What if I am?" I snapped. "It's not like the last time I gave it to someone turned out all that great."

"So lock up those girl parts, sister," Lottie said dismissively. "And we'll be done with this. Because . . . no."

"Is there an energy for being a cop-out?" Ryn asked.

Evie snickered.

I was the one glaring now, at Ryn . . . and Evie.

"You know, just let him off the hook so he can move on. This is getting to the point it's . . . not nice," Hattie said quietly.

And there it was.

I had half a cinnamon roll suspended on a plate in front of me, and I sat motionless, horrified.

Because I was already one of those bitches that had fucked with Auggie's head.

I had not told a one of them I'd had sex with him.

I did not share that now either, for obvious reasons.

But...

What was I doing?

Ryn cut into my thoughts.

"And let's hark *way* back to the whole Juno-trying-to-fix-you-up thing. I mean, as you know, I'm not a mom either. But I think she's trying to tell you something."

"What she's trying to say is, she sees all her mom's girls loved up and settling in and she's a part of this world," I returned. "She understands partnering up. She undoubtedly remembers what it was like back when her dad and I were together. She wants me to be happy like that. She wants me to be happy like you all."

"I think the takeaway from that is *she wants you to be happy*," Ryn stressed.

"Don't dismiss that," Evie said hurriedly. "Really. Because, straight up, for the people we love, that's all we want for them."

"I am happy," I asserted.

No one had anything to say to that.

I pushed it.

"You don't have to have a man to be happy."

"No. You don't," Lottie agreed. "But do you want Juno to be an only child?"

Shit.

I didn't.

I loved babies.

And I loved kids.

Every age Juno was, was my favorite age.

Kids rocked.

And true, my relationships with my brother and sister had not turned out great, as they had gone on in their lives to do things I wasn't at one with.

But when we were growing up, there was love. I was tighter with my brother, but my sister and I had our moments.

A lot of them.

Juno was getting older, but a sister is a sister, no matter the age.

I wanted her to have that.

"Do you want to be a dancer all your life?" Hattie asked, cutting into my thoughts.

No, I didn't.

As noted, I wanted to open a meditation/yoga studio.

"I can move on from dancing myself," I stated.

"You can, I'm just pointing out that maybe you have to think on things, Pez. Are you happy? Are you *really* happy? I mean, anyone can be happy. And I believe you're happy. But why not reach out for something and be happi*er*," she urged.

Happi*er*.

Auggie was loyal to his buds.

What would it feel like to have a man loyal to me?

He was funny.

What would it feel like to have more laughter in my life? In my home? Giving that to my daughter?

Work was not all to him. On any given group occasion, from the important ones, like standing up for Mo at his wedding to Lottie, to Mag grilling pizza, he was always there.

What would it be like to have a man who understood the important things in life were not even close to being about how much money you made?

Not to mention, I might melt into a puddle on my crocheted cushion if I thought about what Auggie could do if he had time and an alternate, more comfortable location, considering how well he did when he fucked me hot and quick against a wall.

And my baby girl wanted him for me.

"I'll call him tonight," I mumbled.

"What did you say?" Evie asked.

I cleared my throat and looked across my four girls.

And louder, repeated, "I'll call him tonight. He asked to get a bite to eat after the meeting about the Thanksgiving show at the school is over. I'll say yes."

"Oh. My. *God*," Ryn said, smiling broadly.

Hattie jumped to her feet then jumped on her feet, her dark, curly hair bouncing, all while she clapped and shouted, "Yay!"

Evie reached across and gave Lottie a high five.

I should be freaked out.

I should be scared.

But I couldn't stop the twitching of my lips becoming a grin at seeing how happy they all were.

Happy about me taking a shot at love.

Ryn tugged Hattie down as Lottie focused on me.

"Okay, that's done, and I could try to find the words that describe how thrilled out of my goddamn mind I am that it is, but I can't so I won't try. Now, what are you gonna do about your mom, your sister and your brother?"

Right.

Of course.

The scary part done, onward to the other scary parts.

"I don't know about Birch," I admitted. "Maybe leaving that alone might be a good idea. However, I need to think on that. Because Juno has cousins, and I have nieces or nephews. And that's a big thing to turn my back on along with Birch, especially also keeping Juno from it. But regarding my mom and mostly my sister, I have a plan."

When I hesitated, they all leaned slightly toward me.

And I knew, whatever my plan, they were either in, or they were in for the long haul to discuss it, modify it, refine it and then participate in it.

God, I loved these chicks.

I felt lighter inside.

The heaven energy was flowing for me that day.

Being supported.

Unrestricted.

Mighty.

I was going to take a chance with Auggie.

And suddenly, I felt the fear and trepidation leak away.

I felt buoyant.

Bubbly.

Excited.

I felt...

God, I felt like I used to feel, back in the day, before Corbin, before even Juno, when I was free of my family and out on my own.

Like the world was full of possibility.

All I had to do was reach out and grab it.

*   *   *

Hours later (many of them), when it was late enough pretty much anyone, including Auggie, would be off work, I was again pacing.

This time with my phone in my hand.

Office zone, kitchen, office zone, living room, office zone...

On about trip seven, I stopped midway to the kitchen when a memory flashed of not too long ago, when the girls were giving me guff about not going out with Auggie, and Ryn had called me chicken.

"Oh my God, I'm totally chicken," I breathed in horror.

I then lifted my phone and engaged it.

"I am no chicken," I said to it. "I am mighty."

On that, I opened my contacts, going down to "H," finding

Auggie's name (I had his number because we had a group text string going, mostly funny GIFs, hangout invites, things like that, this would be the first time I used his number outside that string) and then hitting the little phone icon.

I'd read somewhere you never put your phone anywhere near your head (or left it resting in your lap, or in your pocket, or your bra—EMFs were a bitch).

So I hit speaker.

It rang once.

In that minuscule amount of time, I considered hanging up, rushing to the sliding glass door and throwing my phone in the backyard, so I not only couldn't hear Auggie ringing me back, if he used some of his commando resources to locate my phone, he'd see it in the backyard and think I lost it there.

Sadly, as I contemplated this preposterous notion, he picked up.

"Pepper?"

God!

What did I do now?

I went for casual.

"Hey."

"Is everything okay?"

He sounded worried.

He was so...totally...*a mountain*.

"Yes. Everything is...well, I just, you know, I dance at night so there won't be a lot of time to grab a bite after Juno's Thanksgiving thing."

"Right," he said softly.

"So I'm going to take a personal day. We have Holly in the show now, and she's good at filling in."

Holly was our new MC and house comedian.

Leave it to Dorian (the manager at the club where I worked, Smithie's) to hire a gorgeous female comedian to MC a sexy revue that used to be a strip show.

She'd been a hit.

Then again, everything Dorian touched at the club seemed to turn to gold.

"You're taking a personal day to go out with me," Auggie said.

"Do you...I mean, do you still want to grab a bite?" I asked.

"Abso-fucking-lutely."

At his response, I suddenly felt so giddy, I almost giggled.

What was the matter with me?

"You got a place you wanna go or do you want me to pick?" he inquired.

"You pick. And before you ask, I like practically everything," I told him.

"Great."

"Yeah, great."

Okay.

What now?

"I'm glad you decided to say yes, sweetheart," he said.

"I'm, uh...glad you're glad. I'm glad too."

He sounded amused when he replied, "Good we're both at that place."

"Mm-hmm."

Man, I completely forgot how hard this was.

"So, did this decision happen over cinnamon rolls?" he asked.

I felt my eyes get big.

Then I started laughing, not giggling, but genuinely laughing, and I wandered to my pink couch and threw myself on it.

"My cinnamon rolls are magic," I shared with no attempt whatsoever at humility.

"I've heard that about them."

"I'll, well...make you some sometime."

God!

Did that sound like I was alluding to the fact he'd spend the night sometime?

"I'll look forward to that," he said, not sounding lewd, just like he was looking forward to it.

Okay, well...I was being a dork and he couldn't miss it.

So, since I took this step, might as well face the rest head-on.

"You're going to have to go easy on me," I stated. "Because it has just occurred to me that I haven't flirted for nearly a decade."

I heard his chuckle, then, "Just be you, Pepper. I've been waiting for this call for three years. And that's what I've been waiting for. To connect with *you*."

How sweet.

"Three years?" I queried.

"Has it been five?" he teased. "It's felt like five, but I didn't want to go there."

I laughed again. "It's only been months."

"A lot of months."

He was right.

And I was still laughing. "Okay, a lot of months, but not three years."

"No," he agreed. "Not three years." Then, "Juno back with her dad this week?"

I turned to my side to get more comfortable, set the phone on the cushion and started playing with my hair as I replied with a glum, "Yeah."

"Sorry, baby. That sucks."

"Every other Monday it's hard not to throw myself a pity party."

"I can imagine."

And then...

It happened.

After that, Auggie and I talked for nearly two hours.

I knew what he was in the middle of on Netflix (*Mindhunter*). He knew I was doing an epic catch-up of a show my parents wouldn't let me watch back in the day (*Girlfriends*).

I knew he was born and raised in Denver.

He knew I was too.

I knew he was renting his pad, a duplex in the Baker District, from some mutual friends/acquaintances, Indy and Lee Nightingale.

He knew I'd bought my place two years ago and just a few months back put the finishing touches on the décor (for now, there was never any *true* finish to décor, something else he knew since I told him).

I also spent a fair amount of time waxing on about how perfect Juno was.

He spent that time listening to me wax on, as well as agreeing.

And so it went.

It was only when he said, "Sorry, baby, but I got a thing I gotta do for Hawk that means I gotta be in the office at five tomorrow. I need to get a shower and hit the sack," that I realized how long we'd been talking.

It was after ten at night.

I thought of Auggie in the shower.

We'd had sex but I hadn't seen his body.

Even not knowing what that visual was for certain, I shivered.

Then I said, "I'll let you go."

"It's safe to say I'm pretty fucking happy you called tonight, Pepper. And I don't wanna push things. But still, phone date tomorrow? Same time?"

That didn't cause a shiver.

It made my chest feel warm.

"I'd love that," I said quietly.

"Good," he murmured.

"Sleep well, Auggie."

"All right, baby. Talk to you soon."

"'Night."

"'Night."

My screen registered his disconnect and it took me not even a second to say out loud, "To hell with EMFs," pick it up, roll to my back and hug it to my chest.

I stared at my ceiling.

And it took me a lot more seconds before I started laughing in a way I was actually giggling.

Because my baby girl had it going on.

She might be eight, but she knew.

This was what she wanted for me.

Hugging my phone.

Giggling.

And happy.

CHAPTER EIGHT
Day Made

PEPPER

Yes, I can do that. No, I won't be doing that."

Evie's voice was coming over my speakerphone, and the things it was saying were messing up my master plan.

She wasn't on speakerphone because of EMFs (well, she was, but not only). She was mostly because the girls and me were in my blue Hyundai Tucson (the girls being Lottie, Hattie, Ryn and me), and I wanted everyone to hear her.

It was Tuesday, late morning.

It was also go-time on another part of my master plan.

The day before, once we sorted out the Auggie thing, the girls and I did what I said we'd do.

They listened.

We discussed.

Refined.

And now it was time to activate.

"It'd be super helpful if you did a wee bit. Not a lot. Just a *wee bit*," I cajoled.

"Pez, hacking is a crime," Evie stated.

"You're a genius," Ryn pointed out from the backseat (and this was true, literally, Evie's IQ was off the charts). "Be genius at not getting caught."

"And I don't want you to hack *everything*," I added. "Just enough to prove Reverend Clyde is the creepiest creepmeister living."

I was hoping . . . porn.

My father would seriously frown on porn.

So would my sister.

"I will repeat, I was the one who was consistently against us wading into this," Evie's voice said. "The boys can do it, probably in a fraction of the time, and undoubtedly they won't ef it up."

I was mildly offended by her suggesting we might ef it up.

This was only mildly because, the truth was, there was likelihood we'd ef it up.

Which was why we needed a genius hacking Reverend Clyde's computer.

However, she had, indeed, said this, and reiterated it, then did that some more.

On the one hand, as noted, she was a genius. We should probably listen to her.

On the other hand, I had no idea how much effort it took for Auggie to amass the kind of information he amassed in the short time he had between our situation at Juno's school and our discussion at my house. But I had a feeling, with the sheer amount he'd been able to gather, it took a lot of effort.

I'd just agreed to an official phone date to be followed by an official date-date with Aug.

I didn't feel in the place to ask for favors.

"And as *we* consistently said," Ryn began, "the boys are busy with earning a living and other somewhat important things, like, you know, *investigating a ring of dirty cops*."

"Ryn, you've been kidnapped...twice, and shot at," Evie reminded her. "Have you not learned your lesson?"

"I haven't been kidnapped," Lottie, sitting up front next to me, cut in. "You guys have left me out of all the fun stuff. There's one fixup left, one last chance, and I'm all in."

Just to say, I'd been kidnapped. And during it, had a gun pointed at my head.

As such, I could testify that it had not been fun at all.

And I didn't want a repeat.

"We're not gonna get kidnapped," I said.

"All right. Then if we're not gonna get kidnapped, and you're not gonna hack into this guy's computer, Evie, then we're doing this," Lottie decreed. "I mean, for God's sakes, when my sister's friends got hooked up with their men, there were car bombs, high-speed chases and grenades exploding. Not that I was wanting it to go that extreme for you guys, but a couple of measly kidnappings and we're done? We need to shake things up."

And now I was having second thoughts about my master plan.

Because outside the hacking and my family being hella pissed at me if I did what I'd recruited the girls to do (though I hoped, in the end, they'd be enlightened), there wasn't a ton of real danger involved in this.

At least I didn't think.

"Fine," Evie snapped. "Just keep the line open to me so when I hear you all screaming, I can call in the boys."

Ryn gave me an *Evie's so dramatic* eye roll in the rearview mirror.

I agreed with her.

This wasn't the dangerous part of the master plan (the hacking was).

"Okay, that's a go for me. I'm going in!" Hattie announced.

She then threw open her door and walked in her graceful but still girlie Hattie walk up the sidewalk, hair swinging and skirt swaying on the cute, long-sleeved, short dress she wore with knee-high boots.

Hattie being a classically trained dancer, she sometimes did her routines *en pointe* at the club. She'd trained so much, every movement she made was poised and elegant.

It was beautiful.

And super cool.

It was also why we picked her for this assignment.

Lottie looked like, well...a stripper. Not only because she was, it was also her aesthetic. And she soooooo rocked it. But the stripper look didn't really go hand in hand with what was about to happen.

Ryn was stunning. But she was edgy. World-wise. And she didn't hide either. No way she could do what needed to get done without someone wondering why she was doing it.

Hattie was curvy and had long, curly hair, big eyes and she was also a dazzler, but in a more innocent and cute way.

She was perfect (though, that short dress might cause some waves, but part of her remit wasn't being incognito, she was heading in supposedly to *learn* about the church, not like she knew all about it, if she did, she couldn't ask questions).

"I don't have a good feeling about this," Evie's voice said over my phone as we all watched Hattie walk down the sidewalk toward my family's church.

I'd never been there. It was a new-ish build. But I'd noted the minute we'd reached our destination that Reverend Clyde had been busy after I'd escaped his flock.

I already knew this because my parents were very excited when they broke ground, and then even more so when they sanctified their new place of worship.

According to Dad, it did not have all the "obnoxious trappings" of those TV evangelists' churches. It was, as he said, "simply fit for purpose."

I didn't know what that meant, and I didn't ask because I also didn't care, seeing as I wasn't a fan of their "purpose."

And at the time, I didn't know about the multiple-wives thing.

I just knew you weren't allowed to cuss (not unusual), take the Lord's name in vain (that *was* a commandment, so even though I did it, the fact they seriously frowned on it was no big thing), and you weren't allowed to have sex before marriage (um…no one gets to tell me what to do with my body).

You also had to worship *a lot*.

It was seriously frowned on to miss prayer practice and missing a Sunday sermon was treated like a high crime.

But more, there were a ton of events, fellowships, revivals, baptisms, plus courses (these, though, were only for the men, which I always thought was shady).

Hell, if someone claimed they'd sneezed a righteous sneeze, Reverend Clyde would gather us all to hear his words on the subject, and you'd feel the censure if you didn't show up.

However, although none of that was fun, the big thing that was my issue was that the man was the "lion of the home" (Reverend Clyde's words).

In other words, what the head of the family said—the *male* head, that was—went.

The end.

Like seriously, *the end*.

Once we got involved in the church and settled in, Mom never made a peep against Dad's wishes.

It was gross.

And disturbing.

And women could not dress as they saw fit. They covered up. They did not wear pants. Nothing tight. As little skin showing as possible.

No makeup either.

No high heels.

No dyeing of hair. Also no short ("boyish") hair.

And so many more rules for women, it was *not* funny.

Now I was seeing that the "obnoxious trappings" Dad had talked about when it came to their new church did not include size.

In other words, the building was big. Far bigger than needed for a simple sanctuary, an admin office or two and perhaps some rooms for fellowship and Sunday school.

Which made one question why they'd need that much space.

The parking lot was large as well. And it currently had a number of cars in it, trucks, a couple of vans, and three seriously kitted-out RVs.

But I'd positioned my car down the street so we had a view of the front door, and thus could have eyes on Hattie until she went in.

"She's just going to gather information. Leaflets. Brochures. Talk to someone about services. Feign interest in joining. Whatever," Ryn reminded Evie. "It's not like she's going to—"

Ryn cut herself off to gasp.

I gasped with her.

And Lottie exclaimed, "Holy shit!"

We did this because three things happened at once.

The first, in front of the church, Axl appeared out of nowhere, hooked Hattie, who was making her way up the walk, by the waist, and dragged her around one of the RVs, out of sight of the church.

The second, Mo, also appearing out of nowhere, was suddenly standing at the hood of my Tucson, beefy hands on muscular hips, Oakleys over his eyes, his bald pate shining in the sun, his massive shoulders blocking it out, a look on his face that would make small children burst into tears (though, this was his normal look, Mo was scary—albeit a sweetie, however, in this moment, I could tell he wasn't feeling sweet).

And the last, my door was abruptly pulled open.

I looked that way in time to see Auggie leaning in.

He undid my seatbelt, and I cried out as it zipped back into place.

And then my ass was no longer in the driver's seat because he'd dragged me out.

It took me a second to get my feet coordinated.

It took me another second to fully comprehend what was happening.

And in the next second, I demanded, "What the hell?"

He turned, stopped and used my hand in his to yank me hard so I slammed into his chest.

I looked up and noted two things immediately.

One, he also was wearing sunglasses—polarized, tactical wrap-arounds, and he looked good in them.

Two, so much was happening during his visit last Sunday, I had not completely processed the fact that his thick stubble on Thursday had become thicker stubble that day. But I was right then processing that two days further of non-shaving meant his black stubble had gone from a significantly shadowed jaw, to what could only be described as a beard, and that was *hot*.

"Shut your mouth, we'll talk in a second," he growled.

Then he was off again, and I was too, considering he still had hold of my hand.

At that time, I noticed my Tucson driving by me, Mo's huge body wedged in behind the wheel, Lottie glaring at Mo, Ryn grinning and waving out the passenger window at me.

What in the—?

Auggie tugged me around a corner. I fumed down half a block. And then we went off the sidewalk toward the cars parked on the side of the street. Here, he pulled me in front of him, let me go, but only so he could put a hand on my belly and press my back against a very shiny, black Hummer.

In other words, his and the boys' ride. As I'd seen the guys in them before, I knew it was their company vehicle.

Before I could say a word, he demanded, "You wanna tell me why you're here?"

I opened my mouth to do precisely that, and then go on to ask him why he was manhandling me and acting like a big jerk.

"No," he went on before a single noise escaped my lips. "I don't care why you're here. What the fuck, Pepper? Do you not think we're on this?"

Okay, now I wasn't seriously miffed he and his bros had horned in on me and the girls activating my master plan *and* Mo had stolen my car *and* Auggie had dragged me down a sidewalk.

Now I was confused.

"You're on what…exactly?"

"That mess your family is wrapped up in."

Hang on a second.

"What?" I asked.

"Your entire family's finances are tied up in that church. Which only makes sense in the aspect your dad and his wives live in that building, the same with the other eleven deacons, and their wives, as well as their children, including your sister. But she actually works for the church, in admin, also doing what we're referring to as acquisitions, but they refer to as missionary work."

My God.

Well, that explained why the building was so big.

"You left that part out on Sunday," I informed him.

"This is because I didn't know it on Sunday," he informed me. "This information came in this morning. Which is why we're right now doing shit to keep an eye on shit and be able to find out more shit, because everything we discover is more fucked up than what we've already learned."

Obviously, none of this made me happy.

"Now I've changed my mind," he continued. "I wanna know. What the fuck are you doing here?"

"I sense, somewhat the same thing you are," I replied.

"Explain," he bit off.

Um.

Hell no.

"No," I snapped, then poked him in his chest. "*You* explain times two. First, explain why you're being so cranky and bossy. And second, explain why you think I owe you an explanation. No, wait, times three. Also explain what *you're* doing here."

"Have you heard of the Branch Davidians?"

I made a scoffing noise and said, "Reverend Clyde is a creep, but that's hardly a remote compound filled with weapons. So, it's on the outer outskirts of Littleton, it's still a Denver suburb."

"Pepper, every single deacon in that church has a bank account in their own name. An account that Clyde Higgins has access to and is a signatory on. He has his own, no other signatories on that, not even his legal wife. The church has three. And in the last twenty years, this church and its leaders have gone from barely scraping by to drifting just under an income that will jump them into a significantly higher tax bracket. Your father sells insurance and has for the last fifteen years. And he's hovered around making one hundred and sixty thousand dollars a year for the last nine years. The same *exact* income as all the other deacons."

Wild guess, that wasn't a coincidence.

I stared up at him, speechless.

"I'll do the math for you," Auggie offered. "The deacons alone have over two million dollars in their accounts. The church's accounts, which by the way aren't taxed, are even more healthy. And I haven't gotten into the 'wife' situation, considering most of them aren't legally married. So they file separate. Which means they have their own accounts. But I'll bottom line it and share that Reverend Clyde has direct access to over seventeen million dollars."

"Oh my God," I breathed. "How are they making all that money?"

"That's what we wanna know."

"So you're investigating my family's church?"

He drew in a big breath that expanded his (awesome) chest.

Then he said, "Pepper, the last thing I wanna do is freak you. I just managed to nail down my first date with you. And that task took me three years."

Three years.

I couldn't stop the smirk I gave him.

He definitely noted my smirk, if his nostrils flaring in a sexy way had anything to say about it, but he kept talking.

"But like I told you, I'm taking this serious." He flicked a hand in the spare space between him and me. "That means, in my mind, I'm making you mine. Juno mine. You're both gonna be in my life. And I look after the people in my life that I care about. You're out of this mess, whatever is going on there, so it can't touch you in one way. If it's what we think it is, though, it can touch you in another. It can upset you. Upset Juno. And I gotta do what I can to make that not happen. And if I can't do that, make it so the blow is as soft as I can possibly manage."

Ummmmmmmmmm...

"Did you just say that?" I asked, my chest warming, and other places warming too.

"I just said that," he affirmed...*firmly*.

So of course, I jumped him.

There wasn't far to jump, but still, I went at him with velocity, which meant my body slammed into his. Once connected, I wrapped one arm around his shoulders, the other hand I slid into his thick hair that instantly curled around my fingers, claiming them.

I then pulled his mouth down to mine and I kissed him.

A millisecond later I was up against the Hummer, crushed to Auggie, my kiss was taken over and we were making out, hot and heavy, around the corner from my family's church.

I was grinding into him.

He was grinding into me.

I had a fistful of his shirt and a hand cupped around his head.

He had a fistful of my hair and a handful of my ass.

God, he could kiss.

His tongue was magic.

All of a sudden, though, it was gone, and his face was stuffed in my neck.

I could feel his breath hot on my skin.

I was panting.

"We need to cool it," he murmured into my flesh.

We did, for multiple reasons. The primary one being that we'd done that before (including the me-jumping-him part), it had one consequence, and I didn't want the second time we did it being in the back of a company Hummer.

Or in broad daylight at the side of it.

Being arrested for lewd behavior so close to church premises would likely blow my master plan.

"Yeah," I agreed.

He lifted his head and looked down at me.

"You good?" he asked.

No, I was not.

I wanted to spend the next hour kissing Auggie and/or listening to him talk about how he wanted to look after me and Juno and/or having sex with Auggie (though, not in the backseat of the Hummer).

"Yes," I said.

He grinned at me and I got the impression he could read my thoughts.

Then he said, "Your turn."

"My turn, what?"

"Why are you here?" he asked.

"I don't want my sister to marry Reverend Clyde," I answered.

"And?"

"And...we were going to do a little sleuthing."

Woefully, since we were chatting and no longer going at each other, it seemed appropriate to take my hand from his hair and stop holding on to his shirt like he was keeping me upright.

This I did, but I didn't go far because I liked the warm, hard feel of his flesh. It was solid. Stable. And it made me feel both.

And he smelled like sunshine.

So I rested my hands on his shoulders and kept talking.

(Incidentally, Auggie had moved his hand from my ass to my waist, but his other hand was totally still in my hair, but now absentmindedly fiddling with it...*mm*).

"Saffron is tight with Dad," I said. "She's always been his favorite and not because she was a suck-up. They just click. But she's not an idiot and I honestly don't think this...whatever it is that's set up with her and Reverend Clyde, is something she wants. So we were trying to find some stuff I could use to appeal to her rational side. Because the church has changed. Something's off. And she's in it. It's hard to have perspective when you're in it. I wanted to give her some perspective."

For obvious reasons, considering his reaction to me even being there, I did not share about the Evie-hacking portion of my master plan. Fortunately (now), she'd refused to do it, so it wasn't like I was keeping anything from him.

Exactly.

"You're right, something's off," he confirmed.

"Well, yeah," I said. "I mean, they're hardly Scientology with millions of members around the globe. The multiple-wives thing is screwy. The money thing, though, is fishy."

"They have a lot of members."

I shook my head. "It's always been small. Dad says—"

"Pepper, sweetheart, they have a lot of members. And one of the reasons they do is because your sister is their top recruiter. She's your sister, so it might not have registered on you, and she's not as gorgeous as you are, but she isn't hard to look at. And she's not the only one. Higgins has a good number of hot babes dragging mostly men in, and it isn't the promise of being closer to God that's bringing them in. It's the access to hot babes and approval direct from God to have however many you want under your thumb and in your bed that's bringing them in."

"I can't...I don't..." I couldn't spit out the depth of my disbelief.

"It's probably not a surprise to you that there are a lot of losers out there who will find God in the idea of having four or five wives that look like your sister," he continued. "But that's not the primary hustle. That isn't going to get you seventeen million bucks. We just haven't had time to find out what the primary hustle is."

"How are they getting hot babes to do that?"

"We don't know yet."

"Have you seen Reverend Clyde? I mean, the dude is hardly Pierce Brosnan."

Auggie's perfect lips quirked. "Pierce Brosnan?"

"Ask any breathing female on this planet if they'd do Pierce Brosnan, right now, at his current age. The answer will be, 'yes.' Some might whisper it, but others would scream it."

Auggie started chuckling.

"Including you?" he asked.

"I'd scream it, but I think we made enough of a scene while you and the boys thwarted my master plan."

He kept chuckling but queried through it, "Master plan?"

I didn't answer that.

I pointed out, "If this hot-babes situation is true, you do know Hattie is perfect for undercover work on this operation, don't you?"

He was smiling but also shaking his head.

"I won't even tell Axl you suggested that. He wasn't real hip on her being in the car with you, seeing as we all knew you were up to something. He was even less hip on her hauling her ass out of it and heading to that building. No way is Hattie going undercover."

This was probably true. I'd noted that the girls' guys were protective.

"Well, my family is always asking me to go to church…" I muttered, trailing off thoughtfully, since this was actually a cool idea.

I mean, not to use my mom's illness to uncover some possibly felonious behavior of Reverend Clyde.

But it'd be the perfect excuse to tentatively (albeit fakely) come back into the fold.

Two birds, one stone, I'd be able to spend time with my mom and maybe ferret out some good intel.

As I was contemplating my new master plan, I was also lightly rubbing the stitching on the collar of Auggie's t-shirt.

I should have been paying attention to his face, because when I did that, I saw he'd turned into a Greek god statue wearing kickass wraparounds.

A beautiful one.

But a pissed-off one.

"What?" I asked.

"Are you insane?" he asked back.

"No," I answered.

"You've got a kid, Pepper," he reminded me.

"Uh…*yeah*. But I said *I'd* go back into the fold. Not Juno. No way for Juno."

"What I mean is, you've got a kid and you don't need anything happening to you," he clarified.

"Anything happening to me? What could happen?"

"I'll try another prompt since maybe you didn't get what I meant by the other one, baby," he said gently. "Waco?"

I felt the hair on my arms stand on end at a repeat of this

incident that had a very unhappy ending, and my fingers gripped his shoulders.

"Are you telling me what's happening at the church is dangerous?"

"How about no phone date tonight," he suggested. "How about I come over with some takeout and we talk."

"No, Augustus," I denied and smacked his arm for good measure. "That's an important question. I can't sit on it, waiting for you to bring over crab rangoon and orange chicken with everything fried rice from your choice of Chinese place."

Auggie grinned again at my completely unveiled order for food for our date adjustment.

And then he got serious.

"Pepper, shit gets real when money and God are involved. For Higgins, my guess is, it's money. For his followers, it's God. There is no way in hell that church has that kind of cash legally. Even if they do have a number of members. Something's very wrong. If you threaten it, Higgins is gonna activate his disciples. He's going to be protecting what he has that he does not want to give up. They're proceeding in the name of God. Both are volatile. Together, they're radioactive."

Okay, this made sense.

I mean, one could not argue that religion, and money, had been the root of a lot of very bad shit for, I didn't know, say, the last ten or twenty centuries (and longer).

"I just don't want my sister to marry that guy," I shared.

"I can imagine, because I've seen him, and I've looked into him, and the dude is not right. But if you intervene the way you were going to, you might be playing with fire."

"So instead, *you're* going to play with fire?"

"Sure. I do it for a living, babe. It's just another day at the office."

Ummmmmmm . . .

It was safe to say, when your business card (if he had one)

said, AUGUSTUS HERO, COMMANDO, your days weren't filled with sharpening pencils for your boss and developing surveillance photos in their company darkroom.

However, I had not thought on this because I had not gone far enough to consider a date, much less having this man in my life.

And as such, needing to deal with what he did for a living.

"Later on that," he muttered, watching me closely.

That would be wise.

"Agreed," I said. Then I noted, "There's also my mom to think about. Now I know why she's not letting me come visit. But she's sick. She's my mom. I want to see her."

"And she won't come to you?"

I shook my head.

"We can hash that out later too."

I exhaled a restless breath.

"You haven't talked about your brother," Auggie remarked cautiously.

"That's because I decided to focus on only one section of the crazy pie that's my family. I'm not gonna shove my full face in the pie, that's just gonna leave me with pie on my face."

His perfect lips were quirking again. "Interesting metaphor."

"It's also made me think we need pie after Chinese tonight."

He started laughing.

Okay.

Not all better, but watching Auggie laugh?

It was a little better.

When he quit laughing, he said, "Though that's probably smart, not biting off more than you can chew."

I shot him a grin as he took my metaphor and ran with it.

"You do need to get in touch with him," Auggie went on. "And you didn't ask for his contact details. But I have them."

"Thanks, but I haven't decided if I'm going to get in touch with him," I shared. "On the one hand, Juno has cousins. It might be a mess of dysfunction we're stepping into, but she doesn't have a huge family and what she knows of it is looney tunes, and as I've learned today, maybe worse. On the other hand, it might be a mess of dysfunction we're stepping into and I don't want my daughter buried under that. So I need time to think on this."

"And then there's Birch," Auggie replied.

I shook my head. "I'm even less decided about whether or not I want to see my brother. But I'm leaning on the *not* side of that. That said, I don't know how to meet his kids without him being involved. So as you can see, this is a conundrum."

But Auggie was looking at me quizzically, and I didn't think he was quizzical about my conundrum.

So I asked, "What are you thinking?"

"Pepper, sweetheart..." He lifted a hand, wrapped it around my neck and smoothed the pad of his thumb along my jaw before he went on, "It's his mom too."

Holy hell.

I hadn't thought of it that way.

And the girls hadn't thought of it that way.

That was because your girls thought about you, and your kid, not the best interests of your nefarious, prodigal, long-lost, now-found brother.

But the new guy in your life could still look after you (we could just say the thumb maneuver was effective) at the same time giving you an important new angle, shedding light on a different side of things.

Damn.

"I'll leave you with that and we'll talk about it over crab rangoon and orange chicken with everything fried rice tonight," he confirmed he got my order.

I smiled at him.

He did not smile back.

He asked, "What kind of pie do you want?"

Right.

It was time to file away the work it was seeming I might need to do to stop myself from kicking my own ass that I waited so long to let this guy in.

I did.

There was reason.

He got that reason.

We were here now.

Onward.

"I'll get the pie," I declared. "Or I'll make one. Do you like French silk?"

"Did one of the women tell you about that?"

My head ticked. "About what?"

He backed off that question and just said, "Yeah, I like French silk pie."

I didn't allow him to back off, and noted, "You didn't answer my question, Auggie."

"It's my favorite pie."

Uhhhhh . . .

"Seriously?" I asked.

He nodded.

"It's my favorite pie too."

He didn't respond.

"And Juno's," I kept going.

Auggie said nothing.

Okay, I'd learned, if you listened, the universe spoke in a lot of different ways.

But an all-'rounder of us having the same favorite pie was not, in my estimation, the universe speaking.

It was the universe screaming.

Case in point: Corbin wasn't a big fan. The raw egg component freaked him out. The caloric content did too. He avoided chocolate (and cream, ditto butter and sugar). In fact, he avoided pie on the whole. And desserts.

Juno loved cooking with me, and I tried my darnedest to be a good mom, so I taught my daughter to eat healthy. I did it with her. But we also had regular treats.

She also loved her dad, but if there was one thing she'd grumble about when she was back from his place, it was that he made her eat healthy all the time, there were no fun treats at her dad's pad, and he encouraged her to keep that up when she was with me.

With this French silk pie info, I was feeling significantly balanced with my energies as I gazed up at Auggie.

"Are you going to kiss me again?" he asked.

"I'm not feeling backseat Hummer sex and I wasn't all that hip on you stopping the last time. I don't want to court another go."

"That's probably good since Hattie and Axl have been hanging twenty feet away for the last five minutes and we got shit to do."

I jerked and looked right, seeing he told no lies.

Hattie and Axl were standing on the sidewalk not close, not far. And if Axl was perturbed about Hattie being involved in my master plan, he was over it, because they were in each other's arms, Axl's head bent to Hattie, who was saying something to him.

Seriously.

I loved Axl for her.

They were *so* cute together.

I looked to Auggie. "Do you have eyes in the back of your head?"

Another grin from him.

Day further made.

"No," he answered.

"The heightened senses of a commando?"

Still grinning. "Something like that."

"I should probably stop hogging your time, and we should probably save Mo. Lottie looked none too happy you all thwarted my master plan. She's been itching for some action. She's felt left out of the kidnappings and whatnot."

Auggie's chest started bouncing before his laughter became audible and he shifted to my side so he could slide an arm around my shoulders.

"Then we best rendezvous with them, save Mo and reunite you with your car," he said.

I looked up at him to see him catching Axl's eye and jerking up his chin.

"Right," I replied.

He looked down at me when I did.

"Pepper?"

"Right here," I pointed out.

"Just to say, no worries on the flirting. You might be out of practice. You're still a master."

What a nice thing to say!

I smiled brightly up at him.

He aimed his shades at my mouth and warned, "Stop smiling at me like that or Axe and Hatz are taking a walk and we're having backseat Hummer sex."

I forced my smile upside down.

He didn't laugh at that.

He *busted out* laughing at that.

Nope.

Now my day was made.

CHAPTER NINE
Crispy Duck

AUGGIE

Carrying a bag of Chinese food, Aug walked up to Pepper's house, thinking the same thing he did the last time he did that.

Her autumn decorations were the shit.

He hit the doorbell and prepared to wait and possibly have to hit the bell again.

Her outside lights were on as well as the Christmas lights that trailed through the pumpkins and pots of flowers up her brick steps. He'd also texted to say he was on his way, and she'd replied *Great! See you soon!* so she knew he was coming.

He was still prepared to wait because women did that shit. The waiting thing. For whatever reason they had, making it clear you didn't matter, she was good in her own zone, her own space and she had the power to let you in whenever it pleased her.

Even if she knew you were coming over to hang or pick her up to take her out.

His mom did the same thing. Not only to his dad, but when his parents were on the outs, and she lived somewhere else, and his pops was taking Aug over for her visitation time, she'd do it to Auggie, her own son, as he was standing outside her door.

He didn't get it then.

He didn't get it now.

What he got was a jolt when the door opened on these thoughts within seconds of him ringing the bell.

And Pepper was standing there wearing what she'd been wearing earlier that day. A slouchy beige sweater that hit her at her waist and fell off her shoulder. Under it was a white cami or bra that had a high spike of some lace that you could see and a spaghetti strap. And she had semi-distressed white skinny jeans covering her legs.

She'd been wearing some ankle boots earlier that day, but now her feet were bare, her toes painted a wine color. Also, her hair had been down earlier, and now it was up in a mess at the top of her head, tendrils floating around her face and neck.

Pepper had honey-colored hair, a lot of it, and unusual clear, olive-colored eyes that had a defined dark blue circle around the edge of the iris.

With her eyes, hair, flawless skin and fine features, all of this topping a tall, slender body with perfectly proportioned hips and tits, wearing cool clothes, with that look of welcome on her face, she was honest-to-Christ the full package.

And because of this, on sight of her, his cock jumped.

"Hey!" she greeted excitedly, already moving to open the storm door.

His cock jumped again.

"Hey," he replied, feeling his lips curve.

She held open the door, he moved through and she remarked in the direction of the bag he was carrying, "That seems like a lot of Chinese food."

He stopped just inside and stated, "I like noodles."

She smiled up at him. "Right."

"And egg rolls."

"Awesome."

"And crispy duck."

Her body swayed back. "Whoa, pardner. That's some fancy food you're totin' there. That's, like, Christmas-dinner-type food. Warning, food like that gives a girl ideas."

She could have any ideas she wanted, especially as pertained to him.

Fuck, he needed to kiss her.

Kiss her hard then fuck her harder then find some way to claim her in a primal way that could not be mistaken by her or anybody.

It was bizarre and actually unsettling, but by that, he found that he was thinking things like branding, tattoos, just something... *permanent*.

In other words, fucking caveman shit.

He'd wanted her before.

But this funny, honest, flirty chick who opened the door to him without any bullshit and let him into her house that, at a glimpse, he saw was ordered and mellow and smelled like...

He sniffed.

"Sweater weather," she said.

"What?" he asked.

She shot him another smile, closed and—he was happy to see—locked the door. "The scent. The candle I'm burning. It's called 'sweater weather,' and that's the perfect name for it, don't you think?"

He didn't care what it was called, he just cared that it smelled fantastic, which it did.

It was not a question to answer so he didn't, and not only because it wasn't. But because she took his hand and guided him out of her foyer and into her house.

And while she did, he experienced another part of Pepper.

The home she created.

More...

The home she gave to Juno.

He'd spent some very good time in the foyer, in the dark, but that did not end well.

And he'd been up the stairs to her room.

That was it.

Seeing the bulk of it...

Damn.

His mother's places were always temporary.

Dumps, or she'd move in with some guy who lived in either a bachelor pad or his own dump.

Auggie's dad's place was more permanent, since he never moved (his mom mostly left them, though sometimes she'd switch it up and kick his dad out, but these times heralded when she wasn't quite feeling it, because she made Aug's dad do his penance and then let him come back fairly quickly).

Still, his father's house seemed transient, since his mother was consistently moving in and out, taking things with her she might not bring back, and if she did, she might put them somewhere else. Or she'd have a fit and smash something, rip it up, take it to the backyard and burn it. Or his father would do that.

Pepper's place was...

Not even close to that.

"You unpack, I'll get plates and drinks and stuff," she ordered as she let him go when they were at her island.

Pepper went to a cupboard.

Auggie put the bags of food on the island.

"What do you want to drink?" she asked.

"Got beer?"

"Yup," she said, taking down big plates that matched her kitchen, setting them by the food he was putting out, then heading to her fridge. "I got tomorrow off work, but I have to go in tonight. I called Ian and he moved the dance schedule, so I'll be the last in the lineup. I still need to leave around eight thirty, latest nine." She glanced at him. "Is that okay?"

He set the carton of lo mein down, saying, "Of course, baby."

That earned him another smile, and she turned back to the fridge, opening the door. "Choices, Fat Tire or Blue Moon."

It took him a minute to answer, primarily because he saw a mound of whipped cream sprinkled with shaved chocolate covering a pie dish in her refrigerator.

She'd made French silk pie.

Christ.

That was something else he'd never seen in his mom's house.

Homemade pie.

Or anything she made special for Aug.

First face-to-face date, there it was.

With effort, he got out his answer to her question.

"Fat Tire."

She grabbed a bottle of beer, as well as a big green bottle of Perrier.

She came back to the island with their drinks, set them down, and asked, "Glass or drink from the bottle?"

"Don't dirty a glass."

She gave him bright eyes and went for a drawer.

Aug popped tops on food, and she finished her gig, uncapping his beer, getting utensils, cloth napkins and pouring herself a glass of Perrier, to which she added already cut slices of lemon and lime she had in the fridge.

"I don't drink before I dance," she explained. "Because, if I don't keep drinking, alcohol makes me sluggish. And if I keep doing it, it makes me drunk."

That earned her a smile. "You don't have to explain it, Pepper. I'm not the I'm-drinking-so-everyone-has-to-imbibe guy."

"Cool," she murmured, shoved spoons in all the food that needed them and handed him a plate.

They loaded up then hiked their asses onto stools at her island.

"Did you successfully put the Tabernacle of the True Light under surveillance?" she asked.

He swallowed the food he'd stuffed into his mouth and answered, "Something like that."

She nodded, then went on, "I'm sensing from the financial information you've gathered, you have ways and means. So are you also hacking their communications?"

"Considering what we've found so far, Hawk's putting this situation on the agenda for tomorrow's team meeting," he told her instead of answering in the affirmative, which was the honest answer. "Wanna come?"

She perked up on her stool. "Can I?"

He grinned at her. "No."

She faked a frown that was hilarious.

Then she got serious. "Is Hawk really doing that?"

"Yeah, he really is."

"Okay, then I'm feeling weird about this."

He got serious too, and asked, "Why?"

"I don't know. But your time is worth money. I sense it's worth a lot of it. And Hawk needs some coming in to pay out what his men earn. Not them doing a bunch of stuff for some broad that isn't being reimbursed."

That was when Auggie got *very* serious.

"If you're suggesting I get Elvira to invoice you, don't. One, Elvira would never do that. This is in the family. Her fingers might melt on the keyboard if she tried to type out a bill for you. And I'll repeat, this is in the family. So Hawk would never ask her to do that."

Elvira was their office manager, and he did not lie about what might happen if she attempted to ask someone close to the crew to pay for their services. Though, her fingers wouldn't melt, she'd just make her thoughts known on the matter and refuse to do it.

But Hawk would never allow it.

"This is our first date, Auggie," she said quietly. "And it's at my kitchen counter, and in a couple of hours, I have to end it to go to work. I'm hardly in the family."

He put his fork down and grabbed his egg roll, but before biting into it, he said, "Then you don't get the concept of family."

He was concentrating on chewing his food, but when he caught sight of her expression, he concentrated on her.

"Babe," he said, but it was a question.

She read his question and answered, "That's maybe the coolest thing anyone has ever said to me."

Right, it was a risk. So far, it seemed anytime they got too close in proximity, things got out of hand.

And he was hungry, and she eventually had to get to work.

Still, he took that risk, leaned into her and touched his mouth to hers.

He liked the expression on her face when he pulled away a lot better than the one she had when he'd been going in.

He grabbed his beer and took a slug.

"Speaking of family, I'm going to call my brother and tell him about Mom," she announced.

Swallowing was difficult, because he was surprised she'd already made this decision.

But he did it and focused on her. "Yeah?"

She nodded, but now she didn't look so hot.

She'd made the decision, but she wasn't at one with it.

"This is too deep for Chinese at your kitchen island," he said. "But some insight without diving into the full story, I don't get on great with my mom. I'm sure it doesn't surprise you we have lingering bad history. I shared a little of it with you. I still would want to know if anything was wrong with her. If she had trouble financially. If someone was causing her problems. And definitely if she was ill."

She nodded and picked up a rangoon, shoving it in the sweet-and-sour sauce.

"Do you want me to spend some time watching him?" he offered.

Her gaze came to him. "Sorry?"

"Life sucks, Pepper. The shit I found out about your brother paints a pretty dark picture. But neither of us know what was behind any of it."

"Beating his wife?" she asked.

He shook his head. "I'm not defending him. But at my urging, you're about to open a door that was pretty seriously closed. I'd feel more comfortable having a better handle on the man he is today before you call him and open that door. Even to share about your mom. There are other ways he can find out, and it won't involve you."

He did not share it would involve him, or a member of the team.

Just not her.

"Auggie, if you do your job, ferret out and then take down a ring of dirty cops, uncover whatever nasty is happening at my family's church, *and* put time into finding out what kind of man my brother is today, when will you find time to date me? And equally importantly, be at Juno's school to build Thanksgiving sets?"

He chuckled.

She reached out and squeezed his thigh then took her hand away.

It was friendly.

He still felt her touch in his dick.

This was because she was her.

It was also because, when they'd had sex, it'd been fucking *awesome*.

But knowing she got that hot during sex, and she was unfettered, willing and able to go for it, give it, take it, and get off on it was not going to be helpful in his mission to take this slow.

And he'd vowed to himself they were taking this slow.

Because he did not want to do anything to freak her, and he didn't know her enough to know what would freak her.

So even though he wanted more of her physically—and he wanted that bad—he thought it best they put a lid on it and build something solid between them before they went there again.

"Thanks anyway," she continued. "I think with Birch I just have to take my chances."

"I hope you get, even though I urged you to consider this, why right now I'm rethinking that."

At that, she bumped her knee against his as well as reaching out and squeezing his thigh again.

And she said, "You're sweet, Auggie, but I'm a big girl. I'll play it smart. But can I count on you for backup?"

"Absolutely."

She shot him another smile and turned back to her food.

He returned to his but got out his phone, and eating as well as using his thumb on his phone, he looked up and then sent her the info she'd need to get ahold of her brother.

He'd put his phone back in his jeans and had fully concentrated on eating when he realized he didn't hear her cell chime with his text.

"Just texted you your brother's deets," he said.

"Cool, honey, thanks," she murmured distractedly, focused on piling orange chicken on some fried rice.

She'd just called him "honey" again.

He liked it again, especially now, when it was not in a scenario that pissed him off.

But something tweaked him.

"Where's your phone?" he asked.

She gave him her attention. "In the office zone."

"Say again?"

"The office zone," she repeated, then said, "Shit. Sorry. I didn't give you a tour. Though, I have an excuse." Another grin. "I was hungry."

"It'd be cool to have a full tour, sweetheart, your pad is freaking awesome—"

"Wow, thanks," she cut in.

"But where's your phone?" he finished.

Her head kicked to the side.

"I told you, Auggie, it's in the office zone."

"Is that upstairs?"

"No, it's that room we walked by at the front of the house."

He had been concentrating on her holding his hand and the feel and smell of her place, so he hadn't noticed that room.

"Is it out of juice?" he asked.

She sat straighter and gave him her full attention.

She then opened her mouth.

But she closed it, and something moved over her face.

Then she opened it again to speak.

"You're an adult, so when you're here, you can make this decision for yourself. And you have a job we have yet to talk about that might mean you have to have comms close," she began. "But I have a rule. Electronics remain in the office zone. I turn the sound off on my phone, and if I'm home for a while, I'll go in and check it. Make sure no one has called or texted. But I also might be the only person under eighty that still has a landline. If folks need me, they can get me on that, and I don't have to have my phone with me all the time, or have it buzzing and beeping, again, all the time."

She stopped.

He said nothing as he digested this information.

She started again.

"And Juno doesn't have a phone. But she does have a laptop

and a couple of handheld games. I'm also considering getting her an iPad for Christmas. But that stuff doesn't enter our living space or resting space. Our living room is for living. Our bedrooms are for sleeping or chilling out. Screen addiction is not conducive to any of that."

Auggie still had no response.

Though, he thought it was fucking cool.

Pepper studied him in his silence then remarked, "You think I'm weird."

"No, I think that's fucking cool," he replied. "I gotta tell you, at least half a dozen times a week, I wanna toss my cell in the garbage."

"I know, right?" she asked, no longer concerned about his reaction, therefore becoming animated. "It seems like everyone's got their head down and they're staring at their phones everywhere they go. I wanna stop them and say, 'The sun is shining, it's gorgeous and warm, and you're missing it.'"

That wasn't why he wanted to throw his phone in the garbage.

And it was weird, but not in a bad way, that she read that on him.

"Work stuff always pressing into life?" she asked.

He dug his work. He dug who he worked with.

So that was not it.

But he wasn't sure it was time to lay any heavy on her.

"Or something else?" she pressed when he didn't reply.

"My parents drag me into things," he admitted.

She sat back and he watched her mouth get tight.

"It's okay," he assured. "It is what it is. I'd probably flip out if it stopped happening." This time he bumped his knee to hers. "What I mean is, I'm used to it."

"But it makes you want to throw your phone in the trash a dozen times a week," she pointed out.

"Half dozen, tops," he joked.

"Aug—" she started.

But she didn't get more out because the front door opened and Juno shouted, "Mom! I forgot my pink sweater!"

Auggie stood up, not knowing exactly why he did, but the apprehensive look on Pepper's face told him he needed to be prepared to do anything she asked.

Juno had definitely been angling for him to be right where he was.

But, even if he and Pepper hadn't talked about it, he knew by the expression on her face that Pepper hadn't told her daughter she was going there with him. And he could see why Pepper wouldn't want her to know he was there.

At least, not yet.

They heard Juno's feet hitting the stairs and it was then Pepper snapped out of it and gave the cue as to how she was going to handle this.

She did it by shouting, "You don't even come..."

Auggie sensed something, tensed then stepped to the side of the island.

"...and hug your mother?" she finished yelling.

But the last word sounded strangled.

Because the reason Auggie tensed and stepped to the side of the island came into view for her.

Aug had caught him walking down the hall.

And he had caught sight of Auggie while he was walking down the hall.

Dark haired. Seriously built. Good-looking.

The man had thirty, maybe forty pounds on Auggie and it appeared to be all muscle.

Even so, Auggie would obliterate him.

He stopped in the kitchen, tore his irate gaze off Aug and looked to Pepper.

"What's going on, Pepper?" he asked.

Aug did not like the tone of his words.

Hell, he didn't even like the words.

This had to be Juno's dad.

And seriously...

Who the fuck did he think he was, walking into Pepper's home and asking shit like that?

Auggie shifted, he felt Pepper's attention on him and heard her say, "Auggie, it's okay."

He looked over his shoulder at her.

She was also standing.

Further, she was pale and openly freaked.

"Is it?" he asked.

"Who's this fucking guy?" the ex demanded to know.

"Auggie, this is Corbin Patrick. Corbin, this is Augustus Hero," she introduced.

Game to make a go of it for Pepper, Auggie took a step forward and offered his hand.

Corbin stared down at it like it was a snake he was about to land a boot on.

He dropped his hand.

"Corbin—" she tried.

The man seared Pepper with a look. "You fucking lied to me."

"Corbin—" she tried again.

"Careful there, friend," Auggie warned.

Corbin turned to him. "Fuck you."

"Corbin!" Pepper snapped.

"Remember where you are," Corbin advised Auggie.

"I know where I am, man, do you remember where you are?" Aug asked.

Pepper was on the move, about to round him.

He stepped in front of her, looked over his shoulder and said with a shake of his head, "Unh-unh."

"Honey," she whispered, though her face had gotten soft and

her eyes had lit in a fuck-me-now way that was phenomenal but straight-up in that moment not helping shit at all.

He knew the first time she called him that, if he ever managed to make her his, she'd get away with a lot if she used that word on him.

But not this.

"This is my daughter's kitchen," Corbin sniped, regaining Auggie's attention.

"It is. It's also her mother's and her mother pays the mortgage," Auggie stated.

Pepper came up close to his back, but was smart enough not to try to get in front of him, and she said, "Corbin, you need to—"

"*Auggie!*" Juno shrieked.

Aug looked beyond Corbin to see Juno had rounded the stairs and was sailing down the hall in his direction, the pink sweater in her hand flapping as she went, her expression open and happy.

He braced but still bumped into her mother behind him when Juno hit him full-bore and he had to fall back on a foot.

He wrapped a hand around the back of her head. "Hey, sweetheart."

She kept hugging his middle and looked up at him.

She had what he now knew was her father's hair, but her mother's build, also her mother's eyes.

It was striking.

But her face was all little girl, and she was cute as fuck.

"What're you doing here?" she asked.

He felt Pepper's hand press in the middle of his back and that was it.

Great.

No help there.

"Having dinner with your mom," he answered.

"Cool!" she cried, let him go, bopped away and then attacked her mom. "Hey, Mom!"

"Finally. She remembers I exist," Pepper teased.

Juno didn't let her mom go as she arched back and gave Pepper a little-kid *shut up* look.

Pepper's face changed to a *Get used to it, I'm your mother and I'm gonna give you loving guff until you die* look.

Juno bobbled her head on her shoulders in a *whatever* gesture.

Pepper mimicked it then tugged playfully on her daughter's hair.

Auggie nearly burst out laughing.

Then again, that was his constant state when he was around these two.

He'd never seen anything like it, and he loved how they interacted.

"Juno, go out and sit in the car." Corbin interrupted this silent, hilarious and awesome byplay to issue this order.

Still not letting go of her mom, Juno looked to her father.

Auggie did too, his eyes narrowing.

"But...Dad." There was a whine to it, not full-on but it was there. "Auggie's here and—"

"What'd I say, Juno?" Corbin demanded.

She continued to look at her dad, and when it was clear there'd be no quarter given, she glanced through Auggie in an embarrassed way that pissed Auggie way the fuck off, then up to her mom.

"Do what your dad says, Dollface. Okay?" Pepper urged, smoothing her daughter's hair. "But not without a hug and a kiss. Yeah?"

Juno didn't move immediately. But when Pepper bent to her, she gave her mom a hug she got in return, same with the kiss.

"See you later, gator," Pepper said, her voice having a forced lilt that wasn't there earlier.

Yeah.

She was pissed Corbin was essentially kicking their daughter out of her own house.

Maybe also pissed that, to be a decent parent, she had to keep her mouth shut and not countermand his order.

"Later, Momma," Juno mumbled then looked up to Auggie. "Later, Auggie."

"Later, sweetheart," he replied.

Her mouth was moving, and he didn't know if she was struggling to smile at him or struggling not to cry.

She turned away, and with a gentler voice, Corbin said, "Take the keys, Button."

She went to her father, got his keys, then trudged, like the wood floors had turned to sludge, down the hall and out the front door.

When it closed, the adults refocused, laser sharp, on each other.

Pepper got there first.

"I don't like the idea of my daughter sitting out in your car by herself, Corbin."

"Does this guy sleep in your bed when my daughter is in this house?" Corbin asked, completely ignoring what Pepper said.

"Maybe I need to define *how* you need to be careful, Corbin," Auggie suggested.

"You are not fucking in this," Corbin bit at Auggie.

"I'm standing right here, and I was invited," Aug fired back.

"Stop it," Pepper hissed.

But she did this doing something he thought was odd.

She moved from where she'd been standing, at his back, off to the side. She shifted her body right to his side, pressing in there and wrapping her arms around him.

Jesus, fuck.

She was claiming him.

In front of her ex, she was claiming Auggie.

And the ex did not miss it.

The vibe of the room, already not good, disintegrated.

It got worse when Aug slid an arm around her shoulders.

"Corbin, you need to go," she ordered.

The man's eyes darted from where Pepper held Auggie around the middle up to her face.

"You stood in this room, not a week ago, listening to me say shit to you—" he began.

But he didn't finish.

"I'd just learned my mother had cancer," she shot back. "And you showed up unannounced. And I'll remind you, I did not leap at your offer of reconciliation. Because that isn't a possibility, Corbin. And it isn't because you broke my trust in a way that it's impossible to repair. Regardless, I don't want you to repair it. I've moved on. And incidentally, I didn't lie about Auggie. We weren't seeing each other then. We've since changed that. It isn't your business, except for the fact Auggie has been a part of my life for a while, and in the way he was, as you know, he was a part of Juno's. Now, he's in it this way, and I hope that means he'll be in Juno's life in another way. So you'd eventually need to know."

"You didn't mention that was a possibility when we discussed *him*," Corbin spat.

Right, this guy wasn't getting it, and this was going on way too fucking long.

"You didn't mention you were fucking your high school girl-friend for six years while you had a woman and child at home either," Auggie put in.

Corbin made a move toward him.

Auggie shoved Pepper behind his back.

She was fast, though. Fast enough to whip around and get in front of him.

She had both arms up to hold them back, but Aug hooked her at her ribs and drew both of them away from Corbin.

"Okay, this is not happening in my house or *anywhere*," she declared. "Corbin, we're done. I'm sorry if you've had second thoughts about that, but if you think about it further, we were done before we even began. And you," she turned to look at Aug, "*behave*."

That was cute, and she had a spark in her eye that was both annoyed but also something else.

Still, he clenched his teeth.

Because this guy was an asshole and Auggie itched to land a fist in his throat.

"You're lucky she got in the way, buddy. I'd fuck you up," Corbin threatened.

It was then, Auggie relaxed.

Because the dipshit believed that, and only a fool made threats, and only an even bigger fool underestimated his opponent.

Surprisingly, he felt Pepper relax too.

She also said, "You really don't want to go there."

"You don't think?" Corbin asked snidely.

"No, I don't think," she clipped out. "Because, first, if you got physical for whatever asinine reason you think is your right to get physical with a man I'm seeing, you will be reduced to nothing but the guy my daughter spends every other week with. And second, because he's a former marine and a current commando, and you might have some weight on him, Corbin, but he'd wipe the floor with you."

Alerted to Auggie's possible skill set, the guy probably didn't even know he was doing it, but his aggressive body language backed right off.

"Now, *please*, our daughter is sitting in your car. Go to her," she finished.

Naturally, with a dude like that, he made to move.

But he did it getting in the last word.

"We're not done with this, Pepper."

And she knew enough to wait for him to almost have the door closed behind him before she called out, "We are for now."

Corbin shut the door.

Auggie walked to it and bolted it.

He then walked to Pepper and stopped five feet from her.

"Not-so-breaking news, my ex wants a reconciliation," she announced.

"I got that," he said, though he already knew that. He just didn't share.

"I do not want that," she stated unequivocally.

"I got that too."

"He heard you did career day for Juno. He got territorial. I thought that was all it was, I swear," she went on.

"You don't need to explain this, Pepper."

"Auggie, I…" She looked away. Then she looked back at him. "He might be a problem."

That was when he went to her.

Assessing her reaction as he did it, he carefully took her in his arms.

She came without hesitation, sliding her hands up his biceps and over his shoulders, loosely linking them behind his neck.

Nice.

"How do you foresee this problem manifesting itself?" he asked.

She laid it out.

"Scenario one, he intends to continue to be territorial and is right at this very moment revising his strategy to win me back, keeping in mind the new obstacle of you."

"Mm-hmm."

She started fiddling with the ends of his hair.

Very nice.

"Scenario two, he's ticked someone moved in on his turf, turf he realized he cannot win back, and he's going to act out."

Auggie tensed. "Juno in that line of fire?"

She stretched out her lips in an *I don't know, could be, but I hope not* gesture.

Shit.

"Is there a scenario three?" he prompted.

"He could have matured in the years since we were together, be mad now, but once he calms down, he'll think it over and realize his best bet is to let it go and move on."

"Categorize these scenarios from most likely to least," he commanded.

"Is this the commando way to tackle a potential problem?" she queried.

"Yes," he told her.

She grinned up at him.

He gave her a gentle shake to get her mouth moving.

"All right," she said. "It's a guess, but I'd say two is most likely, then one, and three is only vaguely possible in an alternate universe."

Fucking shit.

"Juno's pink sweater?" he asked.

She shook her head morosely. "Normally, if she forgot something, she'd do without or call me, and I'd take it to her school. Since the beginning, I don't think they've ever just popped by."

They'd be getting into the "since the beginning" part, just not now.

"But she has a key." He stated that, but it was a question.

"Yeah."

"And Corbin knows that. So this was an ambush in order for him to see you, or for him to engineer a situation where you'd all be spending time together."

"Yeah," she muttered.

He looked over her head, drew in a breath and then let it out.

"Auggie, I'm sorry," she whispered, and he focused on her.

He also gathered her closer.

"Why are you sorry?" he asked.

"We're just kind of, you know, at the starting line and I haven't been the easiest person to get there. And we have my mom, and the church, and my brother to deal with, and I'm sure you have shit in your life—"

He interrupted her. "Pepper?"

"Yes?"

"You get that life is a game of dodgeball, right?"

"Wh-what?" she stammered, staring up at him with an alarm he didn't like.

So he explained, "You keep sharp and pivot, adjust, run, duck, jump, whatever you need to do to dodge shit being hurled your way. But eventually, you're gonna get hit by a ball and that stings."

She said nothing.

"That's when you get to go sit it out, find a way to shake it off. But inevitably, you're right back in the thick of it again," he finished.

"Do you really think that's the way life is?" she asked softly.

"Do you think I'm wrong?"

She didn't answer for so long, he kept talking.

"What I'm saying is, shit happens. Shit is always going to be happening. We're always pivoting, running, ducking, jumping. The bottom line for me is, we're at that starting line you mentioned. And right now, that's not only all that matters, that's my priority, so that's got my primary focus."

She was still talking softly when she said, "That's very sweet."

"Good you think so."

"And I've noticed we not only both love French silk pie, you and me are hell on wheels with metaphors."

He grinned at her.

"Though your dodgeball one is scary," she murmured.

"Babe?"

"Yes?"

"We need to eat so we can spend some time making out before you gotta go to work."

She brightened. "We're gonna make out?"

"Yes. But we're gonna practice restraint since we're taking this slow."

She dimmed. "We're taking this slow?"

"Yeah."

"Boone and Ryn were going to take it slow. That lasted, I think, a day."

"We're not them."

"Axl and Hattie took it slow, and in the end Axl took it so slow, Hatz had to beg him to fuck her."

Christ, he hoped she never begged him to fuck her—that would probably end well, but he might scare her when he went at her.

"We're not them either."

"I'm sure Mag and Evie would have taken it less slow, if he hadn't been shot. Then again, if memory serves, the first time they did it was the night he got shot."

"Pepper?"

"Yes?"

"Are we gonna finish eating?"

"Can we discuss this 'taking it slow' concept further over food?"

"No."

She scrunched her face at him.

He bent and touched his mouth to hers.

He didn't pull back far when he said, "When it's time for us to go there again, we'll know."

"It kinda feels like that time right now, right here where we're standing," she noted.

He started laughing and through it said, "It's not."

"Bummer."

Good to know she was ready to roll with that.

It just wasn't time for them to go there.

He communicated this by touching his mouth to hers again. He then broke out of her arms and took her hand to guide her back to their food.

"You want me to nuke any of this?" she offered.

"We're good."

"Awesome call," she said, sliding back onto her stool and taking up her fork. "If I nuked it, that would delay us making out."

"Stop talking about making out. Tell me more about this Thanksgiving show I'm gonna be making sets for."

"I know nothing about it, except if anyone's dressed as an Indian, we're walking off in protest."

"Word," he agreed, shoving lo mein in his mouth.

They ate for a bit and then he heard her voice coming at him quietly.

"You're cool, Augustus Hero."

He turned to her, saw she was in profile, diligently eating her food to prove to him she was focused on it, not him, when he knew she was focused on him.

It was then he realized the toll that scene probably took on her, which was significantly magnified from what he experienced, and he hadn't liked it in the slightest.

So he bumped knees with her and replied, "You're cool too, Pepper Hannigan."

Her lips turned up before she shoveled fried rice in her mouth.

Aug reached to open the foil that would expose the crispy duck so he could start ripping it apart so they could start eating it.

Pepper let out a dreamy sigh.

Auggie started laughing.

And they finished dinner.

CHAPTER TEN

Dynamite

AUGGIE

The next morning, Auggie was glad the only men in the office he had to face when he first walked in were Billy, Marques and Axl.

Billy and Marques were younger, newer to the team, and hadn't been roped into Lottie's fixups (yet, but Auggie had seen her eyeing them at her wedding reception, so he figured, once he and Pepper got their shit sorted, she'd be buckling down for round two).

So it was only Axl around first thing to give him shit that he and Pepper were finally getting it together.

And Aug knew Axe was going to give him that shit by the stupid-ass grin that spread on Axl's face the second Auggie walked in.

He didn't even bother to wait for Aug to get close.

He called, "Word is, you actually went over to her place. Means I lost my bet that you'd hit eighty before you break bread with Pepper at the assisted living place you'd both eventually shack up in."

Both Billy and Marques, standing together higher up in Hawk's theater-style control room, looked down at Auggie.

And at a glance to his left, where Elvira's office was, he saw she was in and her stick-your-nose-in-everyone's-business antennae had received the signal.

She was staring right at him.

Aug said nothing. He just walked toward his station.

"How'd it go?" Axl asked when he was closer.

"It was great," he shared.

And it was.

Even if her ex left a pall over the evening that they both felt, she did her best to keep things light and positive. She remained funny, flirty, open, all of which he dug about her. And after Corbin left, they didn't let anything get heavy and it ended up being a good night.

And making out and feeling each other up on her pink (but comfortable) couch was awesome.

"Date two still tonight? That is, after you meet at Juno's school to dive right into those important stepdad-but-not-yet-stepdad things," Axl kept at him.

It was usually Auggie who gave shit when it was warranted.

But he was rethinking his place as the shit-giver in their crew.

He didn't get the chance to tell Axl to kiss his ass.

Elvira had wandered out.

Damn.

"So, obviously, last night Gwen, Tracy, Camille and me decided it was high time we hit Smithie's for a sisterhood session," she remarked.

Of course they did.

Gwen was Hawk's wife. Tracy and Camille rounded out that posse. It often included Hawk's best friends' women, Tess, Mara and Tyra.

Fortunately, last night it wasn't the whole crew.

But still...

"Seemed to me, one of the dancers was dancing on air," she went on.

Absolutely.

He was done giving shit.

Marques was coming toward them, likely to get in on the act.

Billy was not.

This wasn't a surprise.

Billy was edgy. Billy didn't banter. Billy's version of getting-to-know-you time was asking if you had a backup clip or checking the straps were secure on your Kevlar vest.

Therefore, Billy, right then, was studying the bank of screens that made up the front wall, where their workstations pointed. Screens that had a variety of real-time footage playing on them for missions they were currently involved in.

This was because Billy was all business all the time

Aug didn't know Billy's story. Nobody did. Except Hawk. And maybe another member of the team, Hawk's Number Two, Jorge.

"There were some cute girls up on that stage, Marques," Elvira noted when Marques made it to where Axl was standing at his station (that was next to Aug's), still grinning at him. Elvira was in front of that space. And Auggie was booting up his laptop and ignoring Axl grinning at him.

"Not ready to be tied down yet, Vira," Marques replied.

"You boys never are," she muttered. "Then you meet the right woman and *boom!* down for the count."

Finally, something that made Auggie smile.

Because that sure was the truth of it.

The door opened and he stopped staring at his laptop so it could read his face in order to boot up and he looked that way.

Mag and Mo were coming in together.

Mo was usually taciturn.

But his expression stated he was all in to break from being a man of few words in order to bust Auggie's chops.

Mag already had his mouth open.

Auggie beat him to it. "It went great, all right?"

Mag was undeterred.

"Who woulda thought that we should have enlisted an eight-year-old to get both of your heads out of your asses?"

Auggie let out an exaggerated sigh and crossed his arms on his chest so he could be comfortable while they all gave him stick.

"What're you gonna do about the ex?" Mo asked.

Misread.

Mo's expression didn't say he was going to bust Auggie's chops.

It said that Pepper shared with the women last night and Lottie had shared with Mo.

"What about the ex?" Axl asked.

Auggie sighed again.

Then he told them, "Pepper's ex wants her back. He stopped by last night. Juno forgot a sweater, and instead of calling Pepper and asking her to take it to the school, they showed without warning in the middle of dinner. He wasn't thrilled I was there."

"Ambush," Mag noted.

"Absolutely," Aug concurred.

"Where's Pepper at with this?" Axl questioned.

Aug shook his head.

"You don't know?" Axl pressed.

"Yes. I do. She's not on board. She doesn't want anything to do with the guy. Not in that way," Auggie stated.

"I can't believe I'm saying this, but there's always a connection between parents," Mag commented. "Are you sure she's over him?"

"She is one hundred percent over him," Aug assured.

Mag gave Axl a look.

Mo and Elvira were watching Auggie.

Mo knew the history, Auggie could tell.

The rest, apparently not.

Including Elvira, and she wasn't liking what she was hearing.

And normally, he'd be where Elvira was, because Mag was right. You shared history, a kid, you found ways to make things work.

This was not that.

But they would worry it was.

So Aug gave more. "He cheated on her."

"Women forgive cheaters, especially if there's a kid involved," Mag said.

"For six years," Auggie added. "He was fucking another woman the entire time they were together."

He heard a whizzing noise that was Marques sucking in a breath.

"Not a lot of women get over *that*," Marques said on his exhale.

Everyone relaxed.

Everyone, that was, except…

Auggie shifted his attention beyond Marques to where Billy had come to stand close, but not so close it could be mistaken he was standing among the loose group.

In fact, he felt everyone's focus shift to Billy.

That was the kind of vibe Billy gave off.

When he was around, you paid attention to the guy. Not that he said much, he just wasn't a guy you wanted sneaking up on you.

"You cool, brother?" Auggie asked him, even if you could tell by the look on his face that the man was far from cool.

"Perfect world, men like that would be stoned to death," Billy declared.

Jesus Christ.

Corbin was an asshole, but that was over the top.

"By women who'd been fucked over by cheaters," Billy finished. He then moved to march down the rest of the stairs, muttering, "Are we having this meeting, or what?"

Billy disappeared in the large conference room that sat bottom right when you came in the front door.

When he was out of sight, Elvira said, "I just love that guy."

She then walked back to her office.

Mo, Mag, Axl and Auggie all looked at each other with everyone ending up with eyes on Marques.

All of Auggie's crew—that being Axl, Boone, Mag and Mo—were in their early thirties (Auggie being thirty-four), and except for Mo, who'd been with Hawk for a good while, they'd all come on around the same time.

Forming their team, they'd also formed a bond, because they came on together, and because they were all veterans.

Shared experience, and a recurring theme in the shared baggage they all had from that experience.

In other words, his crew had a bond.

Marques's crew (not that Billy was any kind of official member, still, it included Billy and Zane) were in their late twenties. And they too had joined the team around the same time as each other when Hawk had expanded operations.

Marques and Zane were also ex-military.

Billy was not.

He still was in that crew, and in work, Hawk partnered them up according to who knew best how the others worked and the experience and loyalty that came from that.

The distinction was minimal.

But it was there.

So essentially, without words, they were all asking Marques *what the fuck* with Billy.

"I don't know," he said. "All I know is, the guy's intense. And we all know the kind of intense he is, it's the kind you want either at your back or taking point."

That was the truth.

On this, Boone strolled in the front door and his gaze came right to Auggie.

"Save it," Mag advised. "We got there before you and then

found out Pepper's ex was an unwanted interruption at their dinner party because he's making a play to get her back. So it isn't fun anymore."

Boone's eyes shot to Auggie. "Are you serious?"

Before Auggie could answer, Boone looked over Aug's shoulder and up, so Aug looked that way.

Hawk was coming out of his office.

Marques was manning the monitors that shift, so he headed back up to his station.

Axl and Aug walked along the row then down the stairs toward the conference room.

Boone met them at the door.

"It's all good, man. She's over him. She's into me. It was a great night. She's fantastic," Auggie told him.

Boone studied him, saw what he needed to see and then nodded.

When they hit the conference room, Billy was at the Nespresso machine.

But Boone, Mag, Mo and Axl had travel mugs undoubtedly filled with coffee, so they moved right to seats at the table.

It struck Aug then that he didn't remember ever seeing any of the men with travel mugs before they got with their women.

Maybe he did and it didn't register.

Jorge, another member of their crew, was married.

And in the mornings if he was in, he came with a mug.

But Auggie was heading to the Nespresso. Billy, as mentioned, was getting his. And if Zane was there (instead of at home since he'd done night duty), he'd be at the Nespresso too.

Because they were all single. They hadn't been domesticated.

Only Mag's woman, Evie, was probably up and getting ready to face the day at the same time as him, since she worked computer support at the same time she was studying to get her engineering degree.

Ryn, Lottie and Hattie danced and didn't get home until the

early hours of the morning. He doubted they got up to share breakfast and coffee.

It hit him then it was just...

That was what you did when you had a partner.

You had food in your house because there was someone other than you there who might need to eat.

And you made coffee in the morning because you weren't the only one drinking it.

Toting a travel mug of coffee said *I have someone who cares about me*.

Billy moved out of the way and Auggie stepped up to the Nespresso, sorting his pod and mug, remembering while growing up, going to the kitchen and grabbing a bag of Chex Mix or some Cool Ranch Doritos, and if he was lucky, there was peanut butter and some bread to make a sandwich or some Hot Pockets in the freezer.

In other words, their cupboards were filled with snack foods or quick fixes that got nowhere near a pan, a stove, an oven or a homecooked meal made with love.

His mother cooked on occasion, and when she did, she made certain you understood it was under duress, or alternately expressed what she considered appropriate gratitude, which meant kissing her ass.

His father's method of cooking was heating up a frozen pizza.

As far as Aug knew, his mother and father to that day didn't own a travel mug.

And their coffeemaker probably hadn't been used since the '90s.

Which brought him to the fact that Thanksgiving was coming up, the holiday Auggie dreaded only slightly less than Christmas.

Because Christmas was prime time for a big family drama.

With Thanksgiving being second on that list.

"Aug."

Auggie jerked himself out of his thoughts when he heard Hawk calling his name.

"You with us?" Hawk asked.

Fuck.

Auggie nodded.

Hawk eyed him a beat, and Aug felt that, mostly because he'd never had to have Hawk bring him mentally into the room.

If you worked for Hawk, you were mentally where he wanted you to be when he wanted it.

Needless to say, if he called a meeting, he wanted your head there.

Auggie grabbed his filled mug and took a seat at the table.

"Jorge's on something, so he's not coming to the meeting this morning," Hawk began. "But I just got off the phone with him. He ran some things down for me to bring to the meet."

As mentioned, Jorge was Hawk's Number Two, and not only because he'd been with Hawk the longest, even though he had.

The man was married. Kids. Great guy. Solid.

"He's uncovered some history on Clyde Higgins," Hawk went on.

And yeah.

There it was.

Jorge was a solid guy.

He was good at everything he did for Hawk, and he had a wide range of talents.

Auggie had slammed into a brick wall with Higgins and the Tabernacle of the True Light that only reconnaissance, bugs and hacking might put a crack in.

Auggie's dead end was that the man had ceased to exist prior to 1986.

Jorge'd had a day and he had something.

"What'd he get?" Auggie asked.

"Higgins had a flock before he started the Tabernacle of the

True Light," Hawk said. "It was called the Church of the Sacred Dawn."

"Man can stick with a theme," Mag murmured.

"It was in Montana," Hawk kept going. "And it disbanded because one of his wives lost a baby in childbirth. A childbirth he was attending, without any other medical practitioners. No midwife. Definitely not a doctor. Not even a doula."

"One of his wives?" Auggie asked. "He's done this bigamy gig before?"

Hawk nodded.

It was then, unusually late, that Auggie noted Hawk was looking grim.

Shit.

Hawk kept sharing.

"The death of this child shed some light for local officials on what was happening at Sacred Dawn. The woman's parents were not happy. They were this not only because their daughter lost her child. And not only because she was one of three other wives this guy had, something they didn't know. In fact, they didn't know she was married at all, much less wife number three. But regardless all that sucked for them to learn, the big thing was that she'd hemorrhaged significantly post-birth without a professional anywhere near to tend to her."

Hawk took a second to take a breath and none of the men interjected.

This was because all of the men were considering this nightmare scenario.

Including the idea of a man "attending" the birth of the woman he was supposed to love, a woman who was having his child, and there wasn't anyone who knew what they were doing anywhere near.

But it was more.

Hawk and Gwen's last baby, a little girl, had been a difficult delivery for Gwen. Hawk almost lost them both.

And Hawk's history was even darker going back further, considering what happened to his first wife and their daughter while Hawk was deployed.

Auggie had not been around at the time Gwen had Vivi, their youngest, but it was now lore because Hawk loved his wife, he adored his sons, and he doted on his daughter.

You could just say Hawk Delgado was the kind of man that, no matter what shit they were in, or how deep it was, Gwen could get a message to him, and that message could be that Vivi had the sniffles, and Hawk would be gone.

Another reason why he'd assembled the team he had.

Because this very conversation proved where Hawk's priorities were.

Family first, including the one you made for yourself that wasn't blood.

Then work.

And no matter what they were neck deep in, you took each other's backs.

Which was why they were having this conversation first thing at their meeting, a conversation about a case he wasn't making a dime on, but he was throwing all his resources at.

Hawk carried on.

"And if another member of the church hadn't gone against Higgins, who was known as Clyde Dickens then, and taken her to the hospital, it's likely she would have died. The parents were called to the hospital, discovered these things, and did not let it go. The bigamy was outed. Heat landed on Dickens and the whole church. This meant, in 1984, Dickens disbanded it and moved to Colorado. Here, he hung tight and laid low for around two years. And then he started True Light."

And this was why, in 1986, this guy suddenly came into existence.

"Did the other wives come with him?" Boone asked.

Hawk shook his head. "No. He cut himself loose. Including from five children he'd fathered on two other women. He was also careful to keep the past in the past and not just by changing his name. And incidentally, that would be the second time he did that. He was born Jonathan Clyde Bottoms. Jorge hasn't had time to get into that one. That name is back to you."

Hawk said the last with a nod toward Auggie.

And more reason why Aug hadn't found much on him.

The guy wasn't young, but three name changes in seventy-five years were two more than most people had.

And unless you did it when you got married, most people did it to leave a life behind.

Sometimes for reasons out of their control.

Sometimes for shit that was entirely in their control that got out of it.

Hawk kept talking.

"He was hard to gather history on because he put shit in place to make it hard to find him. He's used three different socials, one for each name. Now he's using the social of a man who died in 1985. But along with that, he changed his appearance, dropping forty pounds, getting contacts. Until fifteen years ago, he also didn't have his name on anything. Contracts. Rental agreements. Credit cards. Deeds. Nothing."

Well, shit.

Hawk kept going.

"His wife, that being his fourth one, but his first in Colorado, had her name on everything. Until three years ago. Jorge found two properties purchased by Jonathan Bottoms with his own, that being personal, not church, funds. One is a mountain house in Park City, Utah, and the other is a high-rise condo in Fort Myers, Florida."

"He's preparing for retirement," Axl guessed.

"Maybe," Hawk allowed. "But Jorge activated some connections we have to poke around in both areas. And according to some locals, the properties are in use. In other words, he isn't hiding he has them, or that he uses them. Someone is on both properties regularly. The head pastor of a church doesn't take that many vacations. Definitely not to high-end accommodations. Or he shouldn't. They have to know where he's going. Or at least those closest to him likely do."

Hawk took a second.

Then, with his attention on Auggie, he finished, "So, either those closest to him, his deacons, understand the long con he's on and support it, and him, or they're so deep under his influence, they're happy to give up what little they have just to get him closer to God. Even if that means his high-rise or his three-thousand-square-foot mountain house."

Heard loud and clear.

Pepper's father was fucked up even more than they already thought he was.

"You want me to run with that Bottoms information?"

Auggie was surprised this came from Billy.

"This is a personal project, man," Aug said. "I'm diving in when I have—"

"You've also started seein' that woman. And she has a kid," Billy cut him off to tell him something he already knew. "I don't have either. I got more time on my hands. And I'm good to run with it."

Aug didn't take his eyes off Billy.

The syndicate of dirty cops they were investigating started as a personal project on the heels of Evie getting dragged into that situation and Mag's commitment to getting her out.

This happened on their first date.

That ended with them making affiliations with the guys of Nightingale Investigations, as well as two motorcycle clubs (Chaos and Resurrection), and a handful of good cops because...dirty cops.

That would normally be enough said, but it had gone extreme and had involved intimidation, frame-ups, faked suicides, and murder.

So in the end, it wasn't personal.

It was a job that had to get done.

This situation with the Tabernacle of the True Light wasn't the same thing.

But even so, it was a shocker that Billy was offering to help.

"Billy—" Auggie started.

Billy interrupted him.

"Kids need good men in their lives, and no one should have to go it alone."

Whoa.

That was deep coming from Billy.

Auggie shut his mouth.

Hawk opened his.

"Billy, you take Bottoms. Aug's got other shit he needs to be doing. Connect with Jorge. He'll give you a game plan."

Billy nodded to Hawk.

Hawk moved the meeting to paid work.

And he ended it as they always seemed to end their team meetings these days.

With Hawk reporting on the dirty-cops case, a brief that usually shared not much to nothing was happening.

This time, though, Hawk began this with, "You all know that B delivered the message that they got to her to share the intel with us that they were standing down."

He got nods, because they all did know that one of their informants, a low-level drug dealer, but mostly information-peddler, Brandi, aka "B," had told them just that.

"You also know that since then, B has been vapor," Hawk went on.

More nods because it had been months, and nothing from B, no information, no sightings, she was gone.

She had a tendency to dip in and out of the scene as it suited her.
But they weren't thinking good thoughts at this disappearance.
Either she wised up and got out of Denver.

Or someone took her out.

"And since all that, even with a close eye on Lynn and Heidi,
and aware of what these assholes intend to hit, that being going
after valuable evidence in the police impound, just not when or
who might hit it," Hawk continued, "there's been nothing."

Lynn was Lynn Crowley—the widow of the cop who got dead
investigating the dirt that their team had spent months trying to
uncover, with no result. The hit on her husband, Tony, had been
what Cisco had been framed and later cleared for. It was their entry
to this sitch, since Evie's family had dragged her into that.

Heidi was Heidi Mueller—the widow of one of only two cops
they'd ferreted out as dirty in this mess. Her husband, Lance,
had in turn been framed for not only Tony's murder, but also
for a murder-suicide that would have been impossible for him to
commit, considering how zoned out he was on a date-rape drug
he'd been slipped.

The fact Lance Mueller had been roofied had been reported to
Hawk's crew, but entirely left out of the official autopsy report.

Both women were under their team's surveillance as well as
their protection.

But even if someone had been dicking around with Lynn prior
to B's message that those in play were standing down, it was too
hot, they were hands up, surrendering, neither woman had had any
issue since they'd reluctantly come forward, willing to help.

"But we have something," Hawk stated.

Every man in that room sat straighter.

Hawk didn't elucidate.

At least, he didn't right then.

He said, "Mo, Aug, Mag, I got somewhere to be, and I want
you with me. Billy, you hit up Jorge and then look into Bottoms.

Boone, Axl, stay on normal duties. We'll brief again later." Hawk looked at his watch, then his eyes landed on Mo, Auggie and Mag briefly before he finished, "We're heading out now. Aug, you're in the Camaro with me. Mo, you and Mag take a shade. I'll give you the address and my route. I want you approaching from a different direction. And be absolutely certain you're not tailed."

That didn't sound like they had something.

That sounded like they had something interesting.

They referred to the vehicles they used when they didn't want to be spotted as "shades." They were usually nondescript, but top of the line of their model so they had power under their hoods and maneuverability, just in case.

Hawk switched them out randomly, selling old and buying new (though those "new" could be used). And Aug had noticed they'd never had a shade longer than six months.

Hawk ended the meeting, convened with Mo to discuss approaches, they geared up with sidearms and then they moved out.

The trip to where they were going was not filled with conversation.

But what little was said was important.

The entirety of it included, from Hawk, "You and Pepper trying things?"

From Aug, "Yeah."

From Hawk, "Going okay?"

From Aug, "Great."

From Hawk, after a small pause, "Good."

From Aug, "Juno wants me to help with the sets for her school's Thanksgiving thing. I don't know the schedule, but I might need free evenings."

From Hawk, "You'll get 'em."

There was another pause, and then from Hawk, "I know you all know I dicked around and nearly lost Gwen because of past history."

He did know, so Aug grunted, "Yeah."

"Don't get caught in history, Auggie. Don't waste time," Hawk advised, mostly because he knew things too. Everything about all his men. And he gave more than a passing shit. "You can't get time back. And trust me, you never want to be at a place where you regret you pissed it away."

"I didn't grow up—" Aug began.

"I hate that was what you had," Hawk cut him off. "I cannot express how much. But that's history, Auggie."

Aug shut up.

Because it was.

This was now. A different time. Different people.

And he needed to guard against letting something dark that he'd had no control over break something bright that was within his grasp.

Hawk said no more.

Auggie didn't either.

Then again, when they got closer to where they were headed, Auggie got his head in the game and kept his attention on where they were and if someone was following them.

He didn't like the zone they were in. It wasn't a good part of Denver.

And when Hawk parked, and they hoofed it on foot the five blocks from where they left Hawk's Camaro to where this meet was happening, he didn't like the feel of the place.

But most of all, he didn't like the fact that Ian's black Mercedes GLC SUV was parked outside of it.

To Auggie's knowledge, Ian had dick to do with this case.

So what the fuck was Pepper's employer doing there?

Aug felt Hawk's gaze and gave his boss his own, and neither of them were happy.

This meant Hawk didn't know Ian was going to be here either.

The meeting place was a small box building made of cinderblock painted white. In fact, everything was white. White doors. White trim.

But it wasn't clean, and it wasn't kept up to the point it appeared mostly derelict.

The small parking lot all around was made up of cracked asphalt and broken parking blocks that had also, at some time not close to recent, been painted white.

They did a wide loop around the perimeter before heading to one of the two doors to the building, and as they did their loop, neither were thrilled that all the windows were blacked out.

Hawk pounded twice on the door with the side of his fist and Aug had his hand on his sidearm while he did it.

There was no answer.

Hawk opened the door.

They moved in swiftly and shut the door behind them just as swiftly.

Because Ian was there.

As was Smithie.

As were Rush, Shy and Dutch, all from the Chaos MC.

And Beck, Core and Eightball of the Resurrection MC.

Last, Malik, Elvira's husband, one of the cops on their crew.

Auggie could tell by the line of Hawk's body that this was a bigger meet than he expected, not just with men present, but the importance of what that many meant.

He could also tell that Hawk wasn't a fan of showing somewhere and not having that intel.

"You know what this shit's about?" Smithie, the least patient of any of them, asked.

"Not yet," Hawk answered.

Another double pound on the door and Mo and Mag came in.

Both men scanned the players then looked right to Hawk and their faces settled into how the rest of them looked.

Unhappy.

Fortunately, they only had to wait a few minutes before there was another pounding on the door.

Three knocks this time.

And in came Lee Nightingale, and his right-hand man, Luke Stark.

With them were Eddie Chavez and Hank Nightingale, both cops.

And sandwiched between these duos was a tall, slender Black woman with a great ass, close-cropped hair, insanely beautiful bone structure, big eyes and a presence that, if literally physical, would have pushed them all back on a foot.

At her entry into their scenario, two things Auggie did not like happened.

One, Beck grunted, "Nope."

This meant she was bad news.

All of them, Hawk and his men, Nightingale and his crew, Chaos and their brothers, but especially the cops, would like to lay claim to the fact that they knew the streets the best.

But the truth of it was, Resurrection did.

You played the game their way, that was what happened.

They knew the good.

They knew the bad.

But they rubbed elbows most with the ugly.

The second thing that Aug didn't like was the vibe that shot between the woman and Dorian.

Christ, if anyone got between their locked gazes, they'd be incinerated instantly.

Which meant Smithie growled, "*Fuck.*"

"Are you fuckin' shittin' us with this bitch?" Eightball demanded of Lee, Luke, Hank and Eddie as a whole.

"It's time you all met Dynamite," Lee stated.

At that, the room went static.

The word "dynamite" was the only lead in the dirty-cops case Tony Crowley left them before he died.

"Not so well known as Lieutenant Stephanie Fortune, deep cover, Denver Police," Eddie finished.

"The fuck?" Beck whispered.

Well...

Shit.

CHAPTER ELEVEN

Bee's Knees

PEPPER

The good thing about the one, two, three, four punch of a life that included making the decision early that you were going to leave the nest and never look back, plus the man you thought was the love of your life betrayed you to the point you lost all dignity which meant you had to build it back from scratch, plus you spent years stripping for a living, and finally, you meditated...was you owned yourself.

I owned myself.

And what I was owning right then was not hiding that I was hanging at my desk in the office for the sole purpose of seeing Auggie drive up, get out of his SUV and walk up my path.

Bonus, I was close to the door so I could rush to it and throw it open to provide myself the opportunity to finish watching him walk to my house with no obstructions.

All of this, I did.

Did this say I was excited to see him?

Yes.

Was I excited to see him?

Hell yes.

As such, I saw no reason to hide it, and not only because I (inadvertently, it was important to note) led him a merry chase up to this point and I didn't feel he needed any more of that.

I was just really excited to see him.

"Hey!" I exclaimed when he was halfway up the front steps.

"Hey," he responded, his lips curled up.

Still, he had that look on his face that he'd had the night before when I'd opened the door.

A look that said he didn't quite know what to make of me.

He got a kick out of it.

But he didn't get it.

I wanted to ask about it but maybe not now.

Now was the time for...

He got close.

And I threw myself at him, got on my toes, wrapped my arms around his neck, putting pressure there, and I laid a wet one on him.

Like both times before when I'd instigated things, it was mine for a nanosecond before Auggie's arms around me clamped tight and he shuffled me inside.

I heard the door slam (not shut... *slam*) when he kicked it closed.

I was then whirled and pressed to it and we made *way the fuck* out.

God, he even tasted like summertime.

When I had both my hands up his sweater at the back and my nails were exploring his hot skin, and he had his hand curved under my breast, wrapped around, not cupping, but like he was about to do that and more, he broke the kiss.

No!

"Auggie—" I started to protest when he slid his hand from where it was an awesome promise to my waist, where it just felt sweet.

He caught my eyes. "Baby, that was one helluva hello, and there are no complaints coming from me about it, but we gotta be at Juno's school in fifteen minutes."

"It's a ten-minute drive away."

I mean, if I could be hot and bothered and do the math, so could he.

"And you were one minute away from being drilled in your entryway again."

I considered this, and in considering it I realized it was essential in that moment for me to make another substantial sacrifice as a mom.

And that was to stop snogging Auggie so we could get to the school on time, not get there late and with me having sex hair.

However.

"Only one minute?" I teased.

Auggie wasn't in a playful mood.

Thus, in all seriousness, he declared, "You're gorgeous. You taste good. You feel good. I haven't fucked anyone since I fucked you two feet away from here. And I've never in my life had someone open their door to me that way. So yeah. I'm already hard, *very* hard, and that's all for you, so I wanna give it to you. But I'm not gonna."

There was so much there, to properly address all of it, I'd have to light a few candles and put on some calming music.

I didn't do that because I didn't have time to do that.

I quickly prioritized and focused on the top of that list.

"You've never had someone open their door that way to you?"

Suddenly, he looked uncomfortable.

Very uncomfortable.

Awkward even.

It was weirdly cute.

It was also alarming.

"No," he said like he had to force that syllable out.

Okay.

This was impossible.

Someone who looked like him, kissed like him, fucked like him.

Someone who was funny and protective and liked kids.

It wasn't just impossible.

It was unbelievable.

But at the look on his face, I believed it.

"You wanna grab your bag so we can go?" he suggested.

"Sure," I said softly, giving him a squeeze before I let him go and headed into the office.

Even if it wasn't far away and he could have hung at the door, Auggie followed me.

Then again, after dinner last night, we got into groping and making out. Thus, he still hadn't had a tour of my house.

"That's cute," he said, gaze to Juno's side of the room.

I glanced at him and then to my daughter's space and saw that he seemed to have his attention centered on a Polaroid resting on one of Juno's shelves. It was of me and Juno. Our neighbor Len took it on Halloween.

I'd gone for it in a full-on Wonder Woman outfit (I wasn't going to have this body forever, so while I had it, I was gonna flaunt it, and it was a hit, because ... *Wonder Woman*).

Juno had surprised me by wanting the collared catsuit of Black Widow.

It was a kickass selection for my girl. No Elsa for her (not that there was anything wrong with Elsa).

So I'd hit up Lori from down the way who was a great seamstress (and, not incidentally, Len was her husband).

And there the Black Widow was. Red wig and dangling utility belt and all.

"I know," I agreed with Auggie. "One could say Juno was the only Black Widow on the block on Halloween."

He turned to me. "That's definitely cool, Pepper. But I meant her whole space." He tipped his head that way. "It's cute. It's awesome she has that. You're a great mom."

Uhhh...

I frowned at him. "If you don't want to be jumped, you can't say stuff like that."

He grinned at me at the same time, and since I'd nabbed my bag, he took my hand and headed us to the door.

"So noted."

I went with him and tried not to skip to his SUV.

Like he did that night he'd driven me home, Auggie opened the door for me, which was utterly adorable, and when my ass was planted in his seat, I gave him a smile to communicate that.

His lips quirked and he shook his head as he shut the door and walked around the hood.

I took that moment to shimmy my behind in that seat, really going for it.

It was a personal celebration, but since it was something to celebrate, being in Auggie's car again, with Auggie, I was going to celebrate it.

He got in, and I stopped shimmying because the ritual was complete.

We belted up and he backed out of my drive.

"So, let me guess," I started. "You haven't had a long-term girlfriend."

"I was with a woman almost throughout my time in the marines."

Wait.

Seriously?

I looked his way. "How long was that?"

"Nearly five years."

Whoa.

"That's a...it's a..." I was too surprised at further info on Auggie that had not been shared by anyone to get the words out. Finally, I got them out. "That's a long time."

He glanced at me before looking back to the road. "Pepper, I'm thirty-four. I'm a bachelor. And I've never been married. But I've been committed a few times. Marie was just the longest term."

"What happened with Marie?" I asked.

"She cheated on me," he answered matter-of-factly.

But I'd stopped breathing.

That night was the night of impossibilities, for certain.

"She ... *really*?" I queried, and I couldn't keep the disbelief out of my voice.

"It's rampant in the armed forces. Lots of time away from each other. You can get stationed in different places. For women, they're spoiled for choice. For guys, they think being a real man is getting your wick as wet as you can as often as you can with as much variety as you can get. Not to mention, shit can get real, and if you think at any moment you could die, you live it up while you have the chance."

"Cheating is rampant outside the armed forces too," I murmured, and he reached out and squeezed my knee.

He then sadly released it and said, "Maybe, even now, I'm trying to find excuses for her."

"Been there," I replied with feeling. "But it happens everywhere, no matter what job you do."

"Yeah," he muttered.

"Did you live with Marie?" I asked.

"Yeah, for about four years."

Holy hell.

"Why didn't you ... are you not a marrying guy?"

"We were engaged."

Holy hell!

Did none of the girls know *any* of this?

I mean, why was I just learning all of it now?

I did, of course, get that there were things that Auggie might want to share that they shouldn't.

But him having a former fiancée, committing to another woman like that, wasn't a state secret, for goodness sakes.

I stopped asking questions.

I did this for so long, and obviously I didn't tamp down my shock, which meant Auggie felt it, which was probably why he spoke.

"Babe, I'm over her. *Way* over her. That was years ago. It didn't end well, obviously, and I haven't heard from her in a while. Mutual friends share where she's at, but trust me, I don't care."

"All right," I replied.

There was a pregnant moment of silence before he did something huge.

Something extraordinary.

Something profound.

Something I would not forget for *the rest of my life*.

He hooked his pinkie with mine.

That was it.

That was the something huge.

A small gesture.

A pinkie hug.

That didn't mean it wasn't colossal for all the things it was.

Intimate.

Cute.

Tender.

Thoughtful.

But then he made it even bigger when he said gently, "Pepper, I didn't cheat on her. I'd be deployed. She was in the marines too, so she'd be deployed. We'd be separated months, back together for weeks, separated for months again. And in all that time, she had all of me. I never considered it. Never looked at another woman in that way."

Yes.

Oh yes.

That made it even bigger.

Auggie kept talking.

"She didn't want to end it. She said it was a moment of weakness. She said she was lonely. She said it happened once, and she regretted it the minute it was over. She confessed. I didn't find out, she told me. She couldn't live with it between us. She wanted to go to counseling, alone, and if I was willing, also as a couple. But she didn't lay any blame on me. She said it was her thing. She just wanted me to hang with her while she worked shit out at the same time try to work it out together."

I said nothing.

Auggie finished, "I didn't hang. I packed my shit and got out."

At that, I turned my head his way.

"You didn't give her a shot?" I asked.

"She let another man slide his dick in her body. That's sacred space, Pepper. She'd gifted that to me. There is no moment of weakness that can explain that."

Wow.

Those were beautiful words.

Especially the "sacred space" part.

And, well...the "gifted that to me" part.

Still...

"That's an extreme point of view, Auggie," I noted carefully.

It felt like he was going to take his pinkie away, so I tensed mine and he stopped.

But he inquired, "Are you gonna take up for her?"

"No. Your feelings and thoughts matter to me. I don't know her. She doesn't matter to me. Also, I agree with you. Things can go sideways in a relationship, and there is no definitive right or wrong for every person in every couple as to how they deal with it. But that's an intense betrayal."

He let my pinkie go then, but only to grab my whole hand and murmur, "Maybe we shouldn't talk about this."

He was thinking about me. About what Corbin did to me.

This was not about me.

This was about Auggie not ever having anyone open the door to him like they were excited as all get-out to see him coming their way.

"What happened when you were deployed and came home?" I queried.

"Sometimes she was home. Sometimes she wasn't. Why do you ask?"

He didn't get my question.

I didn't answer his.

"And she cheated on me when she was in the field," he explained.

I didn't say anything.

"Pepper, let's leave it at this. Cheating is a dealbreaker for me."

I squeezed his hand. "It is for me too. I didn't give Corbin a shot either. Then again, he didn't only do it to me once. But even if he did, I know I'd find it difficult, if not impossible, to bounce back from that."

"Then we're down with that."

"Yes," I agreed.

He returned my squeeze.

Then he noted, "You two were together for a long time too."

"We were," I affirmed.

"But not married."

That was leading.

"No, not married," I said. "I wish I could tell you I sensed something wrong, but I can't. I just didn't have a good example of marriage. It kinda freaked me out. And when Corbin asked, I told him I'd have a commitment ceremony, go all out. Dress. Cake. DJ. The works. Just not official. I guess, if he turned out like my dad, I wanted an out."

"He asked?"

"Yeah."

"And you said no."

"Yeah."

"Mm," he hummed meaningfully.

So I looked at him.

"Do you want to get married?" I asked.

"Yeah, I want that. I also want my kids to have the feeling of safety and stability that would give them."

I stared at his utterly perfect profile.

And I couldn't believe it (I blamed the pinkie hug, though the perfect profile was part of it too), but it couldn't be denied I was thinking I could marry this man.

"It wasn't out of the question," I said quietly. "Corbin jumped on us having a commitment ceremony somewhere down the line. We just never did it. I should have known then."

"Never shoulder that kind of blame, Pepper. That's on him. All on him. The end."

He was so right.

And there was something more than a little cool about the fact he got where I was coming from, a little bit.

I didn't want him to be hurt, betrayed. Obviously not.

But he understood that hurt. It was a dealbreaker for him, as it was for me.

Also for me, that was *huge*.

To communicate all of that rolling around in my head, I whispered, "The end."

He let my hand go, but not entirely. He hooked our pinkies again.

Yeah.

I had a feeling I was going to be blaming the pinkie hug for a lot of things.

He then finished driving us to the school, found a parking spot, slid into it, and shut the vehicle down.

When he did, I turned right to him in a manner that his attention came direct to me.

"All day long, I couldn't wait for you to ride up my street, park in my drive, and walk up my front steps," I declared. "I was waiting in my office for you so I could witness it happening from start to finish. I don't know how this is a world where the women in your life did not do the same. And I can't say every time you come to me, I'll be in that space. Just that … Auggie, you're a man to get excited about."

He didn't move, not a muscle, not his eyes, which were glued to mine.

All right, perhaps that was too much.

"Maybe we should—" I began.

"If you don't wanna get fucked stupid in my car outside your kid's school, don't say shit like that."

"Okay," I whispered.

"I'm super fucking pissed at you," he declared.

What?

"Why?" I asked.

"Because you're fuckin' fantastic and you dicked around and we lost months and that pisses me off."

Shit.

"Does it help that I'm super fucking pissed at myself for the same thing?" I asked.

"Yeah." He finally cracked a smile and I relaxed. "It does."

I smiled back at him.

"Get over here and kiss me but don't stick your tongue down my throat or we'll be banned from school premises," he ordered.

I was smiling bigger before I did as told, including (woefully) keeping it chaste.

He caught me when I was pulling away, cupping my jaw to do it.

"Takeaway from that, sweetheart, is you're fantastic," he said.

"You're fantastic too," I replied.

"Glad you think so," he muttered to my mouth, the soft, sexy look on his handsome face muddling my head.

Fortunately (kinda), he let me go, and got out of the car, so he wasn't in close proximity to muddle my head anymore and I was able to get out of the car too.

And my unmuddled mind caught on the fact he'd said, *Glad you think so*.

Not a cocky, *Yeah, I am*.

Not a, *Thanks, baby*, which would still say in a less arrogant way that he knew he was.

But, *Glad you think so*.

Something was really not right about that.

I couldn't roll it around in my head, since he'd rounded the car and was nonverbally sharing he wasn't a fan that I exited the vehicle on my own steam. He did this by doing a mini-scowl at the closed door and then at me.

I burst out laughing.

"What's funny?" he asked after he'd grabbed my hand and again started guiding me someplace, this time to Juno's school.

"You," I told him. "You're like a throwback to the forties."

"What?"

"Guys don't open women's car doors anymore, Aug."

He stopped us both and looked down at me.

"Does it offend you?"

"No. It's sweet."

"Then why do you find it funny?"

I suddenly didn't.

"Did I offend you?" I asked cautiously.

"No."

Uhhhh . . .

"Okay, here we are," he stated, words that were clearly preamble to a proclamation.

Oh man.

"I open doors for women," he continued. "To cars. To buildings. If you don't want me to, I won't. But my dad taught me to do that.

In whatever fucked-up neural pathway in his head that led him to this opinion, one of the few on which we agree, he said it was respect, to treat a woman like that. And a man should always do that. Even if, on another pathway, he'd find it in himself to think it was okay to fuck around on my mom and do other shit to screw with her and play games with their marriage and their lives."

I stood staring at him, feeling each word like a puncture wound to the heart.

Because his dad did this to his mom.

At the same time he did it to Auggie.

"So I open doors," he continued. "Not only because my father taught me to, but probably because my mom on more than one occasion told me, if he wasn't a 'gentleman,' she would have left him for good a long time ago."

I gave him the truth.

"It was very sweet, Auggie, and I loved that you did it for me. And I'd love it if you'd continue. I wasn't laughing at you in a bad way. I was laughing because...well, I don't know why. Maybe because I liked it but it's old-fashioned and you're not old-fashioned."

"My father is. Because in his time, a man could treat a woman like dirt, but God forbid he didn't help her into a car."

I was suddenly thinking we could catch up on the school Thanksgiving show sitch.

For now, we had more important things to do.

"Maybe we should—"

"No," he stated implacably before I could make my suggestion. "We're doing this for Juno."

Okay, I loved that he was all in to make sure he didn't let Juno down.

However...

"I know I just laid a ton on you," he said. "We can finish it later. Now, we're doing this for Juno."

He was right, of course.

He'd laid a ton on me.

But now we needed to do this for Juno.

I nodded.

He held my hand as we walked into the school.

And he didn't let it go when we hit the assembly room and both of us immediately saw that our night was about to go further awry.

Because Corbin was there.

And to my knowledge, he wasn't supposed to be.

Indeed, Corbin never did this kind of thing. Corbin was too busy making money to do this kind of thing. You couldn't build proper elementary school show sets with a mobile phone glued to your ear while you made a deal.

Thus, Juno had quit asking him, and unofficially, this kind of thing was what I'd get roped into doing.

I could not claim master craftsperson with a hammer.

But I could take direction.

And I always wanted Juno to know I gave a shit about something she gave a shit about.

That said, considering the fact this show preparation was going to happen at night and last a couple of weeks, I wouldn't have volunteered for it primarily because I worked nights, and right then, I was only there to hang with Auggie and make sure he was cool with what was going to be expected.

"Fantastic," Auggie muttered, attention on Corbin.

He could say that again.

"Momma!" Juno shouted when she caught sight of me.

She ran from where she was standing with her dad, hurtling our way.

She hit me with a hug.

I hugged her back.

She arched away and whispered loudly, "Come here."

I bent to her.

"I don't know how he found out!" It was still a whisper, softer than her first, but even so, it had an exclamation point.

So there it was.

Corbin was pulling some Corbin crap.

"It's okay, honey," I whispered back.

"It's gonna be weird because you're with Auggie," she said.

"It's gonna be fine," I lied.

"Hero."

"Patrick."

The men were greeting each other.

Tersely.

I gave my daughter a reassuring squeeze before I straightened and Juno cried, "Auggie!" and threw herself at him.

He gave her a one-armed hug and ended that with his hand on top of her head.

He kept it there when she looked up at him.

"Thanks for coming," she said.

"All hands on deck, right?" he asked, giving her (and her father) an out for horning into what Juno had clearly declared Mom's Domain This Time, or in this instance, Auggie's Domain.

He also did this circling her head in a jokey way that had her worried look melting into a genuine smile.

"Right!" she chirped.

"Pepper," Corbin greeted, calling my attention to him.

I tore my eyes from my girl and looked to her father.

Shit.

Shit.

Shit.

I had been wrong the night before.

The likeliest scenario wasn't going to be Corbin messing with me and/or Auggie and me just to be a jerk.

It was going to be Corbin doubling down on winning me back.

Shit!

"Corbin," I said, fighting punctuating that by leaning into Auggie and/or taking his hand.

There was a message that needed to be relayed to Corbin.

But at that juncture, that message didn't need to be relayed to Juno.

Oh, I *so* got she wanted Auggie and me together.

That said, how that would happen and how our growing relationship would be communicated to her would not be because my hand was forced by Corbin.

"You look great," Corbin said.

I did, because this was a highly unusual beginning, but it was still a date with a hot guy.

So I had on a cute sweater and jeans that did fantastic things to my ass and my hair was curly, messy, beachy perfection.

In other words, I'd gone all out.

But a compliment from Corbin?

Ugh.

"Thanks," I replied.

"This meeting is early," Corbin noted.

Oh shit.

Oh shit.

Ohhhhh shiiiiit.

"We didn't have dinner before we came," he went on.

Oh shit!

"Would you two like to go somewhere with us after?" he finished.

Goddammit.

It was a good play, pretending we were all friends, but still, interrupting my date with a hot guy at the same time sucking my time, at the same time giving Corbin the opportunity to show Juno mom and dad could get along and see how great we are all together?

If she wanted it, I'd say yes.

Corbin couldn't know this, but if she wanted it, Auggie would also say yes.

I looked to Juno.

Then I blinked at Juno.

She looked like a Disney villain kid who was about to do something obnoxious, like kick her father in the shin or let loose several dozen caged turkeys that would run him out of the assembly room.

It took so much effort not to laugh out loud, I snorted.

Auggie brushed my fingers with his and said a warning but still amused, "Baby," under his breath.

Juno was so busy fighting the urge to act like a brat, she missed this.

Corbin did not and his eyes narrowed on Auggie.

"We have plans," I felt safe to choke out, still fighting my own urge, that being to laugh.

Corbin's narrowed gaze came to me.

But rainbows and pixie dust flew up from below (not literally, alas) so I looked down to my daughter, who was beaming.

Oh yeah.

She wanted me to be with Auggie.

The fates took a turn for the better in that moment when a male teacher interrupted this awkwardness by calling out, "Parents! Can I have your attention?"

Auggie leaned into me, and his lips brushed my ear, he was so close when he murmured, "He so fucking can."

I snorted again.

He moved his lips away, but I felt his touch on my hip, there and gone, and again felt magic coming from my daughter's space, so I returned my attention to her.

She was smiling largely at me, all worries gone.

I was glad she was feeling that, and I wished I could be there with her, totally and completely.

But in a very short car ride a lot had been unleashed from Auggie and we'd walked right into an unwanted declaration from Corbin, so I couldn't.

Even so, that was where she was in the now.

And I was there with her in the now.

And it was a good spot for the both of us.

I felt Auggie's arm brush my shoulder as the teacher started to make general announcements and I turned my gaze to Aug.

I'd gotten the shoulder brush because he was close and he'd crossed his arms on his chest (a position I right then noted was kind of his "at ease" because he was in it a lot). His handsome face was alert and attentive, his eyes to the teacher, but he seemed relaxed.

So it was a good spot for all of us in the now (except Corbin, but whatever).

That meant, I was good settling there.

So I did.

* * *

"I just don't know what to make of this. It's so much, I might need to meditate for a month to be at one with it," I joked.

"Babe, El Tejado is totally better than Las Delicias," Auggie replied, stating a preference I already knew, since my ass was in a booth at El Tejado, waiting for my combo #3.

"I can't. I can't." I closed my eyes, settled both hands on my chest, fingers of one resting on the others, and started breathing deeply with exaggeration.

He wrapped a foot around the back of my ankle, and lifted it until he could catch it with his hand between his splayed legs.

My eyes popped open.

Since I was wearing a pair of low-heeled mules in fake-fur

leopard print, it was easy for him to slip the mule off so the ball of my foot was *oh so close* to another set of balls.

With both hands, he started massaging my ankle and calf.

"As good as that feels, it's important I note that isn't how you're supposed to play footsie, Augustus Hero."

He shot a glamorous smile at me.

I kept blathering.

"It's also important to note that providing me with a massage will, indeed, get me to shut up and stop giving you shit about something. However, it is one thousand percent not going to be conducive to me doing my part in practicing restraint. To wit, if you think you can sit across from me, all hot, sexy *and* tactile, I think it's fair to warn you that you will get jumped somewhere between the parking lot and my front door."

He kept smiling at me.

"God, you're gorgeous," I whispered.

His smile froze as did his fingers.

"Aug?" I called.

He put my shoe back on, squeezed my ankle, and gently shoved my foot down, saying in a way he was trying to be humorous, but his heart wasn't in it, "We both need you doing your part."

I placed my foot on the floor but leaned into the table.

"You should know, I know a little bit about how women screwed you over, and we're not talking Marie. We're talking the others who did fucked-up shit because you're all that's..." I threw a hand up between us, indicating him, "*you*."

"Pepper—"

I cut him off and asked, "When I haven't been giving you an in, why didn't you find someone else?"

That question appeared to perplex him. "Sorry?"

"You said I was your last."

"You were," he confirmed.

"Why?"

Now he started to look annoyed. "Not every guy needs to fuck everything that moves."

"Of course not, but—"

"And I wanted in."

I shut up.

Auggie didn't.

"I didn't know until recently that your ex did what he did. But you were aware I wanted you. Does it say to you, 'I want to give us a go' when I'm fucking some other chick?"

No.

It did not.

"No," I said quietly.

"Ryn wasn't ready, and Boone moved on, and that nearly fucked them up. Hattie *really* wasn't ready, and Axl moved on, and that nearly fucked *them* up. You weren't ready. And I wasn't going to do dick to fuck up the possibility of an us."

Oh my God.

I was going to start bawling in El Tejado.

"Pepper?"

I waved a hand in front of my face and demanded, "Cease speaking immediately."

He looked concerned, then he started to look cocky.

Fortunately, the second look eased my need to start bawling.

That need totally evaporated when he announced, "You do know, if we work, by definition through this being our first away-from-your-kitchen-island date, El Tejado is going to be our place."

I flopped against the booth and tipped my head back to say to the ceiling, "Why do you challenge me so, sweet Lord?"

I only righted myself when I heard Auggie chuckling.

"Just to point out," I went on, "it's awesome here."

"Glad you think so."

Glad you think so.

On a repeat of these words, I got deadly serious.

"And you're gorgeous, Auggie. I know that opened the door to bitches treating you like shit, but it doesn't make it less true. They're just bitches. And you're just awesome. And they fucked up *big time*. And although what Lottie said they did totally sucked, and I hate that for you, I hate that you went through that. I'm still glad it means I'm sitting right here, across from you. Because you're not only gorgeous, you're the bee's knees. And I'm a big idiot for wasting months I could have been with you. But I'm okay with that too, because I'm sitting here, across from you."

After I finished that, I sat very still because Auggie did too.

But he did it with an expression on his face and a vibe emanating off him that, frankly, it was a miracle our table didn't melt from between us.

He then said, "The bee's knees?"

"Totally," I replied.

"Christ, you're cute."

To get us fully out of the intense, I fake preened, fluffing my hair on one side, the whole shebang, saying, "Why, thank you."

"You're also a huge dork."

"Another thing of note, honey, calling me a dork does not lessen my need to jump you."

He burst out laughing.

I smiled at him as he did it.

When he was done, I remarked, "Now let's talk about how deep our relief is that there wasn't a feather or moccasin to be seen in Mr. Sykes's plans for the Turkey Day show."

"That's hitting my gratitude journal tonight for sure."

My eyebrows shot up. "You have a gratitude journal?"

"As much as it appears it's going to disappoint you, I was joking." He studied me a second then asked, "Do you?"

"I journal every day and I begin each day's entry with three things I'm grateful for from the day before." I reached out and patted his hand. "But it's okay you don't have a journal. Christmas is coming."

He laughed again.

I smiled again.

His humor didn't totally leave him even as he said, "Corbin's gonna pull out all the stops to reunite his family."

I wasn't feeling so jaunty, even as I joked with words that were the truth, "Clearly, you're a good judge of people."

"He's not hiding it."

He wasn't.

"This is doomed from the start since, because of him, we never really were a family."

"Sweetheart," he murmured.

"We weren't, Auggie. Let's be crystal clear on this. We weren't. And that means there's nothing to go back to because there was never anything really there."

He nodded.

"Do you believe me?" I asked.

"Even if I didn't, if you looked like you were considering it, Juno might go in search of a voodoo practitioner and have them put a hex on the both of you."

"This is a concern," I said mock gravely.

Auggie wasn't hiding his amusement, but it faded before he said, "What it is, is double trouble, baby. Because if he doesn't get his head out of his ass, it's going to upset her. And he's so intent on what he wants, he's not paying any mind to his girl."

I pulled in a big breath and let it out on a massive sigh, because that was the truth.

"I get involved in school stuff that Corbin isn't involved in, though this isn't normally my thing," I told him. "I only went tonight to be with you and make sure it was all cool for you. She wasn't supposed to be there to see me. It's going to be rough, being at the school then going to work. Ian is going to have to schedule me so I can come in late for the next few weeks."

"Then don't do it, I'll do it. You don't have to be there."

"Auggie—"

"It's every weeknight from seven to nine. You work. You can't do it. She'll understand. And it takes you out of Patrick's space."

"Maybe I should come for this week, so I can have a minute to explain it to her."

"Your call, she's your daughter. But don't take this in a bad way, it might be a relief for her, you don't show."

This was something to ponder, because he might be right.

He grinned to take any sting out of his earlier words and teased, "She didn't hide it messed with her master plan, her dad bringing her tonight."

"We Hannigan girls don't like our master plans thwarted," I concurred.

He reached out and took my hand. "It's all gonna be good, baby."

I rubbed the apple of his palm and mumbled, "Yeah."

And in another stroke of luck that night, that was when the waitress showed with our food.

It was a stroke of luck because I was done with this conversation and thinking of Corbin. I wanted to think about Auggie.

But also, I was hungry.

And El Tejado's food was amazing.

CHAPTER TWELVE

Energy

JUNO

I s everything okay, sweetheart?"

Juno got worried that Mr. Cisco answered the phone that way.

Not that he didn't again answer real quick.

And it wasn't about the words he said.

Just that he sounded like her mom sounded when Juno asked her a question and she was doing something, like making a grocery list.

"Are you busy, Mr. Cisco?" she asked, phone to her ear, covers pulled up on that side, eyes peeking out and aimed in the direction of her closed bedroom door.

She was being careful, even if her dad never came to check on her after he made sure she brushed her teeth and hair and got in her jammies, had her book bag sorted and got into bed.

It was lights out, so he probably thought she was sleeping, and he was downstairs, doing whatever he did when Juno was in bed.

Still, he might hear her talking.

"Give me just one second, Juno," Mr. Cisco replied.

Juno gave him that one second, though it was more than one.

Finally, he came back to her and his voice was different.

He wasn't writing his grocery list anymore (or whatever).

"Okay, honey, is everything all right?" he asked.

"Dad's ruining *everything*."

Now it was *her* voice that was funny. All bumpy and hitchy.

"Juno, take a deep breath for me, okay?"

Her mom would say that to her when she got upset about something.

So she took a deep breath.

Like always, it helped.

"Now, what's happening?" Mr. Cisco asked.

"Well..." she began, then told him about how her dad somehow found out about the Thanksgiving show, and even though he never, ever, *ever* did anything like that, he showed up at the school and took Juno with him.

But that was Auggie's.

That was Juno's way of showing her mom that Auggie liked Juno. Mom didn't have to worry about how he felt about Juno. He would be good for her, for her mom, for *them*.

And her dad was *ruining it*.

When she quit talking, Mr. Cisco said, "Okay, sweetheart, leave this to me."

"Wh-what are you gonna do?"

"I don't know yet, but like any complicated operation, it's good to know all that's happening so I can create an appropriate strategy."

That sounded like hooey he said just so she wouldn't be upset anymore.

"Dad's acting funny, Mr. Cisco."

"Hmm."

"And he broke up with his girlfriend. I can tell."

She could always tell when he was done with one of them, because her dad was on the phone even more than normal, finding another one.

But this time, he wasn't on the phone or texting with that silly smile on his face.

This time was different.

And Juno didn't like it.

"Juno, I want you to listen really close to me."

"Okay."

"Are you listening?"

Of course she was listening. What else would she be doing?

She tried not to sound mean when she said, "Yes."

"Good. Because this is important," he replied. "You see, there are some things in life that we can't control. And some of those things are things we really want to control. They might even be the things we want to control most of all. But we just can't. No matter how hard we try. The important part about this is realizing when that is and then stop trying. It takes a lot of energy to try to control things that are out of our control, and in the end, it's wasted energy. But more, that energy can be directed at something that we *can* control. Are you with me?"

"I'm with you," she told him.

And she was because that made a whole load of sense.

Mr. Cisco kept going.

"In this scenario, we cannot control your father. We don't know what he's thinking. What he wants. But we're getting sidetracked. He isn't our primary objective. Auggie was there tonight with your mom. That's our primary objective. So *that* is what we focus on. Because another thing it's important in life to always be certain to do, is take a moment to savor the victories. And right now, honey, you've had a victory. But you aren't savoring."

Okay, now he was losing her.

"What's savoring?"

"Celebrating."

Oh.

"I can't celebrate, Mr. Cisco. I'm supposed to be sleeping."

She heard him chuckle.

Then he said, "Yes, you should be sleeping, not worrying about this. Even so, take a minute tomorrow not to think of your dad going to your school tonight, but think about Auggie and your mom being there. Think about how it felt when you saw them walk in. Not the part where you were worried your dad was there. The part that's just about your mom being with a good man you like for her. That's not only a better thought, it's what this is all about. Am I right?"

He was!

"Yeah," she answered, grinning.

"Do you feel better?" he asked.

"Yeah," she repeated.

"Good. Now don't think of this. It takes up too much energy. You need that for school and to keep on top of our operation, the important parts of it. You with me?"

"I'm with you, Mr. Cisco."

"All right, Juno. Goodnight, sweetheart. Sleep well."

"Okay, 'bye."

"Good-bye, Juno."

She hung up and took another breath before she touched the button to make certain the phone didn't make noise (the button was still in the position it was supposed to be, thank goodness, even though Mr. Cisco never phoned her, she had to be careful). Then she hid the phone between her mattress and the thing under it that wasn't a mattress.

After that, she pulled the covers up to her neck and thought of her mom walking into the assembly room with Auggie, her mom's hair curled in that special way she did it only when she was going out with her girls or when she came to one of

Juno's events or when they went to Christmas Eve services at the church.

But this time, she did it for Auggie.

And Auggie looked really nice in a black sweater and jeans. Juno had only ever seen him wearing t-shirts and stuff, except, of course, at Aunt Lottie and Mr. Mo's wedding. He wore a special suit to that.

Mr. Cisco was right.

That was the important part.

That was where she should put her energy.

Because her mom and Auggie looked real good together.

And her mom looked happy.

CHAPTER THIRTEEN
Space

PEPPER

Late the next morning after my El Tejado date with Auggie, I walked in the back door to Smithie's in order to get some rehearsal in.

And I did this with my head bent to my phone.

This was because the date hadn't really ended.

It had gone on via text.

It started with a message from me approximately one minute after I lost sight of Auggie's SUV down my street:

I'm mad at you.

From Aug sometime later, hopefully when he wasn't driving:

Why?

Because you just left.
And you're way too good
at practicing restraint.

He had been.

At my house, an end-of-the-night beer for him, glass of wine for me, a little convo, a little snogging on the couch, and then he left.

So yeah.

I was not happy.

About that.

Because I was totally happy since the date had again been amazing, even if the beginning was deep and intense. It was a good deep and intense. And to get to know Auggie, we were going to have to get deep and intense.

Might as well start out with a bang.

Though, it went without saying I was hoping for another kind of bang.

Poor baby.

> I am.
> I'm a very poor baby.
> Because my boyfriend
> is mean.

Obviously, I freaked out after sending that because Auggie's three dots kept going for a really, really, *really* long time without a text coming through.

And in that long time, I realized we'd had one phone date, one at-my-kitchen-island date and one going-out date that started with him going to a meeting at my daughter's school.

And I'd just called him my boyfriend.

While his dots were forming, I quickly texted:

> I didn't mean boyfriend-boyfriend.
> I was just being funny.

There were not a lot of dots to that, before I got:

**Shame. The boyfriend bit was
my favorite part.**

Yes!
That was his reply.
Of course, it took off from there and it could not be denied
that our fourth date was a text date that lasted from after he left
me until we mutually agreed to stop texting in order to pass out
and started again this morning with him texting me so early, it
was criminal.
But I did not care even a little bit.
And this was what his text said.

Morning, sweetheart.

Call me crazy, but that was the most perfect text I ever got
in my life.
Now it was just after 10:00 and we'd been texting on and off
since 5:30.
And yes, I broke my own rule and had my phone by my bed
all night.
To hell with EMFs.
"Pepper."
Ian's voice saying my name, doing it sharply, and in close prox-
imity, had me stopping in my tracks as well as ceasing looking at
my phone grinning like a loon.
The reason my name was sharp and close was because he said
it right before I ran into him.
"Hey, sorry," I said.
"Hey," he replied, and his usually deep, rich voice still had an
edge to it.

Ummm...

"I'm glad I caught you," he continued. "Dominique gave notice yesterday. She's going back to Milwaukee."

I said nothing since I already knew Dominique, one of our solo dancers, and a veteran of Smithie's, was considering this. She'd rekindled a flame from back home. She'd gone back, he'd come to Denver, and now they were done with long distance and were going to give it a real go.

"So we're hiring and I'd like you, along with Lottie, Hattie and Ryn, to sit in on the auditions."

Righteous!

That would be a blast.

I grinned at him. "Right on."

"We'll actually be hiring two, maybe three dancers. So be prepared. This could take some time."

I did not grin at that.

Mostly because we didn't need two, maybe three dancers.

Dominique was fantastic, but we already had a good lineup of soloists.

This was evidenced by the fact that we had a packed house every night with a line around the building to get in.

Ian had done a revamp of the show, taking us from stripping with only Lottie having several marquee performances a night, to being a revue. That included all of us taking the stage for solos, ensemble burlesque performances in between, and with Holly on board doing two to three comedy bits a night and engaging the audience between dancers so the stagehands could set up for the next, we had it down.

The frosting on top was that now they served food. Gourmet tapas that had been a huge hit.

It all had been a huge hit.

The VIP section was booked until March, *that* big of a hit. And the rules to reserve VIP were, you had to book it for the entire night, you had your own server and could get whatever you wanted from the bar, but menu options were extra.

And it cost fifteen thousand dollars.

A night.

We absolutely needed to replace Dominique, but unless he was letting go of the ensemble performers, or adding to them, we didn't need more soloists.

And this was a concern to me because I was not Lottie. She not only was an artiste exotic dancer, she was famous. She'd been famous before she started at Smithie's. She'd been his headliner for years and only increased in popularity in that time.

It was also a concern for me because Hattie was an exceptionally talented dancer, and not just the exotic kind. She was so good out there, her routines so spectacular, she'd organically taken over the headliner spot. (Lottie didn't mind, because that was the way Lottie was.)

And Ryn was like me. We got the job done, enjoyed it and put our all into it.

But Ryn had a man and was working on having another source of income. She was building her business flipping houses, and so far, she'd done well at it.

She had a plan.

Unlike the others (and I hadn't told anybody), I'd taken a hit to my tips when we'd gone revue. Not much, but it wasn't the same as before when it had been straight stripping with the occasional (but lucrative) lap dance thrown in.

I wasn't Lottie or Hattie, and I didn't have a backup like Ryn.

I couldn't skip a dance a night for more variety in soloists.

I needed the tips.

This all on my mind, when Ian spoke again, I focused on him to see him studying me closely.

"Hattie's gonna be gone soon, Pez. Sadie sold another of her pieces yesterday. And she just told me it looks like that show in Aspen is a go. She's going to need more time in her studio, and she prefers being there. Not to mention, Ryn's eventually going to make a move. You can't dance all night and lay tile all day. It's going to wear her down and I know which one she'll eventually give up. I have to be ready. We'll add to the ensemble. Good dancers, women with potential that Lottie, Hattie, Ryn and you can mentor so I can move them up when the time comes."

Okay.

Phew.

Crisis averted.

Because Hattie's talents didn't only lie in dancing, she was a sculptor. She'd recently had a kickass show at Sadie Chavez's art gallery, and it was kickass not only because her stuff was spectacular, but because she'd sold well.

And her art was priced in a zone where I couldn't buy a thing.

In other words, her selling another of her pieces could mean thousands of dollars for her.

Like, five to fifteen of them.

"I'm all in when that time comes, Ian."

"Everything else good?" he asked.

"I had the best date of my life last night," I answered. "Which is weird, since the night before I'd had the best date of my life. And that was weird, because the night before *that*, I'd had the best date of my life and it was a phone conversation."

A smile formed on his mouth, but when it did, it was me who was studying him closely because Ian was a cool dude, a good man, an awesome boss, a great friend, open, honest, approachable, and I didn't think I'd ever seen him smile at me with a conflicting light in his eye.

A light that said he was happy for me, but something else was on his mind and whatever that was might not be great.

"Is everything good with you?" I asked.

"Perfect," he lied.

And I felt my stomach squeeze, because that was totally a lie and I wasn't sure Ian had ever lied to me.

"Sure?" I pressed.

He nodded.

"Sure," he stated firmly. "I'll let you get to your rehearsal."

He started to move to go out the back door, but I caught him with a hand on his arm.

He looked down at me.

He wasn't just all that stuff I'd said he was before.

He was tall, and immensely good-looking, with beautiful eyes, broad shoulders, gorgeous chocolate skin. On top of that, he dressed great, and he had an amazing manner.

It was kind of a miracle he wasn't taken yet.

Then again, I wasn't sure there was a woman in the world good enough for Dorian Walker.

Which was probably why Lottie (or none of us) had tried to fix him up.

It'd have to be someone special. A superhero.

A wonder woman.

"You know, if something's up, I'm here to listen. Anytime, yeah?" I said.

His face relaxed, he looked and felt more like Ian, before he said, "Thanks, Pez. But really, I'm good."

"To reiterate, offer's always open."

He bent down and kissed my cheek.

(See? Amazing manner!)

"Honest, I'm fine," he told me after he'd straightened.

I nodded.

He went out the back door.

I headed into the club.

Lottie and Hattie were in one of the killer new booths that rounded the stage.

Ryn was on the stage with some chick I did not know, a satin rope suspended from the ceiling, and a big mat underneath it.

Oh man.

Ryn had said she was going to try an aerial dance, and here we were. She'd hired that coach she'd told us about and she was going for it.

Awesome.

I kept my eyes on Ryn as I moved to the booth at the end of the catwalk where Lots and Hatz were hanging.

"Yo," I said as I slid in with them and watched as Ryn, one foot wound around the rope, the same with a wrist, did a backbend/splits maneuver that was damn cool.

I got a "Yo" in return (Lottie) and a "Hey" (Hatz).

Ryn came out of her position and her coach moved to her, so I looked to Hattie.

"Congrats on the sale."

She beamed at me. "Did you run into Ian?"

I nodded. "Happy for you, babe. And Aspen is happening?"

That was when she nodded with a cute little bounce in her seat. "I'm excited. But Sadie's sold so much, I need to get to work."

Yeah.

Ian had been right.

Hattie wasn't going to last long at Smithie's.

Not to mention, Ryn definitely wanted her life to be about flipping houses (and Boone).

And Lottie and Mo were moving along at a good clip. It seemed like just yesterday when they'd met. Now they were married, and I knew she wanted kids. You couldn't dance the way we did when you started showing. She might even retire (though, I didn't think she would, but I'd seen her with her nephews, she doted on them—I could totally see her saying, ef it, I wanna be a stay-at-home mom).

And then there was . . . me.

I couldn't dance forever either.

I was sure a bangin'-hot seventy-year-old woman could do a smashing job, but the tips would probably be crap and half of them would be pity tips.

I needed tips, lots of them, and none of them from pity.

God.

I, too, needed a backup plan.

"How'd the date go?" Lottie asked.

I buried my thoughts and smiled at her. "Awesome."

"Do you feel like a big dufus you put him off for so long?" she asked.

I didn't stop smiling at her. "Totally."

She did a small headshake and rolled her eyes, but her lips were tipped up.

"Did you hear about Dominique?" Hattie asked.

"Yep," I answered.

"We need to be at one with that," Lottie stated confusingly.

"At one with what?" Hattie inquired, obviously as confused as me.

"At one with who's hired," Lottie said. "If they hire one woman, it's about Billy. If it's two, then I say Billy and Marques. But I'm open to discussing Zane. If it's three, we're golden."

Hattie and I looked at each other.

Then we looked back to Lottie and it was Hattie who got there first, but I knew when she did, we had the same thing on our minds.

"Do you mean, we need to be at one with our selections of new dancers so you can fix them up with the rest of Hawk's commandos?"

"Yes," Lottie said. "Though, it won't be just me fixing them up this time. It'll be all of us."

Uh . . .

"I'm not sure we should pick dancers based on who we want to set those boys up with," I put in.

And I wasn't sure we should set those boys up.

I'd met them. They'd been around on a variety of occasions. And even though they seemed like great guys, I didn't know them all that well.

Still.

First, they seemed young. They were probably the same age as me, but dudes matured slower and having a kid accelerated that process (at least it did for me).

Second, I wasn't a fan of meddling in other people's lives.

And last, breaking it down:

Billy was scary. He was hot, but he was scary.

Marques still had a lot of boy in him, and even though he was hot too, no woman liked to hang around while her man grew up.

And Zane seemed...broken. I couldn't put my finger on it, but there was something jagged in that guy. Sure, there were women who were good at smoothing things out for a man, but I didn't think we could find that by watching some chick dance.

"You're not a Taoist, like me," Lottie said.

Hattie giggled.

I grinned at her.

But even if she was being funny, I broke it down for her too.

"Billy's scary. Marques is a man-boy. And Zane is broken. Do you really think we could pick the perfect girls for them just watching them audition to be dancers at Smithie's Revue?"

"I nailed it with you four," Lottie pointed out.

"You knew us and none of the guys had those issues," I returned.

And when I did, both Lottie and Hattie gave me a look.

So I asked, "What?"

"Auggie's broken," Lottie said.

Oh shit.

He kinda was.

Actually . . .

We were getting to know each other, but I still didn't know him all that well.

Though, what I did know was that he wasn't kinda broken.

He just was.

"Axl has a messed-up dad and he watched his best friend die," Hattie told me.

"Mo has bad PTSD, you both know that, and before me, women shit all over him, you know that too," Lottie said. "Mag has PTSD as well, and you also know that. And Boone's best friend committed suicide after he got out. No one is perfect. Everyone has issues. And as funny as it is, I'm no Taoist. I just picked four really good women for four really good guys. And it worked. We just have to find good women. And it'll work."

Okay, Lots was my friend, but it was super nice she called me a really good woman, because she was a really good woman and I was glad she was in my life, and more glad to hear her confirm the feeling was mutual.

And she was right.

There was nothing special about any of us, and yet we were all top to toe to mind to heart to soul special.

And so were the guys.

I felt a spark hit my heart and it felt good.

"Ohmigod, I could totally get into this," I said.

"I could totally too," Hattie added.

"See?" Lottie asked, looking smug. "It's fun."

"I'm not sure Billy should be first though. I'm with Pez. He's kinda scary," Hattie noted.

"Those are the best ones," Lottie replied.

She'd say that. Mo had been scary too.

Before Lottie.

Yeah.

This was going to be rad.

There was a thud of body to mat.

"*Kathryn!*"

We all twisted our heads around when we heard Ian bark Ryn's name like that.

Sure enough, Ryn had fallen off the rope and was lying flat on her back on the mat on the stage.

And Ian was standing behind the row of booths off to the side, face like thunder, and my neck tensed completely seeing it, because even when he was dealing with an asshole patron or a drunk, he was always cool as a cucumber.

"The rope dance is out," he declared.

Ryn jumped to her feet and put her hands to her hips. "But, Ian, it's cool as shit."

"It's too dangerous," he retorted.

"I just need a little practice and it's gonna rock," she returned.

"*What did I say?*" he roared.

The entire room stilled.

And it was a vast room.

Because never, ever had I heard Ian raise his voice. Not ever. Definitely not in anger.

"It's out. Do something else," Ian decreed.

And then he prowled through the huge room with five sets of female eyes on him the whole way, disappearing up the stairs to what had been Smithie's office, but now it was mostly Ian who used it.

When he was gone, I hummed, "Ummmmm…"

"What's wrong with Ian?" Hattie asked.

Ryn was too far away, so she didn't hear Hattie's question, thus her, "What's up his ass?" was semi-yelled at us.

I was watching Lottie.

"Lots, do you know?" I queried.

She was looking over her shoulder, pushed up so she could see over the back of the booth.

She settled in and aimed her eyes at me.

"No clue. But I don't like it," she said.

"Me either," Hattie agreed.

I returned my attention to where Ian had disappeared.

"Maybe give him a minute to calm down and then we can go talk to him?" Hattie suggested.

That was a good idea.

But I caught Lots shaking her head.

"He's always there for us," Hattie remarked. "It isn't cool if something's going down with him and we're not there for him."

"We also need to give the man the chance to have an off day without four bitches getting in his shit about it," Lottie replied.

"I didn't mean get in his shit," Hattie pointed out.

"I'm all about getting in his shit."

We all looked to the end of the catwalk to see Ryn had joined us.

"We're not getting in his shit," I declared.

"He didn't yell at you and tell you that you couldn't do a super-fly rope dance," Ryn returned.

"True enough," I muttered.

"All I'm saying is," Lottie cut in, "we need to let him have some space. He lets us be real. We need to let him be real. If it seems like something's up with him that's not just a bad day, we'll reconvene."

I could agree with that, so I did.

But I wasn't a big fan of it.

Because Ian hadn't seemed right when I was talking to him in the back hall earlier either.

So, okay, that "earlier" was only maybe ten minutes ago.

Still, this was way out of character. There was no way I'd known Ian for years and he hadn't had a bad day in that time. He just didn't shout at anyone.

So that meant this bad day was a *bad* day, and I didn't want him to think we didn't give a shit.

But I had to admit, he was a man who struck me as someone who would want some space if things weren't great.

So I could give him that.

For now.

CHAPTER FOURTEEN
Unless I'm Around

PEPPER

This was what happened between Ian being icky to Ryn at Smithie's and now.

Now being Sunday morning and I was all ready and sitting at my desk waiting for Auggie to show for our date, which was going to last all day (and night?).

And I was beside myself with glee, not only about the upcoming date.

But also about what happened in the time from Ian being icky to now.

And most importantly, that I'd thought we'd done pretty well practicing restraint, so I was all in to stop practicing that and start doing something a whole lot different.

Even better?

Auggie had indicated he was too.

* * *

It began with more texts.

> Weird time at rehearsal.
> Ian yelled at Ryn.

Why'd he do that?

> She's doing an aerial dance.
> And he saw her fall off the
> rope. So he said she couldn't
> do it.

Can't say I don't agree with him.

> Aug! Srsly?

Yes. Seriously.

> It was going to be awesome.

Now it's gonna be safe.

> We're professionals.

I didn't say you weren't. And
don't get pissed at me, Ryn
is great. But she isn't Cirque
du Soleil.

He had me there.

> It's still weird Ian got so
> pissed. I've never heard
> him raise his voice.

When a woman you care about
takes a header, you react.

OMG!

What?

I hadn't thought about that.
We're all pretty tight with
Ian. I could so totally see
how he was upset that
she went splat on the mat.

You need to hang around me
more, baby.

Agreed.
Though I don't know why
you said that in the current
context.

So you'll have more
practice understanding
the way a man reacts and
you'll get with the program.

Ugh.

I texted "ugh."

But I so totally wanted more practice understanding the way a
man (primarily, Auggie) reacted.

More, I really dug having something happen at work, and

then I could text someone who knew the players, and we could talk about it.

For sure, I had my girls. I could, and we did, talk about everything.

It was just nice to have a man, a partner, someone in my life, to talk to about stuff.

No.

It was nice it was Auggie.

Splat on the mat?

Cirque du Soleil?

Are you dissing the Cirque?

**No. Just surprised at
your reference.**

Have you been to a show?

No.

**Weekend away. Vegas and
a show.**

I am SO there.

There was a lot more of that all day, through the evening, and Auggie demanded I text him when I got home so it went into the night. Because when I got home, we continued it until I was in bed and it was time for us both to crash.

*   *   *

The next day, I didn't wake when my phone binged with his text. But when I did wake, the first thing I did was check my phone to see if he sent one.

He did.

Text when you're up.

This I did.

He didn't respond.

Not for an hour and a half.

And yes, I was timing it.

Then, after I'd finished meditating, journaling and was in the kitchen doing my breakfast dishes and pouring my second cup of coffee, the doorbell rang.

This was not unusual in our 'hood. A social development meant anyone could show at any time in need of something or just to chat.

Thus, I didn't hesitate.

I wandered to the door with my coffee cup wearing a pair of brightly patterned sleep shorts and a chunky, cropped sweater.

I looked through one of the windows beside the door and saw Aug standing there.

So, obviously, I threw open the door.

"Hey!" I peeped.

His eyes went down, they came up, and he growled, "Get rid of the coffee."

I froze for half a second before I whirled and ran to the stairs.

I set the mug down on a step, turned, and he was on me.

We made out and we made out some more and we groped and made out even more.

When I had my hand closing in on his package, he captured my wrist, pulled it around to the small of my back and stopped kissing me senseless.

I came out of the fog slowly, and when I focused on his eyes, he whispered, "Morning, sweetheart."

Okay.

That was about 57,897 times better than a good morning text.

And then he said, "Now I gotta get back to work. Have a good day."

After that, he'd given my ass a squeeze (because that was where his hand was) and walked right to the door.

Yes, that was what I said.

He'd come to me.

He'd pounced on me.

And then...

He walked right to the door.

I stood there with hard nipples and more than one set of flushed, swollen, quivering lips and lied, "I hate you."

He turned in the door he'd opened, winked at me, then he closed it behind him.

Hot.

Annoying and frustrating.

But still so freaking totally *hot.*

To his first text to me a couple of hours later, I responded with:

> **I'm so totally not talking
> to you.**

Why not?
☺

Yes!

He ended that with a smiley face!

Because you're a tease.

I worried he wouldn't take that right, considering our history. So I added:

**Of note: I'm not talking to
you, but if you wanted to
come over and make out,
I'm down with that.**

☺   ☺   ☺

Yes. Three smiley faces.
But he didn't come over and make out.
It was Friday, my day on the go. Laundry. Cleaning the house. Getting to the grocery store. Generally preparing for that golden moment that would be Monday afternoon when my baby would be back home.
And I suspected Auggie was busy too, because after his smileys, which I let sit for a while, I'd asked if he might want to grab a quick bite on Saturday before I had to go to work, but he hadn't answered quickly.
However, with spooky synchronicity, his next text came in right on top of one from Corbin.

**Juno and Patrick were here
last night. They aren't tonight.**

By "here," that meant Auggie was at the school on a Friday night building sets for the Thanksgiving show of a kid he didn't know all that well.
And Corbin was wherever Corbin was, texting me:

Do you have any free time this
weekend? I'll get a sitter for Juno.
We have to talk.

I ditched the texting and phoned Auggie.

"Hey," he answered.

"Corbin isn't there?" I asked.

"No," he confirmed.

"He's texting me, telling me we need to meet this weekend and talk."

"Do you want to do that?"

"No."

"Are you gonna do that?"

"No."

"Should you think about that?"

"No."

"Pepper—"

"Auggie, I told you, it's not happening."

"I know, but maybe you need to be as clear with him as you are with me so he'll move on."

"First, he won't move on until he understands with a clarity I can't give him with just words and then he'll be an ass for a while, he'll probably go cold and man-pout for a while and then maybe, if all the stars in the universe properly align, he might get over it."

"What's second?" Auggie asked.

And honest to God, I loved that he did.

Not only because I was ranting and most men didn't prompt a woman to rant on, but also he was keeping track of what I was saying enough to know I had a list (doing this while I was ranting).

"Second is that I feel the need to calm down a bit after discovering that Corbin feigned interest in something at Juno's school only as an opportunity to make some play with me. And now he's out. Mr. Sykes seemed to have some capable volunteers helping, so Corbin not showing probably isn't a loss. Though obviously you are by far the most capable, seeing as you can not only wield a hammer, if there was an imminent threat of attack, you could get everyone to safety and capture the bad guys so the police could have an easy night."

Auggie started chuckling.

I finished, "But you don't pitch up for your daughter and then ditch. It isn't cool."

"You're right, it isn't."

I tried to stay calm and not fume.

"Is there a third?" Auggie asked.

"No."

"Can I say yes now to grabbing some food before you go to work tomorrow?"

That made me smile.

"Yes."

"I'd want more time tomorrow, baby. But things are busy, and I have something to do for work. I'll be done in time to take you to an early dinner, though. Cool?"

"Absolutely."

"It only reflects on him. Not you. Not Juno."

He was back to talking about Corbin.

"I know, but I don't want her disappointed."

"Okay, I didn't want to say anything to worry you, because she handled it great. But she was obviously torn last night, Pepper. She wanted to hang with me. She wanted to hang with her dad. He and I steered clear of each other. She hung with her dad, but she kept smiling and waving at me, like she wanted to be sure I knew she was grateful I was there. Patrick let her give me a hug hello and one good-bye, but it wasn't a mellow sitch. Do you know what I mean?"

"Now there's *totally* a third. Because I'm also not meeting up with Corbin so I don't poke his eyes out or kick him in the groin."

"Probably a good call," Auggie murmured, sounding amused.

"She does appreciate that you're there. And I do too, Auggie. Please know that. It's incredibly sweet you're spending your nights doing that."

And then he did it.

He said it.

He...said...*it*.

And what he said was, "Pepper, for there to be an us, we all need to be an *us*. If this works, where I am now will be part of the territory. Now, I could either be at home, watching TV or out for a drink with one of the guys, both scenarios wishing I was spending the evening with you. Or I could be here, doing something that means something to Juno. I pick door number three."

See?

Totally *it!*

"I...am...*so*...jumping you the next time I see you. Don't *even* think of trying another teasy sneak attack. If I have to tackle you to the floor, I'm paying you back for being so awesome."

"Paying me back by tackling me to the floor?"

"To give you an orgasm."

"Right."

That was totally amused.

I was totally tackling him.

But for now...

"Say goodnight, Auggie."

"Goodnight, baby. Text when you get home safe from work."

"Will do."

And I did.

* * *

Saturday didn't start off stellar because I had set that day aside to use the information Auggie gave me to reach out to my brother.

Also, Aug was busy with work, so even though I got my morning text from him asking me to connect when I woke up, and I did, and he sent an *xx* ☺ in return, he was obviously busy because that was all I got from him.

Which I was taking as good, the universe telling me it was the perfect shot, a clear schedule with errands run and a tidy house and Auggie working, to focus on connecting with my brother for the first time in over a decade. Doing this knowing what kind of man he'd become and having the news I had about our mother to share with him.

Not incidentally, Mom was still putting me off. I'd phoned, texted, reached out to both Dad and Saffron, offered to meet her for coffee, lunch, whatever she wanted.

It was Saffron who said they'd be in touch about the prayer circle and asked if I'd heard anything about Birch.

I had prevaricated about Birch *and* the prayer circle.

This had caused Saffron to woman-pout, which meant she hadn't picked up a call or returned a text since. And that had happened on Wednesday.

Such was dealing with my family.

Which led me to fortifying myself with a good long journaling session (that included me listing more than three things I was grateful for, but Auggie was in my life, so that came easy) and a cup of my favorite tea.

I sat cross-legged dead center of the couch.

And I called my brother.

I was a nervous wreck.

He answered on the third ring, "Yeah?"

"Birch?"

A hesitation, then, "Who's this?"

"It's Pepper."

Silence.

"Birch, listen—"

"How did you get this number?"

Uh...

That was it?

Twelve years I hadn't spoken to him and it was *How did you get this number?*

"Birch—"

"Pepper, how'd you fuckin' get my cell number?" he demanded.

"Mom's got cancer."

Another silence, longer, far more loaded.

"Birch—"

He again cut me off.

"Bet they're not doin' dick. Bet they're dousin' her with holy water or some shit and watchin' her waste away."

He wasn't far off.

"They tried treatment," I told him. "It didn't work."

"Well, fuckin' A. There is a God. 'Cause that's a miracle."

"Birch—"

Again, he interrupted me.

"So, what? They want you to get in touch with me to ask me to fuck a goat covered in sheep's blood or some shit and then they'll use my cum as some sort of miracle ointment?"

Ho...

Lee.

Hell.

I mean, I'd noted the reasons I wasn't fond of my family's church.

But they'd never been *that* weird.

"I moved out when I was eighteen," I informed him curtly. "I'm not in the church. I haven't been for ten years. But I still keep in touch with our family. And please remember, you're talking to your sister so maybe keep your cum out of it."

"You moved out?"

"The minute I could. But now, I'm twenty-eight, so of course. Still, you know me. Or you did. You think I'd stay?"

He went quiet again.

I didn't fill the silence that time.

Until he said, "Listen, Pepper—"

But I was through with my big brother.

And I shared that.

"No, see, the thing is, I have a man in my life who's obviously also a son and he doesn't get along great with his parents, including his mom, but he told me he'd want to know if she was sick. And I thought, my brother, Birch, was a great brother. He tried to be a good son, but they didn't make it easy on him. But he was a great brother. And he'd probably want to know. So now you know. And you can do what you want with it. They built a new church. It's big. It's probably got a website. If you want to get in touch with them, Dad's still a deacon. Call the church. And have a good life, Birch."

"Pepper!" he bit.

But I hung up.

And I didn't block him.

But I didn't answer when he called back three times.

Because...

Twelve years since he'd left me with them, and all that happened in between, and it was *how did you get this number* and some bullshit about his cum?

Fuck that.

*　*　*

"So, fuck that."

Yep.

That was what I announced to Auggie, standing by the stairs in my hall after I'd barely let him in my house to pick me up to take me out to dinner that night.

He'd given me a "Hey" and a sexy look.

I had not tackled him.

No.

I'd launched in about my call to Birch.

"Okay, honey, it's done," Auggie replied. "Over. You did the right thing and now it's his to do with whatever he's gonna do with it."

"Yeah," I agreed.

And then I burst into tears.

I was in Auggie's arms and a few seconds later we were sitting on my couch and I was nearly in his lap.

Still bawling.

"God, I can't have puffy eyes and dance," I snapped, pulling away (but not too far away, Auggie smelled good and felt better). I did this so I could swipe at my face.

"We'll get you a cold cloth when you're done."

"Is my makeup a mess?"

He didn't answer.

It was a mess.

"Shit!" I hissed, moving to push away from him so I could hit the powder room and fix my face.

"Babe," he called, grabbing both my wrists so I couldn't get away.

I stopped moving and looked at him.

"Cry. Shout. Throw shit. I don't care," he invited. "You're dealing with some serious heavy."

I totally was.

"I like you," I blurted.

His head jerked with surprise, then his lips tipped up at the ends.

"I hope so, because I like you too."

"What I mean is, I'm together. Juno and me, we have it going on. Normally, I'm totally laidback. With it. But you're not seeing that. I don't want you to think, you waited so long, now we're doing this, and I'm a mess. Crying. Ranting. Freaking. My family's in a cult. My ex is a douchebag. My brother is a felon and a wife beater. I'm not perfect. But I'm also not this."

"No, you're not *this*, Pepper. Did you just hear yourself? Your *family* is in a cult. Your *ex* is an asshole."

I'd said douchebag.

But...

"Your *brother* is a felon," he went on, letting my wrists go and gliding his arms around me again. "You're none of that. You're just reacting to their shit. It isn't you. I want *you*. Their shit is their shit, but a relationship isn't worth dick if the two people in it don't stick together through good and through bad. Now, you got some bad, that doesn't mean *you're* bad. It just means we gotta get you through the bad."

I glared at him.

Then I stated, "Seriously, if we don't have sex soon, it's gonna kill me."

He busted out laughing.

I felt a whole lot better hearing and watching that.

When he sobered, he shared, "There are other ways to pay me back for being awesome."

"I didn't say you were awesome," I noted (at least I didn't say it this time). "I said I want to have sex with you. You've inferred the awesome. Though I will note, I was inferring that too."

He started chuckling, and said, "Thanks for that correction. But I still want to get my point across that another way to pay me back is never do anything like that again, unless I'm around."

I wasn't following.

"Anything like what?" I asked.

"Anything like calling your brother."

I sat nearly in his lap, in his arms, looking into his eyes, and it felt like blues and turquoises and purples were swirling around in the air, edging out the grays and yellows and oranges that I'd lived with so long, I no longer noticed were there.

In other words, tranquility, protection and wisdom were edging out gloominess, instability, sluggishness.

I had my daughter.

I had my girlfriends.

But in truth—and it was not buried, it was not hidden, it was right in front of me every single day—I knew I was alone. I was the one who was responsible. I was the one who had to take care of myself, my daughter, our health, our home, our happiness.

I could do it alone.

But it was lonely.

Good God.

Auggie *was* my mountain.

"Pepper?" he called.

I had tears welling in my eyes again when I focused on him.

"Baby," he said softly.

"Thank you for that," I replied just as softly.

"You're welcome, and I think something big is happening right now, I'm just not sure what it is. You wanna tell me?"

I shook my head.

I was edging the line of crazy brand-new girlfriend you might need your head examined for seeing. I didn't need to explain how he was my mountain.

Obviously, I couldn't share that.

So I told him the second reason why I didn't want to get into it.

"Can we not do any more heavy? Just for now?"

He nodded his head. "If that's what you need, definitely."

Of course he'd say that and let it go.

Totally my mountain.

I pulled in a deep breath to settle my emotions and then suggested, "Let's go get something to eat, you hungry?"

"How about I go grab something and bring it back?"

"Is my makeup that bad?"

He gave me a small smile. "No. I just want you to feel in a safe place."

God.

He *was* awesome.

"I'd actually rather kick back," I admitted. "So let's go out together and get something to bring back."

Aug got out of my couch immediately, pulling me with him.

So that answered that.

My guy was hungry.

After a brief discussion in his car, we went to Mad Greens, because we both liked it, and it wouldn't be heavy in my stomach before I had to dance.

We were back at my island, shoving food in our mouths, when I shared my new plan about how to deal with my mom.

"So, I'll actually go to their old place, because for me it'll make it real, the fact my family moved without telling me they moved. But it'll also make it somewhat authentic even when I lie and say I went to their old place to visit them and found out they didn't live there. That way, they'll have to tell me they moved to the church. And the occasion is extreme, considering it's been over a week since I learned my mother is ill, and naturally, I want to see her. So it won't seem like I'm being weird, showing up unannounced when I haven't been 'home,' as it were, in years."

Auggie studiously shoved rice, veg and chicken slathered in yummy dressing into his mouth.

What he did not do was look at or respond to me.

Great.

"What?" I asked.

That was when he looked at me.

"Okay, since your day hasn't been that great and shit keeps coming at you, I'll do this fast."

Crap.

"Reverend Clyde is either a bona fide nutcase, a con man, or both," Auggie continued. "His history is hinky and convoluted, but it seems he's setting himself up for a cushy retirement. Info is still coming in on him, and that church. But what we have so far, I'd advise you not to get anywhere near it."

I decided to start closer to the beginning of all of that.

"What's hinky and convoluted mean?"

"He's had three different names, three different identities, two churches. Though, before he hit his second identity, he was involved in another situation. Not a church, a commune where it looks like he got some of his ideas. Particularly men having multiple partners and the general subjugation of women. And when he's left behind identities, he's left behind wives and kids. He did this when it was out with the old, in with the new because things got hot for him."

Okay.

Yes.

That was hinky and convoluted.

"What does hot mean?" I asked.

"Hot means he's practicing bigamy and that's illegal. And he delivered one of his own children, and he has no medical training. The child was lost, and the mother almost didn't make it."

"Holy hell," I breathed.

"I already told you, there's money tied up in all of this, a lot of it. There's also property. It's fishy, Pepper. We've been attempting to set up some surveillance of the actual church and the higher-ups who run it, namely Clyde, but predictably, it's been difficult to get a safe in. There's always someone around and they're watchful. Exceptionally watchful, which tells its own story. It's strategically undesirable to push it, and maybe tip our hand that we're nosing around in their business, because we sense he's going to make a break from it soon. And the way he has things set up, he's golden. The church, though, will be fucked."

And it didn't get any better.

"Now what does that mean?" I queried.

He took in a deep breath, and since he'd been offering me some unfun info, the fact he had to take a deep breath before what he was about to say didn't make me super happy.

Then he shared, "I got the bulk of this information today, and considering how your day has gone, I decided to sit on it. But now were talking about it."

We sure were.

"So," he carried on, "it means the church is mortgaged to the hilt and in debt. Nothing is paid off. Not the building. Not the furnishings. Not the equipment or vehicles. This is the case, even though they have access to millions of dollars that could easily pay it all off. And Higgins personally has access to all that money. So he could wipe them all out and go live in his big house in Utah, or his luxury condo in Florida, and leave them with a mountain of debt."

Although that wasn't awesome, I didn't know why he took a big breath before he shared that, and not before he shared that Reverend Clyde had a hand in the death of his own child.

Therefore, I asked, "Why would I care about this?"

"Because the deacons are the cosigners for the loans. Reverend Clyde isn't personally responsible for dick."

There it was.

And it was worth a big freaking breath.

"Oh my God," I whispered.

"Yeah."

"Dad?"

He nodded.

I couldn't believe this.

"How could he be so stupid?" I asked a question Auggie couldn't answer.

So he didn't, he just shook his head.

"This is..." I couldn't finish.

Auggie could.

"Fucked up?"

I stared down at my food, my appetite having vamoosed.

"It's his bed, Pepper. He made it. Like you said, this has nothing to do with you."

I looked to Auggie. "My sister is recruiting for this guy. My father is a leader in that church. When Reverend Clyde takes off, everyone is going to look at them when they're left holding the bag."

"Yes," he agreed simply.

Yes.

I stared at him.

And that was it.

Yes, all I said was true.

But that "yes" Auggie said meant something else too.

It wasn't my thing. It had nothing to do with me. With Juno.

It was simple.

My family made their bed.

And I'd made mine.

"We're working to gather evidence that, if you want—" Auggie started.

Nope.

No more.

"You're off duty, honey."

His thick, gorgeous brows drew down over his deep-set, hooded, equally gorgeous eyes.

"Say again?"

"My mom has cancer," I stated. "If it'll bring her peace, I'll sit in a prayer circle. Since it means something to her, when I don't have Juno, I'll attend their services. That's all I can do because that's all they're allowing me to do. If she reaches out for more, I'll do what I can for her. If Saffron or Dad need me in a way I can give myself to them, I will. But this..." I shook my head. "It's too messy. I'm done. And so are you."

"You don't want to warn them?" he asked.

"Oh, I'll warn them," I told him. "I'll talk to Dad. But I have to time that right, Auggie. Because if he's in denial, or if he gets mad, he can cut me off from Mom. I mean, do I save him and Saffron from themselves? Or do I do my best to give my mother as much peace and comfort as I can while she's going through this?"

"You look out for your mom."

I nodded. "And if the timing isn't right, and Reverend Clyde takes off before..."

I swallowed.

Auggie gave me the time I needed.

I took it and kept going, "...whatever is going to happen with Mom, then that's just really bad luck."

"Babe—" he began.

But I shook my head and leaned to him to touch my mouth to his.

When I pulled away, I said, "Honestly, this is a relief. A relief *and* a release. It's validation that I knew something was not right with where they'd put their faith. It's the universe confirming what I knew. That I'd made the right decision getting out of there. It exonerates me from the duty of getting too deeply involved in a situation I know won't be healthy for me, which eventually will mean it's not healthy for my daughter. And every line bottoms with Juno. They're adults. They lost a son and daughter, a brother and sister, to that church, picking it above their family. We all have to own our decisions. Including them."

"If you change your mind..." He let that trail.

"I'll let you know," I assured.

"You know that offer's open, but I gotta tell you that I think you've made the right decision about this and your brother. You did what you could do, sweetheart. You did more than many people who were pushed into your place would do. And now, it's not on you."

"I'm glad you agree."

"I don't have to agree."

"I'm still glad that you do."

That hit Auggie in a way that meant something, I saw the hit land.

Then he gave me a movie-star smile and I got him leaning to me and touching his lips to mine.

Obviously, my appetite returned, so I turned to my bowl and said, "Enough about me. How was your day, honey?"

He didn't answer me, so, after I shoved my own spinach, rice, chicken and yummy dressing in my mouth, I looked at him.

To see him grinning at me.

"It was great," he said. "It ended with you."

I swallowed and cried, "Oh my God! Stop being awesome!"

And Auggie started laughing.

* * *

So yeah, it sucked that we didn't have time for a snog session after that. I had to get to work. He told me he was wiped, and he needed to get some shut-eye.

But we did the whole me-texting-when-I-got-home, him-texting-a-good-morning thing.

And now it was ten.

Auggie said he had our day planned, but it was a surprise what we were going to do.

Though, he'd also said we were going to end it at his house, "And bring a toothbrush."

Which sounded insanely promising.

It was my first of two days off. Tomorrow my baby would be back to me.

In other words, it was going to be two days of goodness.

And I was ready to roll.

What I was not ready for was to shoot from my desk to open

the door after I watched Aug drive up, park and walk up my front walk, and have Auggie, who had not even made it up the steps, bite out, "Grab your purse. We gotta hit it."

"What?" I asked.

"Lottie, Ryn and Hattie are right now at services at the Tabernacle of the True Light. And if we don't get to them before Mo, Boone and Axl, shit is gonna get real."

Holy.

Hell.

CHAPTER FIFTEEN

Bastard of the Church

PEPPER

I was pretty displeased I had to race up the stairs to change out of my fabulous sweater, distressed skinny jeans, and sexy, high-heeled booties and into my pullover, slouchy, oversized sweater dress that had a turtleneck and was a heathered tawny shade.

I was displeased because the dress was slouchy and oversized, but it still managed to be sexy (because that was the way of sweater dresses, it was mystical, magical and you didn't question it).

It was especially sexy when I paired it with my chocolate-suede, thigh-high boots (which I had no choice but to do, even if the heel was high and thin and not within the dress code for females at the Tabernacle of the True Light—still, I had to do something to cover up the skin from mid-thigh down, which, hint, considering the dress had a high hem, was part of why it was sexy).

That said, the dress was not casual, ready-for-anything-day-with-Auggie, and although it would be a lot easier for him to take it off (eventually and hopefully), I'd pored over my apparel selections that day and a slouchy sweater dress was not the "I'm ready for anything!" as well as "Take me I'm yours!" look I was going for.

Alas, I had to save the girls because they didn't know what they were doing.

And Reverend Clyde was hinky and convoluted, and if he was alerted to the fact that the cat was out of the bag as to his very long con, he might clean them out and take off faster than he'd planned.

Now, I didn't want the man screwing over my dad and leaving him responsible for a shit ton of debt at all.

But since that was probably out of my hands, if I had my druthers, if I couldn't stop it, he'd do that at a time my mother wasn't counting on a prayer circle she undoubtedly hoped Reverend Clyde would lead to cure her cancer.

Auggie didn't have the memo about church-wear and as such was wearing a pair of army-green pants with a white tee, over which was a blue button-down (that was unbuttoned). A brown-banded, bulky, sporty watch interfered in a cool way with the cuff of his left sleeve.

He looked fantastic.

And if memory served, the men at church wore slightly more dressy clothes than Auggie had on, but they weren't expected to be as formal as the women were.

But Auggie's outfit was a smidge under what was the norm.

I felt this meant I had to go in alone.

Therefore, when we were in his SUV and on our way, I said to Aug, "Since you're not dressed for church, I'll run in, find them, have a word, and get them out."

"The fuck you will."

Surprised at his response, not just the words, but also the tone, I turned my head his way.

"Sorry?"

"Will your family be there?"

"Indubitably."

There was a tightness to his cheekbones, and at my word, he sucked in his lips like he was distributing ChapStick, and when he stopped doing that, they quirked.

"Indubitably?" he asked.

"Yup," I answered.

"You're not going in alone, Pepper."

"They're not going to grab me, wall me up in their compound and Patty Hearst me," I pointed out.

He glanced at me then said quietly to the road, "Baby, take a second and let what I'm gonna say next sink in, okay?"

Oh man.

"Okay," I agreed.

"Your mom is gonna be there."

My body tightened.

Of course she was.

I hadn't thought about that.

And of course again.

Because Auggie did.

"And this is the gig," he went on. "Shit like this, I'm not gonna let you go it alone. Are you understanding what I'm saying?"

Oh yeah.

I thought I did the last time.

I'd even had a moment because of it.

But definitely this time I did.

"Yes, Auggie."

"I said this yesterday, at least I thought I did, and you just said you were going in alone. So just to make sure, do you *really* understand what I'm saying?"

Mm-hmm.

I *really* understood what he was saying.

I wasn't going in alone...

Because I wasn't alone.

"Yes, honey," I whispered.

He lifted his hand palm up between us and demanded, "Hand."

I placed mine in his.

His fingers closed around, he brought them to his chest and pressed them in, the back of mine to his t-shirt.

It was then it hit me.

It was likely I was going to see my mom.

It also hit me I knew how deep the shit was that my dad was in.

And it hit me that I'd spoken to my brother, and I'd told him about Mom, and he might reach out. And since a day had passed, he could have already done that.

Last, it hit me Auggie knew all this when I hadn't thought about any of it.

And as this hit me, reflexively, my fingers tightened around his.

He brought my hand to his lips, touched it there, then dropped it to his thigh, still holding it in his.

We were quiet until we reached the street that led to True Light.

Me, because I was gearing up for what was to come.

Auggie, I sensed, because he was giving me space to gear up.

I didn't remain silent when we got close to the church.

This because there was a one, two, three of Mo's big black Ram truck, Boone's shiny black Charger and Axl's graphite Jeep parked on the side of the street.

And on the sidewalk there was the one, two, three strike of Mo with hands on his hips, Boone with his arms crossed on his chest, and Axl leaning one hand to the hood of his Jeep, his other hand fisted at his waist.

And all their eyes watched us come up the road.

Upon seeing them this way, coupled with the expressions on their faces, I made a mental note never to make a crew of commandos unhappy.

Thus, I broke our silence with an entirely appropriate, "Oh shit."

Auggie didn't respond but he did slow to a stop across from them and slid down his side window.

"We're going right in," he told them.

"Tell Hattie I moved her car from the parking lot and she's to walk her ass directly to me," Axl ordered.

I pressed my lips together, which for some reason made my eyes bug open.

This was partially to stop myself from laughing, and partially to stop myself from speaking, because Hattie was shy, and she was cute, and she was definitely the girlie-est of our bunch.

But even if she'd let her dad shit all over her (families), she'd never let a man do it.

Not that Axl was shitting all over her, but he was being hella bossy, and I wasn't sure Hatz would be down with that.

I mean, sure, the women were going gung-ho with this on my behalf (and because Lottie wanted in on some action). And yes, that was unnecessary at this juncture (even if they didn't know that, I hadn't updated them about my new take on the situation).

But like I'd said to Auggie, they weren't in any real danger.

So I wasn't sure hella bossy was the way for these boys to play it.

"And since Hattie's their ride, Ryn and Lottie best be following her," Boone decreed.

Hmm.

I kept my lips pressed together, because even if Ryn was of a certain sexual bent (and Boone was of the opposite bent, but the two so totally fit together), she one hundred percent was not a woman who liked a man bossing her (in that way, *ahem*).

Aug gave them a nod, hit the accelerator and slid his window up.

"You do know that we're going to need to finesse that because the girls aren't going to be big fans of the guys being bossy and overprotective," I muttered.

"What I know is that any situation is entirely unknown, and

you go into it that way. You can think you have all the intel you'll need. You can think you planned your operation down to the minutest detail. And you can always be taken by surprise and your shit will be in a sling you're unprepared to get it out of. That's what I know. And that's what those men know. So, baby, I'm warning you. They fucked up, nosing into this. So I'm not finessing shit."

And there was a reminder we had not yet gotten into his job.

Now was not that time.

Now was the time for me to mumble, "All righty then."

"Not to make this any more difficult," Aug continued. "People believe the same thing for different reasons. But have you considered the fact that, since she was young, someone has been Patty Hearsting your sister?"

Shit.

It was beginning to get low-key annoying that he seemed to have it totally together and knew practically everything.

Low-key annoying as well as ridiculously appealing.

Whiplash.

I decided my best response was, "Ummm…"

"So…yeah," he finished.

Yeah.

We parked in the big church parking lot, which was pretty full.

So yeah again, Auggie's intel was correct.

They had way more members than they used to.

We got out, and even if I was in high heels, we hoofed it quickly to the front doors.

We did this holding hands.

Aug was a hand-holder.

Totally old-fashioned.

This time, I didn't mention it.

This time, I stayed silent as Auggie pushed open the doors and went in first, still holding my hand, and I followed him.

We got out of the crisp but sunny November day and our eyes adjusted to the vestibule of the sanctuary, which was spacious, but my father had not lied.

High-wearing, utilitarian, commercial carpeting in dark gray covered the floor. All around, bare walls painted midnight blue. Very narrow windows that let in the light, but not a sliver of stained glass to be seen. There were some cheap-looking standing lamps to chase the shadows from the corners. And on the middle wall that separated the two sets of now-closed double doors that obviously led into the sanctuary, there was a not-so-great, but kinda large artist's rendition of that very church.

Other than a few uninviting wooden benches sitting at some walls, that was it.

Definitely none of the ostentation of some of the bigger churches that had television or social media followings. Or, frankly, any of the loyally collected and scrupulously cared for décor of any other church I'd been to.

It was bare bones.

Aug didn't linger to check it out.

He led me to one of the sets of double doors and then he led me right through.

Whoa.

It was *huge*.

And obviously some people were carpooling.

There had to be several hundred people in there.

Doing a visual sweep, I noted another surprise.

It was mostly men.

Now, how did these men think they were going to get themselves multiple wives if their fellow parishioners were also dudes?

Reverend Clyde, with his narrow shoulders covered in white robes and his high, greasy, signature pompadour that was silver-threaded-through-black up top, full silver at the sides (totes vampiric), was pontificating from an equally bare-bones pulpit at the front. And the room was so huge, only those closest to us turned and looked, probably because the ones beyond hadn't noted our entry.

Auggie ignored them.

I gave them an *I'm sorry we disturbed* look, because it was a loopy church, but it was still a church.

Aug was scanning, no doubt for Lottie's distinctive head of big blonde hair.

I was scanning for something else.

He found what he was looking for first, and out we went through the doors we'd walked in, across the front of the painting, and in the next set of doors.

Down the aisle.

And using my hand, he shoved me in first as Hattie, who was at the end of the pew, looked up, startled.

Ryn and Lottie looked up too.

Ryn didn't hide her surprise.

Lottie visibly sighed.

They all scooched as we pushed in.

"Sorry," I whispered to anyone disrupted in our general area.

Auggie didn't say anything.

Once I got my ass to a pew, Lottie did.

She leaned forward and rapped out, "Who had the big mouth? Mo?"

I didn't reply because I didn't know, but even if I did, and it was Mo, I wouldn't say anything because I adored Mo and I didn't want to get him into trouble.

I shrugged.

Auggie, sitting next to me, leaned forward too. "Get your shit. We're leaving."

I counted three gasps in our vicinity, undoubtedly due to his use of the word "shit."

Though, it could be because we were continuing to talk.

"I'm not going," Lottie declared.

"I'm not either," Ryn said.

But I'd lost interest in them because I felt it.

I looked toward the front of the church.

There were three sets of rows of pews angled back with a view to the pulpit, the center one the longest, two aisles cutting through the collective.

We were halfway back, left of middle.

And at the end in the front row of the set of pews at the left, my father was turned and looking at me.

I'd gotten his hair.

I'd also gotten my mother's eyes.

He was almost entirely gray now, but in his forties, his blond had darkened with age and I'd wondered if mine would too.

He was tall and straight and lean, like me.

And he was handsome and retained some of that to this day.

I tore my eyes from him and saw a head of silvery-white hair dutifully contained in a bun next to him.

My mom.

She'd been dark and had started to go silver in her late thirties, the white came through in her forties.

And next to her, a blonde and two brunettes.

No white. No silver. No gray in those heads of hair.

Shining and declaring their youth without seeing their faces.

My father's wives.

"Oh my God, I'm going to fucking kill him," I whispered.

More gasps, a sharp "*Shh!*" a whispered, "Oh my goodness," and Hattie reaching to my knee and squeezing it.

"Let's go," Auggie growled.

"Are you okay?" Hattie asked.

Either we were making a ruckus, my mother sensed me, or she noticed my father had not turned back around, because slowly, *painstakingly slowly*, she looked over her shoulder.

And my world fell out from under me.

I made a very loud noise of shock and sorrow.

People turned to look.

"We're leaving," Auggie clipped.

He still had my hand in his and he used it to pull me up and out of the pew.

I sensed my friends getting up with us, but even if Auggie was tugging me toward the door, I was resisting.

Because my mom was a living skeleton.

She was a breathing horror show.

Sags of skin dripping on her face.

Innumerable deep wrinkles lining her mouth.

Her wispy, silver-white hair controlled by the bun at the back but framing her face.

She was a character from a haunted house.

And she was fifty-four years old.

There wasn't even a nuance of my mom left, and if I wasn't seeing the vestiges of my eyes and the memory of her thick head of hair, I wouldn't have recognized her.

Panicked, my mind harked back, trying to place the time I last saw her.

It wasn't that long ago.

A month.

Maybe six weeks.

I'd thought she'd lost a little weight.

She'd come to that in six weeks.

For some reason, my eyes swung right, to the front of the center set of pews, and I saw several women looking back at me.

A few older.

The rest younger.

My sister with her soon-to-be sister-wives.

"Baby, let's go," Auggie said in my ear.

"If we could please have everyone take their seats," Reverend Clyde requested over what sounded like a very high-quality audio system.

Bargain basement pews.

Bargain basement carpet.

But you sure could hear Clyde in every corner of that big room.

"Pez, honey, let's get out of here," Lottie urged from close.

I looked from Saffron to Dad.

He was now standing, fully facing me.

I did not look at my mother.

"Yes," I called loudly down the aisle to him. "You better damn well follow me."

More gasps, some shocked murmuring, but I turned, pulled free of Auggie, and stomped toward the doors.

They all followed me.

I got to the vestibule and started pacing.

"I don't think now is the—" Ryn.

"Okay, maybe we shouldn't have—" Hattie.

"Hey, hey, hey, look at me," Lottie said from right in front of me, stopping my pacing with her proximity and her hand on my cheek.

I looked down at her. "She's wasting away."

I felt Aug get close to my back.

Lottie's face got soft, her mouth turned down, and her thumb slid across the apple of my cheek.

The door to the sanctuary opened and my father appeared.

I turned on him.

Lottie's hand fell away.

Aug didn't move an inch from me.

"Excellent foresight, Dad, lining up a young harem for when the old model fades away," I snapped sarcastically.

I felt Auggie's hand slide from the small of my back to wrap around the side of my waist.

Dad moved closer to us, hissing, "I cannot *believe* you showed during services, causing a scene."

"And I cannot *believe* I have three *stepmoms*. Do I have more brothers and sisters? Considering your wives' ages, should I get in touch with Santa? Make sure I get access to my baby bros' and sisses' lists for Christmas?"

Dad had stopped a few feet away. "You decided not to be a part of our lives, so you aren't. It's only your mother who wants you in the fold. If it wasn't for her, I would have been happy to let you waste your life in sin and depravity."

I blinked.

A lot.

And rapidly.

Because he didn't answer my question.

"Do I have brothers and sisters?" I whispered.

Dad said nothing.

I looked over my shoulder at Auggie.

His mouth was tight.

"Do I?" I squeaked.

His fingers gave me a squeeze. "I don't know, baby. Honestly."

The door opened again and Saffron came out.

"You didn't tell me how bad she was," I accused loudly, before the door closed.

"Now is not the time, Pepper," she snapped.

"When *is* the time, Saff?" I asked. "I mean, I'm somewhat over the fact you didn't ask me to be the maid of honor at your upcoming wedding…"

Her eyes darted to Dad.

Dad glowered at me.

"…it's your wedding, your choice. But she's…" I leaned forward, "*our* mom. And I should know she's at death's fucking *door.*"

"Do not speak like that in this building," Dad ordered.

"Are you crazy?" I asked. "My mother is *dying!*"

"You need to leave, Pepper," he retorted.

"I think you might have wanted to form the prayer circle about three months ago, *Dad*," I returned.

He looked down to Saffron. "Get her out of here."

"How much time does she have?" I demanded of my dad.

Saffron came my way.

Lottie shifted in front of me. "Do not get near her."

My attention remained locked on my father. "Do I have other siblings?"

Dad turned toward the sanctuary.

"Answer me!" I shouted.

He turned back around. "The doctors say she won't last the year. And my family has expanded by two boys and one girl, but they are *not* your brothers and sister. You are my blood. But you are a bastard of the church. And therefore, I do not claim you as mine so you do not taint them, and you *will not*."

Yes.

He was crazy.

The outside doors opened but I didn't look that way.

I looked to my sister.

And a chill glided over my skin so bad, it was a wonder the fine hair covering it didn't frost over when I saw the way she was sneering at my father.

Actually sneering.

What on earth?

Even as I sensed Mo, Boone and Axl joining this tableau (Aug probably gave the signal and one of the girls texted them), what my dad said hit me.

She won't last the year.

It was November!

"Is she in pain?" I asked.

Dad opened the door to the sanctuary.

"*Is she in pain?*" I screeched.

But I didn't know why I did it, the answer to that question screamed from my mother's every pore.

Saffron came to stand in front of me.

The door to the sanctuary closed behind my father.

I looked to my sister and repeated my question, because I damn well wanted her to admit it.

"Is she in pain?"

"She needs assistance getting to services, yes."

The breath I drew in whistled between my teeth.

Auggie glued himself to my back.

Lottie took my hand.

"We take care of her, Pepper," Saffron asserted.

"She should be in bed. She should have morphine."

"We take care of her."

"How?" I asked then pointed at the sanctuary. "Like that? She looks like death. She looks like she *wants* to be dead. What are you thinking?"

"She's closest to God in there."

"You're mad," I whispered.

She opened her mouth.

"And you're *cruel*," I spat. "Saff, what's the matter with you? You have got to know that's wrong."

"It's what she wants."

"It's what Dad wants."

"Yes, and that's what Mom wants."

We stared at each other, and damn it all to hell, I did it knowing my sister wasn't lying.

I closed my eyes.

Tight.

"Pepper, please. This is definitely not helping her," Saffron said quietly.

I opened my eyes.

Something was in my sister's face, I just didn't have it in me to read it.

I wanted to shake her.

Slap some sense into her.

Punch her and kick her and take all my fury out on her that it's all come to this.

I didn't do any of that.

I pulled my hand from Lottie's, turned, and walking around the girls and boys on the far side from Saffron, I headed to the doors to the outside.

"Have you located Birch?" Saffron called.

I stopped and turned back. "Yes. He knows. It's up to him what he does with that information. I'm out of that." I held her gaze steadily and stated firmly, "But I want time with my mother, Saffron. You arrange that. Sometime next week. I want time with my mom."

She dipped her head. "I'll arrange it."

"Not him," I snapped.

"Not him," she agreed.

"Thank you," I bit out.

Then I turned and walked outside.

Auggie was right there with me, catching my hand.

Lottie came up on my other side.

"I'm so sorry." She grabbed my forearm. "I'm so sorry, Pez. We just wanted—"

I stopped dead and looked at her.

"I'm not sorry. And don't you be sorry. If you didn't do that, I wouldn't have known. I needed to know, Lots. I need to start dealing. I need to figure out how to help my daughter to deal. And I need to do that now."

She stared at me, glanced up at Auggie beside me, back to me and nodded.

I started walking again.

Lottie fell back.

Auggie remained at my side.

"Pepper—" he started.

I didn't look at him, I stared straight ahead when I whispered, "Get me out of here, baby. I'm about to fall apart."

"You got it, sweetheart."

And double time, his hand holding mine tight, he got me to his Telluride, opened the door for me, helped me in, shut the door on me, got in beside me, drove out of the church parking lot and found an open stretch of street two blocks away where he pulled over and stopped.

Then his seatbelt was off.

Mine was off.

I was in his arms.

And I did not fall apart.

Because Auggie's arms were around me.

And as the emotion flowed from me . . .

Those arms held me together.

CHAPTER SIXTEEN

Afternoon Complete

AUGGIE

Aug wasn't surprised Pepper passed out about two minutes after she relaxed into his chest on his couch in front of a football game.

After she got over her crying jag in his car, he asked if she wanted him to feed her. She told him she wasn't hungry, she just wanted to chill out. Then she asked him if he liked football, and when he said he did, he returned the same question.

"Not really," she'd replied. "I like watching games in social settings, but I wouldn't catch a game by myself. But if we watch, you can be doing something you dig while I zone out. Would that be cool with you?"

He wanted her to have safe space to zone out, he also wanted to spend time with her, so he agreed.

They headed to his place while she staved off her friends phoning and texting her, all of them understandably concerned after what went down, and all of them wanting to make sure Pepper was okay.

Auggie knew she was tight with her girls, but that didn't stop him from feeling something settle in his chest that she put them off but wanted to "zone out" with him.

After what happened, she didn't bag on their date, ask him to take her home.

She found something he could do that he liked that she could do with him that didn't take a lot of mental capacity from her.

Yeah.

He liked that a lot.

It wasn't the day he'd hoped to give her, which had included brunch, then a movie, then back to his place so they could kick back, have a few drinks, and she could keep him company while he made her his Philly Cheese Ribeye sandwiches.

Then they would finish the night doing what they both had been wanting to do since the last time they did it.

Have sex.

But this time, they'd be going at each other in his bed with time to explore and discover.

And tomorrow, he'd wake up beside her.

At his place, in his bed, Pepper at his side.

Finally.

That day, obviously, he would have deleted the part where she'd had to confront the extent of her mother's illness the way she did.

But having Pepper cuddled into him on his couch in his living room while he sipped at a beer and she napped did not suck.

In fact, it was awesome.

So awesome, he could do this every Sunday and look forward to it.

Quiet time, doing absolutely nothing with someone you cared about.

He knew the minute she started to wake, because she also started to stir, her body shifting against his.

When she did this, Aug tucked his chin in his neck and looked down at her until she opened her eyes.

At first, she looked sleepy and unfocused, and Aug didn't take his attention from her as she came into awareness.

From the first minute he set eyes on her, he'd thought she was beautiful.

But through the last week, he wondered how he hadn't noticed she was the most beautiful woman he'd ever seen.

He felt her cheek move even as he watched her tip her head back, and she caught his gaze.

"Hey," he whispered.

"Hey," she whispered back.

"You okay?" he asked.

She nodded, shifted a little so she was pressed even closer to him (she was tucked down his side, her back to the back of the couch, her bent leg thrown over his thighs, so she was already close, but he liked the closer) and absently turned her eyes to the TV.

He let her have more time and got off like he'd been doing a lot the last week when he learned something new about her.

She didn't wake up like she normally was: with it, in the moment, full of energy.

She was vague and quiet and cute.

It took a while, and for the most part Auggie watched her that while, before she pushed up a bit and looked down at him.

"You okay?" she asked.

"Definitely," he answered.

"Sorry I passed out."

This brought them to a question he'd had for a while, there was just always so much other shit happening, he didn't ask it.

"When do you sleep?"

"Sorry?"

"You get home from work really late. And you were up today, ready to roll at ten. Since we've been texting, I know that's your

MO. You get home late, but you don't sleep in late. So when do you sleep?"

She shrugged and replied, "I have a daughter who needs to get to school. I like to have time with her whenever I can get it. And I like her to start her day knowing her mom is there for her. I also like her to have good food in her belly before she goes to school. So I get up with her, make her breakfast. I learned a while ago that if I get out of practice between times of having her, sleep in when she's not there, it's not good. So I get up the same time every day. Except weekends."

He quirked a grin at her before he said, "I'll repeat, when do you sleep?"

The sleepy started retreating and she quirked a grin right back. "I nap, honey. I've got power napping down. And Ian takes care of us. For me that means my last dance is always one of the first of all the girls, so I'm usually out of there around twelve thirty, one."

"That's still late when you're up, what? Around six?"

"Again," she pointed to herself, "master power napper."

Maybe.

Mostly, she loved her kid and took every opportunity to show it.

And Juno was going to grow up one of those kids who had no idea, until maybe when she had her own children, just how much, every day, her mom knocked herself out to give her love.

All his life, or until he could get his hands on an alarm clock and do it on his own, which started to happen when he was around ten, his father woke him up. And he couldn't recall a single instance, unless it was some random day one of them decided to make special (but that didn't mean holidays, or birthdays), where his mom or dad would make breakfast.

For the most part it was cereal (if they had milk).

Eggo waffles.

An occasional drive-through at McDonald's to get an Egg

McMuffin, but only if his dad, who took him to school, was hungry.

But, not including the drive-through, it was always stuff Auggie could make himself.

"Auggie?"

Pepper calling his name brought him back to his couch, with her tucked up next to him in it.

A better place to be.

"Are you okay?" she asked again.

"Yeah. Sorry. I'm zoning out too. Sundays can be like that."

Her face got soft.

And seriously, how in fuck didn't he recognize how beautiful she was the minute he saw her?

Off the damn charts.

"I messed up our day," she said morosely.

"Nothing's messed up," he promised. "You missed brunch and a movie. I'm still making you my Philly Cheese Ribeye sandwiches. Are you hungry now? Do you want a late lunch?"

"What time is it?" she asked, looking around the room, probably to find a clock.

"Around one."

Her eyes shot back to him. "Seriously?"

He quirked another grin. "I do not lie."

She looked mildly freaked. "Oh my God. I slept for two hours."

"Correct. Though it was more like you slept like the dead for two hours."

"That's not my usual power nap. Those last twenty minutes, tops."

How she could get maybe five hours of sleep a night, topping that up with a twenty-minute "power nap," and think she was golden, he didn't know.

Except for the fact that she took everything in stride.

She'd started her day with a huge drama, but she wasn't losing her mind. She wasn't throwing a tantrum or milking it for all it was worth.

She'd cried it out. She took a nap. And now they were having a casual conversation.

"Aug?"

He shook his head and refocused on her only to see her eyes narrowed on him.

"Be honest, are you sure you're not pissed that what went down this morning blew our date?" she pressed.

"I was gonna take you to brunch because I wanted to feed you after you hopefully slept in after working late. Then I was going to take you to the movies for something chill and relaxed to do. It's been a serious week for you, and because of that, I designed the day to be low-key. And nothing says low-key better than crashing on a couch with football and naps. So again, no. I'm not upset about our date. I'm upset you had to go through what you went through earlier, but I wanted to spend my Sunday with you. And that's happening."

"I want you to come over for dinner tomorrow night."

She said that like it was a slip. Like she didn't expect it to come out.

And the way her eyes rounded after she said it underlined that.

He just didn't get it since they'd taken every opportunity they could since they started connecting to do just that.

Connect.

So her asking him to dinner, since he'd already had a couple of meals at her house, didn't seem weird.

Therefore, it was careful when he said, "I'm in."

She didn't hesitate to explain it.

"That would be dinner with Juno and me."

Right.

Juno would be home tomorrow.

Definitely a big thing, and fast, for Auggie to be at their house for a family dinner.

"You sure you're ready for that?" he asked quietly.

"She wants us together."

"I'm not asking about Juno. Your girl has made her preferences clear. And I'll reiterate, I'm in. Now I'm asking, are you—?"

He didn't finish because there was a manic pounding on his front door.

He'd heard that frenzied demand for attention often in his life, either with a banging at the door, or a variety of other options.

Hearing it right then, Aug went still and his gut twisted.

Not now.

Pepper jerked in surprise and her eyes went over his head toward the door.

Fuck, *fuck, fuck, fuck, FUCK!*

The pounding didn't stop and Auggie sat up, taking Pepper with him.

"Don't move from here, I'll deal with it," he muttered.

"Deal with—?" she began.

"Boy! I saw your car parked out back. I know you're there. Open the door!"

Yep.

That was his mother shouting through his front door like that was a perfectly normal thing to do on a Sunday afternoon.

Or at any fucking time.

He felt his throat tighten with the need to shout back words he didn't want Pepper to hear.

He also felt his neck at the base of his head go solid with tension that this was happening, especially now, the first time Pepper was at his place.

Last, he felt a prickling of his skin he knew was adrenaline born of acute anger.

"Don't move," he repeated firmly to Pepper as he left her sitting on the couch, got up and stalked to the door.

He opened it, knowing the front storm door would be as it always was.

Locked.

That was the only good thing he knew.

Because it was worse than he thought.

His mother had bags with her.

It was rare she brought suitcases, at least to his house, because she knew that was a no go, no way in fuck with Auggie.

"I'm done with him," she declared upon first sight of her son.

Not "Hey."

Not "Sorry to interrupt your Sunday. Are you busy? I need to talk."

Just, *I'm done with him.*

And honest to Christ, if Auggie had a dollar for every time those words came out of her mouth, he'd fucking retire.

And he'd do it somewhere far away from there, meaning far away from his parents.

"Mom, now is not the time," he told her, and her mass of now-dyed blonde curls piled on top of her head bounced when she jerked with surprise.

"What did you just say?" she asked.

"I said now isn't the time. And you know," he tipped his head to indicate the suitcases, "that isn't gonna happen."

"Augustus—"

"I'll talk to you tomorrow," he said and started to shut the door.

"*Augustus!*" she shrieked.

But he didn't close the door.

He didn't because a situation that was not all that great turned exponentially worse.

This was because his father was prowling up the sidewalk.

Fuck, FUCK!

This part didn't happen often. When she took off, his dad normally let her go in order that both of them could play out whatever scene they were creating to its most drawn-out, but always the same, conclusion.

His father following his mom?

This was gonna be bad.

Auggie had left his keys in the kitchen, but he needed to open the door, step out, and shut whatever this drama was away from Pepper, doing that hopefully moving it from his front stoop, getting them to their cars and getting them away from there.

But he couldn't do that because he didn't have the key to get the door open.

"Dana! We weren't fuckin' done!" his father shouted.

His mother whirled around. "We haven't *ever* been *this done*, you *piece of shit, waste of space!*" She whirled back to her son. "Auggie, let me—"

She stopped abruptly, leaned to the side, got up on her toes and looked beyond him.

Goddamn fuck.

Even as he shifted to block his mother's view into the house, he glanced over his shoulder.

Pepper was lying on her side on the couch. The TV faced the room, the couch faced the windows and door, and if you looked in, which his mother was doing, you could see Pepper.

"Who's that?" his mom asked.

Still turned her way, he caught Pepper's eyes and saw her bite her lip and stretch up her brows.

Yeah, she was beautiful.

Yeah, she could be cute.

Yeah, she was often totally hilarious.

But right now, nothing was going to help.

Except one thing.

"Baby, can you go grab my keys from the kitchen?" he asked.

She nodded quickly, shot up from the couch and headed that way.

"Baby?" his mother demanded of Auggie.

"Dana. Did you fucking hear me?" his father demanded of his mother.

Auggie returned his attention to them.

His father was now on the front stoop, which was more like a short cement porch, painted terra-cotta and running Aug's side of the duplex he was renting.

Aug had a married couple living on the other side. Their names were Tod and Stevie, and they had him over for a special dinner once a month because "You do yard work, including pruning, and that deserves a celebration."

Their lawns were the size of postage stamps so they took about fifteen minutes to mow. There were precisely six pots to plant, which took half an hour to do twice a year. And he probably spent an hour a year pruning their twelve rosebushes.

But Stevie was a fantastic cook.

So he didn't argue.

He wondered now how they felt about him as a neighbor, his mom shouting obscenities on a Sunday afternoon.

"Who's that woman?" his mother asked Auggie, unfortunately bringing him back to their scene.

Demetrios "Dem" Hero, his dad, who hadn't even glanced at Auggie, turned his attention to his son. "Woman?"

"Do you honestly have a woman in your life, and you haven't told your mother about her?" Dana asked, her voice becoming more shrill.

He had a lot in his life, practically everything, he hadn't told his mother about.

"Are you seein' someone special, Auggie?" Dem inquired.

How in fuck could they land on his doorstep in the middle of whatever bullshit was happening with the two of them, and now they were acting like his life was in some way their business?

They'd never made anything about him their business, even when he was at an age he depended on them to do that.

"We're not doing this now," Aug announced. "It hasn't been a good day for Pepper, so whatever is happening with the two of you needs to happen somewhere else."

He heard a low whistle coming from behind him. He turned his head, and Pepper lifted up her hand with his keys in it.

"Pepper? Her name is Pepper? What kind of name is that?" That was his mom.

"Yowza, son. Well done." That was his dad, who obviously got eyes on Pepper, even if she was trying to remain out of sight.

"What the fuck is that supposed to mean?" Again, his mom.

Auggie nodded to Pepper.

Pepper sent the keys sailing his way.

He caught them, unlocked the door and started to jostle with his parents, who were both trying to push in while he pushed out, his mother grabbing her bags at the same time.

In other words, he lost the shoving match and found himself wedged with his back against the open door with both his parents filing into his place...his mom doing it with her fucking suitcases.

That was when he felt his skin start to heat.

Oh yeah.

This was going to get bad.

And he didn't want Pepper to see it.

"Uh...heya," he heard Pepper say uncertainly.

Auggie walked in, practicing patience and rounding his parents as his dad replied, "Hey there, girl."

"So, yeah, of course, first thing, he flirts *with his son's girlfriend*," Dana announced to no one.

Shit.

"What's the matter with you?" Dem asked his wife. "I just said hello."

"I wonder what your girlfriend will think about you panting after a woman young enough to be your daughter?" Dana speculated, giving hints to why this was happening. Either Dad was stepping out, or she thought he was. "I'll tell you what your wife thinks. She thinks it *stinks*."

"Gonna say it one more time," Auggie butted in. "We...are... not...doing...this...now."

Both his parents' attention came to him.

"Son—" Dem started.

But Dana talked over her husband, aiming her next at her boy.

"I hate to cramp your style, Auggie. But I need a place to crash until I can get myself sorted."

Translation: Until I can get one of my former lovers to put me up for a while or find a new one. But if that doesn't work, find a way to patch things up with your dad without losing face so I can move back in with him. Because I've tried all my friends' patience with this garbage, and they're done with me, so you're my last resort. And it's all about me, the fact you've got something on doesn't matter in the slightest.

"Mom, you're not staying here," he told her.

"I've got nowhere else to stay," she shot back.

"We've talked about this before," he returned.

"Aren't you going to introduce us to your girl?" Dem asked.

Dana shifted her attention to her husband. "Of course, all you can think about is the girl. Because your brain has been in your pants since you formed your first thought."

Dem shifted his attention too. "It's your mind in the gutter, Dana. Not mine."

"I live in the gutter, spending too much of my life living with you," she retorted.

"You must like it, you keep coming back," his father stated.

"You make promises, which means you lie," she returned. "And you do it again. And some more. What I gotta do is get my damned head examined, ever believing you."

Then, unfortunately, her attention shifted to Pepper.

And she kept speaking.

"Be careful, girl. They got the looks so they know they can break your heart time and again and you'll put up with their shit."

Auggie opened his mouth.

His father had more practice with this, so he got there first.

"Cut the crap, woman. It isn't my looks that did it, it's my wallet."

This topic of conversation was always an indicator of the deterioration of the situation because both of them could cheat on each other, lie to each other, talk shit to each other, but his mother drew the line at his father accusing her of being with him for his money.

The man maybe made fifty K a year. It was decent bank, but he was far from rolling in it.

But his mother ran through jobs like she ran through tubes of lipstick, which was to say she quickly lost interest, tossed them out and got new. She was never happy anywhere for long. And because her resume was ten pages long, and that only covered five years' employment, any good opportunities had dried up a long time ago.

So the problem in Dana's eyes with what Dem had said was that there was a kernel of truth in it.

Which obviously made matters worse.

"I've hardly gotten bored of my trips on your yacht on the Riviera, Dem," she stated coolly. "And you're right. It isn't your looks. At least not anymore, old man."

"Fuck you, Dana," his father spat.

Yep.

Deteriorating.

Because one thing his mother couldn't stand was to have money thrown in her face.

One thing his father couldn't, was to be reminded of his age and his fading looks. His father's vanity was extreme, and he was not taking his trip through the end stage of middle age at all well.

"I wish. You're too busy fucking *your new girlfriend*, Dem," Dana fired back.

"*Fucking hell!*" Auggie exploded. "*Shut the fuck up and get out of my house!*"

Both his parents looked at him.

He felt Pepper get close and put her hand on his back.

That should make him feel better, Pepper close. Touching him.

It didn't.

It made it all worse.

A lot worse.

Because this was it.

This was them.

This was his family.

Including him eventually losing it just like that.

"Did I hear you speak to your mother and me that way?" his father demanded.

"Get her bags, Dad, get her and then get out," Auggie replied, his voice tight, his brain scrambling to find some calm.

"You got a woman in your house on a Sunday, which means this is something," Dem flipped his hand toward Pepper. "We've never heard word of this girl. We're here. You don't introduce us. Then you cuss at us and kick us out?"

"Pepper's mother is dying of cancer," he stated abruptly. His father's eyes went right to Pepper, remorse on his face, his mother's eyes didn't stray from Auggie, but they narrowed. "She found out this morning that her mom won't last the year. Now, hearing that, do you honest to fuck think whatever bullshit you two are embroiled in that you brought to *my* doorstep and forced into *my* home when I told you repeatedly now was not the time for this means more to me right now than seeing to my woman?"

That shut them up.

He shifted his attention to his mother. "Get your bags, Mom, and go. You know that doesn't fly. I don't have space for you, and you make a mess. He'll clean up after you, I won't. I don't need your shit all over my house and I barely have time to clean up after myself. And right now, straight up, I got other shit on my plate and I can't deal with yours."

His gaze went to his father and he finished.

"Take her, Dad, and go. Now."

Dem looked to Pepper. "Sorry about your mom, girl."

"Thanks," Pepper said softly.

"You know, you, too, can say, 'Hi, my name is Pepper,'" his mother sniped. "I mean, what kind of person doesn't introduce themselves? Especially a girl to her man's fucking parents."

And there it was.

Dana was digging in for the long haul, thrilled at the prospect of dragging a new player into her theater.

Auggie's vision turned white.

Pepper moved and he felt her back pressed to his front.

"Dana, we need to get out of here," Dem muttered the only smart thing Auggie had heard him say in ten years.

"I'm sorry, you're right. I thought it best to let Auggie handle this situation. But I'm Pepper, and maybe—" Pepper started.

"Do not fuckin' apologize to them," Auggie growled.

Pepper got quiet.

"Get the fuck out," Auggie repeated.

"I am not a fan of you speaking to me that way," his mom said.

"You know what?" Auggie asked of Dem. "Honest to God, I don't know why you take her back. She's a piece of work. My advice, get home faster than her, bar the door, call a goddamn locksmith and be done with it."

And after he said that, he ignored his mother's enraged gasp, carefully moved Pepper out of his way, approached his mom, bent and picked up her bags.

He then shoved through her and his dad, went to the front door, opened it and sent them flying down the front walk, one after the other.

They wanted drama.

There it was.

"*Augustus!*" Dana screeched.

"Boy, that was over the top," Dem bit out.

He leveled his gaze on his dad. "You know I can put you both out. Don't make me."

Father and son stared each other down.

It was no surprise to Auggie that he won, swiftly, because it didn't even take three seconds. His father backed down and grabbed Dana's hand.

This was because Dem was weak and every second of Auggie's life, he'd been demonstrating just how deep that flaw ran.

He couldn't even win a staring contest, for fuck's sake.

Which was why, to his mother's muttering and griping, Dem got Dana to and through the door.

Auggie locked the storm door behind them and shut and locked the front door.

He then turned to Pepper.

"Still want me to come have dinner with you and Juno tomorrow?" he asked bitingly.

"Take a breath," she urged.

"I can take a dozen of them, that does not make that bullshit go away."

"Take one anyway."

He drew in a short, sharp breath.

"Another one, honey," she encouraged.

He did it again, it was longer, it went deeper.

It didn't help much, but at least he didn't want to shout or tear apart his living room anymore.

"One more. For me," she requested. "This time, pay attention to nothing but that breath going in. It doesn't have to be a deep breath. Just focus on the in and out of it."

He did that too.

Okay, a little better. Not a lot. But it was something.

"I'm gonna get you another beer," she declared when he'd let out that last breath. "Come with me?"

He looked at her, taking her in.

She seemed calm, alert, watching him closely.

Not like she was biding time until it wouldn't seem too rude to ask him to take her home because she suddenly got a "headache."

So he nodded.

She gave him a small smile and held her hand out to him.

He approached her, took it, and she walked him to his kitchen.

Once there, she got him a beer, rested her ass against his counter, waited until he took a slug, and the minute he dropped his arm, she said, "Talk to me."

"Not sure what to say," he replied. "That pretty much said it all," and he used his bottle to indicate the living room.

"It said a lot about them, but I'm not worried about them. I'm worried about you."

"Yeah, and I'm worried about how you feel about being with a guy who not only has parents like that, but who has no hesitation getting down and dirty with them," he returned.

She sounded confused when she asked, "Gets down and dirty with them?"

He indicated the living room with another tip of his beer bottle, this one a lot more agitated.

"Babe, that didn't do me any favors in there," he noted.

"They forced their way in," she said.

"Yeah, I was the one who they pushed through to do it," he confirmed.

"Auggie, honestly, I was really kinda surprised it took you so long to lose it with them. I mean, you're used to them, but take it from an outsider. That was *crazy*."

He stared at her.

"Seriously," she went on, "it was like you didn't exist, even though they'd come to you. I've never seen anything like that."

"I don't," he stated.

"Sorry?"

"I don't exist."

Watching her react to those words was like watching a slow motion of crash test dummies in a car, hitting a barrier. Her body swayed forward and back, her eyes locked to him.

"We can just say that my mom didn't make sure to get up every day so that I had a good breakfast," he continued.

And that made her wince.

But he wasn't done.

"I'm nothing to them until they decide it's time for my character to enter the scene. I never have been, Pepper. Right now, they've totally forgotten about me. They're either on the sidewalk having it out. Or in their vehicles, racing each other home in order to have it out. Or they've decided who's next to drag into their drama, and they're heading there. The fact they forced their way into this house, into our day, did what they did, said what they said, got the reaction they got out of me doesn't factor to them. He's about him and her, because I honestly think he loves her, it's just fucked-up love. She's just about her, the end. And that's all there is."

"Auggie," she whispered.

"But I should be above that. I shouldn't let it get to me. I should just let them say what they're going to say to each other and wait until they lose interest in me."

"From what I saw, you had no choice but to be in it."

"Everyone has a choice, Pepper."

It was like he said nothing when she continued, "And no child should have to wait until their parents have lost interest in them because no child should ever feel like their parents have lost interest in them. I don't care if you're eight or eighty."

"Pepper, they didn't make sure I had breakfast, they forgot more birthdays than they remembered, and you answer the door faster to me than my mom did when they were on the outs and she lived somewhere else, and I came over for her visitation."

Something clicked in her face, he saw it.

But he was where he was at in his head, and he had to finish giving that to her so she'd get it and not wonder what the fuck was wrong with him.

"That's my life with them, and I wish I could say it's only on occasion that happens, but they fight all the goddamned time and somehow have convinced themselves I give a shit when they do. It's calls. It's texts. It's showing up like you just witnessed. It's asking me out for a beer so they can drown their sorrows but mostly bitch about the other one, to me, their son. Like I'm a bud or some-fucking-thing. I've tried ignoring it. I've tried talking to them in their rational times and telling them I don't wanna be involved. Outside moving, changing my number and making as many plays as I can to disappear from their lives, which honest to God, I've considered, I don't know how to get rid of them."

She opened her mouth, but there was a knock on the back door and a "Yoo hoo."

Auggie looked that way to see through the glass-paned door that both Tod and Stevie were out there.

Fantastic.

He moved to the door and opened it, this time stepping aside without hesitation.

Tod and Stevie came in, Tod with eyes to Pepper, Stevie with eyes to Aug.

"Girl, that sweater dress is *eh-vree-thang*," Tod said to Pepper.

No introductions necessary since they already knew each other. Tod and Stevie were part of the Rock Chick tribe, which was Lottie's sister, Jet's crew.

And there was a lot of intermingling.

"Thanks," she replied.

Tod turned to Stevie and declared, "I need a sweater dress."

Important to note at this juncture: Tod was a drag queen known as Burgundy Rose.

Not missing a beat, Stevie replied, "The sequins of your gowns will snag on the knit when you shove it into your drag closet."

Tod visibly contemplated this, putting an extended index finger beside his mouth to do it.

"Is everything all right?" Stevie asked Aug.

"Sorry, you heard. My parents are having a thing," Auggie told him.

"Heard and saw," Tod stated. "They are right now performing a heretofore unknown Tennessee Williams play on the front walk."

Auggie looked that way, seeing fridge, cupboards and stove, hearing nothing, but not doubting Tod for a second.

"Now, we're here to ask if you're okay but also to ask if we should pop some popcorn in case we get peckish should it do what it looks like it's going to do and take a while," Tod finished.

"Fuck, sorry," Aug muttered, feeling something sour hit his gut and beginning to make a move. "I'll get rid of them."

He didn't get far because, all of a sudden, Pepper was standing in the doorway.

"No, you won't," she said.

"Just to point out, we're here *mostly* to see if you're all right," Stevie amended.

Aug looked over his shoulder at Stevie and said, "Thanks. I'm fine. And I'll take care of it." He turned back to Pepper and ordered, "Babe, please get out of the way. I gotta go out there and try to get them to their cars."

"They've had enough of your time today," she returned.

"And if you make them leave, what are we gonna do with our Sunday?" Tod asked. "I'm all for a lazy Sunday. I'm never all for a boring *anything*."

He twisted to the guys again and said, "You're being cool. I appreciate it. But—"

"No buts," Tod broke in. "And the girl in the fabulous dress is right. If those are your parents, about ten seconds is enough." He waved a hand in the air. "I've lost interest anyway. It's time to talk about how you two *finally* got together. And so you'll be out of their target range should they decide act three involves you, we're doing it at our place." He turned to Stevie. "Do we have Freixenet?"

"Do we ever *not* have Freixenet?" Stevie replied.

"*Omigod!*" Tod did a little jump and looked at Pepper. "We not only have Freixenet, we have a Freixenet Rosé in this cut-crystal bottle. *Perfect* for christening the two of you getting your heads out of your asses about each other."

"Tod!" Stevie snapped.

"Am I wrong?" Tod asked his husband.

"Maybe not, but for God's sake," Stevie returned.

"We have now been together decades, when are you going to stop pretending you're surprised at my behavior?" Tod asked.

"I'm not pretending to be surprised, I'm demonstrating my undying hope you'll learn to behave," Stevie shot back.

"If you wanted a man who behaved, you wouldn't have married me," Tod parried.

Stevie turned to Auggie and Pepper. "I hate that he's right."

Tod assumed a smug expression.

And yet another relationship in Auggie's sphere where the people in it loved each other in a healthy way, even if it came with banter or bickering.

"Are you coming over or what?" Tod asked.

Aug looked to Pepper.

The instant their eyes met, she gave him the sense she was trying to see beyond them, into his brain.

She then said, "I love a good rosé."

Yeah.

She'd read him.

Because he wanted time with her.

But he really dug Tod and Stevie. They were fun to be around. They were kind people. He knew she felt the same.

And if his mother or father knocked on his door again, he wouldn't hear it.

He turned back to the men. "I'm making my Philly Cheese Ribeye sandwiches and I have plenty."

Tod made his way to the fridge. "You'll be guest chef in our kitchen. I'll start packing the ingredients."

Stevie did not hide his grin as he watched his husband move.

Healthy.

Loving.

In his kitchen.

Aug looked back to Pepper and raised his brows.

She got his question.

And answered, "Afternoon complete."

CHAPTER SEVENTEEN
Suspended Animation

PEPPER

It was later than I'd guess we both imagined we'd leave Tod and Stevie's, and it was later mostly because Tod got out the Yahtzee game.

We'd ended up going through more than one bottle of Freixenet while we entered a marathon Yahtzee tournament that took hours, because we were all cracking each other up during it (though Aug didn't drink Freixenet, he brought over his beer because apparently, testosterone-fueled commandos didn't drink sparkling wine—which was okay by Tod, Stevie and me, more for us).

I liked it that Auggie was relaxing, enjoying himself, laughing (even if it wasn't the deep, full-throated laughter I was usually able to get out of him), and for more than that reason, I didn't want the night to be over.

The bigger reason, I didn't want my time with Auggie to be over.

As difficult as it was probably going to be, I also didn't want the conversation about what happened with his parents to be over.

There was so much more to discuss. And this discussion would be centered around how important it was for him to get that they don't reflect on him.

I mean, I wasn't Gonzo for God or a partner-beating felon.

He wasn't a rude, intrusive drama king.

I now got why he seemed surprised I opened my door to him, unmistakably expressing how excited I felt when he showed at my house.

But...

His folks had forgotten more birthdays than they remembered?

It was hard to think about that, even though it rolled around in my head so many times while eating Aug's awesomely delicious sandwiches, drinking sparkling wine, and playing Yahtzee in great company.

So it was often through the night that I'd find myself gazing at him, this sweet, thoughtful, handsome man, and I'd feel my heart squeeze.

As a matter of course, I tried not to think of Juno grown up. I didn't even like to consider the idea that third grade led to fourth, I'd blink, and she'd be in middle school. Then high school. And suddenly she'd be out on her own, making her own life, doing her own thing, living her adventures, maybe getting married, making babies.

I knew one thing about all of that, from now to whenever.

She'd be spectacular.

I'd be proud of her.

And any moment she'd give to me, I'd take it.

And like it was now, as it would be forever, every minute I got to be with her would be a gift.

How Auggie's parents could show up at his door and act like that to him, to each other, to me, I could not fathom.

How it had to feel for him, I didn't *want* to fathom.

But I had to.

I had to hear it, not that I'd ever understand it, but so I could be there for him through however he decided to deal with it.

Tod had kept the vigil, and Auggie's folks hadn't approached his door again (that said, throwing someone's suitcases out onto the front walk made a statement even his parents couldn't ignore). Their situation at the front of the house ran its course and they went off to do whatever they were going to do next.

There was only one good thing about Auggie's parents' visit.

It took my mind off how entirely fucked up my family was.

However, I mentally tucked away the fact that I was going to have to reflect on this.

All of it.

Because what happened with me that morning, and what happened to Auggie that afternoon, bore a shit ton of reflection.

Auggie let us in his back door after we left Tod and Stevie, and I thought it was a good thing that, after he closed it, he used his key to lock it.

So, yes, it appeared I wasn't going home that night.

That was more than a little all right by me.

It was good I had my toothbrush, a pair of sleep shorts, a tank, my cleanser and moisturizer and a clean pair of panties in my bag.

"You want another glass of wine?" Auggie asked.

"I'd like to spend the night," I blurted.

The indicators were there.

But one shouldn't assume.

"I'd like that too," he replied.

"And just to confirm, yes. I still want you to come over for dinner tomorrow with Juno and me."

"Okay," he said softly.

"And I can't believe this is going to come out of my mouth, because I think I've made it relatively clear that I want to have sex with you again," I began.

His perfectly formed lips twisted in a near-grin. "Yeah, you've made that relatively clear."

"However, tonight, if it's okay with you, I just want to be with you," I concluded.

He didn't say anything.

"Or we can have sex," I added quickly.

"You just want to be with me," he stated, like he was trying out words he wasn't certain fit.

"I want you for you," I stated. "I don't want you for an orgasm. I don't want you in order to get something out of it for me. To make myself feel desirable. To end a dry spell. To feel more solid in what we're building," I explained. "I just want you. To be with you. Just for you."

He again didn't say anything.

But this time, he spoke before I could get in there.

"You're making it super fuckin' hard not to jump you right now."

It went without saying it was pretty much all the time that it was super fuckin' hard not to jump him too.

"I'd be down with connecting intimately, Auggie," I said quietly.

He took in a deep breath that expanded his broad chest.

He let it out, saying, "Yeah, and we'll do that. When the time is right. So, to sleep in, do you need one of my tees?"

I felt my throat close, such was my emotion that we were going to do this, he was going to give me this.

That being, letting me give him something.

And he was going to give me...

Him.

That bore contemplation too, how much that meant to me.

But that was also for later.

"I brought some stuff to sleep in, but yes, I want one of your tees," I told him.

Because I so totally wanted to feel Auggie's shirt on my body.

Warmth moved over his face and he reached a hand to me.

I took it.

He led us out of his kitchen.

His place wasn't big, up front, a large-ish room that was living at the front, dining at the back, this fed into the kitchen.

After we hit the living area, I grabbed my bag from where I'd dropped it in one of his armchairs and he led me up the stairs.

Small landing, three doorways leading from it.

"Office at the front," he said. "Bathroom, middle. My bedroom here, at the back."

He then pulled me into his room and flipped a switch that turned on a flush-mounted, modern, overhead light fixture that had kickass black accents.

His room was painted a warm, true blue. The accents were white, other lighter blues, darker ones and grays (these mostly in the striped rug that covered the wood floors).

It was tidy, almost excruciatingly so.

The bed was made, the white comforter turned down at the top exactingly, to the point I had a feeling I could put a level at the edge of it and see how straight the fold was. The comforter was also tucked under the mattress. A stone-blue quilted bedspread was perfectly folded across the end of the bed. Pillows in white pillowcases were stacked precisely with pillows in shams at the head of the bed.

There was nothing on the boxy nightstands, including lamps (there were adjustable wall-mounted reading lights, also black, above the headboard on either side of the bed).

There was nothing on the tallboy dresser except a bonsai tree in a cobalt blue pot.

The only other thing in the room sat in a corner. It looked like a piece of art made of shiny silver metal with holes in it, shaped like an oblong with the top cut off, and if I stood beside it, it'd come up to my hip.

His bedroom was like the rest of the house.

There was style, definitely. And there was something to be said about his minimalistic décor, clean and uncluttered. It gave a sense of peace.

But it was neat and orderly to the point it was regimented.

Something else to talk about.

Auggie let me go to walk to the dresser where he opened a drawer, grabbed a tee and came back to me.

He handed me the shirt, and said, "Do your thing. I'm gonna close down the house. Do you need a glass of water or anything before I come back up?"

There was the thoughtful.

I shook my head.

He bent and touched his lips to mine.

He then took off and I didn't waste time taking his tee and my bag into the bathroom.

I changed, brushed my teeth, cleaned my face, moisturized, and I was out.

I walked into Auggie's room seeing him tying the drawstring of some light-blue, cotton pajama pants.

It was the first time I'd seen his chest bared.

He had a smattering of black hair across his pecs.

He also had shoulders, pectorals, abs and biceps carved by Zeus's own hands.

And we won't get into his ass in those pajama pants.

Yowza.

Seeing him, I experienced a direct hit to my decision not to have sex.

"Be back," he murmured, touching my hand as he passed me to go to the bathroom.

I took a moment to tamp down my sex drive before I moved to his dresser, put my stuff on top, and turned my attention to the bed.

Even if a quarter could bounce off it and hit the ceiling, I got

into it and sat cross-legged in the middle, facing the side of the
bed toward the door.

This was when I noticed the overhead light was out, the two
reading lights over the bed were on, and the piece of art in the corner was actually a lamp, and soft light came through the scattering
of holes in its sides as well as out the top.

Cool.

It didn't take long before Auggie was back, and a little shiver
ran over my skin when he walked into the room and stutter stepped
when his eyes hit me in his bed.

I'd never seen him take a wrong step or do anything with
hesitation. He was confident in his body and the things he used it
to do. So much, until then, I hadn't thought about the fact I hadn't
seen him do something clumsy, a trip, a bobble with his hands,
nothing, since I'd met him.

But seeing me in his bed made him falter, if only for a step.

Okay, maybe it wasn't time to go there. It needed space, for
me, for us, to introduce Juno to it and then for her. It needed deep
contemplation.

But I couldn't help but go there.

I had the strong feeling I was falling in love with this guy.

"Hey," I said when he seemed frozen, standing there.

He pulled himself out of it and replied, "Hey."

He moved to the bed and there was something definitely odd
about his movements then. Like he didn't know what to do.

It wasn't like he was being klutzy, or his movements were jerky.

It was almost like he felt shy.

Oh yeah.

I was falling for this guy.

He adjusted the pillows so they were resting against the attractive black-stained wood headboard and got in bed, leaning back
against the pillows, long legs straight.

He was lounging.

And still, he looked stiff as a board.

"Are you uncomfortable?" I asked carefully.

He was staring at his bare feet as I put my question to him, and he kept doing it for a spell before he looked to me.

"I feel exposed."

I kept my tone soft and cautious when I asked, "How?"

"You saw them."

He meant his parents.

"Did Marie meet them?" I queried.

He shook his head.

Uhhhh...

What?

Holy hell.

They'd been together for years and were engaged.

"Really?" I asked.

"Really," he confirmed, and then explained. "We were both stationed in California. Camp Pendleton. They never came to visit. And for obvious reasons, I wasn't big on asking her home for holidays. For the most part, I didn't come home at all. The only times I did was when my grandfather, Dad's dad, died and when Mom guilted me into coming home because she had thyroid surgery."

Before this information could fully register, he kept talking.

"And just a warning, their big seasons are coming up."

"Big seasons?"

"Thanksgiving and Christmas. Optimal time for drama."

Fabulous.

I shifted position so I wasn't facing his side of the bed with my head turned his way, instead I was facing him dead on.

"If you were safely away from them, why'd you come home to Denver?" I asked.

"Because I love Denver," he answered. "It's my home. Nothing against Cali. But I like seasons. I had friends here. I love the mountains, and not only because I like to board. They never felt like home, but Denver always did."

I totally got that.

When I got out of my situation, I hadn't had the money to venture farther afield.

But even if I did, I didn't think I would have.

"After they joined the church, I honestly never fully felt my mother's love," I announced.

His brows shot up.

"I know she loves me," I went on. "We had moments. There were times. Especially if Dad wasn't around. But he didn't approve of me. I didn't toe the line, even when I was young, living at home with them. And she wanted his approval. That meant she couldn't show she loved me when he was there, because somehow in her head, it would go against his wishes."

"Baby," he murmured.

As lovely as his sympathy was, in that moment, I didn't need it.

I needed him to understand.

"And maybe that's why I make certain that everywhere Juno turns, she sees I love her. She sees how much that is. Having her space in our office. Me getting up in the mornings to make her breakfast. Whatever," I told him.

"Or maybe it's just the woman you are. The mom you are," he suggested.

"Maybe," I acknowledged. "But I know Mom loves me. My father is . . . I don't know. Misguided. Though I think the truth of it is that he's just a follower. He seems very strong in his convictions, but he's not the one who creates those convictions. Someone else is telling him what to think. And he doesn't question it. He doesn't do the research. Ruminate on it and consider how it fits in with the world, his viewpoint of that world, his family, his life. He's told what to think and he thinks that. Before the church, when I was really young, we were a different family. They had a lot of friends.

A lot of parties. Looking back, I realize there were drugs around. Pot. Some hallucinogens. Booze. Music. I was young, but even so, I think Mom and Dad had an open marriage back then, though they were definitely committed to each other. But they were happy. We were happy. We were a family. He loved me then."

Auggie said nothing, but he didn't take his eyes from me.

"He loved me until he was told I wasn't worthy of his love."

He said something then.

"Pepper, sweetheart."

I shook my head. "It's okay, Aug. Really. Truly. It's taken me a long time, but I've come to terms with it. I had no choice. I made some extreme decisions in order to break free. To erase them from my life in a certain way. Build the family I didn't have. I found Corbin. Fell in love with a liar. Got pregnant really fast and too young. All because I yearned for what I didn't have. But being pregnant," I smiled, "meeting Juno for the first time, all gunky and making faces that said, 'What the fuck is this? Put me back.'"

Auggie smiled at that.

I kept talking.

"Her on my chest, squirming, I realized I had to stop messing around. This was real. This wasn't just about me. She was there too. And back then, Corbin. And then he did what he did, and once I got over the sting of betrayal, I took time with it. With the decisions I'd made. What I'd done. Bringing Juno into this world without really knowing the man who was her father. Without even knowing myself. And I realized it *really* wasn't about me. It wasn't even just about Juno. It was that I was part of a much bigger world and my footprint in that couldn't be a shitty one. I had to look after those around me. I had to be a good person. For me. For Juno. For everyone."

"Is that why you didn't cut your family out of your life?" he asked.

"No," I answered. "I didn't cut them out of my life because

they might not love me in a healthy way, or they might not love me at all anymore. But I love them."

At these words, he pushed up, turning to me, bending a knee to sit half-cross-legged, his other foot he put in the bed by my hip, knee cocked. He rested his upper body weight in one hand on the bed, the other he reached out and took one of mine, fiddling with my fingers.

All this so he was touching me, even semi-surrounding me.

I had all his attention.

His closeness.

Him.

God, Auggie.

"Which brings me to this, honey," I kept on. "Do you love them? Is that why you don't cut them out of your life?"

"For the most part, it's because I don't give up," he informed me.

I shook my head. "Sorry? I don't know what you mean."

"When I ended things with Marie, this was the only time she got frustrated and even pissed, after she did what she did, and my response was to make us over. She threw in my face that I never gave up on anything, 'Including those wastes of space that are your parents,' her words. But she'd fucked up once, and I was giving up on her."

"She wasn't in the place where she could judge you for that," I pointed out.

"I know that, but she didn't want us to end. She didn't want to live with the consequences of what she'd done. She was desperate by then."

"Okay, I hear all that, but I still don't know what you mean when you say you don't give up on your parents."

"Strip all that shit, mostly her, that 'her' being Mom, my dad's a decent guy."

He shook his head and let my hand go to shake that between us as well, like I'd said something to refute him, which I didn't.

He then continued.

"Early days, when I was younger, more importantly he was younger, he did some stupid-ass shit. He's conceited. He was a really good-lookin' guy. He knew it. He got married to a beautiful, equally vain woman, but he did not settle down. I even remember being out with him and watching him flirt with women, his young son at his side, his wife somewhere else. I remember feeling weird about that. I didn't like it and I was too young to even get it."

"Yeah," I agreed when he paused.

"And as you and I talked about," he carried on, "I'm not okay with cheating. So I'm not forgiving that in him. I'm just saying, shit got out of control and really freaking skewed along the way. That was on him. It was also on her. She completely descended into the dysfunction. But Dad? He was not father of the year, but he looked after me."

"A parent should do more than that."

He nodded. "What I mean is, when he heard your mom had cancer, he gave a shit. He looked right at you. He doesn't even know who you are, and he felt that for you. My mom didn't even process it. It wasn't about her, so it evaporated the minute the words were said. That's the difference. So I'll amend. I don't give up in terms of not giving up on my dad. Hoping that one day he'll realize he's caught in an unhealthy cycle and he'll get shot of her. Mom, she's a lost cause. I only put up with her for him."

I'd noted he definitely had way more issue with his mother than his father.

And meeting the two of them, even the short time I'd been around them, I got why.

That said...

"I think all of this affects you a lot more than you know it does," I pointed out.

He looked away.

It was me taking his hand then, and when I did, I got his attention back.

"Auggie, you just told me you felt exposed, just because I'd met them. You were engaged to a woman, with her for years, and she never met your parents. You thought I was going to rescind my dinner invitation to you after they played their scene in your living room." I squeezed his hand. "You aren't them. I'm seeing *you*. I want *you* to have dinner with me and my daughter. You're protective and attentive and kind and funny. You're good with kids. You're a great kisser. You are so many things and not any of it has to do with them. But I think you think it does."

"Do you want them meeting Juno?" he asked.

Shit.

That was a tricky question.

I sallied forth carefully, but honestly.

"From the little I've been around them, I'd have to answer, not particularly," I admitted, "But Juno is of this world. She's already experienced things, seen things, heard things, a lot of them, that I would have preferred to shield her from. I'm not doing my job if I cushion her from the bumps of life. Eventually, she's going to deal with dysfunctional people. Rude people. Selfish people. Thoughtless people. She's gotta learn how to handle it."

Abruptly, I felt my skin itch.

And it was because of the look that came over his face and the way he forced out, "It's fucking me up."

His smooth voice was tight, almost scratchy, like there was pain in the act of forming those words.

"What's fucking you up?" I asked quietly.

"Being with you."

Before I could think twice about it, I let his hand go and leaned away, feeling my stomach take an unpleasant dive.

"No, not that. Not that," he said swiftly, reaching with both hands to my face. Once he got hold, he pulled it closer to his. "Not like that," he whispered.

"Okay, now I don't know what you mean, 'not like that,'" I said, my voice small.

"Like it's bad."

"How can fucking you up be good?"

"Because I'm seeing how it was."

"What was?"

"How they treated me," he stated. "How they treat each other. It's coming at me all the time. I can't control it. I'll be in a meeting at work, and I'll be thinking about ridiculous shit that isn't ridiculous. Like how all the guys who have women bring travel mugs into work. How that's what you do when you have someone in your life who cares. How you build a life together. How my parents don't even look after each other enough to have travel mugs in the house. Or food. My dad doesn't get up and make a pot of coffee for the both of them because they both drink coffee, so as a matter of course, one of them makes it so both of them can have it. How even my dad's place, where he's lived for decades, seemed transient to me because she was in and out of it. How I..."

He shook his head.

Dropped his hands from my face.

Looked away.

Swallowed.

"How you were harmed by that?" I suggested softly. "How you needed that as a kid? For them to respect each other and you?"

He didn't answer.

He stared at the coverlet at the end of the bed.

So I took his face in my hands and made him look at me.

"And how you see that if you have Juno and me in your life, you'll have that?" I whispered.

He didn't say anything but there was something burning deep

in his black eyes. Something so intense, it was like his irises were molten. Rippling. Undulating.

Fascinated by that, I kept whispering when I said, "I have travel mugs, Auggie."

"I need to fuck you," he rumbled.

Oh yeah he did.

And I needed that too.

So we'd decided not to do that.

Plans change.

And you roll with it.

I was *so* rolling with this.

"Oh—" I breathed but didn't get the "kay" part out.

I was on my back and Auggie was on top of me.

He was kissing me, and he was touching me, and before I even registered how much I liked the taste of his tongue in my mouth, his weight on my body, his hands were in the tee and it was going up.

He arched away and I lifted my arms for him to get rid of it, and there I was, in his bed wearing nothing but a pair of pink lace panties.

And Aug had a hand in the bed, straight-armed, looking at me like he was about to take a bite out of me when it happened.

The same thing that happened in the entryway at my house.

It was so much, and yet it was still simple.

I needed him.

So I put a foot in the bed, heaved up, caught him on the go with one of my arms, and he was on his back, and I was straddling him.

I went after the drawstring on his pajama pants.

He curled his fingers around my wrists and did an ab crunch up to sitting.

"Pepper," he murmured.

"Get these off, baby," I panted, trying to pull my hands away from his hold.

He could deal with his pajamas.

I was going to get rid of my panties.

"Pepper," he repeated, not a murmur this time, and he shook my wrists gently.

I looked at him.

And I stilled.

Completely.

"Baby, I'm gonna fuck you," he said the words that were stamped in his expression. "You're not gonna fuck me. But first, I'm gonna eat you. Then I'll fuck you. There'll be times I'm down with you going for it with me, but I'm into control so either you chill out and let me take my time, or I'm tying you down and *then* I'll take my time."

I was wrong.

I wasn't panting before.

Because I was panting now.

"You gonna chill out?" he asked.

"Y-yes," I stammered, squirming against the shaft of hardness I was sitting on and wondering if that was the right answer because I also kinda wanted to be tied down.

"Kick off your panties as you roll over, onto your back," he ordered.

"Oh…kay," I whispered.

I did that and I didn't waste time doing it.

Auggie watched me do that.

Total turn-on, him watching.

When I was as he told me to be, he took his time bending to me, taking my mouth, kissing me.

As usual, the heat quotient escalated fast, but when I was about to become swept away by it, I checked myself.

He was into control.

And I was into letting him have it.

I got my reward.

Auggie lowered his weight to me.

In short order, I found that he'd lied.

He was not going to eat me first, then fuck me.

Nope.

First, he kissed me dizzy. He did this while he touched me everywhere he could reach.

Then he cupped my breast under the swell and bent to it, lifting it to his mouth, swirling the nipple with his tongue, before sucking on it until I was writhing under him.

He did the same to the other one.

He spent some time exploring the skin of my belly and the round of my hips with his lips, tongue and teeth, before he spread my legs apart.

So by the time he settled between them, I was so far from chilled out, it wasn't funny.

The only thing I knew outside of feeling the things he was making me feel was that I was going to let him do whatever he wanted to do, because from all experience, he seriously knew how to do it.

But I had no idea.

No idea.

I should have, with the way he kissed. How it made me wild. The way he took over. The way everything but Auggie and what he was doing to me was the only thing in my head.

But I didn't put the two together.

It didn't hit me that, since he could make me wild kissing me, if he kissed another part of me, what would happen.

And it happened.

Not because I hadn't had a non-self-induced orgasm since the last one Auggie gave me.

Because he was just that good at going down on me.

After a while, I had one heel digging in his back, the other foot in the bed, pulsing me up into his mouth, and both arms over my head, hands flat against the headboard, pushing myself down like I wanted him to drown in me.

He didn't drown in me.

No.

When it was there.

When it was close.

When my climax threatened to sweep me away, his mouth was gone.

No!

My eyes flew open, and I saw him on his knees between my legs, yanking on the string of his pants.

They fell down his thighs.

And there was his magnificently formed cock springing up from a nest of black curls.

I barely got a second to admire it, my mouth watering to do just about anything he'd let me do with it, before he demanded, "Condom. Drawer."

My arm was a blur, I moved so fast to twist to the drawer of his nightstand.

I had barely fallen again to my back before he was taking the packet from my fingers.

He ripped it open.

Tossed the wrapper aside.

I watched in stunned awe as he rolled it up his pretty, thick cock (the awe was about his cock, but he was proficient with the rolling too).

And then he wrapped his hands around the back of my knees, fell to his calves, dragged me up his thighs...

Ohmigod.

"Look at me," he growled.

My gaze shot from where my sex was nearly meeting his to his face.

And the look on his face...

Oh…

Wow.

I felt the head of his dick…

And with a smooth thrust of his hips, he was buried inside me.

Auggie was again a part of me.

Taking him, I dug my head in his pillows, my back arced up from the bed, and he commenced fucking me.

It wasn't gentle.

It wasn't rough.

It was *just right.*

"Baby," he called, and I felt his hand leave my leg and a sharp pinch came at my nipple.

Holy hell.

Nice.

I looked at him again.

"You watch me while I'm fuckin' you, yeah?"

Oh my God… *yes.*

"Yeah," I whimpered.

I flexed my thighs, tried to move with his rhythm, but he stopped when I was full of him.

"Unh-unh," he grunted.

Umm…

"I fuck you, you take my fucking," he told me. "I'll let you know when I want you to work."

Oh.

My.

Gawd.

Yes!

"Okay, honey," I gasped.

He started moving inside me again, watching me with that dark look on his face, that blaze in his eyes. I'd never seen a man so beautiful, and I'd already thought he was the most beautiful man I'd ever seen.

Yeah, yeah, yeah.

Holy hell.

He was more gorgeous than even himself when he was fucking.

"Sweet pussy," he murmured, watching my face and my body as it moved with his thrusts.

"Thanks," I pushed out.

His lips twitched.

Then he asked, "You ready?"

"Ready?" I asked back.

"For me to fuck you," he explained.

"I thought...you were...doing...that," I noted, my words hitching because, well, he was fucking me.

"Yeah, I am. But are you ready for me to really fuck you?"

Uh...

"Does it get better?" I asked.

No lip twitch there.

He grinned.

I shivered.

He pulled out, whipped me to my belly, straddled my hips, lifted them slightly, then drove in.

And...

Auggie...

Fucked me.

I was panting and moaning before he tangled his fingers in my hair and used it to turn my head so my cheek was to his sheets and his lips were at my ear because he'd full-on mounted me.

"Feel the difference?" he asked, his voice rough and sexy *AF*.

"Yeah," I gasped.

"Lift your ass, I want more."

I did what he said because I wanted him to have more, and I wanted it too.

His fingers tightened in my hair.

I whimpered.

"Fuck yeah, sweet, fucking pussy," he grunted, driving faster, deeper.

One hand in my hair, the heat of him against my back, his cock fucking me hard, he shoved his other hand under me and found my clit.

It took a roll, two, three, and I jolted under him as my orgasm rushed through me, sharp and strong.

But it lingered, and I was suspended in sensation. The pleasure of the climax. My breasts crushed to the bed, my nipples rubbing against it. Auggie's cock slamming into me. I could hear his harsh breathing, the small grunt of effort that came from his lips, the breath of it racing across my skin with each inward drive.

Finally, the moment of nirvana as Auggie rolled my clit again and I came a second time, before my first even left me.

And he was coming too, louder grunts sounding against my skin, and they weren't breaths, they were so deep, it was a physical touch.

He wasn't finished before his fingers in my hair gave me a gentle shake.

I knew what he wanted, twisted my neck, and he took my mouth with nearly the force he took my pussy.

Okay.

Suffice it to say, the entryway sex at my house?

Awesome.

But an opening act.

The main event was *everything*.

He finished with my mouth and I was breathing heavy, somnolent but buzzed, still tingling but tranquil.

And it was good he hooked my hip with his hand and rolled me over to my back, because I probably wouldn't have been able to do that.

He rested his weight on me again and I stared at his face, which was fuzzy, mostly because I wasn't focusing on it.

I was focusing on his body against mine. The bristly feel of his chest hair, the hair on his thighs scratching against my skin. His flat belly resting on mine. His weight. His heat. His still-semi-hard cock wet with me, lying against my thigh.

"Are you with me?" he asked, his voice an octave lower (an octave I liked), but also holding some amusement.

"No. I'm on a different plane."

I felt that body I was focusing on shake with laughter that wasn't audible.

I finally focused on his face (kinda).

"We can't have sex again," I told him.

His body was no longer shaking, but he was smiling. "We can't?"

"No. Because it can't possibly ever be that good again."

"Wanna bet?" he asked.

Another shiver.

Auggie kissed me, it was wet, sweet and deep, but not intense. When he broke it, he muttered, "Hit the bathroom and I'll be back."

I nodded.

He didn't hit the bathroom and come back.

He tossed the pillows with shams to the floor, adjusted me in bed so I had my head on one of the pillows he left behind, tugged the comforter and sheet out from under me, pulled it over me, located his pajama pants (I hadn't even noticed him taking them off), nabbed them...and *then* he went to the bathroom.

I was in the throes of trying to decide if I'd had two really great orgasms, or one that had phases, when he came back, hair a sexy mess, wearing the pajamas.

He went to the corner to turn off the dope-ass lamp there.

Then he came to bed.

After our day, the darkness of it (his folks, my family), the lightness of it (nap on his couch, Tod and Stevie), I would be super bummed if he wasn't a cuddler. Particularly starting out the night.

I was a girl who could go my separate way once we fell asleep.

But tonight, especially, I wanted a cuddle.

I admired Auggie's lateral muscle as he reached to turn off his reading light, then went long to turn off mine, and when he came to me, I let out a breath as he gathered me in his arms.

"I decided I had two really great orgasms, with a moment of suspended animation separating them, rather than one long one with phases," I announced my decision.

I felt his body shaking again before he pulled me closer and asked, "Say again?"

"I came twice."

"Yeah, I could feel. Suspended animation?"

I tipped my head back and looked at his face through the shadows. "There was this really, *looooong* moment where I was coming, but not coming, still, I think I was coming."

His body shook yet again.

"It was insanely *awesome*," I shared.

"Good," he pushed out, that word vibrating with humor.

"Just so you know, I could still feel you fucking me when I was in suspended animation."

"Thank Christ. I was worried."

"Yeah, no, rest assured, I got it. In fact, I'm pretty sure I still feel you fucking me right now."

He burst out laughing.

And something inside me cleared.

I'd been congested since he came back to me after shutting the door on his parents.

Now, it was gone.

When he was done laughing, he fell a little to his back, taking me with him, so I was partially lying on him, and with a squeeze of his arm around my shoulders, he said, "Seriously, I am glad to hear this, baby. I can get...intense during sex."

Oh yeah, he could.

"Yeah, that came through," I affirmed. "No complaints here."

"If it's too much, tell me to back off."

"Aug?"

"Yeah."

I pushed up, aimed at the vicinity of his mouth through the dark, hit the side of it but he adjusted so my lips were to his.

I kissed him, my own version of wet, sweet and deep (but not intense).

I broke it but didn't move away before I shared quietly, "It was phenomenal. You were phenomenal. I can definitely take initiative, but it turns out that it turns me on to be, not submissive, but..."

"Guided?" he suggested when I couldn't find the word.

"Yeah. With a strong hand."

His voice was lighter, relieved when he replied, "Gotcha."

"So it was perfect," I told him.

He lifted his hands, sifted his fingers through the side of my hair, all the way down my back.

"You sleep naked?" he asked softly.

"Sure, when I have a hot guy to press up against and no kid in the house."

"You don't have to for me."

"I wouldn't if it made me uncomfortable," I assured him.

"I like the feel of you."

Nice.

"I like the feel of you," I shared.

He twined his fingers in my hair and with gentle movements, directed my cheek to his shoulder.

"You need to set an alarm," I told him.

"It's already set," he told me.

It was?

I hadn't seen an alarm clock.

"No," I began to clarify. "I mean for an hour from now, so we can wake up and have sex again."

That got me more of his body shaking.

"Do you need two hours?" I teased.

"Go to sleep, Pepper," he ordered.

"Aug?"

"Yeah."

"Our day was fucked up. But I'm so glad you were with me when my part got fucked up. And I'm glad I was with you when yours did."

His fingers, still in my hair, started skimming through it as he murmured, "I'm glad too, baby. More than I can say."

"I'll go to sleep now," I promised.

"Okay, sweetheart. Sleep good."

"It's impossible not to. My body was fucked into sleep submission."

A slight movement of his frame with his humor and a warning, "Pepper."

"Okay, now I'm going to sleep," I really promised this time.

His fingers kept drifting through my hair, it was crazy soothing, and I wondered if he was getting sleepy.

I didn't ask though.

Because what he was doing was so soothing, I exited straight to dreamland.

CHAPTER EIGHTEEN

Coconut

PEPPER

It was raining.

Distant thunder.

A nice pitter-patter of water droplets.

I felt heat hit my back, then a hand roaming over my hip, my belly, up to cup my breast.

I opened my eyes to a dark room, the alluring presence of Auggie and the outstanding knowledge that his morning alarm (wherever magical place it was coming from, but it sounded like everywhere) was nature noises.

"Sweetheart?" he murmured into the back of my hair.

I did a mini-stretch into him and mumbled, "I'm awake," even though I was, but only just.

"You're doing all the work," he shared.

Before he said that, I was still sleepy.

After he said that, a mental image of his beautiful cock hit my brain, the feel of it hard against my ass hit my consciousness, and I was sleepy no longer.

I turned in his arms.

As I was discovering from Auggie, even if I was supposed to be doing the work, he was in control.

Which was why I didn't kiss him.

He kissed me.

It was gentle and exploratory, it included both of us using hands to wander each other's bodies, and after I delved into his pajama pants, me discovering that his ass felt even better than it normally did, skin against skin.

Then the kiss became less gentle and exploratory and more demanding.

Not long after, Auggie fell to his back, pulling me on top of him.

He had a handful of my ass, another of my breast, when he broke the kiss, his bristly cheek scored down mine, and he said in my ear, "Morning head, Pepper. Want you to wrap your mouth around my dick, baby."

It was not a suggestion.

It was an order.

And I felt my pussy convulse hearing it.

I lifted my head to look into his shadowed face, feeling the heat coming from his gaze, the warmth of his skin, the stiffness of his cock.

Then I dipped my head and kissed his throat.

After I did that, I did not dally.

I moved down and he shifted up, so his shoulders were to the headboard.

He also opened and cocked his legs.

My pussy was pulsing all through this.

It contracted when Aug wrapped one hand around the base of his cock, the other hand he slid into my hair, and I didn't so much go down on him as he took my face by pushing me down on him.

Oh yeah.

He had heft and he had width, he tasted good, and I totally got off that it was less me taking him and more him taking me.

To share my feelings, I licked, sucked and bobbed to the pace he was guiding me with the hand in my hair, as he stroked himself along with my movements.

It was like I was an addition to his morning hand job. I got to watch, feel and directly participate all at the same time.

It.

Was.

Magnificent.

I was so into it, I didn't realize our tempo had escalated until Auggie gripped his dick at the base and shifted up in the bed so I lost him from my mouth.

I looked up at him.

"Condom," he grunted it.

Right on.

I crawled to the nightstand, and we did a repeat of last night. I got the packet. He took it, revealed its contents, rolled it on while I watched through the dark.

And then he said, "Climb on, Pepper."

I did and he held himself steady for me to position and take him.

My body bowed when I filled myself with him.

God, he felt so good, and the low noise Auggie emitted made it all the better.

He wrapped his fingers on my hips and whispered, "Bounce, baby."

I bounced.

Boy, did I bounce.

Auggie bucked and touched, but eventually settled his hips so he could sit up and start sucking my tits.

Oh God.

Yeah.

"Honey," I whimpered.

He slid his lips up my chest to under my chin. "Fuck me, Pepper. Faster."

I did.

He cupped a breast, finger and thumb to a nipple, rolling, and went after my clit with his other hand.

I went faster.

"That's it," he murmured. "Fuck yeah. Christ. Tight. There you go, baby."

He was right, there I went.

I came, gasping and trembling.

Then I was on my back, perpendicular in bed, and Auggie fucked me until he found it.

I was shivering in the aftermath and trolling his body with my hands, discovering the side of his neck and ear with my nose and lips, when he demanded, "Mouth."

I turned my head, he took what he wanted, and when he was done, he slid out of me and rolled us both to our sides, tangled in each other's arms.

The rain was still falling.

"How do I get a magical alarm that makes the entire room sound like rain?" I asked.

His lips hit mine, not for a kiss. It seemed the sole purpose was so I could feel them smile.

I was at one with this purpose.

"I've got a smart home system that connects to the speakers Indy and Lee installed throughout the house. It plays music. Connects to the TV for surround sound. There are hidden monitors around the house so you can ask it to do shit, like tell you the temperature outside or time something when you're cooking. It controls the thermostat. Shit like that."

"I want one," I declared.

"Good that I know a guy," he replied.

I grinned at him and snuggled closer.

But, sadly, it had to be done.

So I did it.

"Do you have to go to work?" I asked.

He sounded as disappointed as I was to ask the question when he answered, "Yeah."

I gave him a squeeze. "Thanks for the bird's-eye view of a spectacular hand job."

I heard and felt him chuckle. "Thanks for accompanying my hand job with a phenomenal blow job."

"My pleasure."

"I noticed."

"I have an IUD," I announced, because things were going to keep up like this, and that had to be said too.

His voice lowered when he replied, "It's been a while since I had a physical. You want me to get tested?"

"Can you do that quickly, like, say, today so we don't have to interrupt you fucking me to deal with that business?"

I could hear the humor come back when he said, "Maybe not today but I'll fast-track it."

"Awesome. Now it's time for you to get creative, since I have Juno and I work nights, so this week you're going to have to find a way to spend your lunch hour in me."

That made him bust out laughing.

And there it was.

The real start of my day.

During it, he kissed me.

And after it, he said, "That will *so* not be a problem."

"Excellent. Now let's do this morning stuff so you can take me home so I'm closer to seeing you again when you come over tonight."

I again heard amusement, but there was something deep and resonant, warm and beautiful, when he said, "She's bossy in the mornings."

"Not usually. But I've got myself a bossy lover and it appears he's fucking the bossy into me."

"I like it. I'll have to keep doing it."

"I hope so."

"Stop being cute and get up, Pepper."

"Stop being hot and get up with me, Auggie."

Apparently, my bossy worked.

Because that was what he did.

* * *

There was someone else I hung out in the office in wait for when they arrived.

And as usual, on the Mondays she was back, lugging the bigger backpack she took that carried anything she didn't already have at Corbin's, I was out the door the minute I saw the school Twinkie drive down the street.

It let out five houses down, and I was at house three when my baby dropped down from the bus.

I smiled big at her.

She smiled bigger and ran to me, her backpack bouncing.

Then Juno hit me and hugged me around the hips.

Okay.

Now my week could begin.

I curled over her and hugged her around her backpack.

As I was doing this, my earlier meditation came to me.

In thinking about all that went down during our Sunday, and the things Auggie had shared with me, I thought about the things I had missed from my family once we went into the church.

And affection was one of them.

We'd been a touchy, cuddly family before the church.

But it wasn't slowly that the cold rushed in, forcing out the warmth.

It'd never returned.

Juno tipped her head back and I straightened up, but she didn't let me go.

Yes.

I had missed that affection.

And I was so glad I fostered it in my daughter, and she took to it.

"Did you have fun at your dad's?" I asked.

Her face clouded over.

Shit, *shit*.

"It was all right," she didn't exactly lie.

I pulled at her hold so I could move to her side to head us home, but we walked close together toward our place.

Once we were two houses closer, and most of the kids had dispersed, so no one was near, I asked, "Was everything okay?"

"I think he broke up with his girlfriend."

Hmm.

"Did you like her?" I asked.

She lifted a shoulder, no other response.

Mm-hmm.

That was the way she'd learned how to play it. She didn't get too close in case they were taken away.

Stupid Corbin.

"You hungry?" I changed our subject.

The light came back to her face, she looked up at me and nodded.

We got in, she went upstairs to dump her bag, and I was in the kitchen, making myself some tea as an excuse to be around her when she tackled the fridge or the pantry for an after-school snack, when I heard the house phone ring.

I wasn't a fan of that because it meant someone who couldn't get ahold of me on my mobile needed to get ahold of me, so they went landline and that could mean urgency or emergency.

I had both of those going on in my life, so when I moved to the cordless handset, I focused on the fact it made me feel very retro since no one had them anymore, instead of what calamity might need to be communicated to me as I took the call.

"Hello?"

"Pepper, you're not answering your cell," my sister said.

"Is everything okay?" I asked quickly.

"You wanted time with Mom?" she asked back dryly.

"Right." I moved out of the living room to have a view to the hall in order to give myself warning Juno was going to show. "Juno's home and I haven't had the time to discu—"

"Tomorrow. Noon. Dad has a lunch meeting. Come to the church. I'll meet you at the front door."

"Oh, um...all right."

"All right. See you then."

And she hung up.

I stared at the buzzing phone, feeling weird.

Because she was all business.

It wasn't unfriendly, *exactly*. It wasn't sarcastic, frustrated or impatient, *as such*.

What it was, was that she was ticking me off a to-do list.

And another part of my long meditation (and, I'll add, journaling session) came back to me.

Because I'd shared with Auggie that I did not cut my family out of my life because I loved them.

But after meeting his folks, seeing the effect they had on him, I felt the need to reconsider my decision not to do that.

I loved them, but I didn't think they were good for Juno. I wondered if there was some strain on her about them. And if (no, it was, sadly, *when*) we lost Mom, I had to seriously consider staying tied to them.

Saffron was never the fun aunt. Or the loving one. Or the supportive one.

In truth, they barely had any relationship at all.

Dad seemed to suffer Juno's existence. He wasn't cruel to her (she'd never be around him if that was the case, obviously). He didn't say ugly things to her (ditto with the never being around him). He also wasn't affectionate or grandfather-y. He would smile at her, listen to her, and once in a while, his face would get soft. But mostly, it was tolerance. Subtle, but my daughter was not stupid. She probably felt it.

It was Mom that lit up (as much as she'd allow herself to do so) when Juno was around.

I had brothers and sisters I had never met.

I had another one I didn't want my daughter to meet.

And it was true, to be the better person, it was up to me to make the effort, and take the hits that might come from attempting to be a part of these people's lives.

But what was that giving me?

What was it giving Juno?

It didn't nurture either of us or enrich our lives.

We couldn't feel the loss of something we never really had.

Could we?

"Mom, who was on the phone?" Juno asked, making me jolt and taking me from my thoughts.

"Your auntie Saffron," I told her.

She made a scrunch face.

Uh...

Yeah.

Not nurturing or enriching.

"Get your snack, Dollface," I encouraged as I put the phone back in its base. "Because we have an errand we have to run before dinner."

She bounced into the kitchen, her ponytail swaying, and I took heart in that.

She could kinda do her hair, but she still wasn't great at it.

Corbin was. Obviously, he'd had to learn along the way, and

when we were together and I'd thought we were solid, I'd also thought it was all kinds of cute how he'd brush her hair and put barrettes in it or pigtails, or when she got older, whatever she asked for.

He still did it now.

She had cute clothes at his house. Alice bands. Hair stuff.

He was mostly a dick.

But it had to be said, he loved his daughter.

I drew in a cleansing breath at that thought, and Juno climbed onto a stool at the island with some hummus and baby carrots, asking, "What errand?"

I went to the electric kettle, having decided how to share this, which was casually, in case me and Auggie got it wrong. Then I could play it as he was just a friend coming over, and later, discuss how to proceed with Auggie.

But if we got it right, I could give her a bit more and see how that went.

"Auggie's coming to dinner so you have to figure out—"

"What, what, *what?*" she shouted, jumping down from her stool and then jumping in the air beside it. "Ohmigod, we gotta make something special," she declared. "And he can cook it with us!"

"Um—"

That was all I got out.

She decided. "Dumplings!"

She loved my gyoza.

"And edamame and teriyaki chicken!" she kept going. "Call him! Ask him if he comes home hungry so he needs to eat right away or if he wants to cook with us."

I was practically blinded, my girl was beaming so bright.

Safe to say, we hadn't read it wrong.

Still.

"Juno, take a breath," I urged.

She went still and her face froze, but it seemed like there was a flicker of fear.

So I didn't delay in saying, "It's important you understand what this is."

The stillness evaporated and she said fast, "You like him, and he likes you. He's your Mag. Your Boone. Your Axl. But he's yours. He's Auggie. And you guys are getting together."

Definitely didn't read it wrong.

Also definitely needed to make note how much Juno didn't miss about pretty much everything going on around her.

The kettle whistled, I switched it off and went to her.

"Yes, honey," I confirmed. "I like him a lot. And he likes me a lot. And we've been seeing each other a bit while you were at your dad's. But we all have to like each other toge—"

"I like him," she chirped. "A whole load."

"Okay. I'm glad. But the reason I want you to take a breath is—"

"Because Dad uses up his girlfriends and things sometimes don't work out and you don't want me sad if they don't work out with Auggie."

I wasn't big on her interrupting me, but she was excited, so I let that slide.

I also wasn't big on how grown-up she was getting, because she definitely had her finger on the pulse of a lot.

In fact, pretty much everything.

To communicate that last, I said, "Yeah."

"Will you ask him to cook with us?" she requested.

In other words, could I ask him to come earlier so we had more time with him.

Oh yeah, I could.

"Can you be careful and pour my tea while I do that?"

"Totally!" she cried, her voice rising.

I smiled at her.

I loved this, even if it worried me.

Not that things weren't going great with Auggie.

Just that life happened.

Parents happened.

Moms got cancer.

Brothers acted like assholes.

Exes interfered.

And I hadn't lied to Aug. If I had my choice, I'd shield her from all of that (case in point: I hadn't yet told her about Mom).

But it wasn't my choice.

She raced to the teakettle.

I went to the office to grab my phone.

Aug picked up after three rings.

"Hey, baby," he greeted.

"Well, Juno is beside herself you're coming to dinner. But she wants you to cook it with us. She also doesn't want you to have to wait to eat if you're hungry after work. So which way do you wanna go with that?"

I wasn't surprised in the slightest when he said, "Cook with you."

Yeah, that was Auggie.

We were doing this.

And he was all in.

"As per Juno's request, it's going to be cornucopia of Asian delights. Pot stickers. Edamame. Teriyaki chicken and rice. We'll probably steam some veggies too."

"You make all that from scratch?"

"Well, I don't make my own wonton wrappers, but...yes."

I heard his soft laughter then, "Sounds good. I'll bring dessert. Anything she particularly digs?"

"She's got a sweet tooth, but not fond of coconut."

"Cool," he said.

"Okay, just let us know when you're on your way."

"No, I mean cool."

"Sorry?" I asked, confused as to why he reiterated this.

"To know that about Juno. That she doesn't like coconut. It feels good to know that." He hesitated and then asked, "Is that weird?"

I shut my eyes.

Stood silent in that moment.

I opened my eyes and said quietly, "It is the least weird thing in the world."

"Cool," he whispered.

"See you later."

"Later, baby."

We hung up and my gaze moved out the window.

My HOA fees were serious. They were also visible. We had great landscaping and beautifully kept shared spaces.

The neighborhood was bustling, and it was busy, and it was pretty, but the units were nearly on top of each other. It never really felt peaceful and serene, unless I was coming home from work, and the 'hood was asleep.

Usually, it felt vibrant and alive even if no one was out of doors. It just hummed.

I liked that for Juno and me.

But right then, it felt tranquil.

Like an oasis.

All because Auggie realized how important it was to know my kid didn't like coconut.

Life happened.

Parents happened.

Moms got cancer.

Brothers acted like assholes.

Exes interfered.

But I had Juno.

And maybe, we were going to have Auggie.

So maybe there would come a time when we three would brave the storms of life together.

Or maybe it was simply that what Auggie brought to the equation was that.

The solidity.

The serenity.

The oasis.

No.

Our mountain.

I moved to the kitchen, to my tea and to my daughter, seriously at one with this thought.

I did this having no idea, in just a couple of hours, and onward from that, how significantly that concept was going to be tested.

CHAPTER NINETEEN
The Goal

AUGGIE

If Pepper's earlier phone call hadn't shared the intel with him, his greeting not quite at the door of her place that evening did.

He'd parked in her drive and the door to her house opened before he'd closed the one on his Telluride.

And Juno was racing to him.

He saw her mom in the doorway.

But he had no choice but to give her daughter his full attention.

She shuddered to a halt in front of him and almost shouted, "Hey, Auggie!"

"Hey, sweetheart," he replied.

That was when she threw herself at him, hugging his hips.

He rested his hand on her head.

In rank, his favorite was Pepper opening the door like she couldn't wait for him to turn up.

But this was a very close second.

She jumped back.

"We did all the prep work," she announced. "Mom said that's

no fun. It's way more fun to put it together and cook it. Do you like cutting stuff up?"

"I'm down with wherever you are in the process."

"Yay!" she said, then nabbed his hand.

They headed toward the door with Juno doing a kind of walk-skip at his side that was a lot more than kind of cute.

When they got to the front porch, Juno let him go, stepped back, and stared at him and her mother expectantly.

He gave his attention to Pepper.

And he saw that night, it was at-home gear: black leggings, white tee that fell loosely to her hips, oversized light gray cardigan over that.

She had makeup on, though, and her hair was curled.

The clothes were communicating something for Juno.

The rest was for Auggie.

"Hey," he said, seeing her, the effort she made, thinking about their morning, the night before and feeling his lips tip up.

"Hey," she replied, then gave him a slight dip of her chin that said, *Yes, we're in that zone with Juno, but keep it cool.*

He did that, bending to touch his mouth to hers, and that was it.

Her green eyes were sparkling when he pulled away.

He grinned at her, and when her gaze started going in that direction, his did too and they looked down at Juno.

Her eyes weren't sparkling.

She was lit up.

This was going to be a fun night.

"C'mon." Juno grabbed Auggie's hand again and dragged him inside.

Like it always did, the place looked good and smelled good, and by the time Juno got him to the kitchen, he knew the second part of that was about the candles Pepper had burning.

"Okay, so the edamame is *eeeee-zeeeee*, so we're not gonna mess with that now," Juno declared. "That means you have your choice. You can make the teriyaki sauce. Or you can put the dumplings together with me. Which way are you gonna go?"

"Totally dumplings," he told her.

She radiated glee and then hopped over to a space at the counter where there was a step stool set up and a bunch of stuff laid out.

"This is our station," she shared as she stepped onto the stool.

"Are you hungry, Dollface?" Pepper asked, and he looked over his shoulder to see her close.

She demonstrated this closeness further by pressing her hand to his back, somehow making a touch you might do to a stranger something demonstrative and warm and communicative.

It said *Welcome to our home*.

It said *Have fun with my daughter*.

It said *I'm glad you're here*.

He'd had versions of all that before from other women, from friends.

But he also didn't miss that this time, it meant more than it ever had.

"Oh no," Juno said, and Aug turned back to her. "Are you hungry, Auggie?"

"I'm good to cook," he replied.

"I'm asking that because you're rushing, baby girl," Pepper said, moving away from him and toward the fridge. "Maybe Aug might want to start out with a beer or something."

"Oh my gosh! Sorry!" Juno cried, jumped off the stool and raced to the fridge. She opened it and called it down. "We have beers. And Mom's wine. And we have grape juice, because that's my favorite. And cranberry juice, because that's Mom's favorite. And fizzy water that tastes like cherries, because that's Mom's *and* my favorite." She turned to him. "Or we can pour fresh tea over ice. Mom says that tastes *heavenly*."

She exaggerated that last word with a roll of her eyes, which meant when she focused back on Auggie, he was smiling.

"Beer, Juno," he ordered. "Thanks."

"Grab that bottle of wine while you're at it, honey," Pepper said, even though she was standing over her daughter at the fridge.

Juno did the heavy lifting.

Pepper popped the cap on the beer.

Auggie took the beer as Pepper asked him, "Good day?"

It was now.

"Yeah," he replied, because they hadn't gotten around to talking about his work, not that he could talk about his work, but right then, even if he could, he wouldn't. "You?"

"*Great* day," she emphasized, giving him a look filled with meaning, then moving her attention to her daughter, which gave her look another meaning.

He touched her hip just because, but also to tell her he read and liked her meaning before he headed to his "station."

Juno was already there.

"Okay," Juno began to boss when he came up next to her. "The cabbage is drained. You put all that together." She circled a hand to the bowls of filling ingredients. "I'll get the wrappers ready and when you finish mixing that up, you can squidge it in the wrapper and we can—"

She stopped talking when a cell phone sounded somewhere in the house.

And then she was staring at the countertop, losing color in her face.

"Did I not turn off my ringer?" Pepper asked from where she was down the counter, making the teriyaki sauce.

Pepper started to move, but Juno moved faster, whirling and falling off the step so Auggie had to catch her before she took a header.

He set her on her feet, and she didn't even notice he saved her from falling on her face.

She yelled, "Mom!"

Shit.

That was the phone Cisco had given to her.

Cisco hadn't managed to get it back and things were such, Auggie hadn't followed up on that.

Pepper turned to her girl.

The phone kept ringing.

"I'm just going to go turn off —" Pepper started.

"That's my phone."

Pepper stood still.

Yeah.

Shit.

"Dad gave it to me," Juno admitted.

Hang on a second.

"He...*what*?" Pepper asked quietly.

"Iwasgonnatellyou," Juno said, running the words together. "But then you said Auggie was coming over and we made the grocery list and went to the store and then we had to put stuff away and cut stuff up and—"

"I was there when we did all that, Juno," Pepper said. "Your father gave you a phone?"

"Yeah," Juno replied, her voice super soft.

And Aug wondered if she was lying to save her ass after connecting with Cisco or if something else was up.

"You guys carry on," Pepper said in a tight voice. "I'll be back."

She then turned and took off.

He looked down to Juno. "Sweetheart, was it your dad who gave you that phone?"

She appeared perplexed. "Yeah. This weekend. On Satur—"

She cut herself off and her eyes got big as she understood his question and that he might know about Cisco.

He covered that by asking, "Why does your mom seem mad?"

"Because I'm not allowed to have one until I'm fifteen, maybe fourteen, if I'm mature enough."

He nodded. "Can you mix the stuff up? We'll fill the wrappers in a second."

"Okay, Auggie," she said.

He went after Pepper.

The double doors to the office were closed, and he hadn't been there often, but in the times he had, he'd never seen them like that.

He knocked, and in about half a second, one side opened.

He saw she had her phone to her ear.

She caught his sweater in a fist, yanked him in and shut the door behind him.

"No, *Corbin*," she spat into the phone, "our decision was that she'd be a lot older when she got—" Silence for a while, then, "That isn't your choice to make." More silence, and, "I cannot *believe*—" She was obviously cut off, then, "How old are you? Are you serious with this?"

She was staring unfocused at Aug's shoulder, but after she asked that, her eyes found his and at what he saw in her face, he rested his hand on her waist, but there was nothing else he could do.

Not a thing.

She was ticked way the fuck off by whatever was happening, and it was out of his power to do anything to help.

"Right then, that's enough said," she stated in a final way. "Just to note, I'll be confiscating the phone. She won't be returning to your house with it." Long pause, then, "As you just shared, it's your prerogative and since Juno's a minor, she can't really own any property, so it will belong to you and as such, you're within your rights to keep it at your house when she's with me. But just to warn you, I'll be having a conversation with her. And I swear, Corbin, if I see any shit happening, like she's being weird about her appearance, or her clothes, or how her hair is, or falling behind on schoolwork, or her attention span takes a hit, whatever, we're gonna have a problem. And it will be a serious one. Because she doesn't need any of that social media shit weighing in her world right now. And you've introduced it. Because you're a child. And that's done. Good-bye."

She took her phone from her ear and then bowed her head to turn it off.

She shifted to toss it on her desk and then she looked out the window.

"Babe?" he called.

"In all that's going on, I forgot to reply to Corbin's text asking me to sit down and have a chat with him. He felt that was rude. And to teach me a lesson about this rudeness, instead of having an adult conversation with me, he decided to give Juno something she really wants, something a lot of her friends have, something I am staunchly against her having until she can process what will be coming at her in all the ways she can use it...a cell phone."

"Right."

She was still looking out the window when she carried on.

"He says not only does she want it, he has the means to give it to her, but also she can have it in case of emergency. I asked him when she'd possibly ever have an emergency, considering she's always one of four places. At school. On the bus to or from school. With him or someone he assigns to watch her. Or with me, or someone I do the same."

"His answer?" Auggie prompted when she stopped talking.

She still didn't look from the window when she replied, "He had no answer to that."

She took a second, tipped her head in a stilted way like she was trying to crack her neck, then she spoke again.

"I think it's safe to say that he's out of the trying-to-win-me-back zone. He's gotten a good look at you, you with me, how Juno reacts to you, and he's realized that isn't going to happen. Now he's in the acting-out zone, which could peter out this week, if he finds some woman to devote his attention to, and he forgets about me. Or it could last until you sit at my side while I weep at Juno's wedding."

"Okay, but, baby, I gotta ask. Why aren't you looking at me?"

"Because, I'm so angry, I'm seething that he felt the appropriate response to not getting what he wants was not only to use our daughter to get back at me, but also to do something that might cause her harm in the long run. And furthering this, he broke an agreement we'd made about this particular subject, one he knows I feel strongly about, doing this on the whim to strike back. And I don't want you to see how deeply pissed I am about that."

This was not good.

Not only all she said.

But because he had no place in it.

And that wasn't because this was his first dinner with Juno and Pepper in their home, time to get to know one another, see if they all fit, and how that might happen.

But because he'd never have a place in it.

He'd had some temporary stepdad- and stepmom-type people along the way.

That didn't cipher into what Aug was currently thinking.

He wasn't Juno's father. He'd never be her father.

It would never be his right to get in his car, drive to this asshole's house, and lay it out for him.

He could not protect Juno. He couldn't protect Pepper.

He could do absolutely nothing but stand there.

And he didn't like it.

So yeah.

This was not good.

"Maybe give him some time, you take some time, and then broach the subject a little later," he suggested.

"He says he's going out tomorrow to buy her another phone and she'll be free to use it when she's with him, but he'll keep it when she comes to me so I won't 'do anything stupid.'"

"Have you disagreed before about this kind of thing?"

She finally turned to look at him.

"We've had our ebbs and flows. In the beginning—"

She stopped speaking and pulled in her lips, which meant Auggie braced.

She let her lips go and her voice was different when she said, "Okay, in the beginning, I admit, I was a basket case. I was angry. I was hurt. I loved him. I missed him. I was also scared to be alone. And there was some time, and sadly it lasted longer than it should, where I was hot and cold with him."

She shook her head vehemently and kept going.

"We didn't get together in that time. But I can't say that I didn't give him mixed signals. My daughter was sad, and I hated that. And I was sad, and I didn't like that much better."

"That's understandable, Pepper," he pointed out.

To that, she nodded, mumbled, "Thanks," and went on, "As a consequence, we were around each other a lot. Or at least he came over a lot. I could act a little...*crazy*. And I think maybe Corbin got it in his head that I did that because I was gone for him, he'd always be," she did air quotation marks, "*the one* for me and the fact that you're the first after him, and it's been years, solidified that opinion."

She drew in a breath.

And kept talking.

"I'm also seeing now that me acting like that, and our residual head butting, gave him the impression I still cared. The passion hadn't died, as it were."

"Yeah?" he asked leadingly when she didn't say any more.

"So I need to give myself a moment to lament this decision and then figure out what's next."

Auggie stood immobile.

He did this waiting for the buzzing to leave his ears.

When it did, he asked with forced calm, "Let me get this

straight. That asshole deceived you in the worst possible way a man can deceive his woman, you had an emotional response to that, he mistook that response because he's got his head lodged up his ass, and you're taking a moment to lament and figure out how to deal with him?"

She stared at him and nodded slowly.

Well, this was good.

Because he sure as shit could do something about *this*.

"Do not take on his shit."

She opened her mouth.

He hooked her behind the neck and pulled her to him so her body hit his.

"Do not take on his shit," he repeated.

Her hands came to rest on his hips, and she stared up at him, but said nothing.

"He's being a dick. That's who he is. That's what he does. It isn't yours. I can listen and help you work out how you'll respond to him using Juno to get back at you. But I'm not gonna stand here and listen to you take on his shit. It is *not* cool that he gave her a phone. She's way too fuckin' young. It's far less cool that you two had made a decision, and he reneged on that for the sole purpose of punishing you for a crime that's only a crime in his mind. He can go fuck himself. You do what you want with her phone. This house is yours. The rules are yours. And if you want me to help, together we can try to come up with a plan to make sure she's good when she has something with her dad she doesn't have with her mom. And as far as he's concerned, that's it. He made a decision, his house, his rules, and it has dick to do with you."

Auggie was so intent on saying the things he had to say, he didn't notice how hard the pads of her fingers were pressing into his hips.

But when he was done, he did.

So he asked, "Sweetheart?"

"I . . . can't even . . ." Her voice was hollow, like an echo, lost in a turmoil of emotions.

He did not like the sound, and in response to it, pulled her fully into his arms.

She put her hands on his chest to stop him from doing anything else and continued speaking.

"I don't have a family. I don't have a mom or a dad to go to and say, 'Look. You have experience. Am I doing this right?'"

Jesus Christ.

He'd never thought of that.

It had never occurred to him how alone she was doing something as colossal as raising a child.

"None of my friends have kids," she went on. She shook her head but said, "I can't even tell you how much it means that you simply validated where I was at with this, but more, offered me a sounding board."

"Anytime, baby."

"It means a lot, Auggie."

"I'm getting that."

"So much, you won't know, until you have a kid."

"Yeah," he agreed.

They stared at each other.

She didn't hide the gratitude in her face.

He felt something he hadn't felt in all he'd done, seen, learned and experienced in his life.

A million feet tall.

"Am I in trouble, or what?" Juno shouted through the door.

Auggie smiled.

He caught a hint of the same from Pepper before she dropped her head and pressed it to his chest for a beat before she lifted it and called out, "No, baby."

"Okay, then are we making dinner, or what?" Juno asked.

Pepper rolled up on her toes to kiss his jaw before she pulled from his arms and went to the door.

She opened it.

And she didn't delay.

"You know how I feel about phones."

Juno's eyes darted to Auggie, her face started to flush, but Pepper didn't let the embarrassment settle in.

"So I'm gonna need you to give it to me. You aren't in trouble for having it or not telling me you did. I believe you were gonna tell me. Then I sprung our dinner plans on you. But you can't have it here and you won't be taking it back to your dad's. It's just my rule. And if he's decided he has a different one, that's between you and your dad. I'll just ask that you use it only for emergencies, or maybe listening to music, and you don't spend a lot of time on apps or games or TikTok. You can laugh at someone who you'll never meet who's probably very funny. Or you can laugh with people right there in the room with you who love you very much." She smiled at her girl. "I know what you're gonna do at our house. How that goes when you're not here..."

She trailed off, shrugged, then bent to kiss her girl's forehead.

When she straightened, Juno asked, "Do you want me to go get it for you now?"

Shit, Juno was a good kid.

And she got that from her mom.

Pepper shook her head. "No, baby. I'm getting hungry. You and Auggie make dumplings."

There was hesitation when she asked, "Are you mad at Dad?"

"I'm not happy with him. But sometimes he does things I don't like. And sometimes I do things he doesn't like. Or you don't like. Or you do things I don't like. It's the nature of the world. The test always is, regardless of that, we find a way to keep on keeping on. You with me?"

Juno grinned up at her mom. "Yeah."

"Am I gonna eat dumplings before New Year's?" Pepper asked.

Juno giggled. "Don't be crazy, Mom."

"I won't be crazy if you feed me."

Juno turned to Auggie. "C'mon, Auggie. We gotta feed Mom."

"I'm there," Auggie replied.

Juno took off.

Pepper stayed where she was, and Aug went there.

He didn't stop as he passed her, but he maintained eye contact when he said, "Well done."

"Thanks, honey," she murmured.

He grinned at her too.

Then he met up with another girl, this one brunette, in order to make dumplings.

*   *   *

"So I'm thinking volleyball. But also softball. I don't know. I did softball this summer. But it's kinda boring. There's a lot of sitting or standing around. You can go a whole inning, and nothing will happen. Volleyball, if you're on the bench, that's boring. But if you're playing, you gotta be *sharp*," Juno chattered.

There were only two stools at the island, so he and Pepper were on their couch, close but not too close, eating, and Juno was entrenched in a nest of cushions and pillows on the floor, also eating.

"So, do you like volleyball or softball?" Juno asked Auggie.

"I like both," he answered, cutting into a pan-seared dumpling that was better than any he'd ever had at a restaurant or takeout.

He was looking forward to the teriyaki.

Juno made a face.

"What?" he asked.

"You don't have to like both because I like both," she said, a thread of impatience in her tone.

He felt Pepper shift at his side.

But he understood that impatience.

It had been a long time, but he'd felt the frustration of dealing with an adult who did shit and said shit only to make you like them.

A kid didn't cognizantly know the ways and means of getting to know someone.

They still knew when someone they wanted to get to know was bullshitting them.

"I'm not," he said before Pepper could get in there and admonish her girl about her tone. "I like both. And I think you already answered your question, because you think softball is boring. All you said about the game isn't gonna change. It's the same game now as it will be if you do it every summer for the next ten years. If you don't like it now, you won't like it then. And it looks like you're gonna be tall. And to be good at volleyball, it helps to be tall."

He shot a smile at her and finished.

"Though, neither of these sports is gonna be banned in the next five years. So you can try volleyball, and if you change your mind about softball, you can go back."

The liveliness had returned to her voice when she asked, "Which one do you prefer to watch?"

"Do they let adults drink beer at your softball games?"

She twittered and answered, "No."

"Then volleyball," he replied.

"You can't drink beer at a volleyball game either," she noted.

He faked shock. "Really?"

She giggled, then offered, "You can hide your beer in a Koozie."

He shook his head and kept his tone light and his lips tipped up when he stated, "No way. I always am who I am and do what I do openly. Hiding isn't my bag."

Juno held his gaze and said, "Me either."

"Good take to have," he replied.

"Yeah," she muttered, and looked down to her food.

She totally knew he knew about Cisco.

The doorbell rang.

Auggie tensed.

"No biggie," Pepper said softly, shifting in the couch like she was going to get up. "FYI, this happens a lot. The 'hood is friendly. Evening drop-bys aren't often, but they happen."

"I'll get it," he replied, also shifting in the couch to get up.

"You eat, I'll get it."

"Is there a reason you don't want me to get it?" he asked low.

She caught his eyes.

Then she settled back.

And she said a lot with one word.

"No."

He felt his face get soft before he put his plate on the coffee table, got up and headed to the door of Pepper's house, which meant whoever was beyond it would know she had a man in that house.

He didn't do it for that reason.

He did it because she was probably the only one who had to get up and get the door.

It was no big thing, but if he was around, he could do that too.

He looked out the side window and nearly cursed, profanely, and loud.

He bit that back and unlocked the door, opened it, and stepped out, which pushed Birch Hannigan back three feet.

Hannigan looked perturbed at having to step back.

Auggie was beyond perturbed the guy was there.

He shut the door behind him.

Then he asked, "Can I help you?"

Hannigan's attention moved to the door then back to Auggie.

"Does Pepper Hannigan live here?"

This was a sitch.

Because he didn't know how this guy found his sister.

But that didn't matter now.

What mattered now was that he didn't know if he should confirm she lived there.

Easy enough for Hannigan to stake it out. Come back at a time Aug wasn't there.

But for now...

"What can I help you with?" Auggie decided to repeat.

Hannigan's brows drew down over his eyes.

He already knew it. He'd seen pictures, mostly mug shots, but the entire Hannigan family, from her dad, to her sister, to this guy, were attractive.

Tall, straight, slim, blond.

"You can help me by tellin' me if my sister lives here."

"She does," Auggie decided to confirm. "But I asked you a question. What can I help you with?"

"Who the fuck are you?"

"Someone who is not okay with you standing on your sister's porch, a sister you haven't seen in over a decade, asking who the fuck the man is who opened her front door."

Hannigan's head ticked. "You her husband or something?"

"I'm seeing that you don't get in this scenario that you aren't the one who gets to ask questions. Now, why are you here when Pepper has no idea that you're showing at her house tonight?"

"She called me, and we got shit to discuss."

Auggie nodded. "Yes, she did. And you were really not cool with her. Now, I suspect you understand who I am and how I'm not big on you showing as a surprise while we're having dinner."

The man started to get even more edgy. "I just wanna talk to my sister, all right?"

"Then call her."

"She isn't answering my calls."

"Then leave a message that you wanna speak to her."

Hannigan's mood deteriorated further. "Listen, bud, I don't got time for this shit."

"You don't have time to listen to me telling you how you might connect with your sister to discuss your mother's illness?"

"No, I don't got time for your bullshit. Now go in there and tell my sister I'm out here and I wanna talk to her."

Aug shook his head. "Right now, I'm gonna ask you to leave. And I'll tell Pepper you were here, and she should reach out again. Then you two can decide—"

Hannigan's voice was rising. "I'm here now, asshole."

Auggie crossed his arms on his chest and kept his tone modulated. "There's no reason to get agitated."

Now Hannigan's face was getting red. "There is, because you're bein' a dick."

"We're not doing this," Auggie told him. "You're gonna go and I'll talk to Pepper about calling you."

"Fuck you," he bit out. "I'm here now, she's in there, what the fuck's your problem, bud?"

"My problem is—"

He didn't finish that because the door behind him opened.

Damn it.

Hannigan looked there.

Auggie didn't.

He knew who it was, and he didn't feel comfortable taking his attention away from her brother.

"Birch?" she whispered, and Auggie felt her join them, hearing the door click shut behind her.

Hannigan heard it too.

"So, what? You're gonna bar me from your fancy-ass house like your husband did?" he demanded.

Aug felt her gaze on his profile. "My hus—?"

He lost her attention when Hannigan interrupted her. "You

could take a call, Pepper. What the fuck with calling me and sayin' Mom's sick then ghosting me?"

"I told you how you could find them," Pepper pointed out.

"Well, I don't wanna deal with that. Or Dad. Or that Stepford bitch we call a sister. I just wanna talk to Mom. And you can get me that."

"I've barely seen her myself, Birch, and I only did for a second because I went to services."

"Jesus," Birch clipped. "I ain't doin' that."

"Saffron's setting it up so I can see her tomorrow," Pepper told her brother what was news to Auggie.

"She is?" he asked, looking down at her.

She nodded up to him. "I didn't have a chance to tell you, what with all the stuff that went down when you—"

"Uh...hello," Hannigan cut in. "Your brother you haven't seen in for-fuckin'-ever." He pointed to himself. "Standing right here."

Auggie wasn't liking any of this.

But he really didn't like that.

"Birch—" she tried.

"You know, it's too bad I don't have a pussy. If I had a fuckin' pussy, I could score myself some dick who could give me a sick pad and would come out and deal with all my shit so I didn't have to do it."

Auggie's back shot straight.

Pepper moved to sidle in front of him.

"I'd advise not pissing Auggie off," she said softly.

"You know, Pepper, I don't give a fuck what you'd advise. I was all right and then you phone and drag me into shit I don't wanna know. I don't wanna care. I don't wanna give that first shit that Mom is dying of cancer."

The door opened.

"Grandma's dying?"

Hannigan's eyes shot in that direction and both Aug and Pepper turned around to see Juno standing there, white as a ghost, staring at her mother.

"Juno, honey," Pepper whispered.

"She's *dying*?" Juno asked her mom.

Stiltedly, Auggie turned back to Hannigan.

He then felt Pepper's hand land on his chest.

Oh yeah.

Good call.

Auggie took a deep breath and paid attention to the in and out of it while Pepper talked to her girl.

"Go inside, we'll talk in a bit," she said.

"Who's that?" Juno asked.

"My question," Hannigan said quietly, staring at Juno.

"Step to your car," Auggie growled.

Hannigan's face shot back to belligerent and he turned it to Aug.

"It's okay," Pepper said.

"It's not," he replied, not taking his attention from her brother.

"It is. Juno, honey, come out here."

He felt her shoulder brush his chest as she stayed close in front of him and Juno joined their huddle.

"Birch, this is my daughter, Juno. Juno, this is your uncle Birch," Pepper introduced.

"I've heard about you," Juno said.

"You have?" Hannigan asked.

"Mom said you were the best big brother ever."

Hannigan had no response to that, but his face got red again. This time, Auggie guessed, for far different reasons.

"You look like Granddad," Juno continued.

"You got your mother's eyes," Hannigan replied.

Right.

Done.

"Okay, sweetheart, do me and your mom a favor and go back inside," Auggie requested.

Hannigan narrowed his gaze on Aug.

"Okay," Juno said. "Nice t'meet you, Uncle Birch."

The man forced his attention to his niece. "You too, girl."

Juno went inside.

The second the door closed, Hannigan asked Auggie heatedly, "What? Is she nine? Ten? You knock my sister up in high school or something? The fuck?"

"Birch—" Pepper started.

"It's none of your business," Auggie stated, and he did it precisely to keep this man thinking Juno was his.

Because there were things he couldn't do for these two females in his life.

But protecting them from this asshole wasn't one of them.

"You think my sister isn't my business?" Hannigan demanded.

"Man, she hasn't seen you in *over a decade*," Auggie shot back. "Do not think you can show at her door and pretend you give a shit." He shook his head. "Now, we…are…done." He looked to Pepper. "Get inside, baby. You can call him to talk when you're down to do that. Now, Juno's in there, probably freaked."

She stared at him.

She kept doing it.

Then she nodded and turned to her brother.

"I'll call you, Birch. After I sit down with Mom. I'll know more then. Okay?"

"Yeah," Hannigan grunted.

"You…I…you look good," she said and finished, "We'll talk."

Another grunt from Hannigan. "Yeah."

"Come in soon, honey," she said to Aug. "Dinner is getting cold."

"Be right in," he replied.

She touched his hand and walked into the house.

Aug remained stationed in front of the door.

Then Hannigan surprised him by saying, "I didn't know she had a kid or that she was listening."

"Well, because you handled this like you did, now we gotta deal with that," Auggie returned.

"She looks..." He didn't finish.

He glanced around, taking in the pumpkins, the sign by the door that said to be grateful, the warm light that filtered through the windows and pooled on the porch.

Hannigan cleared his throat.

"Pepper looks happy."

"That's the goal," Auggie replied.

His faced hardened. "I know you think I got no right, but gonna say it anyway. Don't fuck her over, you know? I think you get she's had it bad enough."

"You're a little late to be sharing that intel, but I hear you. And don't worry. No way I'd fuck her over. Or Juno. Now, I'll ask the same."

"I'd never fuck her over," the man spat.

Auggie just lifted his brows.

And again was surprised when the hostility slid out of Hannigan and he looked contrite before he looked away.

"Juno's a cool name," he muttered to a pumpkin by the door.

"I got two girls in there I'd like to see to. You gonna take off, or we gonna chat for the next half an hour?" Auggie asked, and regained Hannigan's attention.

At first, he looked combative.

That faded and he pushed out, "Let you see to them."

"Obliged."

Hannigan nodded.

Auggie didn't nod back.

He watched the man turn and lope down the walk.

And he waited until Hannigan's POS car chugged down the street before he went into the house.

He locked the door and headed into the living room.

Pepper was curled up into the corner of the sofa, Juno curled into the crook of her legs.

They both held their plates in front of them, but neither of them looked real interested in eating.

And both sets of eyes came to him when he appeared from the hallway.

"Is he gone?" Juno asked.

Aug retrieved his plate, hesitated, and when he saw Pepper indicate with her eyes that he was to share the couch with them at the other end, he settled in and answered, "Yeah, honey, he's gone."

"I'm fed up with stupid stuff happening," Juno muttered to her plate, and he felt tension, just as sure as he felt the same from Pepper.

"What other stupid stuff is happening, baby?" Pepper asked gently.

"You know, Grandma being sick. And you know, Granddad always being all . . . weird. And that kind of stuff."

She shoved a bite of dumpling in her mouth.

Auggie met Pepper's eyes over Juno's body.

"Stay late?" she mouthed.

He was so totally staying late.

He nodded.

"Life stinks sometimes, baby," she murmured to her daughter. "We'll talk about it more tomorrow after I get finished seeing Grandma. But for now, do you think you can have fun with me and Auggie?"

Juno looked at him. "I thought you were gonna bring dessert."

"Juno," Pepper chided.

"I could have grabbed something from King Soopers, and I could still head out and grab something. But I figured you might wanna hit Glacier instead."

Juno sat up so fast from her lounge against her mother's backside and thighs, she almost lost her plate.

"Glacier!" she cried.

It hadn't been lost on him that she'd gone mental when they'd been at a cookout at Lottie and Mo's and Mo had said he was gonna go get ice cream and asked Juno to help him pick flavors from Glacier.

"Work for you?" Auggie asked casually.

"That's my *favorite*," Juno told him what he already knew.

"You're joking. I never would have guessed," he teased.

She shot him a smile even while wrinkling her nose. It was cute as fuck, but that wasn't the only reason he grinned.

"Awesome," she told her plate, returning to it with a lot more enthusiasm.

That was why he grinned.

"Yeah, totally freaking *awesome*," Pepper murmured, and Aug looked at her to see her looking at him with a warmth he felt so deep in his bones, he wasn't sure it'd ever leave.

Then she, too, returned to her plate.

"Next time you come over for dinner, you get to decide what we cook," Juno declared.

That had Auggie grinning at his plate.

"You like ham?" he asked.

"Yes," Juno answered.

"Hash browns?" he asked.

"Yes," Juno answered.

"Then we'll make my ham and hash casserole," he stated.

She turned to him. "Does it have cheese?"

"Yes, lots of it."

She shot him a sassy smile. "Approved."

Auggie started laughing.

And if he wasn't wrong, he heard Pepper let out a sigh when he did.

So he looked at her and saw her eating, her face soft, her attention in the room, her vibe chilled.

Pepper looks happy.

That's the goal.
And it was the goal.
Another goal: that right there.
Safe at home.
With her kid.
And her guy.
People around her that gave a shit.
People around her that thought she was the shit.
People around her that cared a whole fuckuva lot.
So she could be relaxed.
And chill.

CHAPTER TWENTY

Happiness Is...

PEPPER

He'd picked her up.

Picked my eight-year-old baby up and sat her on the hood of his car in the parking lot of a gelato spot.

When he'd done that, she'd gotten stars in her eyes and I think she fell a little bit (more) in love.

I did too.

Then Auggie leaned into a hand against his hood close to her, and they licked ice cream cones in the dry chill of a November night.

Auggie in his blue sweater.

Juno wearing her cute, purple puffy vest over her navy-blue thermal that had big purple and aqua flowers all over it, a purple, teal and pink beanie on her head with a massive hot pink floof on the top of it.

They were adorable together.

In the ice cream shop, he'd encouraged her to try every flavor she wanted and teasingly conducted an interview where he asked her to review them as she was doing it. She got into it, acting all serious even while stifling giggles.

It was fabulous. Like they had their own YouTube channel about ice cream.

He'd bought her a double scoop.

He'd also tipped big so we didn't seem like assholes because we took so much time and tried so much gelato.

Once outside, they talked about the Thanksgiving play.

And they talked about how cool Mr. Sykes was.

And they talked about how all the boys and some of the girls in her class wanted to be marines now.

And they talked about how Juno was a master dumpling folder.

Sometimes Juno would laugh.

Sometimes Auggie would.

And I leaned against Auggie's hood a few feet away from them, quiet and eating my own ice cream.

Because this felt like a different kind of date.

It was going well.

And I was totally a third wheel.

But watching them together, I thought this was it.

This was what happiness is.

* * *

Later that night, after gelato at Glacier, I sat on the side of Juno's bed like I used to when she was little, and I smoothed her soft hair back.

"You gonna sleep okay?" I asked.

"Sure," my girl murmured to the wall opposite us.

She was lying on her side with her back to me, the better for me to get my fingers through her hair.

I drew in breath and let it out, noting, "You sure? It was a big night. Auggie here. Uncle Birch showing." I hesitated. "Your grandma."

"It's okay, Momma."

Right.

Juno said that sometimes.

And when she did, I always wondered if she meant, "I'm okay," or, "It's going to be okay. We'll survive."

I wanted the first.

I'd work for the second.

"Thank you for understanding about the phone," I said.

"I should have told you right off," she mumbled.

"I understand why you didn't."

She rolled to her back and looked me right in the eye.

Then she bossed, "You should be downstairs with Auggie."

"I wanna make certain you're all right."

"I'd be all right if you were downstairs with Auggie."

I started laughing.

"What's funny?" she asked.

I bent closer to her and whispered, "I have a little matchmaker."

"I like the way he looks at you," she whispered back.

A lovely shiver slithered up my spine.

And not only because I was happy she liked that.

But because I liked the way he looked at me too.

"And I liked that he got mad at Uncle Birch for ruining our dinner," she continued. "I mean, I know you haven't seen him in forever, but it's not nice to show up at someone's house and not call first. Unless you're Jenn and you've run out of ranch dressing or something and need to pop over real quick."

She was right and I was glad she had that attitude.

Though I thought it was sweet, how she'd talked to her uncle.

In those moments, he'd become the Birch I knew.

I just didn't want her to get her hopes up that she was finally going to have some good on my side of her family, because if

Birch kept acting like he did, that might be the only time she'd ever see him.

This was why I warned, "I don't know how much he's going to be in our lives, honey. We've grown apart."

"That's okay, we'll have Auggie."

That surprised me.

It also worried me.

"Honey, he and I are just starting to see each other," I cautioned.

"I won't get my hopes up," she promised.

She maybe didn't want to believe that was a fib.

But I knew it was a fib.

I decided not to dig too deep into that.

"And when we lose Grandma, are we gonna grow apart from Granddad and Auntie Saffron?" she asked, not hiding she did it hopefully.

That surprised me too.

Not what she said or that she'd hope for that.

But that she said it.

"I think that's a possibility, Juno," I admitted.

She didn't appear upset about that at all.

In fact, all I saw was relief.

And in that moment, all I felt was sad.

Because they were missing out on my girl.

Mom was going to die, not really knowing her.

And Dad and Saff were going to go on, never having Juno be a true part of their lives.

"We're the dream team, you and me," she announced.

"Always," I agreed.

"Now go be smoochy with Auggie," she ordered.

I rolled my eyes and said, "Don't be bossy."

"You'll never keep him if you make him sit alone on our pink couch while you stay up here, talking to me."

"This seems to be excellent advice," I teased.

"Men don't like pink," she declared with authority.

"I don't know, some men do."

"Okay, but can we discuss that when Auggie's not hanging out alone on our pink couch?"

I kept teasing. "No. Because I think it's important right now at this very moment that you fully comprehend the concept of stereotypes. In this case, saying all men don't like pink. Men can like whatever they like. And some like pink."

"I don't really care if men like pink or not," she replied.

"I don't either," I shared.

"Mah...*um*," she said my name with annoyed exaggeration. "*Go.* Be with Auggie."

I smoothed her hair away from either side of her face. I did it again, and again, then, with her head held in my hands, I bent to kiss her nose and moved away nary an inch.

"I love you with every fiber of my being," I whispered.

"I love you to the moon and back," was her reply.

"Go to sleep."

"Go be with Auggie."

"Goodnight, baby."

"'Night, Momma."

I got up and turned out the little mushroom light that was on her nightstand, this leaving the little crescent moon light that was made of wire and covered in shimmery pink netting to give the room a nightlight glow from the dresser.

I went to the door.

I stopped at it and looked back at Juno.

She had her back turned to me again, the covers up to her chin, tucked there with her hands, snug in her bed, ready to fall to sleep.

Yeah.

Again.

That right there was absolutely, one hundred percent what happiness is.

* * *

Descending the stairs after saying goodnight to Juno, I wandered down the hall and saw Auggie on our pink couch.

I smiled.

He was lounging in his corner, his legs stretched out in front of him, crossed at the ankles. He had one arm thrown long across the back of the sofa, his other hand was held up in front of him and he was looking at his phone.

He was wearing a sweater and jeans, and if he took his boots off, he'd look like he lived there.

That gave me another shiver.

What he didn't look like was bored or impatient that I took my time in saying goodnight to my girl.

He caught sight of me, put his phone down and gave me his attention.

"Hey," he greeted.

I didn't say anything until I got close and plopped my ass in his lap.

He curled an arm around me instantly, shoved his phone in his back pocket with his other hand, and then he slouched deeper into my couch and wrapped that arm around me.

I nestled until I was curled in his lap, head tucked under his chin, one arm wound around him.

"Work or something?" I asked after what he'd been doing on his phone.

"Mom."

My head shot up and I looked at him.

"Your mom?" I asked.

He nodded. "She's pissed about what I said to Dad about her. She's been blowing up my phone all day."

"And what have you been doing when she's done that?" I asked cautiously.

"Ignoring her, which, warning, usually adds fuel to the fire."

"Aug." I said his name, but I didn't know what else to say.

"I'm thinking on this," he shared.

"And what are you thinking?" I queried.

"I'm thinking that I like spending time with you. I like your house. You cook great. You're hilarious. You're sweet. You're together. Your kid is everything. We're fantastic together in bed and I dug waking up next to you. And I need to think deep about what that means when it comes to them. Because I like this so much, I want it to work. I want that a lot. And she's big on breaking things in ways they can't be fixed."

There was a great deal there.

But even though big parts of me were all about him announcing he wanted us to work, I was stuck on one thing.

"My kid is everything?"

He semi-smirked. "Don't act like you don't know that."

I full-on smirked, because I knew that.

"Speaking of moms," he said pointedly.

"We're not done with yours," I told him. "Are you seriously thinking that…?" I didn't know how to put it, so I asked him, "What are you thinking?"

"I'm thinking that I told my father I didn't know why he didn't change the locks and be done with it. And what I gotta think on is why I haven't done the same, figuratively, since she doesn't have the key to my house."

"Because she's your mom?" I suggested.

He grunted out a sigh that I not only heard but felt dug deep.

And then he said, "She's never been my mom, Pepper. I don't have memories like you do. I don't have anything to hold on to that makes me think she loved me. And that really didn't strike me until I saw how you were with Juno. Until the possibility of us being a thing was us becoming a thing. I have no stake in my relationship with her, because she never bothered to form that foundation with me. I'm useful to her on occasion. She isn't to me, ever. So now I gotta figure out if my dad goes out of my life with her, or if I'm gonna try to hold safe something I've got with him. And I have to admit, I think it'd be a whole lot easier in the long run for them both to be gone."

"This is a big decision to make in a day, honey," I said, and he smiled.

"Good I'm not making it now. I'm just thinking about it. Now... you. You're gonna see your mom tomorrow?"

I nodded.

"Want me to come with?" he offered.

I sat still.

"Hawk'll get it, I need a few hours to be with you for that," he said.

"I can't ask—"

"You didn't. But you can."

I thought about this.

I thought about how generous this offer was.

I thought how nice it would be if Auggie was there when I faced whatever I was going to face tomorrow.

And then I realized that it would not be good for Mom.

"She doesn't know you, so I should probably go alone."

"You want me to drive you?"

God, he was just so damned *awesome*.

Still, I shook my head.

"No, I'm good. But be alert. There might be a string of texts sometime after noon tomorrow that could be anything."

"You could just call," he pointed out.

"Be alert, there might be a call sometime after noon tomorrow that might be me ranting, or, alternately, sobbing."

He grinned. "I'll be alert."

Okay, that was done.

And I was glad.

Moving on...

"I'd suggest we commence making out right about now, but Juno was jazzed when she found out you were coming over. Like Christmas Eve jazzed. She seemed pretty relaxed when I left her just now, but she might sneak down to check to make sure Mom isn't screwing things up with Auggie. So we probably shouldn't."

"She seemed relaxed?"

I loved not only that he asked, but he sounded like he really wanted the answer.

So I ran it down for him.

"She thought Birch was rude for interrupting our dinner. But she liked it a lot that you were mad at him for doing it. Which translates to she likes that you stood between him and us and how he would have ruined our night if you hadn't been there. As for other stuff, she's never lost anyone, not like...not like..."

"I know what you're saying," Auggie broke in gently.

I nodded, grateful I didn't have to say yet again that Juno and me were losing my mother.

"So I'm not sure she's really processing what's happening with Mom right now. But she sees it as an opportunity to step away from Dad and Saffron, which, sharing themes with you, I was already considering."

He raised both brows. "Yeah?"

I nodded and explained, "Your father calling you a 'bastard of the church' and saying to your face you'd sully the brothers and sisters you've never met kinda puts a pall on familial feelings."

This "Yeah" from Aug was soft and tender.

I snuggled closer.

"Mostly, she wanted me to leave her and get down here to be with you," I told him.

"You've got a great kid, Pepper," he said.

"I'm glad you think that way, because she really digs you too."

He tucked me even tighter, so I dipped my head and rested my cheek against his shoulder.

"Food was fantastic," he murmured.

"Your cheesesteaks are better."

"Well, yeah, because steak...and cheese."

I laughed softly.

"A lot's going on for you, and you seem good too," he remarked.

I pressed my forehead into the side of his neck and punctuated that by saying, "Because I am."

"Baby."

The depth of those two syllables told me he got what I was saying.

"Thanks for heading off Birch."

"You wanna shield Juno from everything, but you can't. I wanna shield you both from everything, but I can't. That said, when I can, I'm gonna."

I stared at the blue sweater covering his wide chest and told myself I was not going to cry.

In order to take us somewhere to help me with that, I shared, "You know, Juno is a kid and I'm trying to teach her to take care of her things, and she's good about that. And she was the one who recently showed interest in helping me take care of our space. So she helps around the house. But she's still a kid."

"Wanna explain why you're telling me something I know?" he asked.

"Because you're exceptionally tidy." I lifted my head so I could catch his eyes and assured, "I like it. Because I am too. I like my space uncluttered. Clean. Just...you know, Juno might be in a phase where she's interested in helping because I keep our surroundings like I do. And then she'll be out of it. Or whatever. And I'm not one of those moms who rides her kid to—"

"Babe."

"What?"

"I keep my pad, car, yard, life like I do because when I grew up, it was chaotic. I realized that about myself a long time ago. It gives me something not only to see order around me, but to be the one who keeps it. When I have a kid, or if your kid is in my life, I'm not gonna be a drill sergeant. I'm gonna let 'em be kids. I can clean up after them, until it's time for them to learn how to do it for themselves. So if you're worried about that..."

He trailed off, and as he did, it came to me that I actually was kind of worried about that.

Now I wasn't.

Now I was thinking something else.

"I hate that your life was chaotic, honey," I said.

"I do too. But it was, and it isn't anymore. Or at least, it might not be in that way."

That was when I started to get ticked.

And I shared why.

"You know, it would have been cool if we could have started seeing each other, getting to know one another, bringing Juno into that without all this shit swirling around us."

"Maybe," Auggie allowed. "But shit has a way of swirling, Pepper, no matter how hard you try to stop it. I'll run down what I knew about you before we began... you're gorgeous, dress great, seemed cool, and you're a loyal friend. This is what I know now. You're all of those, all the things I said earlier, and you deal with crisis really well. Do I want us to have crisis after crisis thrown at us? No. Is it fucking attractive as all hell that you don't completely fall apart at just a hint of shit going south, much less all that's been thrown at you the last week? Yeah. It really fucking is."

I'd always been pretty proud of my hair.

Now I was pretty damned proud of that.

And part of feeling that way was because he was right. I didn't buckle under pressure. I might bend, but then I got on with it. And that was something to be proud of.

Also, because his mother *did* buckle. She didn't stand up for herself and make positive changes in her life. She didn't stand up for her son and do everything she could so he'd have positive things in *his* life. She hit adversity and fell into a cycle of negativity and toxic behavior.

So the other part of that was that I was pretty proud, when we were hitting crisis after crisis, that I could give that to Auggie.

"It's hella attractive how you dealt with Birch, and last week, Corbin too," I returned.

He shook his head. "I lost my temper with your ex, and I almost lost it with your brother, and you felt that. That isn't cool."

"It is to me."

"Pepper—"

I rested my fingers on his lips. "It is to me, Auggie. You had chaos all your life, I had no one shielding me from *anything* all of mine. I'm not sure you understand how much it meant to me when I shared it earlier, having someone in my corner. But I'll repeat, it means *a lot*."

He held my gaze.

Then he curled his fingers around my wrist, pulled my hand away, and asked, "Are you sure we can't make out?"

I shot him a smug grin because he liked me a lot and he wanted my mouth so I felt all kinds of smug. "Sadly, I am, and we cannot."

"Bummed, sweetheart," he muttered, his lips twitching.

"You missed Thanksgiving play duty at school tonight," I noted.

"I called the teacher. I got a pass," he joked.

"Can Juno and I come with you sometime this week when you do that? I don't want it to be all Auggie all the time for her, or all Juno all the time for you, but—"

"How about Thursday?"

That was when I shot him a big smile.

He dipped in and kissed it off my mouth.

When he lifted his head, he muttered, "Just a little making out."

"Never hurt anybody," I replied.

"You wanna watch something on Netflix?" he asked.

He was staying longer.

Yippee!

"Yes," I answered.

"Where do you keep your remote?"

I got up and got it.

Aug flipped off his boots while I did.

Then I got back down and snuggled in with him, both of us stretched out on my pink couch.

He commandeered the remote from me and flicked the TV on, immediately adjusting the volume low for Juno.

Aug found something we both wanted to watch (*Teenage Bounty Hunters*).

And we kicked back and chilled out in front of the TV.

So, again…

Yeah.

That right there…

Was what happiness is.

CHAPTER TWENTY-ONE
Thanks to Mr. Cisco

JUNO

Juno was worried.

Because Auggie was there and Auggie seemed to notice things that her mom didn't.

And that was big...

Because her mom was *a mom*!

But still.

Even if Auggie might hear her and her mom might not, Juno had to.

She had to call him.

If she didn't talk to someone, she didn't know what she'd do.

She felt funny and gross inside and she knew, whenever she felt like that, she had to share it.

That was what Mom taught her.

Let out the gross.

Just let it go.

But she couldn't let this out with Mom, or her dad, or even Auggie (though, maybe him, but maybe not, which was part of the gross!).

That meant she had to risk it.

So she called him.

He picked up as usual, right away.

"Juno, everything okay?" Mr. Cisco answered her call.

She was under her covers, her eyes peeking over the top of them, aimed to her closed door.

"I did something bad," she whispered.

"Okay, honey, tell me," Mr. Cisco said gently.

Man, she really liked Mr. Cisco.

"Okay, see, my dad gave me a phone. And I knew he was being...well, not cool when he did because Mom doesn't like phones. She doesn't even like her own phone. And I wasn't supposed to get one for years and years."

His voice was different, it seemed stiff or tough, when he said, "Yes, I understand."

"So, I knew that'd make her mad. And my friend Nicole has a phone, so I...I..."

She couldn't even say it.

"You what?" he asked, and when she didn't say anything, he encouraged. "You can tell me. What'd you do, Juno?"

Her breathing was weird and inside felt *so gross* and she just had to *let it out*.

"I told Nicole to call me when I knew Mom would hear and I left the phone somewhere close and turned the ringer up real high to make sure she did. I did that so when Nic called, Mom would hear it and she'd get mad at Dad. And I did all this knowing Auggie was gonna be here."

Mr. Cisco didn't say anything.

Yes, this was bad.

He always said stuff that made her feel better right away.

Him not saying anything meant this was *bad*.

"It was sneaky and wrong, I know it," she admitted. "I mean, Dad giving me a phone wasn't right. He did it to be mean to Mom. But I could have just told her I had it instead of—"

"Showing her how your father behaves while Auggie was there so she'd have support when you did, but also it was made clear that Auggie is not a man who behaves that way?" Mr. Cisco finished for her.

Juno didn't have anything to say then, because … *wow*.

Mr. Cisco figured out everything.

"Juno," he said her name firmly, "I am confident that there will be a time when you'll understand the intricacies of right and wrong. It might not make much sense to you now when I say that there are some things that are wrong that you'll need to do in times that are right. And vice versa. It seems very complicated, and I have to admit, that will never change. It'll always be complicated. You'll learn to weigh the positives and negatives and make decisions on how to move forward. I suspect all people your age start learning that about now. In this instance, how you went about doing what you needed to do was wrong. But the reason you did it was right. Does that make sense to you?"

"Kind of," she mumbled.

"What I'm saying is, it's done, and maybe there were better ways to do it, but the bottom line is, it was done for a good reason. But you can't change it. So put it behind you and move on."

Well, she understood that.

"Okay."

"Okay," he murmured.

"Does Auggie know I have a phone from you?" she asked.

That was the second part of the grossness.

And she didn't know if that was a bigger, or smaller, part.

"Did he say something?" Mr. Cisco asked, instead of answering her question.

"No, but when my other phone rang, he looked at me funny and asked if I was telling the truth about Dad giving it to me."

Mr. Cisco took his time answering that.

But eventually, he did.

"He put a few things together about you asking him to speak to your class during career day and he came to visit me about it."

Slowly, she said, "So yes, he knows I have a phone from you."

"Yes, he knows," he admitted.

Okay...

No.

Nonononono.

"He can't know that, Mr. Cisco."

He sounded not sure when he asked, "Why can't he know that?"

"Because if he knows about me and you, and he's not telling Mom about me and you, that means he's keeping things from Mom and he can't do that. He can't do it. He really can't."

"Juno, calm down for me, okay?" Mr. Cisco asked in that way adults did when they were getting freaked out about how you were acting.

"Dad kept things from Mom," she told him.

He made a noise like, "Ah." Then he said, "I told Auggie I'd get the phone back. So actually, this is on me. He doesn't know you have it anymore, unless you told him."

"But he did know."

"Yes, he did."

"And he definitely didn't tell Mom. Or I'd know."

"I don't know about that, but probably."

"And if Mom finds out—"

He cut her off, which was good. She was freaking out so much, her voice was getting louder.

"Juno, you trust me, yes?"

"Yes," she pushed out through fast breaths.

"Now, I don't want you to be mad at me when I say you're too young for me to fully explain this, and maybe, and I hope this remains the case, you never need to know it at all. But if you trust me, I want you to trust when I tell you that what your father kept from your mother was something that she rightly could not find her way around. It was that big. If she finds out about this, first, it's what you and I did, not Auggie. Second, I made promises to Auggie *I* broke about getting the phone back, so that's on me. Third, Auggie made the decision not to tell her because he didn't want her upset at you, which, if he's put in the position to explain that to her, I think she'll understand. And last, outside how we first met, which has not and won't happen again, you were safe through all of this, so it is not even close to being big enough for her not to get around. Even if she is upset in the beginning, she'll get past it. Do you believe me?"

She really liked that Auggie didn't tell on her.

That was sweet.

And Mr. Cisco was right, Mom would get that.

So yeah, she believed him.

She didn't tell him that.

"I know it was the women," she blurted out.

"Sorry?"

"Dad," she said to explain. "He likes women a lot. And he should like just one woman. Mom. And he didn't. I know that."

"Juno," he whispered, and her name said that way both hurt and felt really good. "How do you know that?"

"I figured it out, 'cause it's kinda the same for me. You know. With his women. Like, him knowing I'm, like...important or something."

"Have you talked to your mom about that?"

"I don't want to make her mad at Dad. Not about that. She'd get *really* mad about that."

Or mad...*der*.

Mad in a way it wasn't about her liking Auggie.

Mad in a way that would just be bad.

"More to the point, have you talked to your dad about it?"

She hadn't even thought of it.

"No."

"Maybe you should tell him," he suggested.

She wondered.

She didn't like that he was always trying to make her eat broccoli (which she didn't like cooked, because...yuck!) and telling her "When you're at your mom's..." what she should do (especially with eating).

And she didn't like him always texting some lady or introducing Juno to one who'd be super (icky and fake) sweet, and then she'd be gone. Or worse, the ones that were cool, and then they were gone.

And she didn't like when he'd do things even Juno could see were stupid, just to get a reaction from Mom.

But mostly, he was awesome.

He came to all her softball games and cheered her on, and not like some dads, who were super hyped up and in your face about it. He always said she did great, even if she just stood in center field like a dummy. And he never looked at a text or even at his phone when he was checking her homework. Her grandma and grandpa and aunt and uncle on his side weren't strange, like her mom's family were. They loved her loads and didn't make faces at her when she wore shorts or pants. He called her Button, which was sweet. And he was a really good tickler. She tried to pretend she hated him tickling her, but he knew better, and he'd make her giggle so much, her stomach hurt when they had tickle matches.

It was just...his ladies.

And maybe she could just...talk to him.

"I'll try that, Mr. Cisco."

"Good. Now, Juno, I think maybe we should figure out how you can get that phone back to me, or maybe just get rid of it."

"No!" she said, that word hard and so loud, she felt her eyes get big as she stared through the dark toward her door.

He didn't say anything.

"I like...um, do you not want me bothering you anymore?" she asked.

"You are never, and can never be a bother," he said in a way, it was like permanent marker on a white board.

And she suddenly realized she didn't feel that grossness anymore.

"We're going to have to figure something else out, though, Juno," he said.

He was right.

"Okay," she agreed easily.

There was something like surprise in his reply of, "Okay."

"I gotta go to sleep now, Mr. Cisco."

"All right, sweetheart. Sleep well."

"Okay. You too. Thank you."

"Anytime."

"'Bye."

"Good-bye, Juno."

She hung up, got out of bed and hid the phone.

She got back into bed, pulled the covers up to her neck and stared at her door for a while.

Hopefully Mom was downstairs with Auggie and they were falling in love so Auggie could be around to help make dumplings and go be with her mom when her dad did something stupid that bothered her mom and her mom would have someone to hang around with after Juno went to sleep.

And she thought of this, and not any of that other stuff, until she was asleep.

So yeah.

The grossness was gone (if it wasn't, she'd never be able to get to sleep!).

Thanks to Mr. Cisco.

CHAPTER TWENTY-TWO

Good-bye

PEPPER

It was probably not a good idea.

But I went to the church early to meet Saffron.

I didn't know why except that I'd had heavy energy all morning, anticipating seeing Mom and all the emotion that might come of that, and it felt better to take off to face it rather than sitting around and waiting for it to happen.

But also, as ridiculous as it was (because it wasn't going to happen), I wondered if I'd run into one of my brothers or sisters.

No, I'll repeat, as ridiculous as it was, I'd hoped I would.

I hadn't fully faced that yet. The idea that I lived in a city where, not an hour from me, I had blood I'd never met and might not ever meet. How I could walk by one of them and never know they were part of my family. How I didn't know their ages. Their names.

Nothing.

This was not in my control. I could do nothing about it. So I needed to do the work around letting it go.

But I knew that was going to take a lot, and I already had a lot to work through.

For Mom's sake, I dressed appropriately, headed out, parked in the church lot and walked into the church.

There was no one in the outer vestibule, and after I went in, I found no one in the sanctuary.

This seemed to speak to me.

Churches should be alive. With people polishing things or praying, organizing hymn books or setting out flowers. Choirs practicing (the Tabernacle of the True Light didn't have a choir, not even an organ, something else I'd never liked about attending church, there was no joy or exaltation in their worship, just lectures and pontificating). Wedding rehearsals happening.

I knew it was late morning on a weekday.

But still . . .

Something.

A buzz of community.

Spirituality

Not this . . . void.

And obviously there were no tow-haired youngsters tumbling about the pews.

I left the sanctuary thinking it had been a mistake that I'd showed fifteen minutes too soon, because fourteen minutes of that was going to be me hanging around waiting.

On that thought, I heard the voices.

They were coming from the far side of the space, where a hall led to parts unknown.

It probably wasn't my sister coming to meet me because I wasn't supposed to be there yet.

It definitely wasn't my business.

I knew I shouldn't have walked in that direction.

But considering all I knew about that church and its leader, curiosity got the better of me.

So I did.

I peeked around the corner and saw, at the end, Saffron standing with a man.

Not Reverend Clyde, her fiancé (as it were).

No.

A much younger man, close to Saffron's age, tall with black hair. He was also lean, but built.

He was wearing a nice pair of dark jeans and a sweater with a button-down under it. His hair was well groomed.

He looked of the church.

He also looked *way* of Saffron.

And Saffron looked *way* of him.

They weren't in each other's arms or snogging or anything, but they were standing closer than you would with a colleague or acquaintance (definitely closer than a fellow parishioner). In fact, it couldn't be missed they were totally comfortable, so far as cozy, in each other's presence.

He was really tall, taller than Auggie or even Corbin. He had his head bent to her, and the both of them were very into whatever they were discussing.

I was surprised.

I was hopeful.

I was freaked out.

Holy hell.

My sister was engaged.

But it looked like she had a boyfriend.

I was going to vamoose myself, give them space, but my movement caught his eye.

His head whipped my way, then they immediately moved apart.

And yeah.

I was freaked out even more.

Because you didn't make movements like they did unless you didn't want to be seen and/or you were hiding something.

Sure, she was supposed to marry another guy.

But they weren't married yet.

"Don't mind me," I called. "I'm here for Saffron, but I got here early. I'll just go—"

"No, it's fine, it's fine," Saffron called back.

It was a long hall, and they were at the other end of it, but still, I saw from the expression on her face that it was not fine.

She turned to him, said something I couldn't hear, and he nodded, face tight and visibly pissed. He shot me a look, that upon receiving it, it was a wonder the ends of my hair didn't catch fire. He then pivoted sharply and disappeared through a door.

Well, hello, and nice to meet you too. I'm your girlfriend's sister, and until just now, I would have been on your side to win her away from a sleazeball.

This was my thought, but onward from that, even if that guy was a dick, it had to be said, I'd prefer him over a con man old enough to be her grandfather who had a bunch of other wives.

Saffron headed in my direction.

When she got close, I said, "I'm so sorry I interrupted. I heard voices and—"

She cut me off again. "It was nothing."

It was something to him.

And to her too.

She had her phone in her hand and she looked down to it. "I'll text Mom and tell her to expect us early."

She was walking in a no-nonsense way, and as such, I had no choice but to follow her.

"Who was that guy?" I asked.

"No one," she muttered.

Hmm.

It was a sin to lie.

"Does he work here?" I asked.

"Yes."

Okay, my sister was not feeling forthright.

So...

"Do you two work together?"

She glanced at me. "Everyone works together. It's a church."

She returned her attention to her phone, off went the text, and then she looked to where she was going.

I just kept following.

We were close to the doors when she said, "Because of some issues at home, Reverend Clyde has given us temporary quarters—"

It was my turn to interrupt.

"Don't lie, Saffron. I know you all live here."

She stopped, hand to the bar on the door that led outside, and she looked at me.

"How do you know that?" she asked.

"Why would you lie about it?" I parried.

"What the family does really isn't your business," she retorted.

Ummmm...

"Do you honestly think that?"

"You left, Pepper. *You left*," she bit out, a fire suddenly lighting in her eyes the likes of which I'd never seen in my life. "It was your choice."

"I don't agree with you about how to practice my faith," I replied. "If I recall, we also had wildly differing opinions on how we felt about steamed spinach."

Her eyebrows shot up in affront. "You're comparing the practice of worship with how you like spinach cooked?"

"I'm just saying people are different. They do different things. They believe different things. They like different things. But that doesn't mean they can't love each other or get along."

"Well, clearly, we have a differing opinion about *that* as well," she snapped.

"Saffron—"

She pushed out the door, stating, "Let's just get this done."

"Saffron!" it was me snapping now, and I caught her elbow to stop her.

She twirled on me, yanking her arm from my hold, and glared into my face.

"What we're about to *get done* is me having a visit with my dying mother, maybe one of the only ones I'll be able to have before she *dies*," I reminded her.

"Yes, so don't you want that to be over?"

Okay, Saffron could be a pill.

No denying it.

But this?

This was something different.

I looked back to the doors we'd come through, then to her.

"Who was that guy?"

"He's an associate pastor."

Reverend Clyde had associate pastors?

As far as I knew, he never had before.

Certainly not young, good-looking ones.

"Is there something going on with you two?" I inquired.

A rod slammed so far up her ass, it shot up her spine as well. "Absolutely not."

"So you're marrying Reverend Clyde," I said.

She gave me squinty eyes. "How do you know all of this?"

"You told me to find Birch. My last name isn't Drew, so I had to have help with that. And the men I asked to help are thorough."

Was it me?

Or did her face just turn a whiter shade of pale?

"So you know..."

She let that trail.

It wasn't a question.

It was a demand for information.

Precisely: what I knew.

And the words were strung so tight, if I didn't answer it, they'd break, lash out and bite me.

"I know Clyde has a bunch of wives. Dad has a bunch of wives. You all live here. You do recruiting—"

"I'm a missionary," she corrected,

"You're on a mission in Denver?" I scoffed.

"The word needs to be spread everywhere, Pepper."

I had nothing to say to that.

"So that's all you know?" she pressed.

It wasn't.

It was all I'd share.

"Is there more to know?" I asked.

She put a hand on a hip she'd hitched and swung out a foot.

Uh-oh.

Not a good stance from any female.

"You don't want us to judge you for running away from home and getting pregnant by a man you barely knew. Making money by dancing for men in an effort to tempt them to ungodly pursuits. Building a home without a lion at the head to guide your worldly and spiritual journeys. If you don't want us to judge you for that, you can't judge us for the way we choose to live our lives."

"I didn't run away from home, Saffron, I was eighteen and no longer a minor. And I wouldn't judge you for any of that if you didn't try to force it on me, and when I found it unacceptable, openly judged *me* because I'd turned away from your church."

She chuffed out some air and shot back, "We didn't judge you."

"Saffron, you yourself called me a whore when I told you I was pregnant with Juno. And I didn't 'barely know' Corbin. We'd been seeing each other a year and living together six months of that before I became pregnant. And let us not forget, you also told Juno the devil shines from women's exposed skin when she was three. Every bath time for a month after you said that, she'd ask, 'Mommy, is the devil shining from me?'"

Wait.

Whoa.

Hang on a second.

Did Saffron just *flinch*?

"Saff, what's going on?" I demanded.

She dropped her hand from her hip and turned to walk along the front of the church, asserting, "Nothing."

I caught up with her and walked at her side.

As we turned a corner, I said, "I know something is up. *You know I know.* So be careful, little sister."

She stopped dead and scorched me with her own look.

Then she hit me with her best shot.

And it was a doozy.

"If you have any regard for her at all, you should let Mom die in peace, Pepper. She hates the way you live your life. She hates the way you're raising Juno. She despairs both you and Birch went so wrong. And she prays to God every day to provide her with answers about what she did that you turned out the way *you* did."

I stood there, figuratively bleeding out on the sidewalk.

She either didn't notice it, didn't have time to revel in it, or didn't care she'd perpetrated it.

She kept talking.

"Now," she clipped, "we have a narrow window of time. Dad's away at a meeting, but the sisters can walk in at any moment."

"Sisters?" I whispered, too poleaxed by what she'd just said to me to raise my voice higher.

"The others in Dad's flock."

"You mean his other wives," I clarified for her.

"Yes," she stated shortly. "His other wives. And they will tell him. So we have to go."

"And we have to go so I can say good-bye to my mother now, rather than attempting to spend further time with her, this so she can die in peace. Peace from me."

Her head ticked but she said, "That would be best, I think."

"What about Juno?"

She was looking me dead in the eye when she answered, "Pepper, we've been dancing around it for years. But you should know, we all regard Juno as a true bastard of the church, born out of it and out of wedlock. Reverend Clyde doesn't even acknowledge her as part of our family. I can't imagine how it would help Juno, or Mom, for either of them to be around each other in this trying time."

My voice was again small when I asserted, "Mom loves Juno."

"In a week or two, a month, or maybe a couple of days, Mom is going to realize how close to God she is."

"What you mean is, Mom is going to be in so much pain, she wouldn't know if the archangel Gabriel sat by her bed and patted her hand."

Saffron didn't answer.

So the answer was...yes.

That's what she meant.

Good Christ.

"I want to see this entire conversation as a shimmer of light in the darkness that is trying to figure out what to do with my love for all of you, as it absolutely shows me the path to understanding you are not healthy for me or Juno. But I don't see it that way. I don't see anything. I just feel. And all I feel is pain," I announced.

Another flinch.

I didn't care.

I ordered, "Take me to Mom so I can say good-bye."

And then I marched down the sidewalk, even though I had no idea where I was going.

"Pepper."

I stopped and looked back.

"You should have let us go years ago," she said.

"Silly me, I loved you. So I didn't. But you've leaped mammoth strides in taking care of that problem today, Saff. So how about we get this done so I can be out of your hair and I can also just be away from here."

We stood there, two sisters, staring into each other's eyes, and it was not lost on me the way we did.

She was behind me by several feet.

I was ahead of her, not fully turned to her, looking at her over my shoulder.

I knew I'd remember that moment until my dying day.

It was us then.

It was us in the past.

It would always be us.

Me, breaking free.

Saffron, behind, mired in total, absolute *shit*.

She nodded.

Neither of us said a word to each other as she guided me to a door at the back of the building. We went in, and she led me through what could only be described as a dormitory made of large suites that looked like small apartments. Most of the doors were open, but I saw nary a soul.

At the end of this journey was my mother.

And good-bye.

* * *

AUGGIE

Auggie wasn't feeling it after he got Pepper's text of,

> **It didn't go great.**
> **Understatement of**
> **the millennium.**

And on the heels of those,

> **I'll call you after Juno goes
> to bed. Hope you're having
> a good day.**

And he wasn't feeling it because Pepper was a processor. She didn't sit on things. She felt it. Talked about it. Sorted it through. And sorted it out.

Maybe she was doing that and needed space to do it on her own.

But Auggie didn't get that from her.

It was the "understatement of the millennium" part.

He didn't feel better when he asked if she wanted him to swing around and she didn't answer.

Then he asked,

> **Just let me know you're hanging
> in there. Okay?**

And she didn't answer that either.

This was why he was at her door and *really* not feeling it because he rang the bell, knocked, and she didn't show at the door.

She always showed at the door.

There was dark shit happening at that church.

And she'd been to that church.

Now she was a ghost?

Standing at her door, he got his phone out and called.

When he got voicemail, he said, "Hey, I'm outside. Quick status check to make sure you're good. Then I'll leave and we'll talk when you're ready."

And he did this going back to his car and grabbing his kit.

When she didn't call back or open the door by the time he was back, he opened his kit, picked her lock in twenty seconds, and let himself inside.

Quick scan of the lower floor.

Nothing.

But her purse was in the office and her vehicle was in the garage.

He made his way upstairs.

All the doors were open except hers at the end.

Shit.

Maybe he was overreacting.

This could be her power-nap time.

He stood in the upstairs hall, undecided about how he felt about the fact he was acting like a total creeper, breaking into her house to make sure she was okay, when her bedroom door opened.

She made a noise of surprise when she saw him and jumped back a step, hand on her door like she was going to slam it shut.

Fuck.

"It's just me," he pointed out the obvious.

She came out of her room but only a little. "How did you get in here?"

Yup.

Acting like a creeper.

The worst kind.

The kind that had a lock-picking kit.

"You were freaking me out, not replying to texts, not answering the door, having just met your mom and being at that church. So I picked the locks."

She stood unmoving for a beat.

Two.

Then she started laughing.

Okay, well that was good.

In the middle of laughing, she started sobbing.

Right, that was not good.

"Aug," she keened, lifting a hand his way.

He considered that an invitation, didn't mess around going to her and she fell into his arms.

"How awesome is it that my boyfriend can pick locks?" she asked, still crying into his chest.

"If you're glad I'm here, why didn't you reply to my texts asking if you're okay?"

"I texted you when I got home and came right up here to try and find some peace. I left my phone in the office."

"Babe," he called.

She turned watery eyes up to him.

"I get your rule. I dig your rule. I'm gonna follow your rule. But, you know, you go somewhere I don't think is real safe to have an emotional conversation with your mother who's gravely ill, you text me and say it didn't go great, you hang tight for a return text. Or, higher probability, me showing like I did just now, but I wouldn't have to pick the locks. Yeah?"

"I'm sorry," she sniffled.

"Nothing to be sorry about. We're learning each other. It's a learning moment."

She started laughing through her tears.

He asked, "You wanna stand in the hall and cry this out, or go downstairs?"

She didn't want either.

She told him this by taking him into her kickass bedroom.

It was not the time.

But it hit his brain that he could not wait to fuck her in here.

She climbed in bed, tugged him in with her, and as he settled in with her, he noted that he loved it that there was not a lot of clutter in her room, just like with his.

But everything was soft. The chunky knit throw across the bottom of the bed. The snowy-white snatch of fake fur thrown over the chair in the corner. The bubble-knit throw pillows.

He angled himself so his boots weren't on her covers and she snuggled in.

He didn't push.

She didn't take her time.

But when she spoke, she didn't give him what he'd come there for.

She said, "Hawk's gonna hate me if you make a habit of blowing off work for me."

"You obviously need to get to know Hawk a whole lot better."

She snuffled and then sighed.

And then she gave him what he came for.

"I essentially said good-bye to Mom today. They don't want me or Juno around while this is happening. We've been a duty they didn't relish since I left home ten years ago. They let me go, apparently, then. And today, it was made plain I need to get with that program."

Auggie didn't trust himself to say anything.

She kept going.

"I'm trying to see this as good. They didn't get anything from me. I wasn't sure they were healthy for Juno. But it's going to take me some time to get there. My mother would prefer to die without her daughter around. I have siblings I'll never meet. Whatever is happening with that church is happening and they might end up in deep shit sooner or later. But I have no control over that. So..."

Her letting that hang was a verbal shrug.

"What about the prayer circle?" he asked.

"What?" she asked back.

"I thought you were supposed to be involved in a prayer circle."

Her body tensed.

Then she lifted up from cuddling into his chest.

She caught his eyes.

On her left side, her mascara was swiped across her temple.

On her right, which had been against his chest, it was smudged all around the corner of her eye.

She was still gorgeous.

"Saffron nor Mom mentioned the prayer circle."

No mention now. But two weeks ago, they're pushing Pepper to find her long-lost brother to complete this all-important circle.

That was so fishy, he could smell it in the room.

He didn't say anything.

"Maybe they've re-thought and decided I'll taint the circle," she suggested.

"Maybe," he murmured.

But he didn't think so.

He thought, in between then and now they could have seen her and her friends there, the men also there, several of them definitely showed up at services and Pepper had made a scene.

He also thought people doing slimy shit that was also potentially felonious didn't like people around who thought they were slimy and could potentially be felonious.

Definitely not snooping around, and the women weren't covert about their operations.

But yeah.

Maybe.

More likely, not.

"She doesn't want to say good-bye to Juno, Aug."

He focused on her.

"How whacked is that?" she whispered, her voice clogged and gutting him.

He reached.

And then he found something.

"She could be hiding behind all the church stuff, honey. You didn't have a good reaction when you saw her. She could be protecting Juno from that same thing."

She brightened at that.

"Oh my God, you might be right. She was...she..." She shook her head, drew in a sharp breath through her nose.

"You don't have to finish," he told her.

She looked to his chest, where she was pinching and releasing his tee.

"So...yeah. Yeah," she said that twice and lifted her gaze to his. "Good take, honey. Because, honestly, if the world was perfect, Juno would never see her grandma like that. She was...up close...she was..." She swallowed. "*Worse.*"

Fuck.

"Sweetheart," he murmured.

She went back to concentrating on pinching and releasing his tee.

He gave her time.

Then he asked, "You gonna be good, just Juno and you tonight? Going to work? All of that?"

She nodded.

She probably wouldn't, but she'd push through anyway.

"You gonna talk to Juno?" he asked.

"I think maybe, I don't know...it might be good you're around when I do that. You're a distraction. You're healthy and vital. And no offense, honey, but you're a shiny new toy."

He grinned. "No offense taken."

"Not that she sees you that way," she said hurriedly.

"I know what you mean. She likes me. I'm exciting. It's hopeful to her. And it's a balance. Bad with your mom and I get to be good."

"Yeah, that," she said, her lips turned up ruefully.

He tucked her hair behind her ear. "So tonight and tomorrow, you get through. I'm a text or phone call away if you need it, and I want you checking in anyway. Thursday, we'll do an early dinner and go build sets. And this weekend, we can do something all together and you can have a talk with her then."

"Sounds like a plan."

"I hate this for you."

Her lips turned down. "It was awful, Aug."

He pulled her back in his arms and held her close.

"That feels better," she said into his neck.

"Good," he muttered roughly.

"Do you have to go back to work?"

"I can, if you're okay for me to go. I can make a call if you're not."

She shook her head against him and said, "No. I'm okay now. Or better." She lifted her head. "Go."

He moved in and kissed her.

When he moved back, she moved in and kissed him.

When she finished hers, she didn't shift far away before she invited, "You can pick my locks anytime, Auggie. Though it'd be a lot easier if I just gave you a key."

And to that, he didn't do it loud, or long.

But he laughed.

Yeah.

She might not be okay.

But he'd done his job.

She was better.

CHAPTER TWENTY-THREE

Something Better

PEPPER

I was sitting in Auggie's car, with Auggie, at 3:45 on Thanksgiving Day, reminding myself about how proud I was that I could bring peace and calm to Auggie's life.

I was reminding myself of this, because for the last two-plus weeks, I'd accomplished that.

For him.

For me.

For Juno.

And I was reminding myself of this, because I was in danger of obliterating that in ways that I might never be able to get it back.

* * *

Allow me to share...

To begin.

It was not fun dodging Juno's questions about her grandmother. Telling her things that were the truth: Grandma was not well, she was very weak, she didn't look much like herself anymore as the illness was running its course.

All of this, but not going *there*.

As in, Juno was not invited to spend time with her grandma to make memories, even painful ones, before she died.

But as she and I were prone to do, we got through that.

And I'd used an evasive maneuver to help that along, this being enlisting her support to make Thanksgiving an awesome day for Auggie.

"He's not close with his parents," I told her. "They've never been very..." I struggled for a word, and found it, "traditional. But he's all about family so I think he'd like us to do it up with him."

Just like my girl, she got excited immediately.

"You mean, like, a tablecloth on the island and fancy glasses and stuff?"

I nodded. "Just like that. And lots of food. We'll go out and buy another stool so we can all sit together."

"And we need to buy cloth napkins," she planned. "And those things that hold napkins that look like big rings."

I swept an arm to the island. "We can design a whole thing. Do it up big. The works."

"Oh my gosh! This'll be fun!"

She was not wrong.

We'd planned and gone shopping and it had been fun.

In fact, except for one part of it, the rest of that week was fun.

Including meeting Auggie for dinner before we all went and helped with the sets. Me going straight to work from there because Auggie could take Juno home to Flossy. That meant we had an extra bit of time together as a three, and Auggie and Juno had the same, just those two.

Then hitting the bad part, on Saturday, when Auggie came over because I was going to give Flossy an unusual Saturday off because Aug was going to hang with Juno that night while I was at work.

And he was going to do this because of the conversation I had planned to have with her.

He smoothed the way by making his ham and hash casserole with Juno as his sous chef.

They worked great together in the kitchen and I loved watching them because they just, well...*clicked* (and it had to be said, his casserole was delicious).

And then, after Auggie told her they were going to start a binge of *The Mandalorian*, making popcorn and watching as many as they could that night before they passed out, then continuing on the next time they had an evening to do it, we sat her down when she was excited and had something to look forward to.

And I gave it to her.

"Me and Auntie Saff have decided that it's probably a good idea you don't see your grandma while she's sick," I told her.

She looked confused, and more.

Eight-year-old-girl shock. Upset. Maybe disbelief.

Thus, I was unsurprised when she asked, "Why?"

Fortunately, I'd prepared and had my answers ready.

"Because sickness like this can last a long time and it can take its toll. It's taken its toll on Grandma." I explained how she didn't look like herself. "She's also in pain, and that makes it hard for her to focus. And Saff and me think it'll be more peaceful for her if she doesn't have to think of you seeing her like that."

"I don't care what she looks like."

That was my girl.

"I know, Dollface," I said gently. "But in times like these, it's not about what you care about or what you want. It's what's best for the other person."

Juno thought on that and I exchanged a glance with Auggie.

Or I tried to.

He had his attention glued to my girl.

I looked back to her when she said, "But I have things I want to say."

Aug cut in then.

"Write her a letter."

Juno turned to him. "A letter?"

He nodded.

"You can write her as long of a letter as you want. You can tell her how much you love her and how bad you feel this is happening to her. You can tell her you miss her and you're thinking of her. And she can write you back and do it whenever she has the energy. On top of that, she doesn't have to worry about how upset you'll be, seeing her as she is. She can just read your words in her time, know you love her and spent time with her, even if you weren't with her, and if she wants to reply, share hers in her time," Auggie said.

Okay.

Suffice it to say, that was freaking brilliant.

Honestly, I wished I'd thought of it.

Then he went on to offer, "I can help, if you want."

And okay.

This guy was the best guy *in the world*.

"I...thank you, Auggie," Juno replied. "But I know what I want to say. I don't need any help. But that's nice you offered."

"So you're gonna write her?" I asked.

Juno nodded.

"Do you wanna do that now?" I went on.

Juno shook her head. "I want Baby Yoda now. I'll do it...later."

I refrained from telling her not to procrastinate too long. That convo had already been tough enough, though it'd gone loads better than I expected it would, thanks to Auggie.

Still.

"Okay, then let's do Mando and the Kid," I suggested, mostly to turn her mind and get her settled for the night with Aug.

"I'll start the first episodes with you and go to work when I have to."

Aug put his hand on her head, tousled her hair and said, "I'll cue it up. We'll make popcorn at intermission."

"What's intermission?" Juno asked.

"It's when we stop the binge when your mom leaves."

"Cool." There was a bit of a chirp to that, not Juno's normal, which was understandable.

But she was like her mom.

Take the hit, and onward.

Aug got up to sort out the streaming, and Juno followed him.

I watched them go and let them settle in (Aug, what had become his corner of the couch, Juno, her usual, the cushions and pillows on the floor) before I joined them.

The Mandalorian wasn't exactly light viewing.

But it was fantasy, you could turn it off, and although things could get scary, for the most part good prevailed and hope abided.

After we started, Auggie and I exchanged another glance, this one, he caught.

His was about taking my pulse on how that went.

Mine was about relief and gratitude, because he was there with me when that happened, he provided what he could (distraction and more, an outlet for Juno to communicate with her grandmother).

And finally, I communicated the not insignificant fact that I was happy not to have had to do that alone.

*   *   *

Auggie left that night when I got home after work because I felt we were nowhere near Juno waking up to a man in the house.

But he came over late the next morning for cinnamon rolls.

After we ate those, he took us to his place for football, which led to Tod and Stevie coming over, more Yahtzee and pork rind nachos.

Juno loved Tod and Stevie. And she declared Auggie's nachos the best things she'd ever eaten (Tod concurred). Aug told her next up was his pimento cheese hush puppies, which she ordered me to add to our Thanksgiving dinner.

I tensed because this was an unknown.

For about two seconds.

I looked to Aug.

Aug said, "I'll be ready to fulfill that order."

In other words, Juno had invited him to Thanksgiving dinner, and Auggie had accepted.

Needless to say, that was way okay by me.

Also needless to say, Sunday had been a great day.

* * *

Juno went to her dad's on Monday, something that sucked no less than it normally did even with Auggie in my life.

Nevertheless, it was tempered by the fact that Auggie, no other way to put it, temporarily moved in that day.

This began with me texting him about five minutes after she left to catch the bus.

> Understandably, due to
> circumstances, you failed in your
> appointed task last week to
> spend your lunch hour with me.
> Now, prepare to devour me at
> your earliest convenience.

And if he didn't understand that, I added,

I mean sexually.

I did not delay in this invitation because, seriously, when you got the good stuff, and barely had a dose of it, then it was taken away, you wanted it back the minute you could get it.

Auggie texted back,

I know what you meant, baby. ☺
Though, I got something on that will
go late tonight.

I was undeterred.

Can you meet me after work?

He was feeling like I was.
Because I got,

Abso-fucking-lutely.

Since I'd already given him a key, the house was softly lit and Aug was in his corner of the couch, watching late-night TV, when I got home that night.

I delayed our reconnection long enough to ask, "Did you bring a bag?"

He stood, answering, "Nope."

"Tomorrow," I ordered.

He'd given me a look that was the equivalent of thirty-three-point-seventy-five minutes of foreplay.

In other words, I was pre-orgasm just standing there staring at him.

Then he'd grabbed my hand, dragged me up the stairs, took me to my room...

And fucked me.

It went fast, so it was good he'd given me that look to prime me, because it also went phenomenally.

He brought a bag the next day.

We had dinner together every night before I went to work.

And he spent every night beside me in my bed.

This was good, not only because I liked to climb in bed beside a warm body (if that body was Auggie's) after getting home from work, having him wake and sleepily pull me into his arms for a cuddle. I also liked being woken by a warm body who wanted things from mine that I was happy to give.

And I gave them.

Freely and as copiously as possible before Aug had to get up, take a shower and tackle his day.

* * *

It was also good Aug temporarily moved in because Corbin decided that, in the month of November, he was going to make a bid for father of the year.

This came Wednesday, when I got a text at work from him that said,

Was in your neighborhood for a late showing. His car was in your drive. He better not be spending the night when my daughter is there.

Considering the fact that Corbin had a revolving door of women spending the night when Juno was with him, I forced myself to give it twelve solid hours (anything less would have had me losing my mind and saying things I wished I hadn't).

Once that time was up, I replied,

I will address this one time.
At the moment, Auggie is not
staying over when Juno is here.
However, there will come a
time when he will, and it will
be none of your business.
Just as it's none of your
business should he be doing
it now.
But please, be more aware of
the things you say, the things
you expect and the things
you do.
I won't talk any further on
this subject.

Of course, within the hour, I got,

We need to sit down in person.
Without J and without that guy.
There are important things
to discuss.

Please name them.

I will at dinner on Sunday
I'll get a sitter for Juno.

I'm unavailable on Sunday.

You don't want this to
get ugly.

Are you threatening me?

I just want to talk to you.

Was that a threat, Corbin?

Dinner.
Sunday.

I'm spending Sunday with Auggie.

From then on, nothing.
Nothing bad.
Nothing good.
However, I shared that text conversation with Auggie.
And after I watched him visibly wrestle with then conquer the urge to find Corbin and punch him in the nose (or whatever), he said, "Do you have a lawyer?"

I shook my head, then nodded it.

"I don't know what that means," Auggie pointed out, his eyes having followed the movements of my head.

"It means, I wasn't working when we broke up. Not really. I had a part-time job, but mostly for play money. Corbin didn't want the breakup. He said he'd end things with her, and we'd sort it out. Then, when I didn't fall in line with that, he got pissed and it got ugly. I was doing hair, trying to rebuild my clientele, nowhere close to full time. I had no money, no family to ask for help. That was when I started stripping."

"All right," Auggie said when I took a breath.

"He kept being ugly, so I got a lawyer," I continued. "I was making a lot back then, and I had my days free to do research. I did that and found a shark. She was awesome. She made things unpleasant for Corbin. Unpleasant enough he stopped being ugly and started to negotiate. In the end, it wasn't that bad. He gave me everything I wanted. Joint custody. Healthy child support. He put her on his insurance. Flipflop shared holidays and equal distribution of her school breaks."

"What are flipflop shared holidays?" Auggie asked.

"Since she was so young, neither of us wanted to miss anything," I told him. "So, say, one year, I have Thanksgiving Day until three, and he gets the rest of the day and the night, even if she's supposed to be at my house. That way I could do an early dinner, and have her, and he could do a later one, and have her. She doesn't miss either of us, we don't miss her. Then he gets Christmas morning, and I get the afternoon. And we flipflop the times the next year."

"Thanksgiving this year?"

"I have her that week, but Corbin will pick her up in the morning, and I get her at three."

"He caved to be the good guy," Auggie abruptly changed the subject.

"Sorry?"

"He caved, not because you got a shark attorney, but so he wouldn't do anything he couldn't go back on. Or, more to the point, anything else," he explained.

I still didn't get it.

So I told him that.

Aug elucidated.

"He didn't stop being ugly because you had someone in your corner. He stopped because he wasn't going to be able to win you back that way."

I shook my head. "He had a glitch, honey. He felt threatened. He's competitive. But, Auggie, I promise, it's been three years and a lot of women in between. He's not pining for me."

"He's pining for you."

I felt my heart pinch.

"He's not," I asserted.

"This is what I know from what I've seen from my parents and from being a guy," Auggie began forebodingly. "If I've moved on from a woman, I move on. You have a kid, but you can move on and still share a kid. You do not find ways to stay in that person's life and in their face. You do not give them a hard time. You don't because you don't give a shit. If things are cool with how the both of you are dealing with your kid, you never have to give a shit. When it's over, Pepper, it's just over."

Oh man.

That made sense.

Aug kept speaking.

"From what you describe, he's never really been gone. He's been fucking with you, he's been in your face about things, and he's done that to stay relevant to you for when you were ripe for him to make his move. Now, I'm in the picture, and he's on his back foot. He didn't expect you to find someone else. He expected things would work out. He's playing the long game not realizing you weren't playing along. Now he's realizing you aren't. And when he understands that what he wants is permanently out of his grasp, he's going to strike back."

I had nothing to say to this because it was flipping me out.

"So, how do you have an attorney, and not have one?" Auggie asked.

"I had her, but I haven't needed her in at least two years."

"She's still your attorney, Pepper."

"Oh," I mumbled.

"You should call her to warn her, share this shit with her, so in case he turns, she's prepared."

This was not good since I didn't want to have to deal with Corbin being more of a jerk.

It was also not good because I didn't have the money to pay her.

She was excellent at her job and her hourly rate reflected that.

Since I had needed her, thanks to Smithie's pay, excellent benefits package and my tips, Juno and I had gone from a house that I'd kicked Corbin out of but he owned (and he didn't make waves about that, but it wasn't mine and it felt unsafe, because he could make those waves whenever he felt like it), to a three-bedroom house that was mine.

I filled it with furniture.

I made it pretty.

Now, my nest egg didn't cover Corbin being an asshole and me needing to go back to my attorney to ask her to get his shit in line.

Maybe I shouldn't have bought that pink couch.

"You okay?" Auggie asked.

I was not.

I didn't share how I wasn't, though.

We'd see if Auggie's prediction panned out.

In the meantime, I needed to come up with some killer routines, try to up my tips, maybe see if Dorian could fit me in for another dance a night, and tighten spending.

Just in case.

* * *

There was no football that Sunday.

Also no cinnamon rolls.

It was our first full day off together with nothing pressing in.

No families. No heartbreak. No exes.

In fact, nothing dramatic had happened since Corbin's texts.

Three full days of life just being life.

Bliss.

Sweetening that pot, the coming week, Smithie's was closed

Thursday, and the revue at Smithie's was on hiatus (it was just straight stripping) on Friday. So I had two extra days off with pay (but not tips, yikes), back on Saturday.

Not to mention, I had my girl with me again on Monday.

So there was a lot to look forward to and a lot to look back at that was happy.

For Auggie and me, it had been a rocky start, with winds blowing from multiple directions, but as I was fond of a mixed metaphor, I was happy to note that Auggie and me were sailing ahead swimmingly.

I liked him.

Not just the gorgeous part and the good lover part, how awesome he was with Juno, how good it felt to make him laugh, the fact that he could cook.

I just liked the guy.

He was easy and attentive, affectionate, wise, and he had a great sense of humor.

We just fit.

His parents were crazy, but after Auggie unloaded on them and his mom tried to draw him back into the drama, but he resisted, it had been crickets.

And it seemed Saffron told no lies.

I hadn't been in touch with any of my family, and they had returned that favor.

So that, until Juno sent her letter, was done.

Birch had also vanished (again). I'd texted him, and after that big show on my front porch, he hadn't replied.

Now it was just a naked Auggie and a naked me in my bed after he'd had an orgasm (and it's important to note, this was after he'd given me one too).

We were under the covers, touching and kissing and nuzzling, and there was nothing to do all day, except eventually get up to get some food.

Nothing pressing.
Nothing distressing.
Just us.
In my bed.

"What'd you mean when you said you were making a lot back then?" Auggie asked into my post-sex, lazy-day, more-sex-to-come, nothing-to-do-all-day happy reverie.

"Sorry?"

"When you talked about having to get an attorney, and you started at Smithie's because of it, what did you mean when you said 'back then' you were making a lot. You're still at Smithie's. Are things different?"

Ummmm...

Seeing as this mental um lasted a long time, my non-verbal um did too.

Which meant Auggie's brows cruised together, and his next question had a definite edge of growl to it.

"Pepper, is there an issue at work?"

At least I could answer that quickly and honestly.

"No."

"So what did you mean?"

This was the thing.

I had my dad, who was the "lion of the home" and acted like it.

That explained that.

Then I had Corbin, who was kind of the same way, without the full-on subjugation and multiple-wives part (well, with the multiple-women part, just that neither of us knew about the other).

I had been in lala land of new-mommy, functioning-family, away-from-my-childhood-filled-with-hippie-free-and-breezy whiplash to Gonzo-for-God-and-everything-was-suddenly-a-sin. I was happy to quit doing people's hair for a living (though I'd loved doing hair) to be a stay-at-home mom who, when Juno went into kindergarten, went back to hair part time in order to have something to do with my days.

That said, Corbin would have pushed it if I wasn't all of that. He wouldn't say something like, "I'm the lion of our home and you do as I say." But we could just leave it the fact that if he and I had worked, and I eventually made more money than him, it would have been a problem.

So with that as all the history I had with men, I didn't want to get into messy money issues with Auggie.

We were new, but that was business that I'd learned the hard way after getting caught short with no man, a kid, and not enough income to survive, to make certain I always took care of.

Auggie had demonstrated a pretty strong bent to being protective. Not off the hook, but the man had picked a lock to get to me after I'd had a difficult meeting with my mother.

So, you see where I'm coming from with this.

"Baby, are you okay?" His voice was a lot different then, concerned, even troubled.

"I do what I do to pay the mortgage and keep my daughter in cute beanies with floofs on the top," I shared. "I don't do it because I love it. I don't do it because I'm good at it. Lottie is good at it. Hattie is a born performer. Ryn doesn't give a crap what anyone thinks about her. She's gorgeous and knows how to use her body, that confidence comes off onstage. I'm...not them."

"You're telling me this because..." Auggie prompted.

"Because when Smithie went to revue, my tips took a hit. It's only a hundred or so a week, but that adds up. Most of that went to fun stuff, some of it went to savings, so it's not like I'm hurting. But less money is less money."

Auggie said nothing.

"So that's what that meant when I said, 'back then,'" I mumbled my conclusion.

"You don't dig your job?" he asked.

I shook my head. "I dig who I do it with and for. I don't dig the actual job."

"You're good at it."

He'd seen me dance.

He'd also seen me strip.

Before we were together, that bothered me a lot.

But now, for obvious reasons, I was over it.

"Thanks," I replied.

"Would you rather be doing hair?" he asked.

I bit the side of my lip and thought about it.

Hair didn't come with Ryn, Hattie and Lottie.

"I liked doing hair. But I want to open a meditation and yoga studio."

He did a slow blink.

"I know, sounds stupid," I muttered.

"Would it be like this room?"

That was an interesting question.

I thought about it and answered, "Yeah. Not exactly, but defo the vibe."

"Defo the vibe," he murmured, his lips quirking.

I quirked mine back and shared, "Meditation is what got me out of the Corbin spiral. I think I was eating sugar-cookie dough, sobbing and lamenting my fate after I had to hand Juno over for a visitation, and some talk show was playing in the background. Someone said something about it that caught my attention. Right then and there, I downloaded an app on my phone, went to my bed, climbed into the middle of it and gave it a go."

I paused and saw Auggie, his head resting on the pillow opposite mine, watching me intently.

I also saw he was interested—in me, in what I was saying.

I had his full attention and it had nothing to do with my naked body pressed up to his, our legs entwined, the designs he was drawing on my ass, the way I was playing with the ends of his hair.

There was something beautiful about that moment—pensive and profound—that I marked because I wasn't certain I'd ever had anything like that.

And I loved it.

"I did a how-to session," I kept talking, now softly, because what I was feeling from him was still stealing into my soul.

"Yeah?" he said softly in return, encouraging me to go on.

"I was shit at it."

He grinned.

"Monkey mind," I told him. "Pinging everywhere. But before I quit, I thought, 'I'll do this for three days and see.' Day three, I had a moment that was…" There was no describing it, so I said, "Really spectacular. Powerful. And that was me, hooked. And eventually, giving myself still space every day, centering on breath, from my practice learning to be able in any given moment to pull myself back just by remembering how I gently tug myself out of monkey mind, I was in."

"And you want to teach others to do that."

I nodded. "I'm no master. No one can be a master. That's why it's called practice. And I'm not gonna be all dramatic and say it saved my life. But it changed it. And it did that in big ways that were positive. I can't claim I'm always together all the time. That I don't have moods. That I'm drifting through life *om*ing and clinking finger cymbals."

He chuckled.

"But I give myself time to sort through things," I continued. "I do it every day. Sometimes I do it for ten, fifteen minutes. Sometimes I do it for much longer. Sometimes I'll also do it at night. But always in the morning. It's a ritual, with journaling. It isn't a 'when I need it' thing. It's daily practice. It's non-negotiable. A lot of people don't do that. A workout is non-negotiable for them. No sugar in their diet is non-negotiable for them. But taking fifteen minutes every day to be with themselves and sit in stillness, take a mental breath from life and all its pressures, allow yourself to feel that freedom, rebalance things mentally, they think it's new-age hooey."

"I'm ready to sign up for a class now."

I laughed and offered, "I'll teach you how if you want."

"No, I'm serious."

My humor left me.

"I'm convinced," he told me. "With what you said. But also, just this room, Pepper. I feel better in this room. There's something about it that makes me..." He shook his head on the pillow. "The world is outside this room. In here it's something else."

"What a nice thing to say," I whispered.

"I'm not blowing sunshine, baby. I felt it the first time I walked in here."

He did.

He'd even said it.

"I'd go to your place. I'd take a meditation class," he reiterated. "I could use a mental breath."

Of course, this prompted me to say, "You're damned awesome, Auggie."

"I'm not feeding you a line of shit," he restated.

"I know, and you're damned awesome."

He shut his mouth.

I kissed his mouth.

He let me roll him to his back and kiss other parts of him.

He stayed on his back and dragged me up his body so I was sitting on his face and he kissed other parts of me.

But in the end, I was on my back and Auggie was still kissing me.

But he was doing other things to me as well.

* * *

Monday, my baby girl was back, Auggie was over, we'd had my steak tacos with fried corn and Peppadew peppers drizzled with my lime sour cream (a hit with Auggie).

He was over not only to eat, but so we could decide the Thanksgiving menu.

This was an important task as it'd be Juno's second dinner and I didn't want her to explode, but I did want her to have everything she wanted for the day.

I also wanted Auggie to have everything he wanted.

In our time together, I hadn't pressed about it, but he'd shared more of his life with his parents.

So it was safe to say, I had been correct in what I told Juno.

Aug didn't have a lot of heartwarming holiday memories under his belt.

Corbin's mom, Melissa, was serving up Juno's first Thanksgiving of the day, and fortunately Corbin's mom was cool. She'd been pissed at Corbin for doing what he'd done, not at me for trusting he'd never do any such thing.

So when I'd called and asked what she was serving so I could plan, she told me (and we also had a nice chat).

Thus, I went into the Thanksgiving menu discussion armed with what I needed to cover all Juno's bases, double up on the things she loved, and make sure Auggie was getting what he wanted, culinary-wise, from T-Day.

We three had found ourselves simpatico (not surprising), save for the fact that Melissa was making pumpkin pie, so Juno wanted pecan, but Auggie and me wanted pumpkin, so I was going to make both and have a ton of pie left over.

That was okay by me.

We were all planned out, it was time for Juno to hit the sack, Auggie was leaving, and I was walking him to his car so I could make out with him a little bit.

I didn't make out with him.

He unearthed his phone, pulled up some pictures, gave it to me and said, "Scroll through those."

I did that.

When I did, I had no clue why I was doing that.

They were pictures of an empty warehouse.

There was a kitchen and there was a loft in one corner and there seemed to be an under-loft space that was a living room because it had shelves on the walls.

But it was empty so it was all really nothing.

"What am I looking at?" I asked.

"I bought that from Hawk a year ago. I was going to put in a new kitchen. Redefine the living spaces. Cut it in half, live in one side and rent out the other. But I don't like debt. So I bought it in cash. It wiped me out. This means I've been saving to start some reno."

I offered his phone back to him with a smile and said, "Cool, honey. Nothing says, 'I'm Batman' more than living in the Batcave. What no one thinks about is that Batman had to do massive renos to the Batcave before he could move in."

He laughed but shook his head and didn't take the phone back.

"Look at it," he urged.

"I did," I told him.

"Look at it for a meditation/yoga studio."

I grew still.

"It's early, too early, with us being an us. I get it," he stated. "I'm just telling you to think about it. Because if I end up with this chick I'm seeing, and she has a kid, and we make more kids, I can't be living in a warehouse. So now I have a massive warehouse space and nothing to do with it. Except, maybe, this chick I'm seeing could use it."

"*Hot* chick," I corrected quietly.

"Sorry, yeah, hot chick," he agreed, grinning at me.

I did not grin back.

I asked, "Are you serious?"

"I wouldn't show it to you if I wasn't."

No, he wouldn't do that.

"I can't—"

"I'm not offering it to you that way," he stated. "All I'm saying now is think on it. If you and I keep working and it's something you want to explore, I'd want a business plan. I'd want to know what it would cost to renovate. I might invest and we'll partner up. You might not want that and need to go for a loan. If you do, you'd need a business plan anyway. All I know is, my plans to renovate are on hold because I really dig this hot chick I'm seeing and there's no point dropping a load on that space if it might be used for something better."

Something better.

My voice was croaky when I asked, "Can you send me those pictures?"

He was watching me closely when he answered, "Sure, sweetheart. Take you to the space too, if you want to see it."

I absolutely, one thousand and one percent wanted to see it.

I just nodded.

"Now kiss me," he ordered.

I kissed him.

Hard.

I knew he felt it when we broke away because his arms were tight around me and he was watching me intently again.

He proved he got it when he murmured, "It's just a warehouse, Pepper."

"No one has stood beside me. No one has protected me. And as such, it's safe to say, no one has ever believed in me, Auggie. So I looked at some pictures. And you said what you said. But the bottom line is, you believe in me. It might not happen, but I know one thing for sure. It'll never be just a warehouse to me, honey."

That was when Auggie kissed me.

Hard.

But we had plans for him to come over Wednesday night to have dinner, go to the school and watch Thanksgiving play and make pumpkin and pecan pie with me and Juno.

So I had less than two days to wait until I would see him again.

*   *   *

We'd made the pies.

And Aug didn't hide how touched he was that Juno and I had not only gone out to buy the ingredients for our T-Day dinner, we'd also bought another stool so we could eat it all together at the island.

We'd attended the play, and Juno had seemed relieved (and I just was), that Corbin didn't show.

On the other hand, this was sad. Because she had a cute part playing an armchair quarterback in a short play about where food came from, gratitude and what's important during a family holiday.

The sets, it must be said, were stellar.

And since Aug had Thursday off too, and since Corbin was an ass, Aug came early on Thanksgiving so he was the one who answered the door when Corbin came to get Juno at nine for her time with him that day.

This did not go over well.

I saw it myself.

Auggie might want to be my shield, but that didn't mean I wasn't going to show up for the fight.

I stood at the end of the hall with my shoulder against the wall, watching them silently stand off.

Juno broke this up, but even in the presence of his daughter, Corbin did not douse the heat ray he sent with his eyes down the hall in an attempt to incinerate me.

Our daughter tugged him out of the house.

Aug and me both hung out in the office to watch them drive off.

And Auggie waited around seven-point-two-five seconds after we lost sight of them to carry me upstairs so we could engage in activities to peremptorily burn off some of dinner.

One could just say, I was pretty certain I earned an extra piece of pie.

But Aug earned two.

* * *

After that, we got to work on some cooking.

Once dinner was sorted (ish), Auggie showed me the warehouse (I was trying not to get excited, but just to say, it might not be perfect, but I could *so work it*).

And then we went to pick up Juno.

Which led to now.

Forty-five minutes past pickup time.

We had a bird in the oven it had been safe to leave in the oven but wouldn't be safe to leave there for too long.

Corbin and his family were scheduled to eat at 1:00.

We'd planned for Juno's second Thanksgiving to commence at 6:00, and to have time for the turkey to rest, and for us to use the oven for other things, the turkey needed to be out a bit before. Not to mention, I liked leftovers, Juno did too, and Auggie had never really had them so I wanted to introduce him to them.

In other words, we had a huge-ass bird.

I had my guy.

I should have my girl.

I might have a warehouse to build a dream (as supplied by my guy).

All was on point for dinner at the house.

Dinner that was, not unimportantly, maybe the first of many important holidays we'd share all together.

But it just plain was (I was determined, damn it) going to be one of the only really good ones Auggie had ever had.

Auggie's hush puppies were set to be our starter and they were singing to me like a siren song.

I was at one with the universe and the universe was at one with me.

I did not need my ex messing with my mojo.

But we were supposed to pick Juno up from his house, even if Thanksgiving was at his parents' house.

At 3:00.

And I'd knocked on the door.

No one answered.

I'd texted.

No reply.

At the fifteen-minute late mark, Auggie had done what he called "recon" (but what looked to me like he just walked around the house, looking into windows). When he rejoined me in his Telluride, he said Corbin's car wasn't there and no one was home.

I was on text six, of

Where are you?

With no reply.

And this was when Corbin's car pulled up his drive.

He was forty-five minutes late without giving me a heads-up he'd be even ten minutes late.

We were half an hour from my house.

I had potatoes to boil and mash. A homemade green bean casserole to cook. A table to set at the island with other stuff Juno and I bought to give Auggie a perfect Thanksgiving. A table I didn't want to set until the last minute because I didn't want to spoil Juno's and my surprise for Auggie, and I wanted my girl to be there when he saw it.

I mean, we couldn't hide the stool.

But the rest of it was meant to be special.

Not Juno throwing stuff on the island while I maniacally whipped potatoes and Auggie's and my stomachs rumbled angrily because we might have worked off extra pie, but in preparation for the gorge-fest, we'd had a light lunch.

I did not need Corbin pulling shit with me.

And what made it something I was oh-so-close to losing my mind over was that he was using our daughter to do it.

She knew three o'clock was the time.

She knew I'd be waiting for her.

She knew Auggie would be waiting with me.

She knew this was a special day for Auggie, as well as her and me, and she looked forward to playing her part in making that special.

She would fret about this.

And that...

That...

Nothing would stop me from losing my mind about *that*.

So when, with a panicked expression on her face, Juno ran from Corbin's garage to my car like she was at tryouts for the Olympics, and Auggie said a soothing, smooth, low "Baby," that, spoiler alert, did not soothe or smooth, I did just that.

I got out of his car.

And I...

Lost.

My.

Mind.

CHAPTER TWENTY-FOUR

My Peeps

PEPPER

One thing my father gave me.

When I was seriously pissed, I did not scream and shout. I went stone-cold.

This, I thought from experiencing it from my dad, was far more terrifying than someone shouting at you.

And because of that, I never wanted Auggie to see it.

I wished I could say Juno had never seen that side of me, but although she hadn't elicited it, she'd seen it.

She had because Corbin had provoked it.

Like he'd just done.

This was probably why she hit me with a desperate hug before I was even halfway to his driveway, and cried, "Momma!"

Her way of stopping my advance.

"Hey, baby," I replied, not taking my eyes from Corbin, who had appeared from the garage and was making his way to me. "Go get in the car with Auggie, okay?"

"Momma."

I looked down at her. "Do as I say, please."

The uneasiness she was exuding penetrated, but not enough.

No.

Not near enough.

She reluctantly nodded, let me go and moved away.

I zoned in on my target, who had stopped about ten feet away, and I walked to him.

Corbin spoke before me.

"You were supposed to meet us at Mom and Dad's."

"Don't give me that bull," I snapped. "You said to meet you here."

He shook his head. "Why would I say that, Pepper? They live more than half an hour away. It'd barely give us enough time to eat if I had to leave in time to meet you here."

I'd left my phone in my purse in the car, or I'd whip it out to show him his text telling me to be right where I was right then.

But he'd have his.

"Check your phone, Corbin."

"I didn't tell you to meet us here," he maintained.

"Check your phone, Corbin," I repeated.

"Pepper, it makes no sense to meet you here. It cuts half an hour off family time for Juno."

"Fine," I spat. "Even if you didn't tell me that, which you did, I've been texting for forty-five minutes that I was here."

"Yes, and at first, that confused me because you said you were 'here,' which I thought was Mom and Dad's, but you weren't there. When I figured it out, we got in the car to drive to meet you here."

"And you couldn't text me to share there'd been a misunderstanding?" I asked.

"I don't text and drive when Juno's in the car."

"Juno knows how to text."

He blew out an exaggerated sigh. "There's no point in doing this."

"I disagree," I returned. "Because you did this on purpose. You wasted forty-five minutes of my Thanksgiving, Auggie's Thanksgiving, and you did it to piss me off. You did it to strike back. You did it to get a reaction. Well, here's your reaction, Corbin, be careful. I'm not playing your games and I am," I leaned toward him, "*absolutely* not going to allow you to use *our daughter* to play them."

He sneered and retorted, "You're delusional. As usual."

"I'm not. Read your goddamn texts."

"Again, *it makes no sense to meet you here*," he bit out.

"You're right. This is a waste of time. But I'll reiterate, Corbin. Don't pull this shit again. Especially using Juno. It won't go pretty for you."

I was about to move to leave, but he caught me fast by stating, "It's you who needs to worry, Pepper."

I shouldn't engage.

I should leave.

Calm down.

Chill out.

There was still plenty of time to make potatoes and the turkey had a full hour and a half left to cook.

I was overreacting because I was letting him push my buttons.

And there was nothing to be gained by this.

But in the headspace I was in, I didn't leave.

I engaged.

"Why would I worry, Corbin?"

This time, he leaned toward me. "Because we don't have to get into the collective whack that is your family, and I never liked Juno being around any of them. But I've also never been a stripper and I don't know who that fuckin' guy is," he jerked his head toward where Aug's car was, "but preliminary reports from my investigator said his employment is nebulous and I'm not a fan of that being around my daughter."

My job?

His...*investigator*?

Now *that*...

That made my head explode.

Which meant I went sub-zero.

"You're threatening me," I whispered, frost forming on each word.

"Don't push me, bitch," he whispered back.

"Fuck you," I spat.

"You have been, from the minute I fucked up and you didn't give us a chance, to right now, being at *my house* with *that fucking guy* in *his fucking car* at *my curb*," he shot back.

Oh my God!

Auggie had been right.

Corbin had totally been pining for me!

"I don't like your ladies and I'm gonna live with Mom."

Hearing Juno's voice coming from close, a frisson of electricity zapped through me, it was deeply unpleasant, and Corbin and I both stepped away from each other like that feeling came from a lightning strike between us.

I turned, seeing Juno standing not two feet away.

It was then my insides went cold, and I heard Corbin make a noise like someone punched him in the stomach.

Vaguely, I noted Auggie was out of the car and standing at the curb.

But my attention was for my daughter, whose face was red, her eyes were bright with tears, and she was staring at her father.

"I don't like you calling Momma a bitch either," she stated.

Oh no.

"Button—" Corbin tried, his voice suddenly hoarse.

Juno shook her head. "No. Mr. Cisco said I should talk to you . . ."

Mr. Cisco?

Who was Mr. Cisco?

". . . and I should have. But I was chicken," she went on. "Now I will. I don't like all your ladies coming over and then leaving and I don't like how you're always on your phone with them and I don't like how you're always finding ways to be mean to Mom and I don't like that you totally didn't notice I was upset because me and Mom wanted to make this a special day for Auggie, and you made us late for it."

"It was a misunderstanding, Juno," Corbin lied.

"You're lying," Juno called him on it. "And you called Momma the b-word, Dad. Right in front of me."

"I didn't know you were there," he pointed out.

"Does that matter?" she asked.

Good freaking question.

I wanted to intervene. I wanted to help her.

But I was sensing she needed to do this.

So I stood there with her and let her do it.

"I shouldn't have said that, you're right," Corbin murmured.

"I don't want you two back together," she announced. I pressed my lips together, and I heard Corbin's sharp indrawn breath. "You're not nice to her and you kept things from her to break us up and you have too many ladies. You should have just one lady. Not one after another. I want her with Auggie. Auggie looks at her in a sweet way. And I want you to find somebody special you can look at that way too. But it can't be Momma."

"You're really too young to—" Corbin began.

Unexpectedly, she lifted her hands in fists at her side and jerked them down like she was planting two ski poles in the snow.

Okay, maybe I needed to end this.

I didn't get that shot.

"*I'm not too young!*" she shouted. "I'm *not*. I'm not too young to know you hurt Momma. And I'm not too young to know you hurt *me*."

Oh *God*.

Corbin was so silent, it felt like the air around us had been deprived of its ability to carry sound.

"So, I wanna live with Mom," she kept flaying him. "And when her dad was being mean to her mom, my friend Kyra had to talk to a judge and say what she wanted, and I will too, if I have to. I'll tell him all this. And Mom might dance at a place you don't like, but Mr. Smithie is sweet and always gives me a twenty-dollar bill when he sees me."

He did?

"And Auntie Ryn and Auntie Hattie and Auntie Evie are *a million times* better than Auntie Saffron could ever be."

I had to admit, that was true.

"And Mr. Ian is super handsome, and I might marry him when I grow up."

Uhhhhh...

"And I wouldn't have any of that if Mom didn't dance there. And if you love me, you'd love that Mom gave me that. So do you love me, Dad?"

Oh man.

I looked to Corbin.

His expression was ravaged, and his voice was raw when he said, "Of course I do, Button."

"Then stop being mean to Momma!" she demanded, stomped to me, took my hand then dragged me toward Auggie's car.

That was when I really took in Auggie, and when I did, it was a shot to the heart, because I could actually *feel* the hum of fury mixed with frustration liberally dosed with anxiety that was vibrating from his place at the curb.

This was because his place was at the curb.

He crouched the instant we got close, though, and Juno broke from me and ran to him.

She stood in his arms between his splayed thighs, held him around the neck, and I hustled to them in time to hear her say, "Let's go home, Auggie. Can you drive fast?"

She wanted to set his special table.

She wanted to give him a good day.

Ugh.

But yeah.

Her father had deserved what he just got, even though I hated Juno had to give it to him.

"Yeah, sweetheart, I'll go fast, but safe," Auggie replied.

Okay.

Time to get this situation in hand.

I lifted my gaze to the heavens and gave myself just enough time to see a cloud drift.

I had missed all this in my girl, or at least how deeply it ran.

As sure as Corbin had, even if I'd tried to tell him about the women.

But we needed to set about making it right.

I drew in breath, tipped my chin, and caught Auggie in the throes of preparing to pick her up.

His eyes were on me.

I shook my head, glanced over my shoulder to see Corbin still standing there, staring at us, immobile, face pale, and then I squatted too.

"Dollface, look at me," I urged.

She did and I could see she was still fighting tears.

"Can we go home, Momma?" she requested.

"Yeah, baby, but first, I need to ask you to do something that's gonna seem really hard on you right now. You'll look back on it later, though, and you'll be really, *really* glad you did it. I promise."

"What?"

"Go give your dad a hug good-bye."

She visibly balked.

"Trust me," I said hurriedly. "Go give him a hug. It can be fast. You don't have to say anything. Just a quick hug and we'll go."

She didn't move a muscle.

"Sweetheart," Auggie called.

Juno looked to him.

"Always trust your mother," he whispered.

She was undecided. She hesitated.

Then she broke free from Auggie and ran to her dad.

Both Aug and I stood up and I moved to him, watching Corbin instantly bend toward her, opening his arms.

Juno ran into them.

Corbin wrapped them around her and lifted her up.

My throat closed.

She might have wanted a quick hug, but Corbin was holding on tight.

"What happened?" Auggie said under his breath.

I didn't know if it was good or bad that he couldn't hear.

But I was leaning toward good.

"Juno made some things plain. I'll tell you about it later."

He didn't respond, except to take my hand.

And yeah.

There it was.

I was grounded, standing by Auggie's side, with Auggie holding my hand.

I heard his phone bing with a text that he unsurprisingly ignored, and we watched Juno and Corbin hug while Corbin was saying some things in Juno's ear. He ended this shoving his face in her neck.

Then he kissed her cheek and set her on her feet.

She looked up at him and shared her own words. They were

short and I hoped it was something like *I love you anyway*. Then she came running back to us.

Auggie had her door open by the time she arrived.

He helped her up while I moved to my door.

I glanced back at Corbin to see him still there, watching us.

When he caught my glance, he lifted his hand—and as pissed as I'd been at him for the last hour, not to mention all the things he'd done in the past—my heart broke for him as he gave me an awkward wave.

His daughter had just spoken to him like that.

And his actions were the sole reason we were driving away from him on Thanksgiving.

I returned his wave and pulled myself into Auggie's car.

I heard Auggie's phone ringing as he pulled himself in beside me.

He tugged it out of his back pocket, glanced at it, then hit the side button to stop the ringing.

While he put on his seatbelt (mine was on already), I looked behind me at Juno.

"You belted in, baby?" I asked.

She was staring at her lap. "Yeah."

"You going to be okay?"

A pause and then, "Yeah."

"You need some space?"

A big breath that seemed to expand her whole body and a repeat of, "Yeah."

"Okay, Dollface," I murmured.

By this time, we were on the road.

I needed to give her that. Then we needed to explore some of the things she said.

In that mix was also finding out what she was doing with those twenties Smithie gave her as well as who the heck "Mr. Cisco" was.

Though, this could wait until after we salvaged Thanksgiving.

I watched the road and Auggie gave her space too as he drove us toward home.

We were halfway there when he said to Juno, "It's all good, sweetheart. Your mom and I did some stuff, but you and I have some cooking to do and the turkey won't be finished for at least an hour."

"Okay, Aug," she mumbled.

He glanced at me.

I made a *yikes* face.

His mouth got tight.

And his phone rang again.

He looked down at it, sighed, and this time, took the call.

It came up on his dash and it was Tod.

Which I thought might be a good distraction for us all, because if Tod wasn't being hilarious, he was just being awesome.

"Hey, Tod. Happy Thanksgiving," Auggie greeted.

"Um, kind of, though I've been calling and texting because, with your mom having broken the front window of your house to get in, I'm thinking for you it won't be."

Auggie hit some buttons to take Tod off speaker and put the phone to his ear.

"*What?*" he barked into it. Pause and, "Right. Thanks. I'll take care of it. Sorry for this disruption." Another pause and, "Okay, no. Don't. Don't go over there. I'll take care of it." One last pause and, "Right. Thanks again. Later."

He ended the call, the air in the cab was stifling, and Juno asked, "Your mom broke into your house?"

Fabulous.

"I'm gonna take you two home," Auggie gritted out. "Then I'll go deal with that. I'll be back by dinner."

"No way!" Juno exclaimed. "Thanksgiving is about being together."

It was.

But not being together with his mother involved.

I didn't want him to go by himself (like, *really* didn't), but I didn't think I had the choice. He couldn't let his mother break into his house. He couldn't have his window like that when he wasn't there.

He had to deal with this.

But Juno couldn't be there when he did.

I mean, seriously.

What in *the* fuck was the matter with that woman?

I kept a tight rein on my anger and looked around the seat again to my girl.

"We can get some things sorted Auggie won't want to do while he's away. Then you two can hit it when he gets back."

"No!" she shouted, and I blinked, because she hadn't shouted when she wasn't getting her way since she was a little kid. Or a littler one. "Family sticks together!"

"Juno," I said mollifyingly.

"I know what you meant, *Mom*, when you said Auggie's family isn't normal."

I didn't say not normal.

I said not traditional.

Though I meant not normal, of course.

Still.

I didn't correct her and not only because she kept going so I didn't have the opportunity.

"It means his family is like *our* family and when it's like that, the good parts of it have to stick together. Like you and me stick together. We gotta stick together with Auggie."

I loved that she thought that.

However.

"I don't think—" I tried.

"We're going with him," she declared.

"Juno, really—"

"*We're going with him!*" she shrieked.

Right.

I was not a fan of that.

Then again, I'd missed that she was clearly suffering as much as she was with what was going on with her dad. That was fresh for her, so maybe...

"You can stay out in the car," Auggie murmured.

"No, your mom gets to know you have people," Juno refuted.

Auggie's lips thinned.

As much as it sucked—because even if my girl was being a bit of a brat, she was still being sweet—it was time to nip this in the bud.

I looked around my seat again. "I know you've just had a rough go of it, honey, but whatever is happening, Auggie gets to make the call with how it's dealt with."

"Is Auggie ours?" she demanded to know.

Ummmmm...

"He is," she answered her own question (correctly, I'd add). "And we take care of what's ours, don't we, Mom? You take care of me. I take care of you. We take care of *what's ours*."

Shit.

Now I felt like crying.

"It'll be fine," Auggie said in a weird, strangled voice that was tight, but also rough, and I knew by that how much it meant that Juno had just claimed him.

I wasn't certain we should give in to this behavior, but the feel of the cab hadn't gotten any better, Juno just laid out her dad, Auggie's mom had broken into his freaking house, and I had two people I loved on my hands who were dealing with some heavy shit.

Two people I loved.

Oh man.

Okay, I had three people I loved, because I loved me, and I

was now dealing with the fact I just figured out I was in love with Auggie.

Holy hell.

I decided to remain quiet.

But while I did that, I reached for Auggie's hand, and he gave it to me.

Auggie drove to his house.

He parked in one of his two spaces in the back.

We all then trooped through his back gate, his backyard, and he let us in through his back door.

When we got into the dining area of his front room, we saw his mom had made herself at home and was watching a movie, flat out on his couch.

I knew this when her head popped over the back of it.

Oh, and there was glass all over the floor under the window she'd broken.

She'd helped herself to a towel from the bathroom to drape over it to contain some of the cold getting in, like she'd helped herself to *his house*.

I inhaled the deepest breath I'd ever taken.

So deep, it was a wonder I didn't pass out.

"So, you haven't ceased to exist," she said, her eyes taking in me and Juno, as well as her boy. "Happy Thanksgiving, not that you give a shit whether mine is happy or not. Oh yeah, I forgot, this is because you don't give a shit *about me*."

Auggie made no response.

To her.

He pulled out his phone, engaged it, dialed a number and put it to his ear.

He then said into it, "Yes, hello. I need to report a break-in."

Dana jumped from the couch and screeched, "*What?*"

Auggie continued speaking into his phone.

"It's a member of my family. My mother. She's broken a

window to gain entry, but she hasn't disturbed anything else or taken anything. However, we're estranged, and this break-in was made with ill intent. She's still here."

"Hang up that phone, Augustus," Dana ordered, rounding the couch to get to us.

"Yes, please send some officers. I'll be pressing charges," Auggie said into the phone, gave his address and then finished, "Thank you."

"*Hang up that phone, Augustus!*" she yelled, moving double time to get to him, her hand up like she was going to try to grab the phone.

Or something else.

I shot in front of him, and since I did, she and I bumped chests.

"Don't touch my mom!" Juno shouted, moving to wedge herself between me and Dana, doing it pushing back.

I stepped back.

Auggie stepped back with me.

When he was done doing that, he planted his feet, and one by one (Juno first, he reached around me to get to her), we were shoved behind him.

"Who's the little girl?" Dana asked, leaning to the left to look at Juno.

"I'm pressing charges, Mom," Auggie told her.

Her attention shot back to him. "You're pressing charges against your mother?"

"No, I'm pressing charges against an unwanted intruder who broke my window who is also the woman who gave birth to me."

"Yes," she spat. "Your mother."

"No, you're not my mother," he returned.

Well, damn.

He was doing this now.

Better now than never, I supposed.

"I can hardly forget pushing you out, Auggie," she bit back.

"That's the only thing you've ever done for me," he returned.

I watched her face and I wanted to say she was offended. I wanted to say she was hurt. I really wanted to say that destroyed her, like what Juno said wrecked Corbin.

I couldn't say any of that.

She was into this. She was loving this.

She'd come there for just this.

Yes.

On Thanksgiving.

"Okay, so now, according to you, I'm a bad wife *and* a bad mom?" she asked.

"Yes," Auggie answered.

She opened her mouth but Auggie wasn't finished.

"You think I'm going to do this with you, but I'm not. I'm going to make a report to the cops. I'm going to board up the window. And I'm going to do that as fast as I can, because we haven't had our Thanksgiving dinner yet, and I need to get my girls home so we can do that."

I looked down at Juno on his "my girls" to see her eyes wide and looking up at me like I just told her we were going to Disneyland for Christmas.

I suspected I was looking much the same.

"You and me, though, we're done," he stated. "I'm blocking you from my phone, and anytime you try to contact me or see me, I'm phoning the police. If need be, I'll get a restraining order. If you remain in his life, I'm doing the same with Dad. You don't have to tell him that, I will."

"I'm not talking to your father," she sniffed.

"I don't care. I quit caring a long time ago, Mom. And the thing that sucks most about that is, you didn't notice," he replied.

Ouch.

I saw two uniforms moving up his front walk as Auggie kept talking.

"They might arrest you. I don't know how you're going to play this that might force their hands. But if they do, I advise not resisting. A broken window is one thing. Resisting arrest won't make things easier on you."

"I can't believe—"

She didn't finish that because Auggie walked toward her, by her, and to the front door.

She whipped her head to me. "This is you." She jabbed a finger at me. "You've turned my boy against me."

Juno made a noise.

But I didn't.

I didn't say a word.

In this, I was categorically not going to engage.

There were murmurings of greetings at the door as Auggie ushered the cops in.

"It's Thanksgiving!" Dana shouted at them, apropos of nothing. "What mother's son doesn't make plans with her for Thanksgiving? He didn't even call!" She was still shouting. "I know it was an extreme way to get his attention, but you don't know. With him, that's the way it has to be."

One cop was studying the broken window.

The other one was watching the Dana Show and he didn't appear impressed.

"Ma'am, can you step outside with me?"

"This isn't that big of a deal!" she yelled.

Aug came to me.

"You wanna take my car, go home, check on things, come back in a while and get me?" he offered when he got close.

"We're staying with you and helping you with the window," Juno answered for me.

"*It isn't that big of a deal!*" Dana screamed.

Instantly, like a switch was flipped, the officer went from handling-a-situation mode to alert-and-ready-for-anything mode.

I was impressed.

"Ma'am, calm down," he warned.

I saw Auggie's eyes move beyond me before I felt someone there.

I turned.

"Tod! Stevie!" Juno cried and ran to them.

Stevie got the hug first.

Tod did a mental-health scan of Auggie before he looked to me. "Hey, girlie. Nice cutout cowl."

Only Tod could walk into a situation involving police and his first comment would be about my sweater.

"Thanks," I replied, feeling a hysterical bubble of laughter rising and it was a nice change of focus to make the effort to tamp it down.

"You do look pretty, Momma," Juno said, going in for a sideways hug from Tod, who gave her one right back and one-upped her with a big jostle.

"Thanks, honey," I replied.

"Augustus! Are you honestly going to go through with this?" Dana demanded loudly.

Auggie didn't reply.

He turned to the cop who'd been surveying the window. "What do you need from me?"

"Quick statement, Aug," he replied, moving our way.

I hiccupped, which was actually me swallowing a laugh.

Auggie knew these guys.

"Are you...*friends*?" Dana demanded incredulously.

"Ma'am, please step outside with me," the one who picked the figurative short stick of having to deal with her requested.

"This is ludicrous. He's my son!"

"Ma'am, again, please step outside."

"Do you have a board, Aug, or you want me to ask Dean and Matt next door?" Stevie queried.

"You don't have to—" Auggie began.

"He's trying to get away from *my* family," Tod explained. "And not only because they're over there watching men tackle each other on our TV, this because we lost when we pulled out of a hat, and we're both still upset we're not watching Brandy's *Cinderella*. So help him out. And me. Even though I intend to do nothing but cheer you on when you wield hammers, I'm not returning to our home until I'm certain the tryptophan has set in, they're all passed out and we can switch over to Disney Plus and get our Thanksgiving dose of Whitney."

"You don't like your family, Mr. Tod?" Juno asked.

He looked down at her. "I love them with all my heart, baby girl. I just sometimes love them better when they're asleep."

That did it.

I couldn't control it.

I burst out laughing.

Juno looked my way and laughed with me.

I felt Auggie kiss my cheek, I turned to him, and he was smiling.

"Be back, baby," he whispered.

He went out front with an officer, which fortunately was where Dana now was, with the other officer.

I turned to Tod. "You made him smile so you're my hero today, Tod."

"I'm someone's hero every day, girlie," he replied.

"On that, so I don't have to wade through it as it rises, I'm going to Dean and Matt's. Juno, you wanna come with?" Stevie asked.

"Sure, Mr. Stevie!" she cried, and jumped to him, taking his hand.

They went out the back door.

"It's gonna be okay, Pepper," Tod said quietly.

I turned to him. "I know, honey. Somehow, some way, it always is."

"Do you want wine?" he asked. "I'll brave a return to grab you a glass."

"That's sweet, but I'm good. We'll be home soon, and it'll be just us. Then, I can look after my peeps."

"That's where it's at. You can get through anything, just as long as at the end of it, you're with your peeps," Tod replied.

"No truer words were ever spoken."

"You may not have noticed this, though I'd be amazed you haven't, but when I'm not being a hero, I'm a sage," he drawled.

And again, I burst out laughing.

CHAPTER TWENTY-FIVE
I Choose Them Too

AUGGIE

Aug stood on Pepper's back patio, not seeing her excellent yard lighting because he was focused on what was coming through the phone into his ear.

"She can be a lot, son, but she's your mother and it's Thanksgiving," his dad was saying.

Which gave Auggie the clue as to who Dana called after she'd been taken in for processing.

She'd committed a B&E.

He was pressing charges.

She'd been arrested.

The cops explained there was no getting around that.

And the truth was, Auggie might need it recorded, if she didn't retreat from his life as he'd asked, and he had to take even more formal steps to be certain she didn't re-enter it.

"But having her arrested?" Dem went on. "Your own mother?"

"You're making it clear where you are in your head about this, Dad," Auggie started. "And I'll be honest. You've given little indication you're any more capable than she is at understanding the depths of dysfunction the two of you live in. Recently, it's become apparent that I've played my part in it by assimilating to it. When I was a kid, I had no choice but to do that. I'm not a kid anymore. I can choose not to be involved. And that's the choice I've made today."

"Auggie—" his father began in a wheedling tone.

"No, Dad, with this, you need to listen to me. What I'm building with Pepper is serious. I see a future. I see that clearly. She has a daughter. Juno is only eight years old. I cannot allow harmful and even damaging things into their lives. And your and Mom's behavior is harmful and damaging. I didn't like it for me. But I won't allow it for Pepper and Juno."

Dem sounded offended when he asked, "You're calling us harmful and damaging?"

Auggie tightened the grasp on his patience, something he always had a stranglehold on, an effort he was so fucking done with expending.

"Mom broke into my house today, Dad," he reminded his father in a stiff voice. "She actually broke a front window I had to board up. On Thanksgiving. Just to suck my time and attention."

"She was hurt about what you said a few weeks ago."

Even if his father couldn't see him, Aug shook his head.

"I'm not doing this. I'm not explaining things you should get. I've had these conversations with you before. And I'm done having them."

There was a pause and then his father tried to change the topic, and suck his time. "Juno?"

"Pepper's daughter," he explained shortly. "Now, as you know, I've made the decision Mom is out. If you can't see that a woman, any woman, hell, any *person*, but particularly a mother breaking into someone's house for the sole purpose of getting their attention and causing a scene as very wrong, you need to take some time to reflect."

He paused to let that sink in.

And then he carried on.

"And I won't be around while you do that. I am no longer going to be drawn into your drama. I've made that plain with her today in a very official way. I will do the same with you if needs be. Straight up, if she doesn't change, I don't want to see her again. And if you carry on like you are with her in your life, the same goes for you."

"I cannot believe the words I'm hearing," Dem stated, and he sounded like he meant it, his tone full of shock and hurt.

Therefore, Auggie allowed what he was feeling to be heard in his next words.

And it was only hurt.

"And I can't believe you can't believe them. *She broke into my home today*, Dad. *Broke in.* And you're phoning to defend her. And you both forced your way into my house on the day Pepper found out her mother is dying, and neither of you behaved anywhere near decent human beings. If you don't see these two things as extreme, unhealthy behavior, these on the back of years of the same, there's nothing more for me to say except what I've already said. I'm done. In this game we've been playing of who gets the most time and attention, I choose me."

There was now a bitter thread to his father's, "Sounds like you choose that woman and her kid."

Is Auggie ours?

He is.

"I choose them too."

His father was silent.

Auggie didn't break it.

However, when his dad remained silent, Aug felt a sour hit his gut and he closed his eyes tight.

When he opened them, he said low, "Good-bye, Dad."

And before Dem could reply, Aug hung up on him.

Then he repeated the actions he'd done with his phone earlier, except with his mother's number.

This meant he blocked his father.

He took a second with that, staring at Pepper's yard, again not seeing it.

No.

All he saw was in his head, Pepper jumping in front of him when his mother was coming at him and then he saw Juno push in front of Pepper.

Is Auggie ours?

He is.

He had thought he'd genuinely been in love with his ex-fiancée, Marie.

But when he heard those words from Juno, when he felt what was coming off Pepper after she asked her question, when she took his hand, he knew he hadn't scratched the surface of that emotion.

Is Auggie ours?

He is.

We take care of what's ours.

He'd not been taken care of all his life. In the end, even by Marie.

He was now.

He also knew what that felt like and he knew what that feeling was.

It was love.

With that thought burning warm deep in his gut, it came to him he'd stepped out there to finally end this when his father called.

But they'd arrived back at Pepper's to find the turkey only slightly overdone and then his girls flew into action to sort the rest out, and they'd dragged him along with them.

And when his phone rang, they seemed weirdly eager for him to "sort that out, honey" (Pepper) and "We'll be here when you're done, go outside" (Juno, actually shoving him toward the sliding doors to the backyard).

He figured this was because they wanted this situation off his shoulders and behind him so they all could enjoy what was left of the day without this weighing on any of them.

Auggie wasn't certain the weight was off.

It had shifted, and it sucked to admit, given that he was excising his parents from his life, it felt like it had lightened.

But he knew it was something he'd carry the rest of his life.

He turned to go back inside.

Then he stopped when he looked in the glass doors and saw the island covered in a tablecloth. Their three stools had been set around it. There were some little pumpkins tumbling from a horn in the middle of the island with leaves scattered around and two thin, glass candlestick holders with two orange taper candles stuck in, both lit.

The plates were laid out with cloth napkins and cutlery on top. Champagne glasses sat at two place settings and a bucket filled with a bottle sat on the counter with some bowls covered in towels to keep the food that was in them warm.

And there was a pint glass filled with beer at what was obviously his plate.

His plate.

His place.

That warmth in his gut intensified.

The island had not been like that when he'd walked outside.

The lighting of the room had also been dimmed.

And the turkey was on the counter, resting and waiting for him to carve it, a platter beside it.

Last, Pepper and Juno were standing there, Juno in front of her mom, holding Pepper's wrists that were resting at her chest because Pepper had her arms around her girl.

They'd been busy while he was outside.

But never...

He had to take a second...

Not ever had he seen anything close to this during any Thanksgiving he'd had.

And absolutely not a soul had put this effort into it just for him.

His throat had closed, and something seemed stuffed into the back of his nasal passages. It took him a beat and no small effort to power through it before he caught Pepper's eyes through the glass.

That beautiful woman standing with her beautiful daughter loved him.

She loved Auggie in a way that would never be a weight.

She would always be a breeze flowing through his life, keeping him calm, keeping things fresh, grounding him.

Making him happy.

His throat was tight again when he went to the door and slid it open.

"*Happy Thanksgiving!*" Juno shouted, at the same time her mother said the same thing in a normal voice.

They were both beaming at him.

Christ.

Christ.

He'd known it was happening, but still, it was a shock to the system to realize he'd fallen in love twice in a month.

With a blonde.

And a brunette.

He didn't sound like himself, his voice seemed far away, when he said, "It looks great."

At his tone, Pepper's head cocked, her gaze remained on him, and warmth moved over her face that Auggie felt spread through his chest.

Juno jumped forward, sharing, "We bought the cloth napkins

and tablecloth and the leaves and that horn basket thingie to make the table pretty. And a special beer glass for you to have here all the time *just for you*."

She'd made it to him while speaking, grabbed his hand and was pulling him the two steps to the island.

"It's gorgeous, sweetheart, thank you." He murmured this understatement.

She smiled up at him. "We have to do a Christmas one next. But you can go shopping with us when we make that one."

He was not a shopper.

He was also not missing that.

Not for anything.

"I'm in," he said.

"Okay, let's get this rolling," Pepper declared, watching him closely even as she thankfully moved them along before Auggie did something whacked, like pull one or the other or both of them in his arms and crush their bones by holding them too hard. "I'm whipping potatoes. Aug, you're on carving duty. Juno, you fill up some water glasses and put the butter and salt and pepper on the table."

"Got it!" Juno said excitedly, let him go and ran to the counter, where three glasses were waiting to be filled.

The turkey was sitting close to where the standing mixer was wafting steam from the boiled potatoes.

They got to work, and when Pepper was at his side and the mixer was whirring through potatoes, butter, salt, pepper and sour cream, she bumped her hip to his.

It made him truncate a slice of breast shorter than he'd wanted it, but he didn't give a fuck.

He looked sideways at her.

"Okay?" she asked softly.

"The best I've ever been," he answered honestly.

Her eyes widened at that.

Then her face got soft, he was reminded again just how freaking beautiful she was, and she gave him what he needed in that moment.

She let it go and finished whipping the potatoes mostly leaning into his side.

He stood strong to hold her upright and carved turkey.

Eventually, though, Pepper got busy with putting the potatoes in a bowl, pouring the gravy in a boat, and sorting anything left, with excellent timing because he was finished with the bird.

"Juno! Where'd you go? We're good to sit down and give thanks," she called as Auggie carried the platter to an island that was now crammed with food.

They hadn't had time to do his hush puppies, and with all that food, it seemed like that was an auspicious turn of events.

Auggie was hungry and looking forward to eating.

What Auggie wasn't going to do in that moment was allow it to hit him how he'd never seen that much food on a family table at which he'd had a place.

But he'd decided ten minutes earlier that this, in all its incarnations, was going to be his future.

That meant the time to let the past slide away was while he'd been standing on Pepper's back patio.

And the time to get used to it was now.

"Juno! Dollface! It's turkey ti…"

Pepper trailed off and Auggie went stiff as Juno showed at the end of the hallway.

Gone was the Juno of ten minutes ago who was excited about their Thanksgiving table and Auggie's pint glass.

She now looked scared out of her mind.

And she did because behind her stood Brett "Cisco" Rappaport.

Well…

Shit.

"Okay," Juno said fast, her gaze glued to her mother. "I know this is sneaky and I know sneaky is bad, but I asked Mr. Cisco—"

He felt Pepper tense beside him for some reason at those last two words, and Juno kept talking.

"—to have dinner with us because he helped me make today what it is because he helped me get you and Auggie together, Momma. And you can't be too mad, because you were being silly about it, and now you're not being silly and Auggie's here and we're all happy."

He heard Pepper take in a breath.

Juno kept going.

"And also, Mr. Cisco should have someone to have Thanksgiving with. And I asked him, and he said he didn't. And he should. Because I'm thankful for him. And you should be thankful for him. And I like him, and he's been looking out for me and you guys and I just think...I think..."

Damn.

She was losing it.

Just when he thought he'd have to step in, she found it again.

"I think he should be our friend and friends have friends over for Thanksgiving."

After that, no one said anything, but Auggie put his hand on Pepper's back, preparing to take a hit for Juno, or even Cisco, explaining how this went down, and that he knew about it, if Pepper lost it.

"How...*exactly*...did you and...*Mr. Cisco*...make today happen?" she asked.

Auggie moved even closer to her and began to speak.

He didn't get a word out.

"That was my doing, Pepper," Cisco lied. "With you the last of the four women who had yet to take the plunge, I decided—"

"Mr. Cisco," Juno cut him off quietly.

He shut up and looked down at her.

She shook her head.

He then looked to his shoes when Juno turned her attention back to her mom.

"He's fibbing for me because it was me," she kept talking quietly. "I got his number from Auntie Ryn's phone and I called him and asked him to help me, and he did and he gave me a phone so it would be safe for us to talk to each other because I...I...um, met him at Fortnum's when I was supposed to be at Emily's house—"

Pepper sucked breath.

"—and I know I need to give the phone back, and I will. And I swear, *swear* I never used it for anything except to talk to Mr. Cisco. But I don't want to give Mr. Cisco back because...because..." Juno took Cisco's hand and Aug didn't miss how it instantly engulfed Juno's or how the man got a little closer to her, "...because he's nice to me and he listens to me and he told me to tell Dad how I was feeling and I didn't so it got bottled up and burst all over the place today and he's my friend and—"

"Baby, be quiet and take a breath," Pepper said softly.

Juno's body startled and her expression grew hopeful as she did as she was told.

After she did, Pepper said, "I think there's quite a bit of this to go over, and we'll talk about it some other time. Not now. Not tonight. Today has been a lot for all of us. So I think we need to talk about what we're thankful for and then eat."

Pepper looked to Cisco.

"I'd like you to join us, but we don't have an extra stool. Maybe we can—"

"I told Mr. Cisco to bring one," Juno chirped and looked up at Cisco. "Did you bring a stool?"

He nodded.

Auggie bit back a bark of laughter.

"Can he bring it in?" Juno asked her mom. "I'll get his plate and rearrange the table so he fits and stuff."

"How about we all take care of that before this food gets cold," Pepper suggested.

The smile Juno aimed at her mom brightened the room and it didn't dim when she swung it to Cisco.

Then she raced to the island.

"I'll just go to the car," Cisco muttered.

Auggie watched him turn and then he moved into Pepper.

"Baby—"

"I am thankful for you and I am blessed with this home and this food and my daughter and that's all for right now, okay?"

He fought a smile and nodded.

"Okay," she stated firmly then began to help Juno.

Auggie walked to the front door, thinking Juno and Cisco couldn't have timed this better.

He got there and opened it to see Cisco carrying a stool up the front steps.

When the man came abreast of him, he said under his breath, "Juno and I have decided your knowledge of this situation is best left unsaid."

"I won't be keeping anything from Pepper."

They locked gazes and Cisco replied, "Your call."

It was, so Auggie didn't confirm.

They were broken up by Juno shouting, "C'mon, you guys! The faster we eat, the faster we get to the pecan pie."

"Says the girl who's already had one turkey dinner today," Pepper's disembodied voice came from somewhere in the kitchen they couldn't see.

Cisco walked in.

Auggie closed and locked the door and followed him.

When they made it to the kitchen, they saw Cisco and Juno would be crunched together at a narrow end that had space under it for their legs and Auggie and Pepper were down the long side.

Aug suspected Cisco wouldn't have a problem with this.

Cisco put his stool where it was supposed to be, and Pepper approached them.

"Hands, now, because we can't all hold hands at the table," she ordered, taking Auggie's hand, and reaching out for Cisco's. "We'll sit down after we share what we're thankful for."

Cisco hesitated, looking at Pepper, then Auggie, before he took Pepper's hand.

Without hesitation, Juno latched on to Aug then Cisco.

Pepper looked at her daughter.

Aug caught Cisco's eyes and thought that, when it was his turn, Cisco didn't have to say a word.

Clear as day, this guy was happy to be here. It was definitely about Juno. It might be that he didn't have anyone else.

But he appreciated where he was standing right then, and he didn't hide it.

"Today is the most beautiful day of the year because its sole purpose is to remind us to be grateful," Pepper began. "To be grateful for the bounty of the earth and to be grateful for the loved ones we share our lives with. But I will say right now I'm especially grateful to have the best daughter in the world, even when she's being sassy and yes, even when she's been sneaky. She's the light of my life and always will be."

Pepper squeezed his hand and he looked at her.

"And I'm grateful..." a meaningful pause, "...however it came about that you're here with me and Juno, Augustus. Because you're amazing and you make me happy."

"You make me happy too, Auggie," Juno chimed in.

"Thank you, sweetheart," he muttered to Juno.

"And I'm always," Pepper continued, and Aug turned again to her to see she was gazing at Cisco, "grateful for new friends."

Auggie grinned.

Cisco nodded to Pepper.

"I'm thankful for Momma, *always and forever*," Juno declared. "And I'm thankful for Auggie because he's sweet and makes Momma happy and me too. And I'm thankful for Mr. Cisco because he's a good listener and he brought the right stool that fits at our island."

Pepper let out a small laugh and Juno squeezed Aug's hand.

"Your turn, Auggie," she prompted.

He nodded to her.

"I'm thankful for two beautiful girls who taught me what real family is," he said, and heard a different sound coming from Pepper. He looked right at Cisco. "And I'm thankful for the reminder that you should always stay open, because you never know when friendships will form, and with who, and you don't want to miss them when that happens."

Cisco stared at him a long beat before he dipped his chin.

"You now, Mr. Cisco," Juno urged.

Cisco cleared his throat. "I'm thankful to be with good people during a holiday." He looked to Pepper. "And I'm thankful for kind hearts that have the extraordinary capacity for forgiveness."

That was when Pepper and Cisco stared at each other.

Then Auggie noticed she shook Cisco's hand and was holding it tight.

"Can we eat now?" Juno piped.

"Absolutely, Dollface," Pepper said.

They broke hands and turned toward the island.

Juno danced there.

Pepper strutted there.

Auggie clapped Cisco on the back then walked there.

Cisco joined them there.

And they ate Thanksgiving dinner.

CHAPTER TWENTY-SIX
End All, Be All

AUGGIE

Aug felt Pepper get out of bed, but he was too wiped to do anything about it.

He didn't even hear the water go on in her bathroom before he'd fallen back to sleep.

He had no idea how long she let him sleep before he was awake again.

Very awake.

Because she'd landed on top of him.

He was on his stomach, but he rolled immediately, rolling her off.

Just as immediately, he pushed an arm under her and pulled her back on top.

He stared up at her hazily.

She beamed down at him brightly.

"Fuck," he muttered, because his woman was flat-out on top of him and he still felt half-asleep.

"Do I need to talk to Hawk about how hard he works my man?" she asked teasingly.

"No," he grunted.

Though, he'd be interested to see how that convo went.

But now, having been warned off the dirty-cop thing weeks ago by Lieutenant Stephanie Fortune, street name Dynamite, which had freed a ton of their time (for now), Hawk had been doubling down on jobs that actually paid.

This meant Auggie and Mag had been up all night on a stakeout, which was his least favorite thing to do. He'd even prefer being on night duty watching the monitors than on a stakeout.

This was mostly because, when you were on a stakeout, you couldn't move. You sat in a vehicle and you stared at your focus and you fought off the urge to get out, drop and pump out forty pushups.

Needless to say, he wasn't a fan of being sedentary.

He was less of a fan of doing it for eight hours through the dead of night and having to be alert that entire time.

He found that more exhausting than a ten-mile training run carrying a pack on his back.

Making matters worse, now he had somewhere far better to be.

In Pepper's bed.

So it made it torture.

"What time is it?" he asked.

"Ten," she answered.

Shit.

He'd been asleep for two and a half hours.

No wonder he still felt foggy.

Christ.

"And I need to leave soon so me and Lots can go over some routines. But I needed to go over some things with you first."

This caught his attention and he asked, "How soon do you have to leave?"

She smirked. "Do you think I woke you up not factoring in time for you to do me?"

He smirked back.

Because the answer to that was a huge-ass *no*.

She'd had Juno last week, which had been Thanksgiving week, so he hadn't been spending the nights.

Juno had gone back to her dad yesterday in a return situation Pepper and Corbin had had a conversation about in order to sync up how they'd be paying close attention to how this went for Juno.

Corbin had instigated that call on Sunday afternoon.

And after spending twenty minutes in the office with the door closed while Juno and Auggie broke the seal on the second season of *The Mandalorian*, Pepper had come out with a look on her face he couldn't read.

She also couldn't tell him until Juno went to sleep.

But later that night, snuggling on the couch, as they'd started to make a habit of doing after Juno was upstairs, she said, "He started by apologizing."

Studying her face, he noted, "You seem shocked by that."

"He's not an apologizer."

"Hmm," he hummed, not surprised at this information.

"He also told me he had a rough night of it after we left on Thanksgiving. He felt like a jerk."

"Because he is one?" Auggie suggested.

She'd given him the full skinny Thanksgiving night, including the fact that Corbin was investigating him.

She'd been worried about this.

He had not.

Lee Nightingale and his men could investigate Hawk and his crew, and Lee was the best in the business. He'd still come up with zilch.

So yeah.

Corbin had been a jerk, an ass, and a motherfucker, partly to Pepper, mostly to Juno.

But that part wasn't a concern.

On the couch, Auggie was in Pepper's arms, as she was in his, and she gave him a jostle to tell him to shut up.

Then she kept talking.

"On Friday, he called and tried to have a conversation with his mom, who wouldn't go there with him because she's been pissed at him for three years. So he talked to his dad, who chewed him out."

"What you're saying is, he's an anomaly because he comes from decent folk, but he's a dick."

"Auggie," she murmured, her tone remonstrating, her eyes bright with humor.

"Go on," he prompted.

"His dad told him to get his head out of his ass. To move on from me, because he'd fubared that, though I doubt he used the word 'fubar,' and instead went gung-ho with the fullness of the F-word. He also told Corbin it was high time he learned how to be a father first, before anything else. Himself. His relationships. Until he found a woman he was serious about, the only serious person in his life was Juno. Corbin took this on board and admitted to me he hadn't fully taken into account Juno's feelings."

"No shit?"

"Aug!" she snapped, but she did this fighting a grin.

He shut up.

"He also admitted that he thought eventually we'd get back together."

Aug didn't even try to hide his smug look.

He was pretty certain she strained her eyes with how big she rolled them.

When she'd again caught his gaze, she continued.

"He admitted to being really hurt that you were at his place, with me, to pick up Juno at all, but especially Thanksgiving. And I had to admit, I hadn't really thought that through—"

"Don't take that on," Aug growled.

"I'm not, honey," she said pacifyingly. "But the truth is, we're new for each other, and we're new for him. It's a broken family, but it's still a family and we all have to respect one another. He'd moved on with so many women, even if I knew he had an issue with you, years had passed, I just assumed he'd get it in some senses when I moved on too. I honestly didn't think about his feelings. But I should have."

It sucked, but Auggie couldn't argue that.

He never would have wanted her to endure that scene without him at her back, then get behind the wheel of a car with Juno.

But it probably hadn't helped that Auggie was there, and maybe him being there had made something bad even worse.

"He says he's going to try to be a better father," Pepper carried on. "And when I shared you and I aren't casual, it was grudging, but he promised to try to come to terms with you and me."

"We're not casual?" he joked.

She tipped her head to the side. "Sorry, did you just want to be my fucktoy? I'm *soooo* down with that."

They'd been nestled in the corner of the couch, but when she said that, he un-nestled them and got her on her back with him on top.

"We're not casual," he whispered when she was underneath him.

"No, honey, we aren't," she agreed.

He was done talking about her ex.

"Did I say thank you for the Thanksgiving table?" he asked.

Her expression grew sweet and warm. "Yes. Twice. This makes three."

"It was beautiful."

"The look on your face after you saw it was a lot more beautiful."

That was when he decided they were done talking about anything. They started kissing, and after they enjoyed that, he'd had to go home.

He hadn't seen her awake until now.

"I checked in with Juno last night, and she said her dad picked her up from school. He took her out for some boneless wings, it's her favorite snack. And they had a chat."

Auggie's body tensed.

"All good?" he asked.

She stroked the beard he'd grown out because he was being lazy with shaving, and kept, because Pepper demonstrated in certain ways, like that one, that she liked it.

"All good," she said quietly. "But I don't think this was just a wake-up call for Corbin to get his shit together. It was one for me too. Her going to Brett, taking that risk, doing something so unsafe—"

Shit, shit, fuck.

They were here.

And he had to give it to her.

He started it with, "Cisco would never hurt her, babe."

"I know. I saw how they were together. But her just going to Fortnum's on her own that way..."

She didn't say more than that, but he got it.

And now it was time to give what he knew.

"You gotta know that I figured out it was Cisco the day we both talked to her class. And I confronted him about it that night. He promised to get the phone back, but I made the decision I wasn't going to tell you Juno had done what she'd done because, in the end, she'd been safe. Cisco assured me he made her promise never to try anything like that again. But also because I didn't want her to be in deep shit with you."

After he made his confession, he was again tense.

Pepper didn't say anything.

So he said, "I should have told you."

"I don't know," she said like she wasn't exactly talking to him.

He gave her a squeeze to get her attention.

When she focused on him again, he asked, "What do you mean?"

"I have to think about this, but I was feeling like a crap mom, that Juno had to go to Brett for help. She talked to him about other things too. And now I think, I don't know, maybe it's life. I want it to always be me for her. The person she gives everything to. But that's unrealistic. It's not going to be. There were always times she'd go to her dad. You're in her life now, and there will be things she takes to you. She clearly feels safe with Brett, and wants to 'keep him,' as she put it, so she has him. She seems especially tight with Ryn. Lottie as well. She's going to grow up. Have more things to process through. I think I have to let go this idea I have to be the end all, be all for her, and rest in the knowledge that I am, in a way. I gave her a life where I also gave her all of you."

She sounded conflicted about this.

Understandably happy, and sad.

So on that, he rolled her so he was pressing down her side and said, "Yeah, baby. That's good. It's healthy. And anyway, you get to be the end all, be all for me."

A look so beautiful washed over her face, it was breathtaking, and she asked, "I'm your end all, be all?"

"Like you didn't know that," he grunted.

"You're not my end all, be all, Auggie," she whispered.

His gut twisted.

Okay.

Everything she did, and said, told him this was as deep and meaningful for her as it was for him.

Had he not read her right?

"Because I have my baby girl," she went on. "And maybe, one day we'll make babies. But that doesn't mean I haven't fallen ridiculously head-over-heels in love with you."

Aug didn't move.

He'd read her right.

But fucking hell.

He had no idea how good it would feel for her to say it out loud.

He also had no idea how long his inability to move lasted, until Pepper called his name uncertainly.

"Auggie?"

"We'll have Juno," he pushed out. "And we'll have kids," he informed her, and another expression of sheer beauty washed through her face. "But you gotta know, Pepper, you will always be my end all, be all."

Her eyes filled with tears.

Auggie kissed her.

And he was pissed as fuck when his hands encountered the leggings she had on, which were hard to take off.

She came to him to talk, and to get herself some.

What had she been thinking?

He bested that while she took off her long-sleeved dance tee and sports bra.

Totally nude, his woman went after his pajama bottoms.

And once they were both naked, they went after each other.

He let her have some time. She liked the feel of his dick in her hand, the taste of it in her mouth, and for obvious reasons, he liked to give those to her.

But inevitably there was that time when she had to be all about letting him.

Letting him kiss her.

Letting him touch her.

Letting him position her with her cheek to the bed, on her knees, while he whispered shit in her ear that made her pant and played with her pussy, which made her whimper.

Letting him roll her to her back so he could suck on her tits until she was squirming and eat her cunt until she was begging him to let her come.

And then she let him cover her as he slipped inside her.

The heaven of her tight, hot pussy clamping around him as she wrapped him up with her arms and legs and looked into his eyes. Watching him watching her as his strokes became thrusts, his thrusts became drives, and then he grabbed hold of the back of one of her knees and cocked it high and drilled her.

He did this until her lips parted, her head pushed back into the pillows, and her pussy milked his cock when she came.

And suddenly, that was all there was in his world because he was shooting inside her.

Their aftermath was as slow and soft as the sex was fast and hot.

She took her time with her hands and her lips and her words whispered in his ear, and he did the same.

This time, though, it was Pepper who rolled him to his back and swept his throat, his collarbone, down his chest to his upper abs with her lips before she pulled the covers up to his waist and put her face in his.

She did this because he was about to pass out.

He lifted his hands to gather the curtain of her soft hair away from their faces.

"Sleep, baby. I gotta go," she murmured.

"The leggings were just plain mean," he mumbled.

She grinned at him and touched her mouth to his and he stayed conscious long enough to watch her grab her clothes and head to the bathroom.

But then Aug rolled to his stomach and he was dead to the world.

In ten minutes, he heard his phone go and he was back in it again.

The shower was off, and he could feel the house was empty. Pepper had an energy. Juno did too. The buzz was low, and it was gentle, but it was there when they were.

It was gone now.

He reached for his phone on the nightstand and saw the time.

It hadn't been ten minutes.

It'd been two hours.

And the caller was Cisco.

Fuck.

He didn't want to talk to him, he wanted to sleep.

But even though Cisco had gotten his phone back from Juno on Thanksgiving, she still knew his number. And Juno had been with her dad for less than twenty-four hours. She might have talked things out with Corbin, but what she told her dad, or her mom, might be different than what she shared with Cisco.

So this could be about Juno.

This was why he took the call.

"What's up, man?" he answered.

"Your woman and Charlotte Morrison have been kidnapped by Pepper's brother and an associate pastor of that fucking church," he growled.

Auggie shot up in bed.

And then he shot out of bed.

"I know where they are," Cisco continued. "We've got our eyes on them. Currently, the situation does not seem out of hand. They're waiting for something, or someone. But I don't know why they'd take the women or who they're waiting for. This means I don't know the state of play or how much time we have. Now we're either gonna handle this situation together, or I'm gonna handle it alone. That's your call. But if it's a together thing, you better get your ass here right away."

Cisco wasn't gonna handle it at all, but Aug wasn't going to get into that with him now.

They'd also get into it later how and why Cisco had Pepper under surveillance, which he obviously did.

Then again, he'd had all the women under surveillance at one time or other. After he'd kidnapped them himself, he'd claimed them along the way. So this wasn't exactly a surprise.

And with this happening, at this juncture, it wasn't unwelcome.

"Text me details, I'll be there ASAP," he said, yanking on his underwear.

"See you soon," Cisco stated like he was very much looking forward to that.

Auggie was moving fast.

But that tone from the man called Cisco, who was one thing to their crew, but an entirely different thing on the streets, made him move faster.

CHAPTER TWENTY-SEVEN

Sisters

PEPPER

This is *way* not as much fun as I thought it'd be," Lottie groused.

I could have told her that.

I didn't tell her that now.

I was too busy watching my brother with Saffron's boyfriend standing together at the other end of the garage they'd taken us to.

We were on our asses and tied together back-to-back *à la* characters in a number of TV shows, spy movies and Indiana Jones and his dad (*sans* the chairs).

I had the feeling, regardless of my current circumstances, that Lottie and I weren't in danger.

And because of this, I was not scared.

I

Was.

Pissed.

"Didn't take long to get in on the scam, big brother," I called out to Birch.

He flicked his glance my way but that was it.

"Can we move this along?" I demanded. "We both have things to do."

The two men looked at me that time, but it was Birch who spoke. "We're waiting for Saffron to get here. She wants to talk to you."

Okay.

Ummmm...

That flipped me out.

"Saff is in on it too?"

"In on *what*?" Saffron's hottie boyfriend almost barked.

Lottie pressed closer to my back.

Yeah, that didn't sound good.

"Whatever you're in on," I said.

"And what's that?" he asked.

"Chill out, Jon," Birch muttered.

"I wanna know what she knows," Hottie Jon said.

"And Saffron's gonna talk to her," Birch replied.

"I don't know anything, by the by," I lied. "Though, a good way to find out, you know, without jumping us, manhandling us, zip-tying us and shoving us on top of each other in the backseat of a car is to pick up a phone and call. Both you and Saffron have my number."

"You weren't answering," Birch retorted.

"Then you came over, and Aug told you to call me, and I not only didn't hear from you, you didn't return my texts," I pointed out.

He didn't meet my eyes when he said, "Things got hectic after that."

Hectic as in he somehow got involved in...

Whatever this was.

"You do know this kidnapping thing is a very bad idea," Lottie jumped in.

"Saffron will be here soon. She'll explain. Then you'll be here for a while. Tomorrow, latest the next day, we'll let you go," Birch told us.

Hang on a second.

Tomorrow, maybe the next day?

I felt Lottie's body jolt at that, but I spoke.

"You're keeping us here for *days*?"

"It'll probably be tomorrow," Hottie Jon muttered.

"You can't keep us here for days!" I yelled.

That got Birch looking at me with a *Cool it!* expression and Saffron's hottie looking at me with a totally different kind of expression.

One that had me shutting my mouth.

"You can breathe easy or we can gag you. Your choice," Hottie stated.

"Just hang tight, babe," Lottie advised. "My guess, we'll be out of here in an hour."

Oh man.

This was her first kidnapping, and I was seeing we girls should have given Lottie the Kidnapping 101.

Her words meant both guys continued to watch us, but neither of them had good expressions on their faces.

"Lots," I mumbled warningly.

"What d'you mean?" Hottie Jon asked Lots.

"Nothing," I said quickly.

Too quickly.

The hottie looked at me. "What did she mean?"

"Nothing," I repeated, trying to make it sound more blasé.

"Then why'd she say it?" he asked.

"Because you're going to let us go," Lottie covered.

She'd totally been talking about the fact the guys were going to figure out we were here and come to save the day. That was what they did. That was their job.

And in my current position, I could thank God for that.

She kept speaking.

"Because we don't know what you're up to and we don't care. So you're not gonna make us sit on our asses in this dingy garage for however long it takes you to do whatever it is you're up to."

"Just relax," Birch advised.

"Easy for you to say, you don't have a bony ass sitting on cold concrete," Lottie muttered.

Her ass wasn't bony.

I didn't get into that either.

"Have you seen Mom?" I asked Birch to get Jon's nose off our scent because he still didn't look happy.

"I don't wanna see Mom," Birch answered.

Oh man.

"Birch, she's bad. You should try to—"

Both men's attention shifted, so mine did too.

Lottie was sitting facing a sidewall with two windows that were up high and covered in grime, as garage windows were wont to be.

I was sitting facing a door that was up two steps and undoubtedly led into a house.

Now I saw Saff coming in from the door, and beyond it, a washer and dryer in what appeared to be a laundry room.

She looked down at me as she descended the steps.

I glared up at her.

"I thought we were done, sis," I noted.

"You're so stupid," she replied.

That had my chin back in my neck with affront.

"Sorry?" I asked.

"God, I mean, I couldn't make it any more plain you needed to *fuck off*."

Now I was blinking.

One, she'd taken the Lord's name in vain.

And humongous number two, she'd used the word "fuck."

It was then, I was noticing something else.

She had makeup on.

And a cute white denim skirt that hit several inches above the knees, some brown suede boots that had a kitten heel, neither being True Light approved. Topping this was a navy-blue sweater, under it a white collared shirt. She'd done the French tuck and was wearing a brown belt.

She looked stylin'. Preppy stylin', but stylin'. And although she wasn't flaunting a huge amount of skin, I didn't think I'd seen her knees for maybe twenty years.

She went direct to Hottie Jon and kissed him right on the mouth.

She didn't stick her tongue down his throat, but she put her hand on his chest, he had his hand light, but still mostly on her ass, and it was without a doubt that wasn't the first peck they'd exchanged.

I *so totally* knew he was her boyfriend.

"What's going on?" I demanded.

Saffron turned to me.

Hottie Jon tossed an arm over her shoulders, did a curl, and then she was tucked back to his front with his forearm across her chest.

I'd think that was cute and be super freaking happy for her she'd scored a tall, hot guy and wasn't destined to be with icky Reverend Clyde, if I wasn't on my ass on a cold concrete floor in a pair of leggings, hands zip-tied together, ankles the same, connected to Lottie with rope wrapped around our chests.

"Okay, you didn't catch on," she stated. "But I wasn't being a bitch to you and Juno just to be a bitch. And, as an aside, Pepper, I cannot even *believe* you'd think I'd do that. Not to you. You're my freaking sister. Absolutely not to Juno."

I stared at her.

Hard.

"That hurt," she declared. "I mean, *a lot*."

"I—"

"No," she cut me off. "I get to be the condescending one this time."

Condescending?

"So this is the deal. Dad's a fucking lunatic," she announced.

Birch made an affirmative noise in his throat.

Jon tucked Saffron closer to him.

My mouth fell open.

"And I knew that even, like . . . a *way* long time ago. Like before you left. Then you left, Pepper." She leaned toward me, taking Hottie Jon with her, and repeated words she'd said to me weeks ago, and she did with the heat and anger she had back then. "*You left. And when you left, you left me with him.*"

"You were only sixteen," I said softly. "I was eighteen. I wasn't out of high school yet. I didn't have a job. I stayed at my friend Corey's mom and dad's house for the first eight months after I left. They floated me for beauty school. And I worked at Burger King and saved every dime I earned to pay them back when I could and so I could get out on my own."

"Well, you stopped working at Burger King and got a job then got a man then got a baby, and where was I?"

"I thought you were into the whole True Light thing," I told her, and I did.

In fact, I was gobsmacked that she wasn't.

"Did you ask?" she inquired.

Right.

Uh . . .

No.

We weren't doing *that* shit.

"No, but you've got a mouth," I informed her. "You could have talked to me."

"When? When Dad was around? When Mom was? When he'd moved us into the church and there were people watching my

every move? When he'd foisted me off to Clyde so he could be
head deacon and Clyde watched my every move?"

Shit.

I had a feeling this was going to get worse and it wasn't that
great to begin with.

Lottie had that feeling too. I knew it when she twisted her hand
so her fingers could grab hold of mine.

"I couldn't know something was wrong with you, Saff," I said
softly. "I honestly thought you were at one with the church."

"Because you didn't ask," she shot back.

"This isn't on me," I stated firmly.

"You're right, it isn't. Not entirely."

"Not at all," I returned.

"But whatever." She tossed a hand in the air. "I was stuck there,
and shit was getting real with Clyde and him adding the crazy to
his already pretty fucking crazy of telling the men to build their
'flocks.' And we can just say, not a one of them hesitated and said,
'Whoa, Clyde. Bigamy? Have you lost your mind?'"

I bet they didn't.

Saffron kept going.

"They were all in and Dad was all in and Mom was devastated,
because she'd already had to share him once, seeing as it was his
idea that they could have sex with whoever they wanted when
they were hippies. But what he meant was *he* could, *she* couldn't.
She did a couple of times, and he lost it with her. So, just in case
you were wondering, he started beating her down mentally before
Clyde entered the picture. But he glommed on real quick when
he found a way to brainwash her into him having a reason to
treat her like shit, convince her she lived to serve, and break her
motherfucking soul."

Okay, hip, with-it Saffron had a mouth on her.

And she was obviously closer to Mom than I thought.

I glanced at Birch.

He was watching Saffron, his face tight, lips thin.

"So Dad's always been a dick," I whispered.

"Yeah, Pepper." Birch entered the conversation, turning to me. "Dad has always been a massive, goddamn *dick*."

"Birch..." I said his name, but didn't know what else to say.

He knew what to say.

"This thing with those flocks of wives isn't new. It was just, back then, it was kept from the women. Clyde has been on about that with the men for years. And Dad was grooming you. And Christ, Pep, he was so pissed when you wouldn't come to heel. But you were lucky. To serve your purpose, you had to be untouched."

Ohmygodohmygodohmygod.

"Me?" he asked. "The boy who didn't cow to the lion of the house? Shit was different. My lessons were a fuckuva lot harder than yours."

My voice was small and beaten when I asked, "What'd he do to you?"

Birch turned, reached between his shoulder blades, and yanked up his long-sleeved t-shirt.

And I saw, along his back, there were a number of distinct, lengthy scars. Before he turned again, I'd counted four of them.

But there were more.

Lottie emitted a sorrowful tone.

I was going to throw up.

Birch spoke.

"He liked his belt. He owned only one. I bet you didn't know that. Didn't notice. I did. Because he wore it all the time. It got to the point, I'd see him wearing that belt, and I swear to fuck, I'd nearly piss my own damned pants."

God, I hated this.

Hated it.

"Why didn't you say anything?" I asked.

"Because he told me not to?" he asked back, but it wasn't a

question. "Seriously, there was shit he told me not to do that I did *not* do. He'd keep me out of school for days after he strapped me, so I wouldn't walk awkward and folks wouldn't notice. He told me to fake the flu. I don't even think Mom knew. I had to change my own bloody sheets. After he was through with me, I did that too. I did anything he told me to do. But most of his warnings involved you and Saff. He said you'd get the same, if I opened my mouth to the two of you."

So he protected us, my big brother.

Or he thought he did.

I took in a deep breath, and on the exhale said, "Okay, this is a lot. I hate it for you. I can't even say how much I hate it. I want to hear it. I need to hear it. Anything you feel you need to share with me. But I don't understand why me and my friend have to be tied to the floor while you share it."

"Because you got your man to look into us," Birch bit out and swung an arm to indicate Saffron and Hottie Jon. "All of us."

"Oh shit," Lottie muttered.

"And for your information," Birch went on, "I've fucked up a lot in my life. I'm not proud of it. Far from it. And yeah, things got physical with my last wife, her to me, and it sucks to admit, but because she was whaling on me, me to her too. I'm the least proud of that. I'd give anything to take back that time I didn't keep my shit when Leslie was all over me. But I don't beat women, Pep."

I was reeling about all that was coming at me.

But in that moment, mostly I wasn't a fan of him saying he "didn't keep his shit" with his wife.

"Did you hurt her?" I asked.

"No," he spat.

"Did you hit her?" I pushed.

"*Fuck no.* Jesus," he grunted, glowered at me, then went on to explain, "But when a woman is beating the shit out of you, you can't ask nice for her to stop. You gotta push her off you."

"That's all?" I kept at him.

"Do you even *know* me?" he demanded.

Okay.

I *did* know him (or I used to) and that part of what Auggie told me about him was the hardest to hear *and* the hardest to believe.

"I'm dealing with some shit and I'm dealing with how I handled other shit and that's mine," he continued. "But whatever your man told you, probably all of it is true. Just not that."

And his *just not that* seemed most important to him.

So again.

Yeah.

When it came to his physicality with his ex-wife, it started and stopped there, and not only had he been punished for it, he himself wasn't okay with it.

"Okay, Birch," I said softly.

He seemed to relax a little when I spoke those words.

"So now, years of what Jon has been working on," Saffron picked up the torch, "and I've been working on with him, is about to happen. And we can't have you fucking it up. Hence…" She pointed to us on the floor.

"What have you been working on?" I asked.

"Saff," Hottie Jon grunted his warning for her not to spill.

"I wasn't a fan of it when you came up with nabbing them, and I'm still not," Birch said Saffron and Jon's way. "We can let them go. Pepper would never say anything."

"You haven't been around her in years," Hottie Jon returned. "Saff's been around her all the time."

I wouldn't describe it as *all the time*.

I didn't get into that. There were more important things to get into.

"You can let us go. I won't say anything," I promised, even though I still wasn't sure what I wasn't going to be saying anything about because one thing was clear in all this, they weren't involved in Reverend Clyde's con.

"We're not letting you go," Saffron sniffed.

"Great," Lottie mumbled.

I stared at Saffron's determined face.

Right.

Moving on...

"Okay, as you know, I'm catching up with all of this, but I heard you were going to be married to Clyde," I noted.

Her face twisted and my fingers spasmed in Lottie's.

"That was the grooming Birch mentioned. You were gone, I was up," she shared. "But I would have had my turn anyway."

"Oh my God," I breathed.

"Yeah," she agreed.

"But you hooked up with..." My gaze went to Hottie Jon.

"Fell in love with," she corrected.

My eyes shot back to her. "Really? Wow, Saff. That's awesome."

"Don't try to be my sister now," she bit.

Try to be?

That hurt.

And it ticked me off.

"I've always been your sister," I shot back.

"Ah, hell," Lottie muttered.

"By leaving me in that nightmare?" she demanded.

"I didn't know!" I snapped.

"Keep it down," Hottie Jon clipped.

"I didn't know," I repeated less loudly.

"It doesn't matter now, it's almost over," Saffron replied.

"What's almost over?" I asked.

"It isn't your business," she retorted. "You'll be fine. We'll give you bathroom breaks. Find you some blankets to sleep on. Get you some foo—"

Saffron finished that word on a scream.

This was because three things happened at once.

Mo busted through the door to the house.

Mag dove through window one on the sidewall.

And Auggie dove through window two.

And when I said "dove," I meant he *dove*.

Glass flying, coming in headfirst, he curled in mid-air, landed on a shoulder, rolled and was up on his feet before I could blink.

Then, in a blur of motion, Hottie Jon was facedown on the concrete. So was Birch. And Mag recovered from his tuck-and-roll and had a Taser pointed at Saffron.

Ho…

Lee.

Hell.

How cool!

"Oh my God! *What are you doing?*" Saffron shrieked, her hands up by her head, staring down at her man, who had Aug's knee in his back.

What Aug and Mo weren't *doing*, but what they'd already *done*, was hog-tie Birch and Jon.

I mean, seriously.

They achieved that in three seconds.

Okay, we hadn't had the discussion about his job.

But if he could jump through a window then pin and restrain a guy in five seconds flat, I was thinking he was good to go.

"Please, do not move," Mag said in a rather gentlemanly way (I thought) when it looked like Saffron was going to bend to Jon.

She eyed Mag and then stopped moving.

Aug came to Lottie and me, pulling out a hefty penknife that probably had so many unfoldable gadgets, it could get us from one end of the Amazon to the other, no sweat.

Mo went to the button that opened the garage door.

It started cranking up and I was free, Lottie was free, and Auggie pulled me to my feet.

Pins and needles a-freaking-go-go.

I ignored them and threw myself at him.

He held me close.

I heard Lottie ask Mo, "What took you so long?"

I also heard Mo's low chuckle and then a sound like they'd given each other a kiss.

"You okay?" Aug asked in my ear.

Not even a little.

But I wasn't not okay because of the kidnapping.

"Are you?" I asked instead of answering, surveying him for cuts from the glass, and finding none.

"Fine," he grunted.

"How did you jump through a window and not get cut up?"

He gave me a look and said, "Practice."

Hmm...

"You don't have to tie them up," Saffron said. "We weren't going to hurt them."

The garage door started going down again and I pulled at Auggie's arms to give him the cue to tuck me to his side.

He did this.

And I saw Brett was there.

Oddly (or perhaps not oddly at all), I wasn't surprised in the slightest about this.

"Hey, Brett," I called.

"Pepper," he greeted. Then to Lottie, "Charlotte."

"Yo," Lottie replied.

"Hey, Sly," I greeted Brett's man, who had also joined us.

"Woman," Sly rumbled and then looked at Lottie. "Woman."

Lottie and I turned to each other, and honest to God, I thought we were both going to bust out laughing. Partly hysterics. Partly relief. Partly Sly being Sly.

We didn't when Brett asked, "Do you want me to handle these two?"

I gave him my attention just as he indicated Hottie Jon and Birch with a nod at either side of his head.

He was asking Auggie.

"Who's this guy?" Saffron asked after Brett.

"Shit, *fuck*," Birch groaned, staring up at Brett.

Uh-oh.

"Have we met?" Brett asked, gazing down at my brother.

"No," Birch answered too quickly.

"We've met," Brett said softly.

"Uh…" I cut in. "We were just getting to the good part of understanding what was going on. Is there a way, considering there are three of them, but seven of us, they could finish the story without two of them being tied up on the floor?"

"They didn't offer you that courtesy," Brett pointed out.

"They did not," Lots agreed.

True.

However…

"One of them is my brother and the other one, my sister is in love with. So maybe we can be cooler than they are?" I suggested.

All the guys (well, the guys on *our* side) looked to Auggie.

"Cut the cross rope, keep the hands and feet tied," Auggie ordered.

Mo moved in to do that, one by one cutting the line between wrists and feet then hauling them with one of his big mitts under their arms to sitting on their ass.

He then stepped back not too far away and crossed his arms on his massive chest.

This, I was seeing, was one of those times it was handy that Mo looked like he'd prefer to break you in half than look at you.

Because both Birch and Hottie Jon were eyeing him in a way neither was going to try anything.

"Give my woman what she wants and then we'll figure out what to do with you," Auggie directed Saffron.

"We can go inside, it's comfortable in there," Saffron tried.

"I didn't see you offering your sister a seat on the couch and a glass of wine," Aug pointed out.

"We—" Saffron began.

"Stop it," Auggie bit out. "Whatever is up your ass, you're taking it out on your sister. I get it. I don't like it. You don't want me to focus on it, I promise you. So move the fuck on."

Okay, seemed my guy could be intense outside of sex too.

And somehow, it was even hotter (maybe, I would have to assess this the next time we had sex).

"We've been working on this for years. That's why they're here. For insurance," Saffron said. "We're making some important moves today and tomorrow and we were about to get a message to you to stand down, not get involved, not fuck anything up. I was going to let Pepper call you to tell you she was fine, and you needed to let things play out. I just didn't get the chance. So now you have to promise you won't fuck anything up," Saffron ended on a demand.

"My woman was tied on the floor before I got in here, so I don't have to do dick. Now, we can move on with this, and by that, I'll be talking Pepper into pressing charges. Or you can tell her what she wants to know."

Saffron shot Aug a prolonged dirty look.

I made note of the fact that apparently, Auggie had been vaccinated against dirty looks, because he just stared at her.

"Okay," she pushed out, exasperated, and looked at me. "Mom's covered, just so you know."

"Mom's covered . . . for what?" I asked.

She didn't answer that directly.

She said, "That's why you had to find Birch for me. We'd heard through some acquaintances that he had skills we needed, but we couldn't find him. You found him, told him to contact the church, he did, we had a chat, he sorted stuff out and now she's covered."

I shook my head. "Saff, you're not making any sense."

Brett entered the discussion. "He has a specific skill set, which includes forgeries. Identification, primarily."

My brother was a forger?

Nope.

No time to get into that.

"Why did you all need—?" I began.

"Oh, for fuck's sake, Pepper, get with the program," Saffron snapped. "We didn't need you for a prayer circle. We needed to use your resources," she jerked her head to Auggie, then to Mag and Mo, "to find Birch. And we needed that to happen fast. Because Mom needs care. And we don't want Dad finding her when she's gone. She's going to an old friend from high school who lives close to a hospital that has a top-notch oncology unit. When we're ready, which will be tomorrow, we're getting her out of there, getting her to her friend, and then other things are happening, and we have to disappear for a while."

"You're kidnapping Mom?" I asked.

She looked to the ceiling like I was trying her patience, then back to me.

"No. She's going willingly. The first kid Dad had with one of his other wives, she was done. It just took her a while for her heart to catch up to her head. Sadly, that took so long, she was dying by the time it did."

I gave more of my weight to Aug.

He took it.

"Go on," I prompted my sister.

"So she's ready to roll. It's just that we don't want Dad finding her because he can talk her into things. Like dying with a lot of pain so she can feel the hand of God, or whatever bullshit he's spouting," Saff concluded.

"Okay," I said. "If that's what you're up to, why on earth would you kidnap me? In fact, why didn't you just ask me for help?"

"Because you have Juno, and Dad offered me, his own daughter, up to a piece of shit, grifting lech old enough to be my grandfather," she pointed out. "And I know, because my fiancé is four years older than me, and he's Clyde's grandson."

My attention shot to Hottie Jon.

Whoa!

Plot twist!

My sister kept talking.

"The minute you had Juno, Dad was salivating for his chance to use her to get higher in the hierarchy of the church. And I think you get how he'd use her. Which meant it was an all-out offensive to get *you* back in the church. So I've been being a bitch and doing everything in my power to get you to fuck off and never come back because I was protecting *you* and *my niece*."

She was protecting me.

And her niece.

She was being mean and Gonzo for God so I'd give up on them so she could protect Juno.

Oh man.

I was going to cry.

"But you just *wouldn't go away*," she continued.

"Because I loved you," I whispered.

"I know, you big dummy," she whispered back.

I stared at her.

She stared at me.

My lip quivered at the same time hers did.

Okay.

Oh man.

Oh shit.

Fuck it.

I moved to her.

She came to me.

We met in the middle, collapsed into each other's arms and started bawling.

"Can someone cut me loose so I can look after my woman?" I heard Jon ask.

And suddenly, I wholeheartedly approved of Hottie Jon.

"And me, those are my sisters," Birch put in.

"No," Auggie said.

Totally hot, my man being a hard-ass.

I kept hold of Saff even as I looked over my shoulder at Auggie. "Maybe it's okay."

He held my gaze and slowly shook his head.

Okeydoke.

Not over the kidnapping yet.

Noted.

I turned back to Saff and whispered in her ear, "I'll get him to let them go."

"He was right. I was just being a bitch because I was mad at you because you might be fucking everything up," she whispered in mine.

"Helping Mom?"

"No, scuttling the church, and setting up in Utah. Jon likes to ski."

Uhhhh...

Wait.

What?

I pulled back so I could see her, though I didn't pull out of her arms, and I was staring again.

"You're going to—" I began.

"Clyde thinks I'm his trophy," she explained. "I got him to trust me. He thinks I'm in with him. So he confided in me. He's planning to cut and run by this time next year, taking me and all the money with him, and leaving what he doesn't want behind. His other wives. His kids. He's done it before. It's his thing."

I nodded when she paused.

So she kept speaking.

"He didn't know I was with Jon. And Jon joined the church, as it were, to do what we're doing. Get back at his granddad because he left his grandma and his dad and a lot of other people high and dry a gazillion years ago. Clyde doesn't know Jon's related to him. He's kinda undercover, just not, um...*officially*."

Well, wasn't Hottie Jon a sly one.

"This will be culminating in having everything sorted, including Mom being safe and out from under it, and us taking off tomorrow," she went on.

Wow.

"We're also going to be turning everything over to the Feds. Anonymously," she continued. "Dad's screwed, but he's just the sucker who believed. He won't really be in trouble. But he might be broke. Clyde is fucked. He'll totally go to prison. But Jon and I siphoned enough off, we've got Mom's care covered, and we bought places in Utah, because Jon likes to ski, and Florida, because I like the beach. But also, Jon's grandma needs somewhere to retire, so that condo is mostly for her. I also want to go to college. Be an architect or something. So we'll have to settle somewhere, and we'll probably do that in Utah."

"Has Birch done documents for you?" I asked.

She nodded. "Jon has the properties in his name. But Mom and I have new IDs now so if he looks, Dad can't find us. And the quitclaims are being processed today. Once that's done, the properties will be transferred, and we'll be good."

"Not if they find out Jon owned the properties before you switched the titles over."

"He kinda..." her gaze slid side to side before coming back to me, "...has that covered. The property was all in Clyde's name. His real one. The one he was born with. So now, it looks like Clyde deeded over the properties to his grandson. And we should be good with that, even when the Feds get involved. Because that was all done with Clyde's money. Jon has an old power of attorney his grandma had and was able to...finesse things. But those places were bought from old accounts Clyde was sitting on. They weren't bought with church money the Feds could go after. Or the mail-order-bride money."

Hang the fuck on.

My eyelids went down, and my eyebrows shot up.

I lifted those lids and asked, "The...*what*?"

"You heard me, and I know. It's sick," she said.

"Explain fully anyway, please," I requested.

Saff nodded.

And when she spoke, she did it with a lot of verbal quotation marks.

"That was the long con. Clyde would talk schleps like Dad into joining the church with a substantial 'donation,' so they could eventually 'order' the members who would join their 'flock.' Those who truly believed, like Dad, thought Clyde, along with God, were bringing the women into the True Light. Saving their souls. Showing them the way. Those who were just assholes who wanted to get off with as many as possible of the poor women who found themselves on this website Clyde showed them didn't care about True Light outside the specter of the 'religious freedom' it gave them to 'practice their faith.' Which meant bang as many chicks as possible while having someone cook their meals and massage their feet."

I made a face. "Holy hell, it's a thousand times grosser than I thought."

She nodded. "That said, except getting some for the deacons, including Dad, he never actually ordered any of the brides. Therein lay the big score. There was the membership fee *and* the men had to reach the potential of the True Light. Like Dad and the other deacons spent years, and a lot of money, doing. Clyde had set them up, he was grooming *them* to be the hook. They'd reached their 'potential,' that was why they got their wives. And he could show them to new members. But every level you pass to reach that potential has a price tag. That's where Clyde was really packing it in. Five hundred here, seven hundred and fifty there. It's non-refundable if people fall out of the program, and a lot did. But bottom line, it adds up."

"And you recruited for this?"

She shrugged. "I was in with Jon and we had to keep up appearances. I mean, it wasn't exactly fun to do that, but honestly, mostly they're either morons, but not nice ones, like Dad, or leches, like Clyde."

It appeared my sister was kind of badass.

I could have done without the kidnapping portion of her demonstrating her badassery.

But still, it was cool.

"If the church goes down, Dad might be up to his neck in debt," I told her. "He's cosigned on some of the loans."

"That isn't our problem," she stated firmly. "Mom will be fine. You and me and Birch will be fine. Juno will be fine. That's all that matters."

"But what about our other brothers and sister?"

"Okay," she pushed out, like she didn't want to say it, "really, you and your guys can't get involved. It's all sorted, and you can't fuck it up."

"Saff," I said warningly.

She blew out a sigh and shared, "We skimmed some more money. And all of the women who'd been forced by circumstances to marry these jerks, and have their kids, are gonna disappear too. And do it with enough money to get them where they want to go and take care of them for a while so they can get set up. Including Dad's women and our brothers and sister. And before you say anything," she said the last quickly. "They have to go tomorrow. Everything has to happen tomorrow. Or it might all fall apart. So no one can say anything, or do anything, to fuck it up. Including you meeting them. I'll know where they are, and later, when it's safe, maybe that can happen. Now, the goal is to get them out so they *can* get safe."

"Did Birch do their documents too?" I asked.

She nodded.

Yep, things had gotten hectic for Birch.

And my sister and Jon (and feloniously, Birch) weren't just badass, they were kind of masterminds.

I looked down at my big brother. "So you came to the rescue. And I nearly fucked everything up."

"I connected with Saff, and neither of us wanted your kid involved, Pep," Birch said. "But you didn't fuck anything up. You found me and sent me her way, didn't you?"

That was nice of him, to try to make me feel better.

It hit me then, I had my brother and sister back.

And my mother was going to be free of that nightmare and maybe get some treatment, if that was what she wanted, or die without pain but with some peace.

I looked to Saff.

"I wish you'd said something."

"I got mad at you for leaving. I got mad at you for having a life and I was stuck there. Then I realized I had to be around to protect you, but I was still mad at you."

Obviously.

I said nothing.

"And I think maybe we went a little overboard today because of that," she admitted.

It was harder this time, but I again said nothing.

"But we do need everything to happen as planned, Pepper," she asserted. "Jon and I want to get on with life. Mom needs good care. Those women have been through enough, they deserve a fighting chance. It's taken a lot and it wasn't real safe, doing all of this. But we're almost to the end. I couldn't believe it when your girlfriends and especially your guy friends were showing up outside church or in services. You had the worst timing."

"You asked me to find Birch," I pointed out.

"Yeah. But I didn't ask you to investigate all of us," she returned.

True.

But still... she'd have done the same thing.

I let that go and moved to another topic.

"You had autonomy. You had freedom. You came to my house by yourself. I don't know why you couldn't have shared any of this with me," I pointed out.

She shook her head. "Maybe because it was mine? Maybe because it was good, and it was mine? You had your good. You had Juno. All your friends. And that was mine."

I could see that.

I tucked her hair behind her ear and then tugged the end of it.

"You're preppy," I said.

She did an eye roll and replied, "Not everyone can walk around looking like a model all the time like you do."

Ohmigod!

How sweet!

"You have cute knees," I told her.

"Once the dust settles, I want to get to know Juno," she told me.

"That is one thousand percent a plan," I declared.

"Can I get to know her too, or is your man gonna be up in my shit every time I try to see you?" Birch asked.

Every time I try to see you.

I was not going to cry, I was not going to cry, *I was not going to cry.*

I looked to my brother then to Aug.

Auggie gave me a one-shoulder shrug.

I turned to my brother again. "I have Juno back next week. Wanna come over for dinner?"

His head dropped like he couldn't hold it up anymore, then his shoulders heaved with emotion.

I decided to take that as a yes.

I was not going to cry, I was not going to cry, *I was not going to cry*.

I looked again at my sister. "You're pretty badass."

"I know."

"We both got hot guys."

"I know."

I grabbed her hands.

"I love you," she said.

I looked into her eyes.

"I know."

"Will you untie us now?" Hottie Jon asked.

My sister grinned at me.

And I grinned back.

EPILOGUE

Softball

PEPPER

I can't even with you," I complained.

"Babe, come here," Auggie demanded.

Resting on my knees behind him in bed, I pressed the edges of the tape that was surrounding the bandage that was covering the seven stitches of a wound on his shoulder. With that done, I fell back to my ass and crossed my arms on my chest.

Aug, who was sitting on the side of my bed in nothing but his pajama bottoms, twisted to me.

His eyes went from my face to my lap and back up again.

"That isn't here," he remarked.

"You told me you dove in that window today and were uninjured."

"As much as I'd like to be able to dive through glass, land on glass, and do it unscathed, my skin isn't made of Kevlar," he replied.

"You lied to me," I pointed out.

"If you knew I was bleeding, would you have been about me having a cut or about sorting things out with your sister?"

"A cut that required *seven stitches*," I corrected.

He just smiled.

"Your cut, *then* my sister," I finally answered.

"So, I lied because the cut is insignificant. The shit your sister had to share was not."

"You got seven stitches!" I snapped. "I cannot believe you stood there bleeding while Saff and me gabbed...*gah!*"

I ended that on a surprised shriek because Auggie's hand darted out, his fingers wrapped around my ankle, he tugged it (and incidentally...*me*) his way, which meant I fell to my back.

And Auggie fell on me.

"Are we gonna have a ridiculous conversation about something meaningless, or are we gonna fuck? And before you answer, I'll give my choice. Fuck."

Like I didn't know his choice.

"I will point out right now you bleeding is never insignificant," I stated.

"So noted."

"And should such an incident occur in future, I wish to be made aware immediately that you're bleeding before proceeding further with anything else."

"An incident such as that is never gonna occur again, sweetheart," he growled.

"Promise anyway," I demanded.

"Jesus, I gotta quit fucking you so hard. You're all about the bossy these days."

I pushed ineffectually (though, just to say, I didn't put much effort into it) at his chest, and said, "Stop joking around. This is serious."

Though, my point might have been weakened by the fact I was kinda smiling and also kinda laughing.

He went in, nipped my lower lip playfully, and lifted his head just as he raised his eyebrows. "Are you saying you want me to quit fucking you hard?"

God, he was gorgeous.

"It's really, really good you're hot, you diving through a window makes you hotter, you coming to my rescue makes you even hotter, and you being a hard-ass makes you hotter even than all that, because if you didn't have all that going for you, I'd be off in a huff and you wouldn't have sex for a week."

"Like you could go that long without my dick," he teased.

"Don't force me to perform that experiment."

He burst out laughing.

I kissed him in the middle of it.

A little while later, he fucked me.

Hard.

And it wasn't only awesome because the sex was awesome.

It was awesome because I didn't have to admit out loud that there was no way I could go that long without his dick.

But that message was sent anyway.

*   *   *

The kids racing around screaming in glee echoed in the huge space.

Juno, and two of her cousins.

And Birch and I were hunched together, looking at the screen on my phone.

At Mom.

On FaceTime.

I'd just given her a tour of where I might build my meditation studio: Auggie's warehouse.

"You're going to do what there again?" Mom asked.

She had never been a vibrant woman. Even in my younger years, she'd seemed dimmed by Dad.

She wasn't vibrant now.

So much not, Birch's hand found mine and his fingers curled around so tight, they crushed mine.

I didn't make a peep.

It was the first time he'd seen her.

"Meditate," I repeated. "And yoga. Maybe have a small café. There's definitely the space for it."

"Be careful with some of that stuff, Pepper," she warned wearily. "I'm sure I don't have to tell you that things that seem good can just be trendy and they can end up...not so good."

Gently, I replied, "People have been meditating for seven thousand years, Mom."

"Oh," she murmured.

"And it's not a done deal," I continued. "It'll take a lot of money to switch this place over, and I want to make a living with it, but I'll never get rich on it. I'll have to have a good plan and it might not work."

Her response to that had my heart squeezing.

"You built a life for you and Juno from nothing with no help, Pepper. Don't sell yourself short."

"I won't," I said, but it sounded more like a wheeze.

"I love seeing you two together," she whispered, and I could see her staring at her screen hard, seeing me and Birch on it. "You were always so close."

"And Saff's good," Birch put in brusquely, shifting the subject. "She and Jon are in Utah. Settling in, like you. It all went down like it was supposed to. It went great. We're all good."

We were all good.

Mom's friend got her to the oncologist right away, and the doc was considering Mom for a trial. It was promising, not a cure, but it maybe could prolong her life.

Just a little bit.

And Saff and Jon had been in touch and they were all shacked up and loved up.

Yeah.

All good.

Though, Dad wasn't good.

He'd lost his mind when Mom and Saffron disappeared. And the extent to which he'd done that probably had something to do with the fact his wives, his kids, the other deacons' wives and kids, and several million dollars of the church's money had disappeared with them.

Two things had occurred since then.

Dad had officially met Auggie, on my doorstep, after I'd not taken his calls or returned his texts, and he'd come over, pounding on the door, demanding to know if I knew anything about Saff and Mom.

I had not opened the door. I hadn't gotten anywhere near it.

Aug did.

And he reported to me he'd explained rather thoroughly that Dad was not to contact me for any reason ever again. And the same went for Juno.

Dad, being Dad, did not heed this advice, though he'd never shown at my door.

But the second thing happened after he continued to try to get in contact with me other ways.

He was blocked on my phone.

I hadn't heard from him in a couple of days.

More good.

Mom nor Saff had heard anything at all.

And that was excellent.

"You wanna meet a couple of your grandkids?" Birch offered, the fake joviality in his tone making me give his fingers a return squeeze.

"I do, Birch," Mom said. "But not...Maybe when..." She took a second. "If I get into that trial, and maybe if I feel better."

She meant didn't look like death.

"Or if things progress and time starts runn—" she didn't quite finish.

Birch cut her off quietly, "Okay, Ma."

"But, Pepper, Saffron sent me Juno's letter. Is she there? Can I talk to her?" Mom asked.

"Sure, Mom," I whispered.

"I'll say bye now, Ma," Birch said. "And go get Juno for you."

"All right, Birch. It was...nice to see you," Mom replied.

"You too, Ma. Real nice. Love you."

At his last two words, her head snapped weirdly to the side, like she'd been slapped.

Then she looked everywhere but the screen.

My nasal passages started stinging.

Finally, she looked at us and said, "Love you too, beautiful boy."

Oh shit, oh shit, oh shit.

Hold it together, Pepper!

Birch's voice was rough and hoarse when he said, "Talk later," left me alone with the phone and took off to send Juno our way and occupy his kids (who were, incidentally, cute as all hell, super sweet and I really liked them—it'd only been six days since it all went down, so I'd only met the two, his oldest, Joshua, who was ten, and Arya, who was Juno's age, but I was looking forward to meeting the others).

"Saffron tells me you've found a decent man?" Mom asked.

I focused on her. "Yeah. Auggie. I wish you could have met him before you left."

"She says he's exceptionally handsome," Mom noted.

"He is," I confirmed.

"The last one was too, Pepper," she noted hesitantly. "Please be careful."

"This is why I wish you'd met him, Mom. Because if you had, you wouldn't feel the need to say that."

"Saffron did say he seemed really keen," she muttered.

Yeah.

You could say that.

Dive-through-a-window-to-"save"-your-woman keen.

"Momma," Juno said, tucking her fingers in the pocket of my jeans and swaying me to get my attention.

I looked down at her.

"Grandma is on the phone. She got your letter. She wants to talk to you."

I was going to ask her if she was okay with that, but my girl lifted her hand for the phone right away.

"She wants to talk, here she is," I told Mom.

"Pepper," Mom said quickly.

"Yeah?" I asked, instead of handing Juno the phone.

"I have things . . . there are things . . . to be said."

"No, there aren't, Momma," I said softly.

She pressed her lips together and sniffed.

I blew her a kiss and gave the phone to my daughter.

Juno looked at the screen and didn't flinch, didn't do anything, but cry excitedly, "Hey, Grandma!"

Damn, I loved that kid.

She stepped away and I let her.

Then she stepped farther away, and I didn't want to let her.

I looked to Birch.

He had his daughter dangling down his back, but his gaze was on Juno.

Since he'd left us all those years ago, he'd been working some things out in all the wrong ways.

But seeing him with his kids, how he was with Juno, I couldn't imagine how I ever questioned the true-to-the-bones goodness of my big brother.

I heard sneakers slapping on concrete, turned, saw Juno racing my way and then I felt my phone pushed into my stomach as she averted her face and said, "Grandma had to say good-bye."

I then bobbled the phone since she let go of it and raced outside.

I looked at the blank screen, pushed it in my back pocket, and turned to race after my daughter.

"Pepper!" Birch called urgently.

I stopped and looked at him.

He shook his head.

"She was—" I started to call back to him to explain.

"You don't think I know what a Hannigan woman needs?" he asked. "She's your daughter, Pep. That girl is all you. Let her alone, yeah?"

I shut up.

What he meant was, my girl needed space to work a few things out before I got in said space.

She hadn't let me read her letter, but she hadn't had any problem writing it.

My hand itched to call Mom and ask what went down.

But Birch was right.

Sometimes, we Hannigan women needed space.

Still.

I moved to the door that led outside. It was open. And I positioned myself in it so my eyes were on Juno, who'd crawled up on the hood of my car and was staring at the sea of asphalt that maybe, one day, would be pulled up to put in a garden.

I jumped when, from up close, Birch said, "This is from Cisco."

I looked to him to see he was holding out an envelope.

"What is it?" I asked, taking it.

"No clue," Birch answered.

I started opening it as I turned my attention up to him. "And why, as well as *how*, is he giving you stuff to give me? He's coming over tomorrow night to have dinner with us. He could have given me this then."

"He offered me a job. I took it."

I lost interest in the envelope and stared.

Then I said, "Birch, he's a nice guy, but he's also—"

"So am I."

I shut my mouth.

"I'm good at what I do, Pepper," he stated.

And he did it proudly.

He proudly stated he was good at crime.

"Birch—"

"It isn't safe the way I do it now. But it will be, if I have Cisco's protection."

"It won't be," I said softly. "That kind of thing never really is."

"Trust I know what I'm doing."

"By continuing to forge illegal documents?" I asked, forcing my voice not to rise.

"It's what I do."

"It's a crime."

"Getting Mom safe, those women safe, Saff safe, those are crimes?" he asked.

"So this is entirely altruistic," I noted, and I had to admit, there was some sarcasm there.

"No, what it is, is my life," he shot back. "I got kids I want fed well, in good homes in good parts of town so they can go to good schools. I got women I fucked over that the least I can do, the *very* least, Pep, is take care of the babies I made with them so they don't have the bulk of that responsibility weighing on them. Now, I can get a job at a gas station, or I can do this. I choose this. And for you, Pep, you gotta learn from what happened. You love someone because you love them, not in spite of the things you don't love about them."

Okay, *that* shut me up.

Because *that* kept me apart from my sister.

And she may not have shared where she was at.

But the judgment part was all on me.

"Now, that church sucked," Birch said. "And Dad's a dick.

But Mom wasn't and Saff wasn't. We both gotta learn, because we almost lost them, and with Mom, we might not have much time to let her know we give a shit. So yeah. We gotta learn."

So yeah.

He was right.

The only thing I could do was nod.

He put me in a headlock, which was big brother for hug.

Shit, I missed this man.

I relaxed into it in an *I give* gesture, which was little sister for the same.

My ass binged with a text just as Joshua and Arya came running up to us.

"Where's Juno?" Joshua asked.

"She's—" I started to request they give her space, doing this still pulling out my phone.

"Outside," their father told them.

They pushed through us to race outside.

They really were super cute.

And I dug that they seemed to like Juno a lot.

I looked up at Birch. "What was that about Hannigan women?"

"You need people to fuck off, and then you need to snap out of it."

He certainly hadn't forgotten much about living with his sisters.

I laughed as I looked down at my phone.

And I saw I got from Aug,

Something just came up, baby. Be late for dinner, but there as soon as I can.

So I replied,

Message received. We'll
wait for you to eat
unless informed otherwise.
Love you. See you soon.

Love you too.

Reading his words, I felt it welling up, and he was probably busy, but it was always a good time to give something like this.
So I did.

Just to say you were
so wrong.

Sorry?

You were wrong.

About what?

Life isn't dodgeball.
Life is softball.
Sometimes you just
hang out in centerfield
under the sun, ready
for something to
happen.
And sometimes you race
for the ball hit in your
direction.
You might catch it
and be the hero of
the game.

You might miss it
because it's out of
reach.
You might drop it
and feel like crap.
But in the end,
it's over.
And you go get ice cream.

There were a lot of dots going and then I got,

I was wrong about
something else.
I don't love you.
I love the fuck out
of you.

Is that your way of
saying I'm right?

Absolutely.

Absolutely.

Instead of bursting into happy tears at his response, I sent him a sly-face emoji to communicate the depth of my smugness.

He sent an eye-roll emoji to communicate how adorable he thought I was (or, at least, I took it like that).

Then I turned to my brother and said, "I need to make a pie. You and the kids wanna go to the store with us? Enticement, in the end, there will be pie."

My brother smiled down at me and said a familiar word.

"Absolutely."

* * *

By the by, this was what was in the envelope.

Pepper,

There are things in life you regret.

Some time ago, I ordered one of my men to point a gun at you.

On my list, which I'm sure you can imagine is long, that's very high on the things I regret.

I can't imagine, especially having Juno, what went through your mind in that moment. I don't want to.

But I live with knowing I made you think whatever those thoughts were.

What's in this envelope is not about me making myself feel better, it's about restitution.

It's about forcing you to contemplate the end of your life and what it might mean for your daughter.

It's about making that right.

Don't return this, I won't accept it.

Take a moment of ugliness and make it beautiful.

Auggie's warehouse is the perfect place to start.

Yours whenever you need me,

Brett

And with the letter, there was a check for one hundred and fifty thousand dollars.

I had forgiven him on Thanksgiving.

And we'd be having a conversation about this, maybe when he was over for dinner.

But for then, I tucked that check away and decided, at least, to use it for one purpose.

The universe telling me to follow my dreams.

* * *

AUGGIE

"I got a dinner to be at, what's this about?" Auggie asked the minute he slammed his door after he got in the passenger seat in Billy's truck.

"We got a sitch," Billy said.

Fantastic.

"And that sitch would be?" Auggie asked.

"That pastor is pissed as fuck, Aug," Billy said.

Billy had not fallen down on the job. He'd gotten the intel Clyde Higgins/Dickens-when-he-had-been-Bottoms had belonged to a commune and had a number of partners and kids from that time who he'd left behind.

One of these eventually resulted in Jon.

But Aug had no idea Billy was still working Reverend Clyde.

"Feds might be lookin' into shit," Billy went on, "but they haven't brought it to his attention. All he knows is, some of his wives are gone, one of his trusted pastors is gone, those other women he ordered are gone, all the kids, and a shit ton of his money, and right now, he's about some serious fuckin' fire and brimstone. He's jacked up and looking to strike back."

"He's got nothing to strike back at, Billy, and the Feds will build their case without alerting him to it. If they did, they'd tip him that they've got a case and he would vanish," Aug told him something he should know. "And they can't hold him if they don't yet know what they've got on him."

"Yeah, but that's gonna take weeks, even months, and he's pissed *now*. And him being jacked up means he's getting his people jacked up. They're as restless and ticked off as he is."

"Hawk, Mo, Mag and me spoke with Jon at length about his plan, and the cover he put on their tracks is solid," Auggie told him.

And they had.

After the garage scene was done, they'd sat down to see if Jon and Saffron needed assistance.

By the end, the way Hawk was looking at him, if they weren't leaving, Aug had the feeling Hawk would have offered Jon a job.

In other words, they didn't need any assistance. Jon and Saffron had it covered.

Aug kept talking.

"Those women won't be found, and Clyde has no idea he held two properties in his name before Jon shifted them. He doesn't even know Jon is blood. So even if he could track him, he wouldn't know where to start."

Billy nodded, but said, "I got a guy, I mean, I know a guy. We aren't...he owes me," Billy gritted out, words that didn't give much, but Billy gave the impression he still didn't want to give them. "I sent him in, and to keep him safe, I'm tailin' his ass, as well as Clyde, because Clyde's exposed, and this isn't righteous-indignation shit to cover himself. He's not talking a good game while he's grabbing what he can in order to get the fuck out of Dodge. He's settling in for the long haul."

Auggie watched him closely. "You're telling me this because you've got something else to tell me."

Billy didn't lose eye contact. "My guy's been going to services now for weeks and he's counted four known police detectives are members of that church, Auggie. And a man who has serious shit happen to him to make him realize he needs to cut his losses, up stakes and get the fuck gone, and doesn't do that, instead, he doubles down. That means he's got protection. That means he feels untouchable. That means he's got someone at his back. So my gut told me to keep on him. And when I followed Clyde just now, I saw him have a meet with those cops."

"Shit, Billy," Auggie muttered, worried Billy did this alone, but impressed with his reasoning as to why he did it.

"I broke in after," Billy carried on. "And I found a stockpile of some serious shit. Stolen goods. Lots of them. Decent street value, but under-the-radar type of thing no one would go to lengths to search for it."

Auggie felt the skin all over his body tighten.

Billy kept going.

"And they got files. They're paying a load of attention, Aug. To you. To me. To Hawk. Lee Nightingale. Luke Stark. Eddie Chavez. Brock Lucas. Rush Allen. Dutch Black. Knight Sebring. I don't gotta tell you the rest. All of us. And they got about seven thousand pictures of some gorgeous Black chick who I don't know who she is, but they're all over her ass."

That gorgeous Black chick was need-to-know and Billy, until then, did not need to know.

"Good job, bud," Auggie forced out through a suddenly tight throat, yanking out his phone.

Billy, in command a second ago, looked confused. "What?"

Aug hit go on Hawk, not even fucking believing their dirty-cop sitch might be tied to Clyde Fucking Higgins.

"You know those dirty cops we've been looking into?" Aug asked.

"Yeah," Billy answered.

"I think you just blew that wide open and saved an undercover officer doing it."

"Aug, you got me," Hawk said in his ear.

"And Billy and I got something for you," Auggie replied.

Hawk said nothing.

Auggie did.

"Call everyone in."

He took a deep breath.

And finished...

"And get word to Lieutenant Fortune her cover is blown."

* * *

ELVIRA

The boys weren't there. They were busy doing a lot of other things.

So it was down to Elvira, when it showed in the mail, to put it in its proper place.

It was different from the others.

But she liked it best.

She set it at Auggie's workstation.

It looked like a plaque.

But it was more a frame.

And on the front of it, in white letters on a purple background, it said, HAPPINESS IS...

And next to that was a selfie picture, with Auggie's arm going long to take it, of Aug, Pepper and Juno scrunched all together, grinning at the camera while holding up ice cream cones.

Elvira adjusted it just so and hoped she was around when Aug came in and first saw it.

That boy needed some goodness.

And she was happy as a clam he'd finally found it.

She moved to the front of the workstations, and for obvious reasons, the room was empty.

She looked along the row two down from the top.

Where Zane, Marques and Billy had their stations, all three together.

She smiled to herself, clicked on her heels to her office and got out her phone.

She made her call.

And when it was answered, she said, "Lottie, girl, I been thinking..."

ABOUT THE AUTHOR

Kristen Ashley is the award-winning and *New York Times* best-selling author of more than eighty romance novels. Her books have been translated into fifteen languages, with more than five million copies sold.

Born in Gary and raised in Brownsburg, Indiana, Kristen was a fourth-generation graduate of Purdue University. Since, she has lived in Denver, the West Country of England, and now resides in Phoenix. She worked as a charity executive for eighteen years prior to beginning her writing career.

You can learn more at:
    KristenAshley.net
    Twitter @KristenAshley68
    Facebook.com/KristenAshleyBooks
    Instagram @KristenAshleyBooks

Can't get enough of that small-town charm?
Forever has you covered with these
heartwarming contemporary romances!

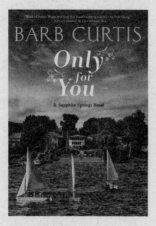

ONLY FOR YOU
by Barb Curtis

After Emily Holland's friend gets his heart broken on national TV, he proposes a plan to stop town gossip: a fake relationship with *her*. Emily has secretly wanted Tim Fraser for years, but pretending her feelings are only for show never factored into her fantasy. Still, her long-standing crush makes it impossible to say no. But with each date, the lines between pretend and reality blur, giving Tim and Emily a tantalizing taste of life outside the friend zone...Can they find the courage to give *real* love a real chance?

THE HOUSE ON SUNSHINE CORNER
by Phoebe Mills

Abby Engel has a great life. She's the owner of Sunshine Corner, the daycare she runs with her girlfriends; she has the most adoring grandmother (aka the Baby Whisperer); and she lives in a hidden gem of a town. All that's missing is love. Then her ex returns home to win back the one woman he's never been able to forget. But after breaking her heart years ago, can Carter convince Abby that he's her happily-ever-after?

Find more great reads on Instagram with
@ReadForever

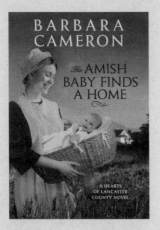

THE AMISH BABY FINDS A HOME
by Barbara Cameron

Amish woodworker Gideon Troyer is ready to share his full life with someone special. And his friendship with Hannah Stoltzfus, the lovely owner of a quilt shop, is growing into something deeper. But before Gideon can tell Hannah how he feels, she makes a discovery in his shop: a baby…one sharing an unmistakable Troyer family resemblance. As they care for the sweet abandoned *boppli* and search for his family, will they find they're ready for a *familye* of their own?

NO ORDINARY CHRISTMAS
by Belle Calhoune

Mistletoe, Maine, is buzzing, and not just because Christmas is near! Dante West, local cutie turned Hollywood hunk, is returning home to make his next movie. Everyone in town is excited except librarian Lucy Marshall, whose heart was broken when Dante took off for LA. But Dante makes an offer Lucy's struggling library can't refuse: a major donation in exchange for allowing them to film on site. Will this holiday season give their first love a second chance?

THE INN ON SWEETBRIAR LANE
by Jeannie Chin

June Wu is in over her head. Her family's inn is empty, and the surly stranger next door is driving away her last guests! But when ex-soldier Clay Hawthorne asks for June's help, she can't say no. The town leaders are trying to stop his bar from opening, and June thinks his new venture is just what Blue Cedar Falls needs to bring in more tourists. But can two total opposites really learn to meet each other in the middle? Includes a bonus story by Annie Rains!

TO ALL THE DOGS I'VE LOVED BEFORE
by Lizzie Shane

The last person librarian Elinor Rodriguez wants to see at her door is her first love, town sheriff Levi Jackson, but her mischievous rescue dog has other ideas. Without fail, Dory slips from the house whenever Elinor's back is turned—and it's up to Levi to bring her back. The quietly intense lawman broke Elinor's heart years ago, and she's determined to move on, no matter how much she misses him. But will this four-legged friend prove that a second chance is in store? Includes a bonus story by Hope Ramsay!

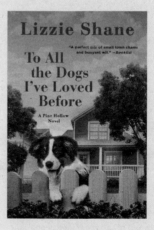

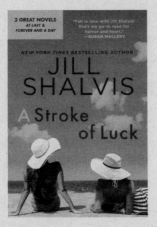

A STROKE OF LUCK
(2-IN-1 EDITION)
by Jill Shalvis

Get swept off your feet with two Lucky Harbor novels! In *At Last*, a weekend hike for Amy Michaels accidentally gets her up close and personal with forest ranger Matt Bowers. Will Matt be able to convince Amy that they can build a future together? In *Forever and a Day*, single dad and ER doctor Josh Scott has no time for anything outside of his clinic and son—until the beautiful Grace Brooks arrives in town and becomes his new nanny. And in a town like Lucky Harbor, a lifetime of love can start with just one kiss.

DREAM KEEPER
by Kristen Ashley

Single mom Pepper Hannigan has sworn off romance because she refuses to put the heart of her daughter, Juno, at risk. Only Juno thinks her mom and August Hero are meant to be. Despite his name, the serious, stern commando is anything *but* a knight in shining armor. However, he can't deny how much he wants to take care of Pepper and her little girl. And when Juno's matchmaking brings danger close to home, August will need to save both Pepper and Juno to prove that happy endings aren't just for fairy tales.